HEALER
TO THE
ASH
KING

REBECCA F. KENNEY

First Edition: June 2022

Kenney, Rebecca F.
Healer to the Ash King / by Rebecca F. Kenney—First edition.

TRIGGER WARNINGS

Violence, brutal contests and battles, death by fire,
torture, threat of rape, monsters, pregnancy of a side
character

1

I live in a land full of memories, fossilized and crystallized by time.

Our kingdom of Bolcan was buried a million years ago by the fiery vomit of the volcanoes that encircle our borders. Most of the volcanoes are sleeping now, though a few still whisper, while smoke curls ominously from their peaks.

In the gullies and along the coal seams, we find chunks of trees that grew lifetimes ago. We unearth pieces gently, polishing them, admiring the varie⸗ colors of the petrified wood—scarlet, soft yell⸗ pale blue, pearly white. Some of it is opalized, go' and rich with minerals. Some pieces have a speckl⸗ spotted pattern, caused by the drilling of tiny cr⸗ es. Our craftspeople hew the largest chunks ⸗ ables or seats for the wealthy nobles of the Capital, ⸗ smaller pieces are polished for clock faces, jewelr⸗ sculptures. Our most skilled lapidary worker, Cear⸗ ok the largest piece of petrified wood ever found ⸗ kingdom and created the throne of the Ash King ' ⸗f.

We also farm th⸗ olcanic soil, producing the most bountiful cro⸗ ne entire continent. Volcanic ash contains valuabl⸗ nts, and it's porous, the perfect density to hel⸗ ⸗ch retain moisture.

I love the volcanoes. I love the way they growl ominously yet give us the fertile ground we need. I love the sleek green slopes, the blue peaks that trail white clouds of steam, and the tall palms with their feathery fronds dotted across the broad landscape.

Though our village is small, I've never felt confined here. In this place we are far from the crushing influence of the Capital and our oppressive ruler, the Ash King. We're far from the Ashlands, the part of our kingdom he razed with fire five years ago, when he was twenty, just before he took the crown.

I have never seen the Ash King, and I don't wish to. All I want is to live here, in this beautiful village on the slopes of Analoir Doiteain, the "Fire Breather," the highest peak in this region.

I am *beireoir uisce*, bringer of water. My magic guides the water from the great river in the valley, up to the fields on the slopes. Which is where I am today, with my bare knees pressed into cool, damp soil, siphoning a trickle of water from the stream running between the potsava beds, coaxing it to curl around a diseased plant so I can cure its ailment and ease its growth.

"Cailin!"

Someone is calling me. The distraction makes me frown; I don't like being interrupted during a healing session, whether I'm treating a plant or a person.

"Cailin!" The voice is young, shrill, insistent. It's Peach, one of the boys from the village. He lives in the house next to mine. I healed him when he had hibernal fever last winter.

"Can it wait?" I call.

"No!" He's coming closer; I can hear him panting. "Cailin, it's the Ash King."

"Is he dead?" I ask brightly. What a glad day that would be. No more fear that he might scorch a giant swath of our kingdom again. Maybe the next ruler will lighten the taxes on our produce, provide funding for more teachers and libraries, encourage advancements in magical learning.

The Ash King doesn't believe in the study or expansion of magical abilities. His Ricters, officers of magical control, are severe and unrelenting in the performance of their duties, which involve traveling the kingdom and doing a mandatory resonance reading of every citizen, to gauge their abilities. Anyone deemed to possess a dangerous ability is Muted—marked with a tattoo that limits the use of their powers.

If anyone needs a Muting tattoo, it's the King himself.

Unless he's dead, and then we might have a chance at a new kind of government—the kind my friends Brayda and Rince want.

"He's not dead." Peach leans over, bracing his palms on his thighs. "He's here, in the village."

Shock drenches me like cold water. "Here? Why in the Heartsfire would he be *here*?"

"How should I know? But you're supposed to come immediately."

"Me?" My hands drop to my bare thighs. "Now? But—I'm not dressed to meet a king."

I wear a simple band of blue cloth around my breasts when I work. My pants used to be long, but I cut them to mid-thigh because the more of my skin is touching the ground, the more clearly I can sense the moisture, and discern what needs to be done with it. My skin, naturally a light brown, has darkened to a deeper hue thanks to my daily sun exposure. My dark brown hair is bundled in a frizzy knot, straggly bits trailing onto my sweat-damp neck. My lower legs and my hands are coated with soil.

I can't meet a king this way.

"Peach, are you sure the Ash King wants *me*?" I say desperately.

The boy nods. "The King's herald said, 'Cailin the Healer.' That's you."

"Rutting ash," I swear, rising. I use a little of the water I've been wielding to bathe my legs and arms. They're still a bit grubby, but it will have to do.

"Hurry," Peach urges. "I don't think he likes to be kept waiting."

I cast a look at the irrigation stream nearby. My magic will linger with it, keeping it flowing upward as I directed, instead of back down to the river. The effect lasts for a few days, and hopefully this odd meeting won't take more than an hour at most.

That's what I tell myself. But my stomach has coiled into a sickening knot, and as I race barefoot across the fields with Peach, I fight the urge to stop and retch.

We pelt across another field and down a slope to the clusters of cottages that make up our village. I'm covered in a light sheen of sweat. The upper curves of my breasts, exposed by the bandeau I'm wearing, are slick with it. I draw some water from a nearby rain barrel, create a fine mist, and walk through it to cool myself. Now I'm even wetter. Wonderful.

"He's in the square." Peach is peering around the corner of a house. "There."

I lean over him to get a peek. Peach is ten, fourteen years younger than me, and much shorter. Since I have no siblings, the younger village children fill that role for me. They look at me with a kind of grateful, loving awe, because I'm the one who can settle their nauseated stomachs, soothe their fevers, ease their coughs, and eradicate the more dangerous plagues that sometimes crawl through our region.

Over Peach's messy brown hair I catch my first glimpse of the King. He's sitting on a horse the color of volcanic ash, and his long white hair flows unbound in the breeze. Set across his forehead is a crown of black-iron leaves. He's young, pale, and handsome, dressed heavily in a black coat of brocade and velvet with dramatically pointed epaulets of metal and leather. At his side hangs a black sheath, from which rises the elaborate gilded handle of his famous sword, Witherbrand. A dark name for a very pretty weapon.

Wicked and volatile he might be, but he's fully dressed and clean, which is more than I can say for myself.

I withdraw into the shadow of the house and press my back to the wall, my heart thundering. "I can't go out there," I whimper.

"You have to." Peach grips my wrist. "Maybe he's going to give you a prize for being such an amazing healer. My mother says you're the best in the land. She says she's never heard of anyone else who can heal putrepox or hibernal fever."

"I'm not the best," I whisper. "I don't want to meet the Ash King, Peach. What if he decides I need to be Muted?"

Peach scoffs. "Why would he think that? Come on."

Peach doesn't know the true extent of my powers— the other side of what I can do. In addition to weaving torn flesh together or reversing its decay, I can also unwind flesh and hasten its corrosion. I can rot, atrophy, and disintegrate as easily as I can cure, renew, or rejuvenate.

When I was younger, I tested my darker powers on plants and animals, just twice, and I immediately reversed the damage I caused and vowed never to experiment with that side of my magic again. Instead, I focus on doing all the good that I can. While I cannot completely stop the effects of time on a person, I can help them stay young and healthy longer than they naturally would. The goodwives of my village attribute their long-lasting beauty to volcanic-ash masks and mud baths, but that's not why the people of my village look so fine and healthy. It's me.

None of the Ricters who have tested me have commented on the flip side of my powers. I'm not sure any of them realized I could do more than heal people and manipulate water. They mentioned the strength of my resonance and requested the standard three witnesses to testify about the nature of my abilities, but there was no further comment. I've never known why, and I've never dared to ask.

Surely I'm not the only healer who can also harm. Or perhaps I am. Magic wielders are rare in our kingdom, and few have dual powers like mine: elemental control and healing ability.

What if someone else passing through our village realized the truth about my powers, and told the Ash King? But wouldn't he just send Ricters to Mute me? Why come here himself?

Peach is pulling me out of my hiding place, and I'm letting him, because I've heard what happens to those who don't obey the king. They disappear into dungeons, and their family's possessions are confiscated. Sometimes they're beaten, mutilated, or executed.

The king doesn't permit rebellion in any form. And I don't wish to anger him, so I follow Peach out of the alley, into the village square. Everyone who wasn't in the fields is here, waiting in curious clusters. The Ash King sits silent on his horse, surrounded by a retinue of half a dozen guards and a herald. Not that he needs the guards—he could level our village and all our fields in one burst of fiery rage.

Another reason I shouldn't resist him or try to run, though every instinct I have is shrieking at me to flee.

My bare feet scuff the stone pavers of the town square. I'm disheveled, damp, soil-stained, barely dressed.

My knees are shaking, so it's easy to kneel in front of the Ash King. I'm not sure how I'll get back up.

Head bowed, I address him.

"Your Majesty," I say. "You asked for me?"

2

I wait on my knees, while the sun presses warm on my head and the fresh breeze whispers across my heated skin. The musky smell of horse mingles with the bitter tang of smoke from the nearby forge, abandoned so our blacksmith can watch my humiliation.

My people won't glory in this, though. Sensing emotion isn't one of my abilities, but I can practically feel their sympathy and concern surging around me, supporting me. These people love me, and I love them. Nothing the Ash King can do will erase that truth.

"Is this a joke?" says a voice somewhere above me— a cold voice with a hissing undercurrent of rage, like red-hot iron plunged into icy water.

Louder the voice speaks. "Is this your healer? The Cailin of whom I was told?"

A throat is cleared, and our village leader, the Ceannaire, speaks. "Yes, Highness," she says. "This is Cailin, our healer. She is a blessing to our village and to those nearby. Her skills irrigate the fields, soothe our elderly, strengthen our—"

"I didn't ask for her biography," interjects the cold-hot voice. "I'm aware of her powers. I wasn't aware she'd be a beggarly orphan."

My head whips up before I can stop it, and my eyes lock with the dark eyes of the Ash King. His upper lip is hitched in a sneer.

"I am neither a beggar nor an orphan," I say.

A hard metal object strikes the side of my face, and I crumple onto the dusty pavers, pain blazing through my cheekbone.

"You will not speak to the king unless directly addressed," says the guard who hit me. "You will not use that tone with His Majesty."

Trembling, I drag myself back into my kneeling position. I don't dare look at the king again.

"Cailin the Healer," drones the king's herald. "You are hereby conscripted into His Majesty's service for the duration of the 'Calling of the Favored,' or as long as he sees fit to employ you. In return for your full cooperation, you will be provided with lodging, food, a clothing allowance, and a monthly stipend. Gather your possessions immediately. Should you refuse to comply, your village will be razed to the ground and your fields burned."

A gasp rushes through the crowd of villagers, and a child begins to cry.

I look up again, desperate. "You can't do this," I say. "These people need me—I'm the only healer in this sector. And I irrigate the fields—"

Slam! Another blow, this time to the back of my head, and I'm flung forward, prostrate on my face.

"Do not speak to the king unless directly addressed," drones the same guard, sounding bored. "You will not resist or rebel—"

"Enough." The cold-iron voice is hotter now. "Do not strike the healer again, fool."

"Your pardon, Majesty." The guard's voice cracks with fear, and the change is so dramatic I want to laugh. I pull myself to my knees again, smiling through the blood trickling from my nose.

But when I risk a glance up, my smile vanishes.

Tiny flames dance at the tips of the Ash King's ring-laden fingers. The flames trickle into his palm, joining into a ball of fire which he snuffs out by closing his fist.

"Gather your things, healer," he says.

The Ceannaire comes to my side, helping me to my feet. She throws a baleful look at the guard who hit me. With her support, I stagger along the street to my parents' cottage. They are both skilled lapidaries, and they left two days ago on an expedition to a ravine famed for its yield of petrified wood.

I wish they were here, so I could say goodbye.

But maybe it's a good thing they aren't here. They might try to interfere, and that would be disastrous.

"My irrigation magic should last a few days," I tell the Ceannaire. My voice is thick and hoarse, unrecognizable to me. I'm stuffing items into a cloth bag—underthings, soap, a few clothes, a book of poems, a hair comb. "You can get Evan from Kuisp to help with the irrigation until I return. He can't heal, but he's a fair hand at shifting the water. And you'll have to get the midwife from Ranis to deliver Elisse's baby."

Tears cluster in my eyes as I think of all the things I won't be able to do for these people—from mending scraped knees to curing more serious ailments. "Ceannaire, I can't go. I can't do this."

The Ceannaire enfolds me, pulls me against her warm breast. She's a big woman, strong and kind. One of the best people I know, and she smells like home, like potsava root and sae-flowers, like earth and baked bread.

"You are our miracle, Cailin, sent by the Heartsfire," she says. "And I know the Fire will guide you in the Capital and bring you back safely to us."

"You can't know that," I mutter through sniffles.

"It's what I hope for. Sometimes belief is all we need to make a thing real. Hold us in your heart as we hold you in ours, and you will be safe." She pushes me back, holds me at arm's length. "Look for the smoke, *mo stoirín*. It will guide you to the truth that lies buried under the mountain."

I half-smile, half-wince at the platitude, a familiar one in this land of sleeping volcanoes. "There will be no mountains in the Capital, Ceannaire."

"Ah, *mo stoirín*." She smiles back, the wrinkles deepening at the corners of her eyes. "Everyone is a mountain."

3

When I return with my bag of belongings, one of the King's guards has "conscripted" a horse. Apparently the Ash King would rather steal a mount for me to ride, instead of bringing along a spare steed from his overflowing stables.

I'm immensely annoyed by the theft of the horse, more than anything else. It's Maken's horse, and once I've mounted I look to him and nod, a wordless promise to bring the mare back as soon as I can.

"Tell my parents I love them," I say to the Ceannaire, but my words are half lost in the thunder of hooves as the Ash King, his retinue, and I ride out of our village.

We ride two by two—a pair of guards, then the Ash King and the herald, then another pair of guards, then me and one guard, while the last guard takes up the rear. I didn't take the time to change, and I'm glad of my scanty clothing because the day is hot. I can't imagine riding in full regalia like the Ash King does. He must be sweltering. I hope he's wretchedly uncomfortable.

As we travel, I siphon water from the air to cleanse my face of the blood, and I heal the bruises the guard inflicted. It's handy, being able to heal myself. Not every healer can, I'm told. But then again, I don't have nearly enough information about my own abilities. Everything I know, I've learned on my own, with some guidance from

Evan, the water-wielder from Kuisp. He's twice my age—not a healer, and not as powerful as I am—but he's a good man. He will do his best to serve my village in my absence.

All day we ride, and into the evening. A couple hours after sunset, we approach the gate of Aighda, a city I've visited a few times, when they had plague and needed help. This is as far as I've ever traveled in my twenty-four years.

"We'll spend the night here," says the guard riding beside me. He's not the one who struck me with his sword-hilt, but he's clad in the same spiky black armor and horned helmet they all wear. All I can see of his face is a pair of bright blue eyes and a nose whose bridge has been smushed flat, possibly during combat.

He keeps talking, even when I don't reply. "Tomorrow the King is escorting one of the Favored from Aighda to the Capital."

Ah yes, the Favored. The eligible daughters of the nobility who will compete to gain the King's affection and become his bride. It's an ancient tradition—ancient and ridiculous, in my opinion. But for centuries the "Calling of the Favored" has been held each time a King or Crown Prince turned twenty-five. A few generations ago, we had a Crown Prince who preferred men, and all the favored noble sons were summoned for the competition. That prince found true love, and he and his prince adopted a foundling who became the grandfather of the current Ash King. It's a beautiful story.

I'm not sure who could love the Ash King. Maybe love isn't a requirement, though.

The guard beside me seems decent enough, so I venture a question. "Does the King escort every Favored to the Calling?"

"No, but he has a previous connection to this one. They say she's his first choice, his preferred match—though of course she will have to compete like everyone else."

If I had to guess, the Favored whom the King is collecting is Teagan, eldest daughter to the Lord Mayor of Aighda. She's vivacious and attractive, with long red locks that must be a beautiful foil to the King's white hair. I've met her before—healed her, in fact—but I had no idea she was close to the King.

"What is my role for the Calling, exactly?" I ask.

"As you know, the competition can be quite brutal," the guard replies. "The noble families are eager to ensure that their daughters emerge unscathed. Hence the need for a healer."

"But surely there are skilled healers in the Capital?"

"Yes, but most of them have political connections, noble sponsors and the like," the guard says, leaning companionably toward me. "It is said that His Majesty wants an impartial healer. Someone untainted by the machinations of Court politics."

"That would be me," I groan. "Oh gods."

"You're worried," said the guard. "Understandable. Your skills will be tested and graded before you're allowed to touch any of the noble ladies."

"Oh, it's not my skills I'm worried about," I say. "I do flawless work."

The blue-eyed guard cocks an eyebrow. "You're very confident."

"I know my powers and my limits."

Maybe this won't be so bad. All I have to do is mend the bumps and bruises of these fine ladies, keep them looking flawless for His Majesty, and return home after he has chosen one of them to be his bride. Poor thing. I pity her already.

Though the King does look rather grand, riding through the gate of Aighda with those pointed epaulets, the black iron crown, and his river of sleek white hair.

"We'll reside in the house of the Lord Mayor tonight," says the helpful guard. "And we'll be dining with him and his family."

"We? As in, me as well?"

"I'm not sure. As the King's personal guard, we're usually offered a seat at the lower table in the hall. I'm not sure where they'll put you, especially looking like that." His eyes twinkle with merriment, though I can't see his smile under the masklike jaw-guard of his helmet.

I smile back without resentment, because he's right. In my present state, I'm not fit for a high table.

The city of Aighda is softly lit with orange lamps, fragrant with the dark, spicy incense that is always burned for royalty. People have gathered along the main street to make their obeisance to the King. They don't hail him or cheer him—they merely sink to their knees in a rippling mass as we ride along. Several of them recognize me, though. With the king safely ahead, a few people dare to call out "Cailin!" in cheerful, excited voices. Smiling, I wave to them, feeling as if I should apologize for my disheveled appearance. To their credit, the people don't seem to care. I saved them from plague, and they remember.

I wonder who recommended me to the king. Was it Teagan, or perhaps her father? I thought my reputation only extended as far as this city and some neighboring villages, but clearly I was wrong. They've heard of me in the Capital. I was discussed by name as the candidate for this position.

A little thrill runs through my chest, and for the first time I think of this as an honor, rather than a punishment. A dubious and dangerous honor—but an honor, nonetheless.

When we pass through the wall surrounding the Lord Mayor's estate, we halt, and grooms rush forward to take the horses' heads. I dismount easily, unencumbered by skirts or armor.

Teagan is standing with her father, mother, and younger sister, ready to greet the King. Her long red hair is elaborately braided, and she wears a stunning silver gown embellished with tiny white gemstones. She's smiling, but too widely, and her eyes are overly bright. She's nervous.

My attention swerves from Teagan as her younger sister Aine sees me. I healed Aine from plague, and we became "best friends," as she informed me afterward, with all the enthusiasm of a nine-year-old. She rushes forward, arms outstretched. "Cailin!"

I hurry forward to intercept the hug before the child barrels straight into the Ash King, who is swinging off his horse. "Aine!" I sweep her into my arms. "You're looking well."

"But I have a splinter." She holds up her thumb, showing a tiny red wound, festering around a sliver of wood deep under the skin. "When I heard you were coming, I wouldn't let anyone else take it out. You can fix it, can't you?"

"Of course." A thread of gold light unspools from my fingertip, and I guide it through her pores, circling the splinter and gently nudging it to the surface. It pops free, and I flick it away, while my magic cools the inflammation and seals up the damaged cells. Within seconds, the child's thumb is in perfect health.

"I love how your eyes turn gold when you do that," she breathes. "Thank you!"

"Aine," her mother says, in a strained voice. "Come here, child."

"Go," I whisper, and she scampers back to her place in line.

I'm conscious of a tall bulk to my left, and when I look up, the Ash King is standing there, watching me. In the lamplit gloom of the courtyard, his face should look softer, less severe than it did in the broad daylight of my village. Yet somehow, the shadows carve his features more harshly than ever. The edge of his jaw is a blade keen as Witherbrand. The hollows of his cheeks and the caverns of his eye sockets are deeper. His eyes seem to glow, lit with a dark red fire from within.

I bow my head quickly, fearing that if I look at the King too long, I'll suffer another blow from the over-zealous guard who hit me before.

"You'll dine with us at the head table," says the Ash King.

Without lifting my head, I look up at him from under my lashes, just to be sure he's talking to me. He is. He's staring right at me.

"I will need time to change," I murmur. "Something else to wear."

"Perhaps that would be best," says the Ash King. "Though this look is growing on me." He nods to my skimpy attire.

He doesn't smile, not even a twitch of his lip. He sweeps past me to greet the Lord Mayor's family, while one of the Lord Mayor's maidservants waves me aside and hustles me into the house, satchel and all. I'm hurried off to what I assume is a guest room, where two servants strip me down and scrub my legs, arms, and face as fast as they can, while another tackles my tangled hair. I feel like a doll they're polishing and arranging—no will of my own, no say in which undergarments are dragged up my legs or cinched around my ribcage, no opinion on which gown is slammed over my head and buttoned in place.

More quickly than I'd have thought possible, I've been cleaned up and crushed into a gown that flares out from my waist in a swirl of sparkling blue. Blue leaves encrust the bodice, and more leaves climb over my shoulders and along my arms by way of sleeves. It doesn't fit perfectly—it was clearly designed for someone with a smaller chest than me—but I'm not bulging out of it *too* indecently, and with my hair braided and pinned, I look fancier than I ever have in my life. My tanned skin fairly glows against the pale blue of the dress.

"Delightful," sigh the servants. "Now off to dinner! We must not keep His Majesty waiting!" And they push me out the door and along hallways until I stumble into a wide room with a ceiling higher than the peak of the Ceannaire's two-story cottage. Two glistening chandeliers hang from the hall's central beam, their chains looping along the ceiling and disappearing behind the damask curtains that shroud the walls. A long table clad in snowy cloths runs the length of the space. Another table, slightly smaller, is already occupied with the King's guards and several other people. Everyone at both tables is standing beside their chairs, waiting for the King to enter.

A butler guides me to a seat near the middle of the larger table and directs me to wait until His Majesty is seated. I clutch the back of the ornate chair and swallow down the bile threatening to slide up my throat. I don't dare soothe my nausea with any water right now, though I can see some in the goblets on the table.

Mere hours ago I was in the place I love best, with my knees half-sunk in soil, the bright sky overhead, water between my palms, and the blue volcanic peak of Analoir Doitean within my sight. Now I'm alone, among strangers and distant acquaintances, trembling because I don't know the rules of this place and these fine people. My visit with them last time was brief and hurried, because the city was in a state of emergency due to the plague. I've never dined in this room with them.

Lifting my eyes, I meet Teagan's green ones, a few seats up the table. She gives me the smallest of smiles and a slight nod.

Something loosens inside me, just a little, and I can breathe easier.

The King's herald steps in. "Announcing His Royal Majesty, the Ash King, Perish the son of Prillian, Ard Rí of Bolcan and High Vanquisher of her enemies."

A laugh bubbles inside me at the fatuous titles the King has given himself. I manage to stifle it, but there's a twitch at the corner of my mouth that I can't stop, not even when the Ash King glances at me as he strides past several seats on the way to his own. When he sees me smiling, his pale brows pull together slightly, and for a second I fear he might incinerate me on the spot and find himself a new healer. But he moves on, taking his place with the stern grace that seems to be normal for him.

Once he is seated, we take our places and begin the meal.

4

The people dining at the Lord Mayor's table are important in this city—merchants, landowners, artisans of superior skill—anyone the Lord Mayor wished to honor with an invitation. I'm relieved that I didn't have to appear at dinner looking dirty and bedraggled. In fact, I feel downright gorgeous, and between that and my confidence in my magic, I'm able to quell my nerves and begin to enjoy myself a little.

I eat cautiously, watching everyone else and taking cues as to which silver I should use first and how I should partake of each course. The food is delicious; of course it is, because much of it is grown in the fields that I feed with my water. The crops will manage with the natural rainfall and Evan's occasional attention, but without my care they won't be as abundant. Does the Ash King know that? Does he care?

As I eat, I try to picture the Ash King enraged, angry enough to send floods of flame across an entire region. He looks so reserved, so cold. Only his voice gives any hint of the molten depths hiding within him.

All people are mountains, the Ceannaire said—or some such wisdom. If people are mountains, this man is a volcano. Lucky for me, I'm used to living near one.

Perhaps I've been looking at him too often. He catches my eye twice, and the third time he frowns.

Panicking, I whip my gaze to my plate, and I'm careful not to look his way again.

That is, until the Lord Mayor says loudly, "Good gracious, my water goblet is empty."

A servant hurries forward with a pitcher, but the Lord Mayor angrily waves him away.

"Oh my, how thirsty I am," the Lord Mayor says again. Once more, the poor servant, looking distressed, edges forward with the pitcher, only to be rebuffed.

I smirk, catching on. My fingers barely twitch as I guide water out of the pitcher in a sparkling arch and let it trickle into the Lord Mayor's goblet. He raises it, triumphant, and everyone at the table claps.

Showing off my powers in small ways doesn't bother me. I enjoy delighting people with my magic. But then the Lord Mayor says, "His Majesty's cup is nearly empty too. Cailin, if you would be so kind?"

I try to keep the antagonism out of my expression as I guide water into the Ash King's cup. But I let the last bit fall a little too suddenly, and several drops splash his doublet. His eyes flick up to mine.

"How clumsy of me," I say softly. "My deepest apologies."

"I hope you will be less clumsy when you are caring for our kingdom's most treasured daughters," he answers.

"Oh, her skills as a healer are unparalleled," says the Lord Mayor hastily. "I am thrilled that you've chosen her. I would have recommended her myself, but I wanted to avoid all appearance of favoritism or prejudice."

"Not that there's a chance of that with Cailin!" his wife puts in. "She has a heart as pure as the clearest lake, my lord."

"So I've been told," says the Ash King dryly.

My cheeks flush, both at the compliments and at his seeming disdain for them. I'm beyond thrilled when the meal is finally over and the guests trickle out of the Lord Mayor's house.

"Any other night I would suggest dancing, drinks, and some entertainment," the Lord Mayor says apologetically. "But Your Majesty indicated that you wished to retire early and get an early start, so…"

"Yes," says the Ash King, rising from his chair. "I will retire now."

He stalks away from the table, trailed by the herald and two guards. I wonder if any of them double as servants, helping him dress and undress, or if he does all of that himself. It would feel strange and awkward to me, being handled by other people every day, helped through the most menial tasks as if they were beneath my dignity. I wonder if his servants wipe his ass for him.

By a stroke of the same terrible fortune that has followed me through this day, the Ash King turns around and catches me smirking at his back. There's a flicker in his eyes—a real flicker of actual fire—and my smile disappears.

But he doesn't shoot flames at my chest and burn me to a crisp. He only narrows his eyes and glides out of the room.

As I'm rising from my own seat, intending to go to the guest chamber where I left my bag, one of the King's guards returns and approaches me. He speaks low and quick in my ear. "Once the house is in bed, someone will come to fetch you. The King would speak with you alone."

5

The King wants to speak with me alone?

I pace the guest room I've been given for the night, scrunching the material of the lovely borrowed dress in my hands.

I am truly terrified, no humor left in my heart. I've heard what the Ash King does to people who displease or dishonor him. Even small infractions are punished with terrible, scarring burns. Underneath the armor, his guards probably have burn marks everywhere. I've heard he brands his palace servants with the print of his scorching hand.

I can't heal old scars. Once a few weeks have passed, my powers can't alter the regular healing process of a wound. Nor can I repair certain deep-seated conditions, the kind people have suffered with since birth, or the kind that grows and mutates within the body. I can help in some cases, but I can't repair systemic bodily failure or continuous damage.

If the Ash King tries to brand me, I can heal myself later so it won't scar. But it will hurt. And after being wrenched from my home and forced into the King's service, I'm not sure I can bear the additional pain.

There's a tap on my door, and I nearly leap for the narrow window. I doubt I could break the thick glass though—I would only end up bruising myself and not escaping the Ash King at all.

"Coming," I say faintly. When I open the door, there's a man outside—the same guard who spoke to me in the dining hall. Mutely I follow him out of my room and through the quiet hallways of the Lord Mayor's house.

My gown swishes loudly against the thick carpet. Maybe I should have changed out of this dress into something simpler. No, best to meet the King in rich attire, just to be safe.

What if he questions me about the extent of my powers? How much should I tell him? Maybe he has summoned a Ricter and I'm to be measured right now…

My anxious thoughts keep swirling until the servant pauses outside a door. "Go on in. He is expecting you."

My fingertips feel ice-cold, and the sodden weight of my fear drags at my lungs when I try to breathe.

I open the door.

The room I enter is elegantly appointed, probably the best guest chamber the Lord Mayor has to offer. There's a somber patterned duvet on the bed, turned back to reveal six fat pillows. Near it is a small fireplace, unlit, and a side table with a glowing bronze lamp. There's another lamp on the dresser, also glowing.

On the cushioned bench at the end of the bed sits the Ash King, wearing a black fitted shirt that tightens across his chest when he moves. His long white hair is secured in a sleek knot at the back of his head. He's taking off his boots.

"Good, you're here," he says, with barely a glance at me. "Let's get to it."

I'm not sure whether to kneel or not, so just in case I sink to my knees, with the blue skirts crumpling and bunching around me. I don't bow, but I keep my head bent a little as I watch the King.

He rises, pulling off the black shirt over his head. With all the layers on his body earlier, it was hard to tell how broad or fit he was. My mouth goes dry and earthy as his torso is revealed—satiny muscle, smooth and sculpted, from his powerful shoulders and swelling pectorals to the planes of his stomach and the angled ridges of his hips.

Why is he undressing?

"Do you need healing, Your Majesty?" I ask.

He looks at me, frowning slightly. "No."

"Then, why—" I clear my throat, willing myself to be respectful. "How may I serve you?"

"Not on your knees," he says, unbuttoning his black pants. "Though it's good to know you are willing. No, I'll have you on the bed, I think."

I look up at the Ash King, shock searing along my nerves. "What?"

His frown deepens as he takes in my expression. "I thought you knew why you were called here."

"I thought I was summoned to—to answer your questions, or to have my magic tested—"

"This late at night?" He arches an eyebrow. "I called you for sex. Why else would a king summon a woman to his quarters at this hour?"

"I—forgive me, my lord, I did not understand."

He sits down on the bench again, his pants half undone and his elbows propped on his knees. I still have to look up at him, but he's closer to eye level.

"You did not understand," he repeats. "The glances you've been giving me, the smiles, the taunting—I thought you were amenable to this."

Heartsfire—he thought I was trying to seduce him? I'm so stunned I can't reply.

"Are you denying your king?" he says, a note of impatience in his voice.

The image of him crushing that fireball flashes through my mind. I dare not refuse him too rudely. "I'm just surprised, my lord. You're in the same house as one of the Favored—a lady you prefer, by all accounts. Why would Your Majesty not call for her?"

"I cannot bed one of the Favored before the Calling," he says. "It would not be fair to the others. And it's not as if I'm married, or even promised. I'm free to seek distraction where I please. And who said I prefer Teagan?"

"People," I say vaguely.

"People say a lot of things about me," he replies.

I have no idea how I am going to get out of this without offending him and getting myself soundly scorched. Maybe I can reason him out of it. "Don't kings usually have women bathed and shaved and scented before deigning to bed them?"

"I'm not difficult to please," he says. "And you look well-groomed enough, now that you're not covered in dirt."

"Oh, but they only washed my arms and legs," I say quickly. "I'm very dirty in other places."

And then my face flames. Because I said that. To the Ash King.

Again his dark eyes spark orange, and this time there's the barest quiver at the corner of his mouth. I have the strangest urge to coax that quiver into a smile.

"You're beautiful," he says, and my heart jolts. "And you're amusing. I want you."

"If I say no, are you going to burn me?" I whisper.

"If I answer yes to that question, will you still refuse me?"

I gnaw my bottom lip. He's handsome, no denying it, with a body most men would envy and most women would crave. His pants are unbuttoned so far it's dangerous, and I can see the outline of his arousal through the taut fabric. But he's a stranger. He's the *Ash King*, and he frightens me. I don't want him touching me, or putting himself inside me—the thought makes me shiver.

"I must deny you either way, Your Majesty," I tell him quietly.

"Do I repulse you?"

"No, my lord."

"And you have done this before, yes? With a body like that, you must have."

I narrow my eyes, unsure what that comment means. But he's right. "Yes, I've been with a man before." My friend Rince, before he and my best friend Brayda left our village to join the Undoing, the rebels who want to bring down the monarchy. They were very zealous about it, both of them. I slept with Rince many times, and I wouldn't have minded continuing the trysts, but he decided his body and mind should be dedicated to the cause.

It's supremely ironic that I'm alone with the very man Rince and Brayda would love to assassinate. Gods, even *I* was wishing he was dead earlier today.

They would want me to try to kill him now. But I couldn't harm him if I wanted to; he'd react too quickly with his fire magic. And besides, I have sworn the healer's oath, not to harm a living soul unless it's in defense of another.

"You keep staring at me," says the Ash King. "Why? Most people fear to look at me too long."

"Maybe they're afraid because your guards smack people's skulls at the slightest provocation," I say sweetly, but my gut clenches, because I know at some point I will go too far. I will anger him, and he will maim or kill me. Or force me into bed.

"It's your mouth," he says, stroking his smooth jaw. "The quick way you have of speaking before you think. The defiance. It flows from you like water. Usually I would punish such rebellion, but when it's mixed with humor, in that body—" He gestures with splayed fingers, indicating my chest— "I'm inclined to let it pass. For now."

"Thank you, my lord," I murmur, relief and rage mingling inside me.

"And you are officially refusing me? Most women are pleased to accept my attentions, and they leave satisfied afterward."

The faintest trickle of warmth traces between my legs at that suggestive promise. But no. "Perhaps one of the other ladies in town would be agreeable."

"I cannot summon anyone else at this hour, nor do I wish to." He waves me away. "Back to your room, healer."

He's letting me go? Thank the gods.

I rise, dipping a curtsy, and his eyes settle on my enhanced cleavage. Damn this accursed gown.

My mother always tells me that one mark of a good man is taking responsibility for his body's reactions, and not placing that blame on a woman's choice of clothing.

By all accounts, the Ash King is not a good man.

"Your Majesty," I breathe. "Good night." I back up to the door, fumbling behind me for the handle. My eyes are trained on the Ash King, as if he is a wild animal and if I look away for one second, he'll attack.

But he doesn't move. He only lifts his eyebrows slightly at my odd manner of exit.

I spend the next few hours lying stiffly in bed, wrapped tightly in blankets, eyes wide open to the dark. What if the Ash King reconsiders letting me go and decides to creep into bed with me? Why does he even want me? I'm not flattered. I'm not. I'm offended, deeply offended that he interpreted a few smirks as some sort of seduction technique. I'll have to be sure to frown at him from now on... though that might get me more blows to the head from his guards... no, I won't look at him at all, ever.

That resolution proves to be easier to keep than I thought, because the next day, the Ash King rides beside Teagan all day. Between me and them are more guards, her two maidservants, and a small cart containing a ridiculous amount of luggage that is apparently essential for her participation in the contest.

I've heard stories about how the "Calling of the Favored" was conducted in previous generations. Some of the rounds of the competition are public, while others are private, and the challenges differ every time—but there are always physical challenges, sometimes involving combat, either one-on-one or in groups. I don't know much about the nobility of Bolcan, but I've always imagined them as soft and spoiled, not worth much in a fight. Perhaps they will simper and slap at each other, and squeal whenever one of them is scratched. Or perhaps I'm being unfair. Teagan doesn't seem like the simpering kind; in fact, she seems like the kind of person with whom I'd want to be friends.

The blue-eyed guard isn't riding with me—instead it's the short steely-eyed guard who struck me those two times. So I have no one to talk to, but I don't mind. The vistas are lovely—sweeping hills, forested valleys, water wheels turning between grassy banks, fluffy sheep nosing about in sloped pastures bordered by neat rock walls.

We pass through a couple of villages. The people bow to the King and Teagan, and they eye me curiously as I ride past. I'm an anomaly, an enigma. I'm wearing one of my own outfits today—my best traveling outfit. It's a simple brown overdress with creamy embroidery, paired with brown pants. My hair is still in the fancy braids from last night—they're a little mussed from the pillow, but they look decent enough.

We pause for a noon meal in a pasture by the side of the road. I'm given a share of food and then ignored, which suits me. A long afternoon of travel follows, and by evening we still haven't reached the Capital. Instead, we turn into the courtyard of a wayside inn. There's much shock and flurry among the owner's family when they realize who their guests are. Again, I'm given food as an afterthought and assigned a tiny room, little more than a closet at the end of the second-floor hallway, while the King and Teagan and their entourage receive all the best rooms.

It's stuffy and windowless in my chamber. Back home, I'm used to sleeping with the windows open so the mountain breeze can flood the room. My sleep was poor last night, and if I can't sleep tonight, I will be a weepy mess tomorrow.

After hours of struggling with wakefulness, I can't stand the suffocating room another minute. I slip out my door, pad barefoot along the hall, and creep down the stairs.

There's a guard on the landing, and he halts me. Despite the gloom, I recognize the blue eyes and smushed nose of the friendly guard, even before he speaks. "Ho there, healer. Where are you off to? Running away, are we? Let me warn you against that. His Majesty will go back to your beautiful village and use it as kindling if you cross him."

"I'm not running away," I tell him. "I can't sleep, and I'm desperate for some air. Please—I just need to open a door, a window—anything. Let me sit in the common room a while, please."

"The common room is occupied," says the guard in a low, warning tone.

"It's all right, Owin," says a voice from somewhere below—a voice like iron and ice. "Let her come down."

A bolt of lightning races through my gut—panic and nerves. I retreat, climbing back up a step. "Never mind," I whisper frantically. "I'll get to sleep somehow."

"Come down here, healer," says the King's voice. Did he hear me whisper? Does he have special hearing powers as well as fire abilities?

The blue-eyed guard, Owin, winces sympathetically at me and stands back so I can pass. I wrinkle up my nose, but I descend the steps, conscious that I'm wearing a threadbare nightdress that's much too short for me, and much too low in the neckline.

I move into the inn's common room cautiously; it's gloomy, and I don't want to trip over the thicket of chairs and tables. The Ash King is sitting at a table in the center of the room, and at first I think he has a candle in front of him, but it's a little ball of flame that dips and swells and shrinks, hovering in midair.

The King lounges sideways, shirtless, hunched down in a chair, one elbow on the table with his hand propping his cheek while the other hand rests on his thigh. He's not even moving his fingers. He's controlling the fire with his thoughts, idly, easily.

His eyes lift to mine, and I gasp. His irises are entirely molten. They've transformed into swirling orbs of scarlet flame.

"Your pardon, Majesty." I start to kneel, and he says, "Enough of that. A bow will do."

"Majesty," I repeat, and bow to him. "Forgive me. I needed some air."

"They've shuttered and barred all the windows in case someone tries to assassinate me," he says.

"What?" My voice shrills in mock surprise. "Who would want to kill *you*?" I hope he notices the wry twist to my tone.

"I am hated," he says. "As all men with power are hated."

My good sense tries to stop me from speaking, but I push past it. "All men with power have not burned an entire section of their kingdom and murdered thousands of their citizens."

"True." His eyes flare brighter, tiny flames escaping and catching on his lashes. "I did do that. I burned thousands of people alive and turned whole towns to ash." He rises, and I realize with dread fascination how tall he is. His long white hair is loosely plaited in a single braid, and escaped strands stir around his face as if caught in a hot wind. He is terrifying and glorious—a glowing, flame-eyed menace in the dark room.

"Thank you for reminding me who I am, healer." His voice is black smoke and burnt bones. "Let me remind you

41

who *you* are. You're a farm girl who happens to possess the gift of water-wielding and healing. I may have found you amusing yesterday, but tonight, I'm wondering if you're worth my trouble." He places a searing palm in the center of my chest, the heel of his hand pressing into my cleavage and his fingers splayed over my collarbone. The heat of his skin scorches mine, and I clench my teeth against the painful touch.

Despite the heart-quickening pain of the Ash King's fiery hand, there is something horribly intimate about his touch against my chest. I can't read his expression through the fire swirling in his eyes, but I can sense his anger building. My burning skin sizzles, and a strange roasted scent rises from it.

This is the end. This is where he burns me to ash.

I'll be damned if I become a living candle without trying to defend myself.

There's water in a bucket across the room—I can sense it as surely as if I could see it. I pull the water and it races to me, coiling around the Ash King's fingers, dousing his fire with a hiss of steam. The Ash King's lips pull back in a snarl and I startle, because flames are licking through his clenched teeth. It's as if his throat is full of fire and it's all he can do to hold it back.

Quickly I splash some of the water across his mouth, pressing the liquid between his teeth and down his throat, quenching the flames.

For all I know, I've committed an unpardonable offense. But he was going to kill me anyway, so... what did I have to lose?

The fire in his gaze dies, and he stares at me, lips wet. He peels his hand from my chest, and I can't help voicing a small pained cry as the contact breaks. My skin is blistered and swollen where he touched me.

So the stories are true. He is every bit as dangerous and wicked as they say.

I release the water-wielding part of my magic and tap into my healing ability. The two skills are different, and I can't use them at the same time. It's one or the other.

Golden curls of light emanate from the handprint on my chest, swirling through my skin, repairing the burnt cells. I can't quite see it happening, but I can sense when it's done, and I can see the effect on the Ash King. His dark eyes are wide, his face gilded in the glow of the magic. Mine is a far gentler light than his.

"I think you've had enough air," he says tightly. "It's time for you to return to your room."

"My apologies for any offense, Your Majesty." I give him a deep bow, even though, king or not, *he* should be apologizing to *me*. Without waiting for an answer, I race upstairs to my room.

For some reason, sleep comes to me quickly after that.

The next day is our last on the road. We should reach Cawn, the Capital City, before nightfall. The blue-eyed guard Owin rides with me, and he assures me that the city will be brightly lit, "from towers to trash heaps," for the king's return. He tells me this while we're lunching by the roadside, a little distance away from the others, and I laugh aloud. He's been making me laugh frequently, but this time the Ash King glances over at us, glowering.

The next second Owin's sandwich explodes into ash and sparks. Soot puffs across his face, and he looks so comically surprised that instead of being frightened, I giggle. He reminds me of some of the boys back home; he can't be more than nineteen.

"Here, have some of mine." I hold my sandwich to Owin's mouth, and he takes a bite, grinning through the ash streaking his features. "Delicious," he says, and crumbs dribble from his lips, which makes us both dissolve into laughter again.

"Stop," he wheezes. "You'll get me in trouble."

"I'm sorry," I gasp, wiping laugh-tears from the corners of my eyes. "I'm anxious, and that makes me prone to nervous fits of laughter. Is His Fiery Highness still watching us with that doomful look?"

Owin swallows, humor draining from his tanned face.

"He's standing behind me," I whisper. "Isn't he?"

"Yes he is," says the Ash King darkly. "Take off your breastplate and tunic, Owin."

My stomach quakes. "Please, it was my fault… I was—"

The Ash King cuts a hand toward me, and a flurry of sparks stings against my lips.

With shaking fingers, Owin strips to the waist and obediently turns his back to the King.

A whip of fire appears in the Ash King's hand, short at first, then longer as he flourishes it. When it recoils it shrinks again, but its flaming tip hangs dangerously close to the tips of the meadow grass. With his dark clothing, and that fiery weapon in his hand, and his pale hair gleaming bright in the sun, the Ash King looks wickedly majestic.

But he's going to whip Owin with that terrible lash.

"No," I gasp. "Please, I'll do it. I'll take the blame. It was my fault."

"A king's guard should be alert, not joking and leching by the wayside," says the King.

"He's young," I protest. "New to your personal guard, right? And I don't know the way of things yet. Please—"

"You confuse me with someone who likes to show mercy," he retorts.

Teagan and her ladies are watching us, and so are his guards. Somehow I know that he won't back down, not in front of them.

"At least let me heal him afterward." I bow low into the grass at his feet. "Please, my lord."

He doesn't reply. Instead his arm snaps back and the whip snakes out, lashing Owin's bare back with bright flame. Owin cries out, but quietly, muffling the sound with his palm.

One more quick lash, and then the King extinguishes the whip and stalks away.

It was a cruel punishment, but I expected much worse than two lashes. I let gold light unspool from my hands, salving the wounds, undoing the damage. Owin turns around, panting, his eyes bright with shame.

"I'm sorry," I whisper, as he puts his shirt and armor on again.

He nods, but he doesn't speak to me again for the next few hours. Neither does anyone else in our company. I ride alone, directly behind the Ash King and Teagan, probably so I'll be discouraged from any further mischief with the guards.

Around mid-afternoon, we enter a belt of shimmering green trees—a dense forest brimming with abundant life. I can sense the dampness of the ground, the sap running liquid through the trees, the dew collected in the hollows of gnarled roots. Birdsong ripples intermittently from the foliage overhead. All of it delights me deeply. In spite of what happened with Owin, I smile.

The Ash King turns around in his saddle at that moment and catches my expression. I wipe the smile from my face as quickly as I can, but it's too late. He has already seen it, and he's frowning, because he hates all happiness and good things.

He pulls his horse up short and falls back to ride beside me.

"Your Majesty." I bow my head. "Forgive me. I did not know smiling was prohibited."

"It's not."

"Thank the gods for small mercies."

He regards me quizzically, then says, "Tomorrow your skills will be tested. We will present you with an enemy spy who has been brutally tortured, and you will heal him."

"Tortured by you?" I ask.

"I have people who do that for me."

"Ah. So a personal torture session with the Ash King is a special privilege."

"That depends on what kind of torture we're discussing. Some torture can be—pleasurable. In that case, yes—it would be a privilege. A privilege rejected too easily by those who don't realize what they are missing."

I sneak a look at him, but he's staring straight ahead, his features perfectly immobile.

"Perhaps they don't care to know what they're missing, Your Gloriousness," I murmur. "Perhaps they prefer the company of people who know how to smile." *And people who don't whip their bodyguards*, I want to add—but I restrain myself.

The King inhales as if he's about to answer, but at that moment I see a shadow shifting in the sun-dappled wood. The shadow of a person with a bow, and an arrow poised to fly.

6

I don't think; I simply react, instinctively sucking moisture from nearby plants, hollows, anything—it all coalesces into a spinning orb of water, just in time—just as the shadow in the woods releases the arrow.

The deadly missile streaks toward the Ash King's head. I fling the orb of water into its path.

The arrow strikes the water with a dull *splorch*, and it's caught, halted, revolving in the ball of liquid. When I release the magic, the arrow falls, and the water splatters on the dusty road.

"Attackers!" shouts one of the guards. The King's soldiers and the Lord Mayor's guards close around me and Teagan, but the King leaps from his horse and shoves his way between our protectors, striding toward the forest. He lifts his hands, and fire streams from his palms, engulfing the beautiful trees in searing flame.

I scream, agonized.

The Ash King's head whips toward me. His teeth are bared, flickering with fire again, and his eyes are ablaze. He's frightening enough in broad daylight; I can't imagine facing him in the woods at night.

I don't have access to enough water to quench that blaze. His palms are still pouring fire into the trees, destroying everything in his urge to kill the person who shot at him. Judging by the screams rising from the inferno, there were several people concealed in that part of the forest.

A shout from behind me. More attackers are coming out of the trees on the opposite side of the road, engaging with the guards. Steel clashes, blades scrape and ring—I'm frozen, my mind spinning in place, snagged on the awful reality of the burning forest. Teagan has pulled a knife from somewhere and she's slashing at anyone who comes near her.

Trapped in the center of so many horse bodies and riders, my horse panics, rears a little, and then plunges down again, her hooves slamming into the road. My teeth snap together at the impact. The reek of burning wood and foliage fills my nostrils—a carnage of nests and blossoms singed and flaking away to ash. My eyes sting with the heat, and with angry tears.

Another arrow whistles past me. One of the guards cries out, blood spurting from a wound in his arm. His horse staggers, shouldering against mine, and I tighten my grip on the reins, but there's nowhere to run, no way to escape. Black-clad figures are everywhere, swarming the horses, slashing at their legs to hobble them. One horse goes down, then another, and the guards on their backs leap off, engaging directly with the enemy. The attackers' heads are wrapped in dark cloths—impossible to see a face, only fury-filled eyes and flashing blades.

I can't think what to do. I've never used my water magic to attack anyone, and I won't use the other side of my healing magic. Desperately I fling out strands of healing energy, trying to mend the leg of a wounded horse. But I can't focus properly—I've never had to do this during a battle. The job is only half done when my concentration breaks—one of the attackers has leaped onto the hindquarters of Owin's horse, right behind him. She's woman-shaped, lithe and deadly, wielding two crooked knives. She drags Owin's head back, exposing his neck—a gleam of savage metal—she's going to cut his throat—

The Ash King is there, seizing her by the collar. Dragging her off the horse. He opens his mouth and vomits fire into her face, and she screams, a piercing sound I've never heard from a human throat, not in all my days of healing. As she staggers into the trees, her head aflame, I siphon the water I dropped on the road and stream it toward her, quenching the blaze—both to help her and to keep her from setting the other half of the forest alight. One of the other attackers seizes her arm and escorts her away, and the rest flee as well.

I'm sobbing, crying for the pretty forest, for the burning woman, and for Owin who was nearly killed. The Ash King saved him.

And I saved the Ash King.

The King swings up onto his horse again, but instead of riding forward he leans over and grips my jaw. "Can you do anything? About that?" He jerks his head toward the blazing trees.

Mentally I scan the surrounding area, as far as my senses can reach.

"Not enough water here," I say miserably.

"Then let it go. It's done," he says. "Heal the horses quickly, and let's be gone."

Trembling, I dismount and unleash my healing magic, mending the sliced tendons of the poor horses.

Afterward, the King orders us to ride on, and as we're moving I let a line of magic flow into the arm of a nearby guard, the one who was struck by an arrow. In moments, I've sealed up his wound.

Teagan is riding beside me now, with her maids directly behind us. They seem all right, if a little shaken.

Teagan herself has that pained brightness in her eyes again. "An eventful journey," she says.

I vent a half-sob, half-laugh. "That's an understatement."

She glances over at me. "Stop antagonizing him," she says under her breath, so low I can barely hear it. "Stay quiet, be respectful, and you'll find he can be pleasant company."

There are two guards between us and the Ash King, so I feel safe enough to reply, "Is that what you want in a husband? Pleasant company, as long as you don't make him angry? And if you do, an explosion of fire? Whiplashes and scorch marks?"

"There are advantages to being his bride," she says. "And you have to admit, he's nice to look at. A thorough lover, I'm told."

"Are you sure he doesn't spew lava when he comes?" I whisper behind my hand. Her eyes flare wide, and her lips pucker like she's holding back a grin.

"Watch yourself, Cailin," she says. "I like you. I don't want to see you get hurt."

My mouth relaxes, my smile fading as I stare at the Ash King's back several paces ahead. I think of his flaming eyes and mouth, of the fire streaming from his hands, scarring the slender trees. I think of his palm searing my chest.

Teagan is kind. But she doesn't realize I've already been hurt.

The capital city of Cawn is even more glorious than I anticipated. Its outer walls with their pointed guard-towers are impressive enough, but the city's most dominant feature is the Triune Arch, three magnificent arches of white stone embellished with gold. They soar into the sky, so tall they seem to touch the clouds, and I feel minuscule as we ride nearer to them. Technically there are only two full arches now—the northernmost arch was broken during the Cheimhold Invasion six years ago.

I remember that time—the fear creeping through the land, the way we trembled as we went about our business in the fields, because the war was coming uncomfortably close to our peaceful home. I was eighteen at the time, and I narrowly escaped being drafted into military service for the Ash King's father. The Ash King himself was a nineteen-year-old Crown Prince back then.

Our army drove the invaders out of our lands, back across the volcanic mountains into their own territory. But there were several mages among the enemy's forces, and one of their wind-wielders broke the third arch. Another mage wounded the king—I'm not sure how. There was never a public announcement as to the nature of the king's wound, but he clung to life for another year before dying and leaving the throne to his son.

A month before the king died, the Crown Prince committed his great atrocity, scorching part of the kingdom and creating the Ashlands. With that memory so fresh in everyone's minds, there was plenty of opposition to his taking the throne, but with no other heir available to challenge him, he stepped into the role anyway. He had just demonstrated his cataclysmic power—no wonder everyone was too scared to seriously oppose him.

When he assumed the throne, the Ash King closed our borders to most trade and diplomacy and turned us into the insular, fortified kingdom we are today. The Undoing, the underground rebels my friends joined, want to open the borders again and resume international trade. And they want other things—various kinds of political and economic change—I heard Brayda and Rince talk about the rebels' goals many times before they left to join the cause. Personally I didn't care quite so much, as long as I was left alone to enjoy my preferred way of life.

As I ride through the streets with the Ash King's company, under a black band of shadow cast by the Triune Arch, I shrink inside, though I keep a smile on my face. I've stepped into the middle of a world far different than the one I know and love. This is a world of nobility and commerce, of favors given and exchanged, of political machinations and marriages of convenience. A world of assassinations and poison, of cutthroat competition between families and utter domination by one all-powerful man.

I'm so far out of my depth.

Throngs of people line our route, waving pennants of scarlet and deep gray. Unlike the citizens of Aighdas, these people cheer for the King, shouting louder whenever he graces them with a brief wave. They're gluttons for his favor, and after what I've seen of his terrible deeds, the blatant pandering disgusts me.

My eyes skip from one side of the street to the other, trying to gobble up all the sights, read every shop sign, scan every window full of fascinating wares. It's the only way to distract myself from the raw ache of homesickness that's starting to gnaw at my gut.

By the time we reach the gates of the Ash King's ancestral fortress, I'm sick of the smell of royal incense. It's dark, thick, overly sweet, and nauseating. I'm relieved when we're done with the city streets and we pass into the fortress by way of a long, torchlit tunnel. The immense thickness of the fortress walls astounds me. No wonder invaders have never been able to break through.

We cross the outer courtyard of the fortress, then travel briefly through an area of fresh-smelling lawns and gardens. By now the sun has set completely, and despite the tall posts bearing lanterns to light our way, I can't see much of the grounds.

The ride from the outer gates to the inner ones is longer than I expected. The guard I'm riding with seems afraid to talk to me lest he anger the King, so I have no one to show me any points of interest or explain the layout of the place.

At last we enter the inner gates, and I see the royal palace uplit in all its glory—white stone and gilded ornamentation, just like the arches. There seem to be a hundred pinnacles and turrets and gables, a thousand windows and arches and balconies. Kings and queens have added onto the place for generations, and though it's a bit haphazard and asymmetrical, it still manages to retain a monumental, regal beauty.

I dismount, and the mare is led away. I'm sorry to see her go; other than the belongings in my bag, she was my last piece of home. Servants and guards appear, ushering our party up the sprawling white steps. The servants focus on Teagan, since she's one of the Favored. They don't seem to notice me.

The gigantic doors of the palace are inlaid with glossy, multi-hued panels of petrified wood, probably from my region. I sidestep out of the flow of people and brush my fingers against them, just to feel a piece of home.

Everyone else is inside now, and one of the four door guards approaches me, stern eyes peering through the slit in his black helmet. "Please enter. We need to close the doors."

"Where did this wood come from?" I ask impulsively.

"I'm not sure, my lady. If you would enter."

"Of course." Hitching my bag higher on my shoulder, I walk further into the creamy gold luxury of the entry hall. The walls are encrusted with beautiful carvings, some of stone, some of wood. Elaborate tapestries and paintings depict scenes from our kingdom's history. Ahead, a broad triple staircase leads to upper floors and different wings of the palace. Candelabra and chandeliers lend a soft glow to the space, but it's still too grand to look homelike.

The servants are guiding Teagan, her maids, and her guards up the left-hand staircase, explaining that all the Favored contestants will be staying in the East Wing. "Bedrooms and privies are on the second floor. Parlors, breakfast rooms, and garden access are on the first floor," explains a tall, crisp woman with a bunch of keys hanging at her waist. Her voice and the voices of the others fade as they reach the top of the stairs and disappear down a hallway.

I'm left alone in the entry hall. Alone is a relative term, because there are at least eight guards standing motionless, in full armor, at different points around this room. That's in addition to the four guarding the palace doors, and I spotted more guards along the route from the outer gates to the inner ones.

Are all kings this well-protected, or is there really a danger to the Ash King's life? The assassination attempt on the road seemed clumsy, poorly planned. If those attackers were part of the Undoing, and that was their best effort, there's no way they could ever make it into the palace itself.

Not without someone on the inside.

Everyone seems to have forgotten about the healer the Ash King conscripted and dragged to his palace. I've been standing in the entry hall for a long time, and my eyes are starting to prickle with angry, humiliated tears.

What am I supposed to do now? Where am I supposed to sleep? The insides of my thighs are sore and chafed from all the riding, and I don't have the heart to heal myself. In a strange way, I *want* to feel the misery, the abandonment, and the loneliness. They feed my hatred for the Ash King.

I'm just getting up the courage to approach one of the stiff, silent armored guards when a voice from above booms, "Healer." The word echoes through the hall.

The Ash King stands on the landing of the central staircase, with a male servant and two guards poised motionless behind him. He has removed the crown of black-iron leaves and he's wearing a loose, silky robe that belts at his waist and trails on the carpeted steps.

"Your Majesty," I say, and bow. It's all I can manage without crying.

"Come here," he orders.

I mount the steps, my cheeks burning.

"Look at me," he says, when I reach the landing.

Reluctantly, I lift my eyes to his.

"I neglected to give the servants instructions regarding you," he says. "My fetching of you was unplanned, so they were not expecting your presence, and they did not recognize your importance to the competition. This oversight will not be repeated."

It's almost an apology. "Shall I follow Teagan to the East Wing?" I ask.

"It would make sense for you to be near the women you'll be treating," he muses. "And yet I do not want you interacting too closely with them after hours, lest you become partial to certain contestants. No, I think I will place you elsewhere."

He looks past me, toward the sound of hasty footsteps and jingling keys. "Mistress Effelin. Just the person I wished to see. We have another guest to place— Cailin, the Healer for the Favored."

"Oh!" The woman looks startled and a little frightened. "Did you come in with the rest of them, dear? I beg Your Majesty's forgiveness—I did not see her. I have a room I can put her in, if she doesn't mind sharing with the maids of the Favored."

The Ash King's features harden. "She is possibly the most important participant in the Calling," he says. "She is responsible for maintaining the health of my future bride. She will not share with the maids."

"Yes, yes, Your Majesty. So foolish of me." The woman is practically trembling, curtsying deeply.

"The Rose Room is clean and well-ordered, yes?" he says.

"The—the Rose Room?" falters Mistress Effelin. "It is, yes. But—my lord—"

"Put her there."

"But Your Majesty—"

The Ash King draws himself up taller, flames sparking at his fingertips.

"Yes, Your Majesty," whispers Mistress Effelin. "Come, my lady."

She guides me along the central hallway, dimly lit by infrequent candles in sconces. I hear footsteps behind us, and I glance back. The King and the three men with him are following us. His face is inscrutable, but his eyes glow scarlet.

Mistress Effelin pauses at a finely carved door and fumbles with her keys. She unlocks it, murmuring, "A moment, while I light the lamps."

I wait in the hallway, pressing myself to the wall while the Ash King glides past. His nearness sends a shiver over my skin. He is pure male power deceptively draped in whispering robes and silky hair.

One of the guards hurries ahead, stopping at a pair of doors a short distance down the hall. He opens the doors for the Ash King, then bows and stands aside.

Ice forms in my stomach, chilling my nerves. Is my room next to the Ash King's chambers?

Right before going through the open doors, the Ash King looks at me, and the corner of his mouth twitches.

The bastard put me on the same hall as him. I'm going to be living next door to the Ash King.

Goodbye to any hope of sleeping soundly during this competition.

"I will send you a maid," says Mistress Effelin, bustling out of the room. "My apologies for the delay, my lady."

"It's no problem. I don't need a maid—"

But she's already hurrying away, muttering something about towels and soap.

I venture into the bedroom, my shoes squishing on a thick, soft rug. Immediately I set my bag down and slide off my shoes. I'm used to going barefoot all day, and my toes are crying for relief from the unrelenting leather. I won't pass up the chance to soothe my tired feet in this plush carpet.

The instant my soles sink into it, I release a soft squeal of delight.

And then I see the bed.

It's beautiful, with satiny, scrunchy, rose-colored covers trimmed with tassels. And there are so many deep squishy pillows. I fling myself face-down onto it, thanking the Heartsfire aloud.

"You should be thanking *me*," says a familiar voice. "I take it you like your room."

I sit bolt upright in the bed, tendrils of hair tumbling over my face.

The Ash King is leaning against the wall of my room, his silky robe parted in a V, showing the slopes of his chest and stomach.

"How did you get in here?" And then I remember myself and gulp, "Your Majesty," with a clumsy half-bow.

With his thumb, he indicates a door nearby, half-concealed by a damask curtain.

"There is a door from my room to yours?" I ask.
"Why?"

"This room used to belong to my father's mistress."

Startled, I survey the room quickly. There's nothing openly scandalous about it—it's a luxurious, well-appointed room for a lady. In our kingdom, sexuality is not shamed as it is in other lands. Virginity is not so highly prized, sex work is accepted as needful, and open marriages or polyamorous groupings are common. Still, I can't help feeling that my presence in this room is inappropriate at best and dangerous at worst.

The Ash King watches my reaction, with his chin tilted down and his eyes still gleaming deep red, like twin fires built far back in the recesses of a dark cave.

"My lord," I say, as calmly as I can manage. "Are you sure it is appropriate for me to be here?"

"Perhaps not. Yet here you will stay."

"But people will think—that I—that we—" I swallow. "They will think you favor me in some illicit way. What if they're uncertain about trusting their daughters' health to me? They might fear that I have designs on the throne and that I'll sabotage the contestants to get it."

"Do you have designs on the throne?" The Ash King folds his arms.

"Of course not."

Again the twitch at the corner of his mouth. "You say that as if it's the last thing you'd ever want."

"Because it *is* the last thing I'd ever want. My lord." The honorific is an afterthought, but he doesn't seem to mind my lack of decorum. "You don't know me. What if I'm an assassin?"

He smiles. It's brief, like a lightning flash. Gone in a blink.

"You, an assassin. The girl with the muddy knees and the tangled hair, who came from the field in her underthings—"

"Those were not my underthings," I gasp.

He looks at me sharply, and I press my fingers to my mouth. I interrupted the King.

"Your pardon, Majesty," I breathe.

"No assassin worth the name would have presented herself to me like that. And no one knew I was going to fetch you until mere hours before my arrival. You could not be a plant of the Undoing. And if you were one of those despicable rebels, you wouldn't have protected me on the road today."

"Maybe I protected you so I could gain your trust," I reply.

"If you were a spy looking to gain closer access, you would have slept with me, to deepen that trust."

I press my lips together, flushing. "So you're saying if I *do* sleep with you, that means I'm a spy."

He lifts an eyebrow. "Your logic is flawed. Suffice it to say that I like the idea of having a protective water-wielder and a skilled healer in the room next to mine, in case any agents of the Undoing make their way to my chambers."

Pulling his robe tighter around himself, he moves to the door. "And in case you have any plans to seduce me— this door locks. On my side."

"Your Majesty," I say crisply. "Again, I was not trying to seduce you during our journey, nor will I ever attempt such a thing."

"That is fortunate, because I am no longer interested in your body or your personality, only your magic."

"Well, that's—that's perfect. I'm glad." *Because I was never interested in your body or personality, you pompous, cruel asshole.* I can't help smirking a little at my inner monologue, and he narrows his eyes, the scarlet glow brightening.

"There it is again," he murmurs. "That smile. You cannot tell me that's an innocent smile. It's too full of secrets."

"I'm afraid you're misinterpreting me, my lord," I tell him. "I have no secrets." Except the alternate side of my healing magic, which he will never, ever discover.

"I think you have many secrets." The Ash King moves toward me. "Things you don't even know about yourself."

"I'm very self-aware," I murmur.

He's drifting nearer, right up to the bed. His ringed hand trails along the covers, catching a tassel and playing with it. His fingers aren't slender and fragile, though; they look strong, ready to close around the grip of a knife or the hilt of a sword. Ready to wield whips of flame, or to blast fire at his enemies.

He killed people today, with those hands.

"How does it work?" The question slips out before I can think better of it.

"What?" He lifts his eyes to mine.

"Your magic. When I wield water, I have to pull it from somewhere. I can't produce it. But your body emits fire naturally."

He holds my gaze so long without speaking that a strange heat flushes over my skin and my pulse quickens. His cheekbones and jawline are so perfectly parallel to each other, and his forehead is so smooth except for a tiny dent between his eyebrows. His nose—just the right size.

A thorough lover, Teagan said. *Nice to look at.*

Why am I thinking of those words?

The Ash King leans forward a little, and a strand of his white hair slips over his shoulder and brushes against my hand. "Have the maid bring some food to your room. It has been a long day, and you must be hungry. Good night, Healer."

He leaves the room, closing the curtained door just as the maid enters.

How odd. Did he hear her coming?

7

The man in front of me has been taken apart.
Literally.

His chest cavity gapes, ribs and flayed skin folded
back to reveal glistening organs still pulsing with life. His
penis lies severed between his legs. He's missing all his
toenails and both his thumbs. His mouth gapes, the
bleeding stump of a tongue quivering helpless in the dark,
moaning orifice.

I retch and turn away, just in time to avoid splattering
the victim in my vomit.

"I thought you were a healer," says the Ash King
coldly from behind me. "Surely you've seen damaged
bodies before."

"I've healed plague victims covered in oozing boils,
and I once regrew a man's hand after he was mauled by an
ash-burrower," I gasp. "But this—the cruelty—"

"Yes, I let my Head Inquisitor do whatever he liked
this time, since the man would eventually be repaired,"
says the King. "He may have gone a bit further than I
intended."

I throw him a scathing look. "A bit? This is
monstrous."

The Ash King takes a step toward me, eyes flaring
red. "Remember yourself, Healer." He jerks his head
slightly toward the two guards in the room.

"My humblest apologies, my lord."

After inspecting me for a moment, he turns to the guards. "One of you call a servant to clean up this mess," he says. "And the other fetch a strong drink for the healer. Apparently she needs it."

The guards hurry from the room.

"Begin, Healer," the King orders.

"I've never done such extensive repairs to a body before," I falter.

"The Ricter who measured you this morning assures me you are more than capable. You have the highest power reading he's ever seen in a healer. In fact, if your abilities were anything but healing and water work, I'd have you Muted. Even now, I'm wondering if I should call a tattoo mage to Mute the water side of your magic."

"Please." I swallow the panicked lump in my throat. "When I return home, I'll need my powers to irrigate the fields."

"Your people have become too dependent on you. That's the trouble with magic, you see. People rely on it, and they fail to innovate other methods of doing the work."

I open my mouth to protest, but he's not wrong. I've had similar thoughts myself—what if something happened to me, and my people had no failsafe, no backup plan, no technology to bring water to the crops when rainfall is scarce?

"You are right, Your Majesty," I concede.

His pale eyebrows rise. "How kind of you to admit it. Now get to work."

I glance at the agonized man. He's almost not a man anymore—just a body full of pain. I'm the only one who can restore him, bring him back to himself.

I start with his penis. Picking it up, I hold it against the stump and lace threads of golden healing magic through it, binding the flesh back together, restoring blood flow, smoothing the skin. My magic soaks into his bruised balls as well, easing the pain, repairing them.

As I'm working, the servant enters quietly and cleans my sick off the floor. One of the guards brings a cup of something and sets it on a nearby table. I ignore everyone and everything, entirely focused on my work, dimly aware of the King dismissing the servant and telling the guards to stand outside.

With one hand continuing the work on the victim's penis, I splay my other hand in midair over his chest and begin winding threads of gold light around each rib, pulling them back into place, filling the cracks. I calm the inflamed flesh and replenish the blood supply. When the penis is finished, I hold both hands over the chest cavity and devote my full attention to its repair.

"Interesting choice, starting with his dick," says the King.

"Men prize their dicks highly, don't they?" There's a bite to my tone, and I omit any honorifics. As I suspected, the King doesn't reprimand me for it now that we're alone. Interesting. He doesn't mind a little insolence from me when no one is around to witness the challenge to his authority. And the tortured man doesn't count—he's unconscious now.

"If someone cut your dick off, you'd want it reattached as soon as possible," I say.

"Not before my tongue," the King answers. "Though I'm equally skilled with both of them."

The suggestive heat in his words sends a tiny ripple of arousal through my lower belly. And then I'm immediately sickened by myself, for feeling that sensation in the face of such horrific torment.

"Of course the women you bed *have* to say that," I muse aloud as I reconstruct the layers of tissue, nerves, and blood vessels for the man's chest.

"The women I bed are not faking their pleasure." The Ash King sounds offended, and maybe a little uncertain.

"How would you know? They'd be too afraid to say otherwise. Now please—I need quiet to do my work."

He grumbles, but I'm too deep in my work to care.

When I finish the man's chest an hour later, I drink a little from the cup the guard brought. Just a single burning gulp, to ease the tightness of my nerves.

When I approach the victim again, the Ash King is leaning over him, inspecting the results. "Impressive attention to detail. Seamless, truly. And he is whole inside, as well?"

"I'll multiply his blood cells at the end and do a last scan of him, just to be sure," I reply.

"A scan?"

"I can sense things that are wrong in the body. Especially when I close my eyes."

We're standing on opposite sides of the victim, bent slightly to inspect him, and when we both look up, our profiles are far too close—so close I can smell mint and herbs on his breath, and he can probably smell alcohol on mine.

The Ash King's hair is tied back today, secured in a loose plait. A crown of antlers and ferns, wrought from black iron and gold, runs from one temple around the back of his skull to the other temple. It settles atop his ears, branching against his cheekbones, and it leaves his smooth forehead bare. His eyebrows are penciled dark, and sooty lines highlight the shape of his eyes. I've never noticed how long his lashes are—or perhaps those have been enhanced as well.

"Your eyes," he says quietly. "They turn gold when you work."

"Apologies, my lord. It is a strange effect."

He hesitates, his gaze averting from mine. His lips part for a second before he says, "It's beautiful."

A jittery, tremulous sensation unfurls through my chest. I'm afraid of him, that's what it is. Nothing else.

"Thank you, Majesty," I reply.

Now that the man is unconscious, his mouth is only slightly open. I press his chin to open it farther, and I let threads of magic wriggle between his lips. Slowly I begin to recreate the tongue. I can feel the phantom shape of it, the edges of the space it used to occupy, the form it took. All I have to do is fill in that space, coax the existing cells to multiply and the new cells to arrange themselves in the right pattern.

It's painstaking work, regrowing something that's been entirely removed. I didn't see the tongue lying anywhere around, and I didn't want to ask for it in case the answer was too terrible.

"I have to greet all the Favored officially this evening," says the King abruptly. "The last two arrive today. I have things to prepare."

"I'm sure you do," I say. "Please do not stay on my account."

"You'll be all right alone? In this—" he glances around at the stark stone room, with its chains and bloodstains— "wretched place?"

"I won't be happy," I reply. "But I'll be fine."

"Good. Because I need to go."

But he doesn't leave. He keeps standing there, staring, and when I finally look up, his dark eyes are fixed on mine with an expression of utter fascination. There's something else in his manner, too—a brittle, panicked energy.

"Are you nervous, Your Majesty?" My fingertips twitch in midair and my golden lines ripple back and forth, making the layers of the tongue.

"Why should I be nervous?" he scoffs. "These women are here at my will, for my pleasure."

"Maybe because the entire kingdom is invested in the outcome of this competition, and the Capital's population has swelled with visitors who plan to attend each public event? Owin tells me all the inns and empty rooms in the city are full."

The King makes another scoffing sound and strides to the table where I left my cup of liquor. He drains it in two great gulps.

"Or maybe you are nervous because you have to choose a lover, a mother for your children, and a companion for life."

"Children. Gods." He slams the cup down, but he doesn't stop me, so I venture further.

"Maybe you are concerned about your own safety. But Owin tells me every contestant was thoroughly vetted, along with their guards and servants. Only long-time, loyal family servants were allowed to accompany the Favored— well-known people, no one new, no one who might have slipped into another person's identity. You need not fear on that account."

"I don't fear," he snaps. "I can defend myself."

"As you did yesterday, from that arrow."

"You saved me, yes. I have already acknowledged it. Do you want some reward? Isn't my trust enough?"

"Reward?" My mind begins to spin through the possibilities. I dare not ask for much, but perhaps I can use his grudging gratitude to my advantage. "The only reward I need is the chance to explore the city alone this afternoon."

He shakes his head, striding back to the table on which my subject lies. "Not alone. As you said, the city is crowded with strangers of every kind. Our streets are haunted by unsavory thieves and ruffians hoping to take advantage of gullible visitors. You would be a kitten among wolves."

"A kitten?" Both my eyebrows shoot up, and I nearly forget my hold on the healing magic. "I'm not a kitten."

"You seemed fairly helpless during the attack yesterday."

"That was—I was taken by surprise."

"As we all were. Yet Teagan managed to draw a weapon and fight back."

Something vicious uncurls in my heart. "Teagan isn't a healer. I'm sworn to help, not to harm, unless I'm defending someone else."

"Or yourself."

"Yes—I suppose." But I don't sound convincing.

His upper lip curls, a spark in his eye. "Kitten."

I strike back with the only barb I have left, one I've been reserving. "Perhaps Your Majesty is nervous because he's afraid of repeating the past."

The Ash King's eyes flare scarlet, roiling with flame. He lunges for me, gripping my shoulder and pushing me away from the table, back against the wall of the torture room. His hot fingers clutch my chin. "What do you mean by that?" he hisses.

There is water on the floor, a small puddle the servant didn't mop up thoroughly. I draw it to myself, creating a liquid ball that I cradle in my palm in case I need it.

"You can't always control it, can you?" I whisper. "Sometimes it's too strong."

"I am the King," he says hoarsely, his breath hot against my face. "I am always in control. Of myself, of everyone in this city, in this kingdom. And I'm in control of *you.*"

He presses tighter to me, until I can feel the surge of his chest against my own. The stiff lapels of his coat rub against my breasts, a rough graze through the light fabric of my shirt, and my nipples peak at the contact. I should have worn a full corset today. My body is suddenly alight, quivering with raw, scintillating sensation.

The Ash King still has my chin in his hand, my face tipped up to his.

"Yes, you're in control, Majesty," I breathe, because it's the only smart thing to say. Teagan warned me to be subservient and quiet. Why couldn't I listen to her?

But as the King himself reminded me, I'm not Teagan. I'm the grimy girl who showed up to his summons in her underthings. No wonder he was shocked at the sight of me. As the memory surfaces in my mind, I can't help it—I smirk a little, in spite of my furiously pounding heart.

"Don't," he says, breathless, his eyes dropping to my mouth.

"You said smiling was allowed," I whisper.

"When you smile, I feel as if there is happiness quivering on your lips, just here." He brushes my mouth with the tip of his thumb. "And if I want it, all I have to do is…"

His mouth dips toward mine.

The man on the table groans suddenly, loudly.

The Ash King throws himself backward, his eyes wide and alarmed as if he can't believe what he almost did. Which makes two of us.

"Do your work well," he snaps, and then he's gone.

For the next two hours I work over the torture victim, repairing the rest of his tongue, regrowing his thumbs and toenails, healing all his bruises. By the end he is fully awake, quietly awed by what I have done for him.

The Ricter who measured me early this morning comes in to watch me finish the process, and he checks over my work. He's an elderly man, a kinder sort than most Ricters I've met. He rakes gnarled fingers through his gray beard and nods. "Excellent work, excellent. You will do well with the Favored. Are you tired, child?"

I'm exhausted. My wells of healing energy are deep, but this task has nearly emptied them. "Yes, I am tired."

"I'm told there is refreshment in the gardens for the Favored and their ladies. The King said you would be permitted to meet the women you'll care for, or if you prefer, that you might venture into the city with a guard as your companion. The guard is just outside to escort you wherever you'd like to go."

"What of this man?" I gesture to the victim. "Will he be released?"

"I believe he will be imprisoned, my lady. He is a spy from Cheimhold, so he cannot be set free. But he will not be tortured again."

The man on the table is watching me, and I meet his gaze. He's in his mid-thirties, with a patchy brown beard and eyes full of gratitude.

"Thank you," he whispers. "For my tongue, and my thumbs, and my—for everything."

"I'll come and visit you if I can," I tell him, laying a palm on his forehead.

He catches my hand and presses my knuckles to his mouth. "I am in your debt."

"You'll have no chance to repay her, lad," says the Ricter. He calls in the guards to take the prisoner away. I sidestep them as they enter, then make my way out of the torture room.

I'm not sure whether I should meet the Favored—who will probably turn up their noses at a simple healer—or go into the city with some surly guardsman. Both options have their perks and disadvantages.

The guard who's been assigned to escort me is standing in the hall, helmet in hand. When I see him, I forget my weariness, and a smile breaks over my face.

The guard is Owin.

The Ash King gave me my reward—an afternoon of sightseeing. And he gave me Owin.

8

Magic-wielders are few and far between in Bolcan, but they pop up randomly, regardless of bloodline or age, which is why the King's Ricters are constantly traveling, testing whole villages at a time. Most abilities surface around the age of seven, like mine—but they can bloom as early as seven months or as late as seventy.

Since the King discourages magical study or advancement, and prefers to rely on non-magical technologies, there's no noticeably high concentration of wielders in the Capital. As Owin and I wander the city, I spot two people with a Muting tattoo on their left wrist, and I see a plump wind-wielder using her air powers to dry her laundry as it hangs on the line. She has no tattoo, so her abilities must be fairly mild. I smile at the chubby toddlers clinging to her skirts and send a thread of magic to heal one child's skinned knee. He stops crying, watching the line of golden light sweep over his injury.

A little farther along the same street, booths and tables cluster at the edges of the road, between the shop doorways. There's a rattle of dice, a merry twang of street music, the smell of hot spun sugar and the cloying essence of *tobak* smoke.

Street performers are everywhere, including a half-naked male fire-swallower whom Owin pauses to ogle. Maybe he thinks his admiration is concealed by the helmet, but I notice, and it makes me smile. The fire-swallower seems to have a low-level wielding ability, but he doesn't produce the fire—he pulls it from several candles arranged in a ring around him, and the flame goes out fairly quickly once he has it in hand or in his mouth. There's a box of matches near his feet so he can relight the candles.

After watching his show, we continue along the street. I pause under one colorful awning to inspect the woven jewelry the craftswoman has laid out, but I have no coin with me. The King's herald mentioned a clothing allowance and a monthly stipend, but no one has discussed such things with me yet.

"Take a look at this fellow, Cailin." Owin tugs at my elbow. I relent and follow him to another shadowy booth, where a man draped in heavy, hooded robes is creating portraits with pebbles. His fingers fly over the array of tiny multi-colored stones on his table, arranging and rearranging them to create the likenesses of the onlookers. It's an ever-changing work of art, morphing seamlessly from one face to the next. Murmurs of astonishment circulate through the gathered crowd, and coins chink into the man's collection mug.

As I draw nearer, my focus shifts from the portraits to the fingers creating them. And my heart jerks.

I'd recognize those slender ebony fingers anywhere. Those fingers used to hold my hand as we ran barefoot through the potsava fields. They dragged me away from an ash-burrower nest filled with newborn monsters. There's a pink scar across the back of the dark right hand—my first healing attempt, imperfect. And those fingers were the first ones to nudge between my legs and tease me into a throat-searing, back-arching climax.

Rince is the portrait-maker.

Rince is here.

I want to push back the heavy hood he's wearing and shout his name, but I stop myself in time. Rince and Brayda went off to join the Undoing. They are anarchists now, possibly living with false names and identities. Which means I need to approach him carefully. Is Brayda here too? I glance around, but I don't see her.

"Do you have coin?" I nudge Owin's arm.

"Coin? Oh, yes—and the King said you were to buy whatever you wanted, in his name. Here." He tugs a small object from his pocket and passes it to me. "He gave me this, for you. I forgot about it."

I raise my eyebrows at him. "Do you forget the King's orders often?"

I can see his shamed grimace despite the helmet. "Sometimes," he admits.

For a moment I wonder if the King's punishment of Owin was—perhaps not deserved, but justified, in part? Owin is charming and fun, but he does seem careless. He's new to this role, though. He will learn, and hopefully not because of more fiery lashes.

The object he gives me is a silver ring, set with a small disc of glossy petrified wood. A tiny pair of antlers has been etched into the surface—the Ash King's symbol, reminiscent of the fire stags of the South. Those creatures have always lived among the active volcanoes along our southern border, and now I'm told they roam the Ashlands as well, ever since the King scorched that part of the world.

I slip the ring onto one of my fingers. It's a perfect fit, and I'm disturbed by how much I love it. I shouldn't be wearing any gift of the Ash King's. For a second I close my eyes, letting the phantom pain of the burning handprint sear my chest again. I can unwind wounds that I've healed, returning the flesh to its damaged state. I don't dare perform that kind of magic now, but perhaps I'll do it later, just for a moment, to help me remember why I need to hate him.

"The ring is lovely," I tell Owin. "But what I need right now is coin, to get that artist's attention. I'll pay you back when I'm given my stipend."

"All right then." He digs in his pocket and produces five coins, which I snatch eagerly.

I shoulder my way forward until I'm right in front of the table, and I hold out the coins. "Payment for a portrait?" My voice trembles a little.

The movement of those quick fingers stutters briefly.

"Perhaps you'd sit for a private portrait?" The hooded man's voice is deep, rich velvet, the words rolling smooth and rounded from his lips. It's not quite the voice I remember, but he could be altering it to suit his persona. My pulse flutters.

"I would be open to a private session," I murmur.

"Please wait behind the booth. I'll be there shortly." The fingers resume their perpetual motion.

I tug Owin around to the back of the booth.

"What are we doing?" He sounds confused.

"That portrait-maker is an old friend. Is there any way you can leave me alone with him for a little while?"

Owin lifts his eyebrows. "*That* kind of friend?"

"Jealous?" I smirk at him. I already know he's not, but I can't help teasing.

"No," he says. "I—you're very beautiful, but—"

"Why don't you go inspect the glorious physique of that fire-swallower again?" My smile broadens as Owin's eyes flare wide. "Just for a little while."

77

"Don't mind if I do," says Owin. "But stay right here."

"We might go in there." I point to a tea shop directly behind the portrait-maker's booth. "But I won't wander anywhere else, I promise."

"You know what will happen to me if any harm comes to you." Owin's blue eyes shine soberly through the opening of his helmet.

"I'll be careful."

He nods and stalks away, back up the street toward the fire show.

A moment after Owin leaves, the portrait-maker comes around to the back of the booth. He catches my arm and hustles me toward the tea shop—but instead of pulling me inside, he draws me into the dark, narrow alley beside it. The space is just a crack between buildings, barely wide enough for two people to stand abreast, and there's rubbish scattered along it, but at least it doesn't smell.

"Rince," I whisper. "That's you, isn't it?"

The man pulls off his hood.

9

With the hood discarded, Rince's features are clearly visible—broad nose, full lips, prominent cheekbones, a jawline that tempts my fingertips. In just two years, he's grown even more handsome. He's lost the boyish softness of his face and gained a bold edge to his features, one that I find very enticing.

"I forgot how beautiful you are," I whisper.

"Cailin." He takes my wrists and slams them against the wall, and he kisses me, his soft lips stealing my breath. I hum into his mouth, my body heating, reminding me of all the things he used to do to it…. before he left me…

I pull back, breaking the kiss. "I didn't expect to see you here."

"It's the 'Calling of the Favored,' love." His teeth flash as he smiles. "Too good an opportunity to miss."

"Then you're here with the Undo—"

He presses his lips to mine again, cutting off the word. His tongue sweeps through my mouth, triggering a wanton tingle between my legs.

"Why are you here, *mo stór*? Was that a palace guard with you?" He presses soft kisses along my neck, moving down toward my shoulder.

"I've been conscripted as a healer for the competition," I gasp. "Heartsfire, Rince—this is quite the welcome. I wasn't sure you'd be happy to see me."

He cups my face, his eyes burning into mine. Always so intense, those eyes, with the rabid light of purpose in them. "I had to leave you. You understand why. My beliefs are everything. The cause is everything."

"So you and Brayda—you're not—"

"Together? Sometimes. We share rooms, and occasionally beds. But I haven't forgotten you, or this." He cups his hand between my legs, and I release a soft whimper in spite of myself. I reach out, running my fingertips along the black braids clustering over his head.

His warm palm passes under my loose shirt, skimming the curve of my breast, then sliding down to my lower belly. I can barely breathe as his fingers nudge beneath the waistband of my pants, questing lower until one finger pushes into the seam of my sex, pressing deep, tempting the little sensitive place he knows so well.

I didn't realize how deeply I've been craving intimate touch. I'm barely conscious of where we are and how foolish this is—my entire focus centers on that one part of my body, and on the sensations rippling from Rince's expert fingers.

"I've missed doing this," he murmurs. "The way you react so quickly—I've always loved that about you. Gods, you're soaked already."

His central finger slides deeper, plunging into my slit, stimulating inner places that haven't been stroked by anyone but me in far too long. I'm paralyzed, helpless to each growing surge of pleasure.

And then he stops.

My eyes blink open, searching for the cause of the sudden halt.

He's staring at my right hand, which he still has pinned to the wall. He turns it so he can see the ring I'm wearing more clearly.

"This is a real palace ring," he says. "Not one of the imitations they sell in the market."

"The Ash King gave it to me."

Rince pulls his hand out of my pants, and I bite my lip to keep from whining my disappointment. "You've seen him? Spoken to him personally?"

"My room is next to his."

Bright, savage hunger wakes in his eyes. "Are you serious?"

"Yes," I say cautiously.

"What a chance!" he exclaims. "What luck! It's as if the Heartsfire itself is supporting our cause!"

"What do you mean?"

"Cailin, surely you see how perfect this is? You have intimate access to the King—"

"I wouldn't say *intimate*," I cut in. "He trusts me. He wants a healer nearby to help him if he's wounded."

"Surely he has a royal healer who could fill that role for him."

"I suppose." I hadn't really thought of it, but there must be a palace healer who already tends to the King. Why did he choose me to live beside him, and not *that* healer, who has an established role and proven loyalty?

"Cailin, listen to me." Rince grips my hands. "You are a beautiful gift from home. The Heartsfire has sent you to join our cause—" he leans in and whispers, "to kill the King."

I jerk my fingers away from his. "You can't ask me to do that. You know the oath I've taken."

"An oath to heal the helpless and protect the defenseless. By doing this, you'd be saving countless lives. The Ash King has killed so many people, love—it's only a matter of time before he does it again. And you could save them all—you, a miracle straight from the bosom of Analoir Doitean, from our beloved mountain."

I tremble against the cool stone wall of the alley, caught between it and Rince's zealous glow.

"Have you seen the King hurt people?" Rince asks.

Pressing my lips together and averting my eyes, I nod.

"He's a cruel, wicked man. And beyond that, his policies are hurting the kingdom, Cailin. They're destroying us as a nation. He needs to go."

I nod again.

"Good girl." Rince strokes my cheek with the backs of his knuckles. "Listen, Brayda will be back any moment. Join us for tea, and we'll discuss a plan."

"We'll have to be quick," I whisper. "My guard will be back soon."

"I'll go wash up." Rince wiggles his damp fingers at me with a grin. "Meet you inside."

With the help of the Ash King's ring, I'm given my choice of tables in the tea shop. I choose a booth in the back corner, with padded benches and curtains half-drawn around it—perfect for a clandestine meeting with representatives of the Undoing.

When Rince enters the shop, he's hooded again, and there's a second hooded figure with him. My stomach ripples with excitement at the thought of seeing Brayda.

But when they reach the booth and she pushes back her hood, it's all I can do not to gasp.

Brayda has light brown skin like mine, tanned to a deep coppery glow. Her hair is straighter and darker, and she's thinner than me, her build more angular. All of that is the same—but her face—

Her features, once smooth, are now seamed with shiny scars. They look like—burn scars.

I can't *not* mention it.

"Heartsfire, Brayda." I rise from the table and reach for her. She hugs me briefly, rigidly, a performative act, not the heartfelt squeeze she used to give me. "What happened to you?"

"Your Ash King happened," she says in a low tone, taking a seat on a bench. "You should know—you were there. I told you, Rince," she snaps at him. "I told you I saw Cailin in the King's traveling party."

Wait—Brayda was part of the group that attacked us? She was the one who nearly cut Owin's throat?

"I thought you were mistaken in the hurry of things." Rince frowns at her. "You were practically delirious with pain after the attack."

"Oh, she was there," Brayda confirms. "She saw him spew fire in my face and light up my head like a candle. Lucky for me our clothes and head-wraps were treated with fire retardant, or I would have died. Of course the fire retardant didn't help our friends in the east woods. They burned alive anyway, cooked inside their skins by the Ash King's inferno. And you, Cailin—you protected him. I saw it."

I'm about to retort, but the tea server comes by our table, so I resume my seat and wait until she takes our order and departs.

Then I lean across the table toward Brayda and Rince, keeping my voice low. "I didn't know what was happening. I reacted instinctively."

"Your instinct should have been to kill him as soon as you had the chance, with a knife, water powers, whatever you had at hand. At the very *least* you should have let that arrow go through his head. We had him, Cailin. We *had* him, and you ruined our one shot. The archer whose arrow you blocked was our best markswoman, and she's dead now. A lot of people are dead because of what you did. And more will die if you don't make the right choice."

"I'm sorry," I gasp. "I'm so sorry. I didn't know. But your face—don't you have healers among the anarchists?"

"We do, which is why I'm not lying in a bed with raw seeping wounds all over my face. Not all healers are as good as you, Cailin. I've come to realize that the hard way. Rince could only find one Anarchist healer on such short notice, and she did her best with me."

"I wish I could help," I whisper. "But you know I can't, once it's scarred over…"

"I know," snaps Brayda. "I'm proud to wear my scars. What have *you* to be proud of?"

It's the worst kind of whiplash—Rince's over-enthusiastic and heavily sexual welcome, versus Brayda's anger. She's treating me like a traitor. Maybe I am.

"If I do what you want me to do—" I begin.

"*If?*" Brayda cuts in. "Is that even a question? Cailin, we've had these discussions before. You know how many people the Ash King has killed, and how his current policies keep our nation from growing, trading, and

85

forming alliances. You know what we stand for—opening talks with other countries, engaging in trade, maybe even pushing our kingdom's borders out farther. We need a fighting military, not just a defensive one. And we'll abolish the Muting of wielders. We'll encourage the open practice of unbridled magic, as well as magical education and expansion. That's something you want, yes? Not this murderous king who holds everyone back."

"So when he's gone, who will be in charge?" I ask.

"No one." Rince reaches to take my hand. "And everyone. That's the beauty of anarchy."

"But these things you want—trade and expansion, a different kind of military—they can only happen with leadership," I counter.

"Leadership will form naturally," he says. "First we have to break down the current structure. We have to demolish the establishments of the past, burn them to the ground, so that the new reality can emerge. Like a child's birth, Cailin. I know you've seen birth before—it's beautiful."

I cock an eyebrow, thinking of the children I've helped into the world. "It's messy, and bloody."

"Yes! Yes, exactly. Bloody and beautiful. New life exploding from the narrow channel of the Ash King's rule. We will be unfettered. Free. We won't have to fear another Massacre of the Ashlands. No lovely face like Brayda's will ever be ruined again. Look at her, Cailin. Look at your friend, at the sickening result of this King's power."

Brayda shoots him a pained glance, and I hasten to say, "She's not sickening."

"Don't try to defend me, Cailin," Brayda snaps. "Rince has been there for me when you weren't. You could have come with us when we left the village. You could have joined up when we did and prevented this. We need someone like you."

She pauses, biting her lip, while the tea server sets our individual teapots and cups on the table. When the girl leaves, Brayda looks up at me again, her eyes bright with resentful tears.

"I didn't go with you because I didn't want that life," I murmur.

"You think we do?" she bursts out. "You think I wanted this face? It's called *sacrifice*, Cailin. We're devoting ourselves to the greater good. But of course you wouldn't understand that. Your pacifism is just another word for laziness and weakness."

Her words lash me like a whip. She's hurting because of her permanent scars, and because I messed up the ambush against the Ash King. But beneath that hurt I can feel the truth of what she's saying—a belief she has held onto for a long time. She believes I'm weak and lazy. She is convinced that's why I don't want to fight back or kill for the cause.

And I can't bear for her to think that of me. We grew up together, harvested the fields together, built playhouses out of boleweed stalks, dressed up in lacy potsava leaves and pretended to be fine ladies. We made jewelry and tiaras out of the iridescent shattered shells of ash-burrower eggs, and we dreamed about becoming rich and powerful. Eventually I realized that all I wanted was my quiet, beautiful life among the villages and the fields, while she realized she wanted to upend the monarchy.

She despises my choice. My best childhood friend actually despises me. And I can't bear for someone to despise me, to hate me. I adore being the healer and *beireoir uisce*, water-bringer, for my people, because I enjoy being appreciated, feeling loved.

But the two friends I used to love best are staring at me like I'm a stranger. In Rince's eyes I see pained disappointment, and in Brayda's I see frustrated rage.

I want Rince and Brayda to love me again.

"I don't think I can kill him," I say softly. "But maybe I can help you in some other way."

Brayda scoffs and picks up her tea, gulping instead of savoring it. But Rince nods encouragingly. "All right, then. We'll work with that. Any information you can gather about the Ash King's habits—when he's alone, who tests his food and drink, where he bathes, how many guards are usually around him and where they are stationed in the palace—oh, and if you find a less heavily-guarded route or a secret passage into the palace. Anything like that. Find out how his magic works, so we can determine his vulnerabilities. You don't have to actually kill him, Cailin. Just give us everything you can collect, and we'll take care of the rest. We have someone in play already, but you're positioned even closer. This can work." He turns to Brayda, nodding emphatically, smiling brightly.

She grumbles into her tea, while I try not to examine the scarred patches and lines across her face. She's still beautiful, through it all—but I know I could have rendered her flawless again, and it hurts that I wasn't there for her. By blocking that arrow, I incited events that led to my friend's harm. I have to focus on the wellbeing of my friends, not on protecting a cruel man I barely know. If I can help the Undoing without actually killing anyone, I owe it to Brayda to do everything in my power.

"I'll do it," I say. "But you should go, before my guard shows up. Meet you here again in a week? Or should I meet with your contact inside the palace?"

"Oh, no," says Rince quickly. "We can't risk our contact. She's in enough danger, being in the spotlight."

"Rince," snaps Brayda. "Gods, stop talking before you give the whole thing away." She shoves herself out of the booth. "I take it you're paying for the tea, Cailin. Or rather, the Ash King is." She looks at my ring, her scarred mouth hitching in a sneer.

"I've got it," I say quietly.

Brayda stalks out the back door of the tea shop without another word. Rince pauses to kiss me on the mouth and he whispers in my ear, "See you here in a week. Maybe we can get a room and I can reward you for your spy work. You take care of that beautiful body of yours for me."

He winks and strides out the back way, just as Owin enters the tea shop.

I draw a long breath, trying to slow my racing heart. With a lifted hand I summon Owin, and he hurries over, his helmet tucked under his arm. "Sorry, I took longer than I expected."

"Did you meet the hot fire-wielder?"

"You could say that." Owin smirks, adjusting the crotch of his pants. "We should return to the palace. You're supposed to be at the Welcoming of the Favored tonight, and I want to show you a few sights on the way back."

Owin hails the tea server and orders us a packet of sandwiches for the return trip through the city. Food in hand, we hire a carriage and take the scenic route to the palace. He shows me the artists' plaza near the Triune

Arch, the Justice Building where the Ash King and his officers hold court twice a week, and the Market of Uniquities, where exotic wares are sold and where most of the city's sex work is centered. He points out the gaudily decorated booths where mutually interested parties can step in and enjoy each other quickly before going about their business.

"There are more of those tryst booths throughout the city, if you know where to look," he says. "The fire-wielder and I made use of one. Very good use. What about you and your *friend*? Did he treat you well? Or she?"

"He was going to," I say. "But we were interrupted."

He winces sympathetically. "I'm sure someone at the palace would be happy to pleasure the Healer of the Favored."

"Thank you, but I'm fine." My cheeks are growing hot, and I fan them with my fingers. The late afternoon sun presses heavily on my skin, reminding me of the Ash King's palm on my chest.

I've never been quite as sexually liberated as some in my village, and apparently I'm old-fashioned compared to many of the people in this city. I wouldn't have stopped Rince from fingering me to climax in the alley, but I'm not sure I would have consented to a full-on coupling with him—not there, not with so many people so close by. When he and I were together back home, we were always in his bedroom or mine, or somewhere far out in the fields, where there was no one to see us. I like intimacy and privacy when I'm with someone.

Back at the palace, I find my maid waiting for me, along with a tailor and a rack of gowns, one of which will be altered to fit me for the night's event. I bathe quickly and yield myself to their hands.

When they're done, I'm clad in a form-fitting dress of sheer dark-blue material that flares gradually outward from my hips. Wave-like swirls of thicker material travel over my thighs, rear and breasts, concealing those areas while my body shows through the translucent blue everywhere else.

My dark hair is pinned half-up, with the rest tumbling in unruly curls. Long gold pendants shimmer from my earlobes, and my upper arms are embellished with gold cuffs. A dozen thin gold chains, like the threads of my magic, lie across my collarbones and cleavage. My maid highlights my natural beauty with a few cosmetics, and when I look in the mirror, I let a quiet swear escape me.

I'm naturally lovely—I don't falsely pretend not to know that. But in this attire, I'm stunning. I'm a goddess of water and healing.

"Thank you," I whisper to the maid and the tailor. "Really, thank you. You're both geniuses."

They smile, but before either one can answer, a garishly dressed man with lavender hair and lots of eyeliner pops his head into the room. "Time to go, time to go! Is the Healer ready?"

"She's ready," my maid replies.

"Good, good." He surveys me, two fingertips resting against his mouth, and then he waves his hand, indicating my entire ensemble. "Marvelous. Just marvelous. Come along, dear. Mustn't keep the Ash King waiting. He set my hair on fire last time I did that. I'm just kidding, darling, don't look so scared. No, he did, he really did set me on fire. Got me the best healer afterward, though. Come along."

I'm hurried through hallways out to the courtyard, popped into a phaeton pulled by a single horse, and escorted by mounted guards through both the inner and outer gates of the royal fortress. Once we're in the city, we take a street lined with more soldiers, one that leads to the Réimse Ríoga, the arena where all public events in the Capital are held.

This place is as old as the tradition of "the Calling of the Favored," built centuries ago when the first contest was held. At that time, it was a fight to the death, with the winner gaining the king's hand. These days the results are less lethal, although injuries can be severe. Last time it was held, during one of the challenges, two women died before they could be healed.

The Réimse Ríoga has a brutal, monstrous look to it. Windows like blank, dead eyes. Stubby towers like hunched stone shoulders. My phaeton rolls through a back entrance, into the lower level beneath the arena itself. I'm hustled out and hurried onto a lift, which is then cranked upward by a man who looks as if he's magically gifted with muscle.

"Just stand quietly in your place, darling, and wave when you're introduced," the lavender-haired man calls up to me. "It's better if you don't speak."

I nod, but he's already bustling away.

I stand on the lift alone, my skin stippled with goosebumps. There's a stale draft of musty-smelling air wafting through the shaft I'm ascending. Through the stone walls I can hear the incessant rumble of the crowd, like the warning growl of a volcano before it vents steam.

And then I'm at the top. The noise crashes over me like an explosion. I'd expected a rush of light, too, but the arena is fairly gloomy—poorly lit.

Shakily I step off the lift. Someone takes my arm, guides me to a spot, tells me to stand there.

The interior of the Réimse Ríoga is a gigantic oval with a flattened end. The egg-shaped floor is thick with sand, but a T-shaped platform has been built across it. The long stem of the T leads from a faraway entrance at the arena's opposite end, all the way to the royal balcony. The top of the T runs parallel to the balcony. That wooden walkway, draped in black fabric, is where the contestants will stand and wait to be welcomed by the King. They'll be slightly below him, but close enough to touch his hand if he advances to extend it.

Banks of seats slope upward from the arena floor, studded with lavishly decorated boxes and booths where the wealthy and privileged can relax and enjoy special treatment while they watch the show. I only know this because the Ceannaire visited the Capital once and told me of it afterward. But I had a child's view of what she described. The reality is far more overwhelming and awe-inspiring.

A few other officials and important people involved with the Calling are standing on this balcony too, poised in front of padded chairs, waiting for the occupant of the largest chair—a seat hewn from an enormous chunk of petrified wood. It's not the actual Throne of Bolcan, but it's almost as impressive.

In moments, the King will take his place there, and the Welcoming of the Favored will begin.

Music rushes through the arena—deep, thrumming music with a hot, sinuous melody slithering along its surface. The music is rivers of lava and boulders of dark stone, scintillating sparks and molten whispers.

Into the swell of that enticing song strides the Ash King, wearing a tall black crown whose spiked tips are sheathed in actual flame. His eyes are scarlet, too, and his lashes are alight. His sleek white hair pours forward over his shoulders, and a great black collar of interwoven antlers flares from his nape. His thick black robes trail from his wrists and torso, sweeping the ground.

As he passes me, his head angles sharply, suddenly, and his scarlet eye sweeps me from head to toe.

Then he's swirling away, his back to me, facing the crowd. From his outstretched palms he releases small orbs of bright flame—a hundred, a thousand, a million—they keep pouring from his hands, rising to cluster beneath the domed roof of the arena, lighting the entire space so dramatically my eyes almost can't bear it.

The crowd roars its approval, kneeling collectively before him. When he sits, they take their seats as well, and so do I.

There's a long welcome speech, during which the King's herald introduces everyone on the balcony. When he comes to me, he says, "The Healer of the Favored, Cailin Roghnaithe, of the village Leanbh near Analoir Doiteain."

I rise and smile, with a little wave. And then, impulsively, I lift my hands and let ribbons of healing light unfurl from my fingers. They have no purpose, no goal, but they snake through the air, dozens of them floating upward, separating from my fingertips as I release them. They spiral and curl aimlessly, twining with the King's orbs of flame in a way that I hadn't anticipated—that I didn't intend. It's a beautiful, mesmerizing dance of magic, and a murmur of appreciation and awe rolls through the audience.

When the ribbons dissolve, their essence sifts down to the crowd in a shower of golden motes. Each person here will feel a little of my healing influence. I've done this before at home, but never on such a large crowd, and never with someone else's magic at play. I can feel the tug of weariness in my soul, the expenditure of my energy. It will be replenished in plenty of time for the first challenge.

As I turn to resume my seat, I glance at the Ash King. His lips are parted, his eyes fixed on me with an intensity that makes my stomach flip.

I need to get close to him and learn his habits, his secrets. He trusts me. He doesn't believe I'm his enemy. But I am. I will see him undone.

More music swells, a sweeping processional, and the women begin to appear, one at a time, from the doors at the far end of the arena.

First comes Teagan, daughter of the Lord Mayor of Aighda, red-headed and regal in a green gown. She's my favorite. If I wasn't cooperating with the Undoing to kill the king, I'd want her to win. But no—I wouldn't wish that fate upon her. Marriage to the Ash King would be miserable.

I picture it for a moment—marriage, to him. Sleeping beside that tall, fit body. Sharing rooms and meals with him, enduring his cold demeanor and fiery eyes and terse words every day. Submitting to his pleasure, lying limp under him while he pushed himself into my body, while he surged against me, his snowy hair brushing my breasts, his striking face contorting with passion, with pleasure—

Gods, I've missed the introduction of the next three girls—I was lost in my personal fantasy. I can feel heat pooling between my legs. I must take care of my own needs *tonight*, once I'm alone. I can't be thinking that way about the godsdamned Ash King.

It doesn't matter that I didn't hear the names of those three girls; I'll meet them soon enough. The fifth Favored is Khloe, daughter of some High Lord of Cawn. She's short, perky, and adorable, with enormous brown eyes and glossy dark-brown hair. She looks about eighteen— probably the youngest of the Favored. She gives the Ash King the most darling smile I've ever seen.

Next comes Adalasia—deep umber skin, rich curves, graceful bearing. Then there's Leslynne, with soft peach skin and abundant golden hair. Morani is olive-complexioned, with short, spiked black hair and several body piercings on display through the cutouts in her gown. A tall, pale blonde with a sharp face and keen eyes—Axley. A small, lithe woman—Diaza—with light brown skin and plentiful freckles. A woman named Sabre with cinnamon-colored hair and powerful arms. She looks as if she could lift the King easily.

I lose track of all the names, cities, and ranks. But I love looking at the radiant gowns, the dazzling jewels, the different shades of bronze, cream, or ebony skin, the unique facial structure and intricate hairstyles of every woman.

At last, all twenty of the Favored are standing parallel to the balcony, waiting to be welcomed. They're all smiling. Some of them look genuinely excited—they flutter their lashes and simper, or grin broadly and familiarly at the King, as if they're already old friends. Others wear polite, tense smiles.

The Ash King rises abruptly, and when he does, I see the edges of even the most friendly smiles crack a little. Every single one of these women is afraid of him.

Good. They should be.

He walks to the end of the balcony and begins to speak their names, one at a time, reaching out to allow every Favored to kiss his fingertips.

There's one girl in the middle of the lineup who is visibly shaking. The closer he comes to her, the harder her body shakes, until I'm afraid she might crumple where she stands. Her smile wobbles, and her eyes are blown wide with terror.

The Ash King pauses in front of her and stands there without speaking. I can only see his cheekbone and the corner of his jaw from my angle, so I'm not sure of his expression, but clearly his stare terrifies the poor girl. She lets out a tiny sob, her smile gone. Her pupils are dilated so far there's almost no iris left.

She's about to pass out.

I'm the healer. I should step in and see to her wellbeing.

Swiftly I rise and move forward to the Ash King's side. I reach out to the girl. "Embri's your name, isn't it? Take my hand, Embri."

Whimpering, she obeys, and golden wisps twine her fingers with mine. I can't alter her emotions, but I can soothe the nausea in her stomach, slow her heart rate a bit, ease the panicked fight-or-flight responses of her body. Within a few seconds, she stops trembling.

Cautiously I glance up at the Ash King.

And in the violence of his scarlet eyes, I see my doom.

10

My fingers are still wound with the girl's, and I continue soothing her nerves even as my own grow taut. The Ash King is staring at me with such implacable rage I can hardly breathe.

The entire audience is silent. The music has stopped. Fear and tension vibrate in the air.

They are all waiting for the King to punish me for my interference.

"She was about to faint," I murmur.

He glares at me a moment more, then turns to the girl, Embri. "You are dismissed from the Calling. You are no longer one of the Favored. Go."

"No!" I exclaim, before I can think. "She was only nervous. She's calmer now—she'll be fine."

The Ash King steps nearer, towering over me. "Silence, Healer. Return to your seat."

For one burning second I hesitate, my jaw tense, glaring right back at him. A guard steps forward, hand upraised to strike me for my defiance, but the Ash King hisses "The fuck you will" at him, and he backs down.

That act of his, protecting me from punishment, is enough to make me yield. With a resigned curtsy, I step back to my seat.

More guards appear, escorting the shivering, weeping girl out of the Favored lineup. The Ash King continues his cold welcome of each remaining contestant, and then drinks are distributed through the crowd. There's a toast, more music, some acrobatics, and a few speeches. I sit silently through it all, while the Favored have to stand in their places for the entire two hours. It must be a test of their endurance and poise.

One woman collapses near the end of the festivities, and then another faints, striking her head on the wooden platform. They are both taken away, removed from the competition—but when I try to follow them to check on their well-being, I'm ordered back to my seat by a guard who says, "They are no longer your concern, Healer of the Favored."

By the time it's all over, when I'm finally escorted out of the arena and taken back to the palace, I'm in a towering rage. My maid brings me a tray of food, and I take savage bites while I pace the room and seethe about the injustice of it all. Now I'm twice as determined to see that bastard king taken down.

I know immediately when he returns to his chamber. I can hear him through the door between our rooms, shouting at his servants to begone and leave him alone.

Furious, I stalk the length of my room, muttering everything I want to say to him. If I were to knock on his door and ask for an audience, he'd probably burn me to a crisp and find himself a new Healer of the Favored. So the most I can do is talk to myself, and pretend I'm calling him out.

"You cruel, selfish bastard," I hiss. "You unfeeling piece of shit. How dare you stare that poor girl down and then humiliate her? You're the worst king this country could have. An abject failure. Heartsfire, if only you'd burned yourself up along with the Ashlands."

I'm halfway across the room again, gnawing a piece of bread as if it's his stupid haughty face, when the door between our rooms bangs open.

The Ash King is bare-chested, breathing hot steam, his eyes flooded with flame. I can see fire glowing molten through the skin and tendons of his throat, flickering under his ribcage. It's swelling inside him, trying to burst out.

"Water," he gasps.

"Don't you have water in your room?"

"Your water," he grits out, while flames coat his teeth. "Water touched by your magic—different."

Quickly I siphon water from the pitcher on the washstand. He opens his mouth, and as fire begins to pour from his jaws, I crush the water against it. With a steaming hiss, the water gushes into him, quenching his inner flame.

He braces one hand against the wall, panting, his lips and chest gleaming wet.

My knees have gone weak with the awareness of what might have happened if I hadn't been quick enough.

"How do you control it when I'm not around?" I ask.

"I have ways. They usually involve the incineration of furniture. This is quicker, and cheaper." He wipes his mouth with the back of his hand. "You're useful. There's something unique about your magic—I may have to keep you around."

Dread ices my veins. "You said I could go home after the Calling of the Favored."

"No. The herald said you would be in my service as long as I saw fit to employ you."

My fists clench. "You can't do this to people. Ruin their hopes, their dreams. Like you're doing to me—like you did to that girl tonight—"

"You think I ruined her dreams?" His laugh is razors and darkness. "I did her a favor. She did not want to be here. You think I crave a wife who is so frightened of me she can barely stand upright in my presence?"

"Of course she was scared the first time she saw you. But you didn't give her any time to acclimate, to get to know you."

"And you think I improve upon acquaintance?"

"Well…no."

He's still bowed over, breathing heavily, but he looks up at me with dark eyes, no longer flaming. A smile quivers across his mouth. "An honest answer."

"The only kind I'm capable of, unfortunately. You'll kill me for it, one day."

His lips part, shock in his eyes. But he swallows and nods. "You're probably right."

The raw truth bleeds in the air between us until I can't stand the silence. "Do you want to sit down?"

"I've been sitting for hours. I'd rather stand, or lie down." But he doesn't move to return to his room.

My own anger has ebbed, oddly enough. I've done him a favor, helping with his overpowered magic—maybe he's feeling grateful. Maybe I can draw information out of him, the way I siphon water.

"What did you think of them? The Favored?" I ask.

He shifts his position, his shoulder blades pressed to the wall and his body slanted. In those dark pants, his legs look impossibly long. "I don't know what to think."

"Did none of them stand out to you? No exceptional first impressions?"

He shakes his head. "What about you?"

"Me?"

"What did you think of them?" He pushes himself upright, his eyes lighting as if he's had an idea—and that makes me nervous. "Ah, why didn't I think of this before? You will be treating these women, interacting with them. I'll have time with each Favored, of course, and I'll be watching them during the challenges—but you will see them in unguarded moments. You can tell me the truth of who they are, not who they pretend to be. Cailin—" He takes me by the shoulders, and my skin warms under his fingers— "Cailin, you can help me choose."

"You want me to help you choose your wife?" I gape at him.

"I have so much on my mind already—so much to keep control of, as you've seen." His hands shift, sliding down the flesh of my upper arms before gliding up to my shoulders again. He repeats the motion absently, several times. It's practically a caress, and I hate that my body responds, warming, yielding, yearning.

He keeps talking, explaining this new idea of his. "You can be my eyes and ears among the women, and let me know who is sincere, who is loyal to the crown. Who might be favorably disposed toward me." He plants both warm hands on my shoulders again, his thumb rubbing along my collarbone. I can barely think through the casual intimacy of the touch.

"It's not a good idea," I murmur. "You brought me here to be impartial. Objective."

"I needed someone untouched by the whims and wiles of the nobility's politics, yes. This is different."

"I barely know you." I manage to meet his eyes, trying not to let the hovering heat of his nearness affect me. "How could I advise you about a good match?"

He licks his lips, and my gaze follows the sweep of his tongue. His mouth looks relaxed and soft right now, not hard and grim like it was during the ceremony.

"What if you got to know me better?" he says.

It's exactly what I need. Personal access to him so I can pass along word of his habits and weaknesses to the Undoing. But how much will this personal access require of me? How much of myself will I have to sacrifice to do this, to earn back my friends' love and do what's right for my kingdom?

"We're both going to be very busy," I say. "I'm not sure how we could get to know each other."

His mouth tightens again, that sleek brow of his pinching together in a frown.

"But," I add, "If my King wishes it, I'm sure I could find the time. And I will be your watcher among the women."

Which means I'm a spy for both the Undoing and for the King. Not complicated at all.

"Good." His forehead smooths again. "I should try to sleep. Good night, Healer."

"Pleasant dreams."

"Unlikely."

He leaves, and I hear the faint click of the lock on his side of the door. There's no lock on my side, but I doubt he'll enter my room again, so I douse every light except one candle, and I strip off the gown and my underthings. Clad in a nightdress, with nothing beneath it, I lie down on the bed and finally, finally, part my legs. My fingers travel through my sex, nudging aside the outer lips, teasing slippery wetness along the seam, circling the bud at the top. It feels so good to finally indulge the hunger I've been enduring. I can't resist a few quiet sounds, but I keep the noises soft so the King won't be able to hear me through the door.

While my right hand trails through my folds, my left passes over my breast, squeezing and pressing. I remember how the Ash King crushed me to the wall of the torture room. I have a choice between a fantasy of him and a fantasy of Rince—but Rince has been the object of my pleasurable focus many times, and the Ash King—he's new, and the idea of being with him is both horrific and tantalizing. Much as I hate him, I can't help feeling secretly flattered by his attraction to me.

I close my eyes, arching back on the pillows, picturing a fight between us. He scorches my clothes off, and I soak his with water and rip them away. Naked we collide, his hand coiled in my hair, my fingers denting his flesh. Our kisses are snarling threats, and when he drives into me it isn't gentle—it's desperate, wicked.

Pumping two fingers inside myself, I whimper and writhe. Close now—I fill my head with the image of the Ash King's harsh, beautiful face and sculpted chest— "Your Majesty," I moan softly—and I come hard, huffing short gasps as pleasure snakes through my belly and thighs.

I press one hand over my mound while the ecstasy eases, and then I draw the sheet over myself and lie limp on the bed. A few minutes later, I tease myself to climax again, then a third time, before finally dozing off.

The next morning, I dress for a day of physical examinations with the Favored. The maid leaves after tidying up, and I nibble at the extravagant breakfast on my tray while thinking about my parents. I need to send them a letter so they know I'm all right. There are pens and paper on the writing desk in the corner, and I can ask my maid about a messenger. But that will have to wait until tonight.

A click, and the door between my room and the King's opens.

He's resplendent in a suit with a long tailcoat—dark gray fabric veined with delicate silvery-white lines. There's no crown on his head, and his white hair is hitched into a high ponytail. Tiny silver rings glitter along his ears.

I rise from my chair and sink into a curtsy. "Your Majesty."

"Did you sleep well?" There's something odd in his tone, a twitch at the corner of his mouth.

"I did, thank you."

"I thought you might, after all that."

I frown, confused. Does he think it cost me a lot of effort to help him quench his fire? "Water wielding doesn't require much energy."

"That's not the activity to which I was referring."

"Oh, you mean what I did at the Welcoming of the Favored? I did drain quite a bit of my healing energy, but it has already recovered."

"Not that either." His eyes never leave my face. "You should know that I have above-average hearing. One might call it a secondary magical ability of mine."

Oh. Oh gods...

"I can hear everything you say in this room, even when you say it quietly," he continues.

Oh Heartsfire, he heard my tirade against him last night. I'm lucky he didn't scorch me into a pile of fluttering ashes—

"I can also hear—other things. Other sounds."

The blood rushes to my face, a gush of humiliation so hot I can feel its frantic haze in my brain.

He heard me pleasuring myself last night. That's what he means. He heard me say *Your Majesty* right before I came.

Fuck. Me.

My hands press to my burning cheeks. I can't meet his eyes.

"Next time, if you want me to join you," he says softly, "all you have to do is ask."

I'm too embarrassed to look at the Ash King, but I hear the rustle of his rich clothing as he leaves my room by way of the hall door.

"I look forward to your report about the Favored," he says. "Until tonight."

Why do those last two words sound like a threat *and* a promise?

I have no more appetite for breakfast, and when my maid returns for the tray, she directs me to the East Wing where the Favored are residing for the duration of the contest. I take along a notebook, an ink bottle, and a quill, partly for taking notes on the physical condition of each Favored, and partly for nefarious spying purposes. I make a clumsy sketch of the palace layout—at least the parts I've seen—and I mark the spots where guards are standing. It's a bit discouraging, since they seem to be everywhere. Security is ridiculously high during this competition. Or perhaps it's not ridiculous at all, since there is a very real threat to the King, as I know all too well.

Rince mentioned that the Undoing already has someone on the inside. He also indicated that the contact is female, in a prominent position— "in the spotlight," he said. It can't be a palace servant, surely—they're selected with great care, judging by what Owin has told me. It has to be one of the Favored or their servants. Despite the vetting process for this contest, it's possible that a sympathizer with the Undoing has slipped through.

I don't really need to know who the Undoing's spy is. But for the sake of my own personal curiosity, I'd like to find out. Maybe I'll discover it during the examinations today.

By dinnertime, I have to examine seventeen women and confirm their ability to participate in the Calling, because tomorrow is the first Challenge. The King isn't wasting any time getting this competition under way. I think he wants to get it over with. Which is sad, both for him and for the hapless girl he chooses.

Of course, if the Undoing has their way, he won't survive long enough to make that choice.

The wing of the palace where the Favored reside looks different from the stately, heavily-furnished hall where I've been staying. This section is airier, lighter, full of windows and colonnades and balconies. Mistress Effelin greets me and leads me to the first floor of the wing, where great doors stand wide open to the midsummer morning. There's a garden outside—not a dull, regimented, neatly trimmed garden, but a vine-draped, floral-scented wilderness rich with lush foliage. Sunlight dapples the flowerbeds and sparkles in the dew on leaves and petals. There's a rain-scented freshness to the air, and I inhale deeply, gratefully.

"You'll work in this room." Mistress Effelin leads me past the open doors, into a long chamber that's also plentifully windowed, though these windows have thick glass. I walk to one immediately and open it wide. The heat of the sun on the sill promises that today will be hot, but for now, there is a lovely breeze.

The room contains cabinets stocked with tonics, herbs, bandages, and medical implements. The white marble counters look spotless. In the center of the room are three thickly cushioned cots and one metal surgical table.

"This room is for non-magical healing." I look to Mistress Effelin for confirmation.

She nods. "At the King's insistence, most of the healing that goes on in the palace is unaided by magical means. He insists that we progress in that area, lest magic disappear from the land."

"Disappear?" I raise my eyebrows. "How could that ever happen?"

"Ask the King." Her thin shoulders lift and fall briefly. "Of course, he understands that some conditions and injuries cannot be remedied without magic, and he allows the palace healer to treat those."

"The palace healer? Does this healer treat the King as well?"

"Sometimes. Our healer is nearing his ninetieth year. It is time for the King to choose a replacement, but so far he has not found anyone to his liking."

"Small wonder," I mutter, running my fingertips along the clean, smooth sheet stretched taut over one of the exam beds. "Please go ahead and send in the first Favored. I have many women to see today."

Mistress Effelin gives me a small bow and leaves.

I wait, twisting my fingers together, rehearsing the speech I concocted for each Favored I'll meet. They're all of high birth and noble blood, ranked far above me in society. They've had more education, they've traveled farther, and they've met more people and had more experiences than me. I'm a simple healer in a blue tunic and loose pants. One of these women will be the future queen.

I can't think about that. I must view them like I view anyone else who needs my healing magic. I need to be objective, kind, and courteous, regardless of my rank or theirs.

A few minutes later, the first Favored enters. It's Axley, the sharp-faced blonde. She's wearing an ivory dress that hugs her slim frame and pools on the tiles behind her.

"Good morning," I say cheerfully. "I'm here to give you a quick scan, ask you a few questions, and make sure you're in optimal health for the first challenge tomorrow. If you have any health concerns or ailments, please let me know, and I'll do my best to take care of those for you."

Axley gives me a sneering smile. "I'm in perfect health."

"That's wonderful. If you'll lie down right here, we can get started."

Haughtily she complies, and I spread my hands in the air above her face. I close my eyes, tuning in to the ebb and flow of her body's systems. Impressing her shape into my consciousness now will make it easier to heal her later if she gets injured.

"The servants told us you're living in the Rose Room," Axley says.

"I am. Only because His Majesty wants quick access to a healer."

"Is that the only thing he has access to? Because we all know what the Rose Room is used for."

She's referring to the fact that my room once belonged to the King's mistress. I can feel myself flushing. When I open my eyes, Axley is watching me keenly.

"It's nothing like that," I tell her. "The King is focused on finding his bride."

"Good. I did not come here to share my future husband with anyone else."

I try not to respond, I really do, but— "Then it's unfortunate you have so many contenders for his affection." I finish her scan quickly. "As you said, you're in perfect health. Any concerns?"

"Just one." She rises gracefully from the table. She's taller than me, possibly because she is wearing dramatic heels. "I hope you realize that magic doesn't equal nobility. Sitting with someone on a balcony or residing near them doesn't make you their equal."

With that, she sweeps out.

The next few girls regard me with the same cool, haughty distaste. It's a relief when Khloe, the adorable Favored with the big dark eyes, steps into the examination room. She hops onto the table without being told.

"Everyone's talking about you today," she confides. "We all saw what you did with your magic, and the way you defended Embri."

"Doesn't seem to have won me any friends," I mutter, spreading my fingers and letting my magic flow over her body.

"You don't understand," Khloe says. "None of us expected a young, gorgeous healer with dual gifts. Seeing you up there on the balcony with him, watching him spare you from punishment, and then hearing the rumors that you're staying in the Rose Room—everyone assumes you're sleeping with the King. Which makes you our competition."

"But I'm not sleeping with him, and I'm not competition. I'd never want to be queen, and even if I did, the Calling is for the high-born."

"Of course. But there's a precedent for others participating, you know. Back when the King's great-grandfather was choosing his husband, there weren't enough noble young men with an inclination to males, so they opened the Calling to men of lower rank. They still had to be important men, well-educated and respected, but they weren't titled."

I'm about to respond, but when the ripples of my magic pass over her stomach, I sense something different. I pause, frowning, and press another surge of magic through the area until I'm sure.

"Khloe," I say as calmly as I can. "Do you know you're pregnant?"

Khloe's dark eyes grow even more enormous. "What?"

"There's no requirement for contestants to be virgins," I say quietly. "But carrying another man's child is a different matter."

"Oh gods," she whispers. "Oh gods—he told me he'd taken a tonic, that we were protected."

"I'd say you're about three weeks along. Does that sound right?"

"Yes." She bites her lip, tears pooling in her eyes. "Oh gods."

"Do you want the baby?" I ask.

She shakes her head at first, and then she nods, pressing both hands over her face. "I don't know. If I decide I want it, I'll have to leave the competition, and my family will be so disappointed. Most of us have waited our whole lives for this chance, you know. We've been groomed for the Calling since birth, knowing that at some point the new king would choose his bride. Some of the girls have retained their virginity so they can tempt him with that."

I snort a little. "Does the Ash King even care if a woman is a virgin?"

"Some men do. And he's so reserved no one knows what he likes. He never drinks much, not even when he's visiting noble houses around the kingdom—and trust me, people have tried to get him drunk, to make him loosen up. He never overindulges, never loses control."

"Really?" That sounds so different from the Ash King I know—withdrawn, yes, but always wavering on the edge of an explosion. Maybe he's more volatile right now because of the stress of the competition and the way his life will change after he chooses a wife.

Or maybe he's more fiery when he's around *me*.

"Some people want him to lose control again," Khloe whispers. "They want to use it against him."

"But not you."

"No. I'm scared of him, like everyone else, but he doesn't seem as cruel as they say. Maybe he just needs someone to make him laugh." She gives me a sweet, watery smile. "I thought maybe that person could be me. I guess I was just being stupid."

114

My heart melts. "There's no need to tell anyone about the baby yet. We have time for you to decide one way or another."

Her eyes widen. "You'd do that for me?"

"I can keep it quiet for a little while, at least." I smile at her.

"Gods, you're so nice." Sniffling, she slides off the bed and throws both arms around me. I hug her back while she releases a few quiet sobs into my shoulder. When she manages to compose herself, I whisk her tears away with my water magic and soothe the redness of her nose and eyes with my healing power.

"The other girls don't need to know you were crying," I tell her, and she smiles gratefully.

When she leaves, I stand rooted to the spot for a moment.

It's not my place to make the decision for her. But I'm grateful that if she decides not to have the baby, I won't be the one removing it. She'll go to a physik who specializes in that sort of procedure.

Diaza, the Favored with the light brown skin and freckles, enters next. She treats me with more respect than the others but less friendliness than Khloe. What I sense from Diaza is primarily caution and a wary distance. Like the rest of the girls, she's in perfect physical condition.

"You're all so healthy," I comment as she rises from the bed.

"We come from families who can pay for the best healers," she says as she walks out.

It's an offhand comment, but it startles me. I've always given my healing magic freely to anyone who needed my help. I can't imagine requiring people to pay for it. Are there people in this city who need healing and can't afford it?

The thought gnaws at me for the rest of the day as I examine more of the Favored. I enjoy my brief time with Teagan, who goes out of her way to be friendly, as if she knows what some of the girls have been saying about me. I treat an infected cut on Adalasia's leg, and I heal Morani of a genital rash she probably got through prolific sexual activity. Samay bears a temporary muting tattoo on her ankle, since magical abilities are not allowed during the contest. I don't question her about it, though I'm deeply curious about her powers.

Next is the big muscled girl, Sabre. She has a small tear of the tendon in her left shoulder. When I ask her how it happened, she blushes.

"I was lifting some of the other girls. Showing off," she concedes. "Even after I felt the pain, I kept going. That's what this contest is about—pushing through pain."

"Well, I'm here to ease the pain." I give her a smile and send threads of magic into the injured area to repair it.

When I'm done, she works the joint and smiles back at me. "Thanks, Healer."

The last Favored, Vanas, is a woman whose bodily energy puzzles me at first—it has an echo I'm not used to. As my magic winds through her, I realize what it is. This body used to be male, but all the male parts were removed, and new female parts have been magically grown in their place.

When I look at her face, she's watching me, her features tense and defensive.

"The healer you hired did very nice work for you." I give her an encouraging nod. "Most healers can only regrow parts that were already there, but your healer created something entirely new, just for you. That's a unique ability, put to excellent use."

Vanas's face relaxes into a smile.

"But you're aware that a healer's abilities only extend so far," I add. "You understand you can't have children?"

"Yes, I do."

"That's something you'll need to disclose to the Ash King, since children are an important part of the monarchy. Of course adoption is possible, and there's precedent for it among the royals, so if you make a connection with him, you could still win this."

"That's what I'm hoping for. Thank you for your acceptance, Healer." Vanas hops off the table and blows me a kiss before walking out.

It's dark outside now. Lamps with clear glass shades light the examination room, and I snuff out each of them before walking over to the open window. The garden beyond is darkly lovely, whispering with night wind, sprinkled with gleaming night insects. Soft music spirals along the paths. Between tall leafy bushes I glimpse a pavilion aglow with light, and I catch the lilting murmur of feminine voices and the chink of cups. Tonight the Favored are having their first private party with the Ash King—just him and them and a few guards.

I wonder how he will act toward them. Will he be harsh and cold, quick to resent any challenge to his authority, or will they see another side of him?

Suddenly I'm desperate to know.

I close the window, latch it, and leave the room. A few steps along the hall are the double doors leading into the garden, and I slip through them, leaving my shoes just inside the entrance.

I've been standing all day, and the cool pavers of the path feel delicious to my tired feet. Impulsively I press one foot into the soil of a nearby flowerbed, moaning softly at the delight of rich earth crumbling around my toes. One foot isn't enough—I plant both feet in the soil and close my eyes, relishing the delicate fragrance of the night, the faint chirp of nocturnal insects, and the breeze cooling my skin. I've almost forgotten about the Ash King and my plan to spy on him.

And then a voice directly behind me makes me jump.

"Healer. What are you doing?"

I startle so violently that I lose my balance and tumble face first into a cluster of broad damp leaves and heavy blossoms. I yelp, trying to disentangle myself without bruising the plants any further.

A strong hand closes around my wrist and pulls me out of the flowerbed. My feet are flecked with soil, and the knees of my silky new pants are grimed with it. I brush twigs and leaves from my tunic and look up into the stern pale face of the Ash King. He's flanked by two of his guards, and he wears a loose black shirt whose scooped neck hangs nearly to his navel, showing off the center of his chest and the first couple pairs of abs.

"What are *you* doing, Your Majesty?" I respond. "I thought you were—over there." I gesture toward the festivities.

"I'm on my way there now. But I happened to see a certain vagabond Healer wading in the dirt, and I got distracted."

"Vagabond?" I giggle. "That's a new one."

"It suits you." A smile plays over his lips. "How did it go today?"

"If it pleases Your Majesty, I'll give you my report later," I tell him. "These girls should have the chance at a first impression that's not colored by anything I have to say."

"As if your opinion carries so much weight with me." But he doesn't say it scornfully, more like he's testing me, pushing me.

"I suppose it's not really a first impression, with most of them, is it? You've spent time with their families before."

"Some of them I've met previously, yes." There's a sudden tension to the lines of his body and the shape of his mouth. "Healer, would you—would you care to join us for the party?"

A shiver of emotion passes through my heart—I'm not sure if it's surprise or delight. "Is that appropriate, Your Majesty? I am only the healer, and this event is private time for you and the Favored. It wouldn't be right." And it will only fuel the girls' suspicions about my relationship with the King.

He hesitates, dark eyes lowered. He's wearing gold paint across his eyelids, and I hate that it suits him so well. I also hate that he's nervous, because it makes him seem vulnerable. It makes me want to protect and encourage him like I would anyone else who needed me.

"They are just girls looking for love," I say quietly.

"No." His eyes snap to mine. "They are wolves hunting for a crown, sirens who crave a throne."

"Not all of them."

"The rest have been pressured to be here, forced to participate. They do not want me."

"Give them a chance. Some of them might surprise you." I yield to an inner urge and add, "Look for Khloe, Vanas, Teagan, and Sabre."

His shoulders relax a little. "I will."

As I'm turning away, he says, "Your full report, later tonight."

"Yes, Your Majesty."

I dine in my room again. I'm sure there are dining halls in this place, but I haven't been invited or summoned to partake in a formal meal—lunch was a quick tray of food eaten while I perched on the windowsill of the exam room.

After eating, I write a letter to my parents and hand it off to a palace messenger, who promises it will be sent to them as quickly as possible.

I don't feel sleepy yet, and I need to stay up to give my report to the Ash King, so I explore my bedroom more thoroughly, especially the bookshelves in one corner. Beneath them are enormous velvety pillows, so I grab a few books with interesting titles and lie on my stomach to read. The books turn out to be extremely salacious, brimming with naughty scenarios. The one I end up reading is about a highwayman and the lass he brings back to his cave. Over the course of several chapters, he and three of his men seduce the eager heroine separately, at different times. I'm just getting to the part where they're all getting naked as a group and they're going to share her when the door to the Ash King's room opens.

I slam the book shut, but I keep one finger tucked between the pages because I'm deeply, dreadfully invested in this story. Suddenly I realize how late the hour is, and how hot my cheeks feel, and how damp my underthings have become. I'm still lying on my belly on the pillows, and I don't rise to bow to him, nor does he ask for the obeisance.

The Ash King comes over to me and sits down on one of the cushions, stretching out his legs with a tired sigh. "Your report, Healer."

"I—um…" I swallow hard, trying to pull my brain out of the world of the roguish highwayman, his naughty companions, and their even naughtier female captive.

The Ash King reaches for the book.

I pull it back, tucking it against my breasts.

"Ah, don't cover up," he says. "I was enjoying the view."

He's right. My cleavage is dramatically on display in this position. Embarrassed, I sit up, casting aside locks of my unruly hair. I keep the novel pinned to my chest.

"Give me the book," says the Ash King, hand outstretched.

"No, my Lord."

His eyebrows rise. "Do you realize how often you deny me the things I ask? I am your king, you impertinent vagabond. Obey me."

"Your Majesty." I hand it over, but when he grips it, I tug a little on my end. "Will you give it back later, so I can finish it?"

"What if I don't?" He leans toward me, dark eyes flecked with sparks. "What will you do?"

Maybe it's the flustered, aroused state I'm in, but he looks different to me in this moment. He has the same clifflike cheekbones and hollowed cheeks, the same haughty arched brows and straight nose, the same razor-sharp jaw—but there's a weary, haunted fragility to his face that I haven't seen before. And mixed with that vulnerability is a hint of humor, as he pulls the book closer to his chest, drawing me nearer along with it. His profile nearly brushes mine, only enough space between us for a handful of words.

"This book belongs to me," he murmurs, his eyes traveling my face. "Everything in this castle is mine, everything you've been wearing is mine, and you—"

"About that—thank you for the clothes, Your Majesty, but your herald mentioned something about a clothing allowance, and no one has explained—"

He presses a ringed finger to my mouth. "Hush. You must learn not to interrupt me, even in private. If you do that when we're with others, I'll have to punish you."

The free-spirited water-wielder from the slopes of Analoir Doitean wants to defy him, but the other part of me—the wise, cautious part—holds the words inside.

When I stay quiet, his expression changes, centering on my mouth. He strokes my lower lip slowly with his fingertip.

Cautiously I release the book and lean back, breaking the contact. The Ash King stirs and frowns slightly, like a man woken from a dream. Then he props a pillow behind him, leans against it, and opens the book at random. In a sonorous voice, he begins to read aloud. "'You'll take all of us, one after another,' said the highwayman. 'We're going to remind you who you belong to. If you're very good, we'll let you take all four of our cocks at once.'"

The Ash King's brows rise high, and he looks at me with an expression of mock horror. "All four? How is that humanly possible? Great gods, Healer. Your taste in books is very shocking."

"I suppose it would be two in her vagina, one in her ass, one in her mouth." My face is on fire now. "But you're right—I don't understand how all the legs and bodies would fit around her."

"The ass man would have to be crouched above her somehow," he muses. "What puzzles me is the other two. They can't stand side by side and penetrate her. It all sounds rather illogical. And painful."

"It's fiction. It's supposed to be fun, not exactingly accurate," I tell him, bristling. "And it's not just about the sex. It's about how repressed she's been, how she hasn't been able to trust anyone or give up control. They're *helping* her."

His face takes on a musing look. "I'm also very repressed. And I haven't been able to trust anyone or give up control. Perhaps I should ask someone to help *me* in that way." His eyes are hooded, his tone sultry and suggestive.

"I'm sure you could find plenty of willing companions." My voice sounds so breathless; I hate it. My pulse is jittery, and my stomach keeps rolling with ridiculous thrills.

"I could. Easily." He tosses the book onto the pillows. "Your report, Healer, and then I will go."

Without divulging the private secrets of the contestants, I tell him a little about each of them. Those who were polite and kind to me, I paint in a more favorable light.

When I'm done, the Ash King unfolds his long limbs and stretches his lithe, muscled body while I try not to watch.

"Earlier you spoke of scanning the Favored with your magic, and you mentioned it again just now," he says. "Does it help with the healing?"

"The better I know the person's body before their injury, the more quickly I can heal them, yes." I hesitate, seeing my opportunity—a chance to get information for the Undoing. "Speaking of which, I should probably scan you, Your Majesty."

Caution flares in his gaze. "No."

"But what if you—"

"I said no." Abruptly he returns to his room and locks the door.

11

The next day, we're back in the Réimse Ríoga—only this time I'm standing on a small square platform in the center of the arena, halfway between the Ash King's balcony and the narrow platform where the Favored will enter the stadium. The arena floor is carpeted with sand, a perfectly smooth expanse. Music thrums through the building, sending vibrations up through my toes and legs.

The Ash King is already on his throne, one long leg hitched over the other. He's wearing deep crimson today, with a shimmering black cloak and his tall black crown on his head. At this distance I can't see his features very well.

Before I was ushered out to this platform, one of the backstage handlers pulled me aside and said, "You are only allowed to intervene if one of the Favored is seriously wounded to the point of death. Otherwise you wait until after the challenge to tend their injuries."

"I understand."

"Good. And you may need to heal more people besides the contestants today. There are other participants in this challenge, but the wellbeing of the Favored is your priority."

"Other participants?"

"Well-paid participants who know the risks," the woman said impatiently.

Moments after that conversation, I was taken to the platform, which rises about a man's height above the floor of sand.

It's awkward, being the only point of interest in the arena. The stands are teeming with even more onlookers today, and they're shouting something—I can't quite hear it at first. Then I notice a man in one of the front rows leaning over the rail and bawling, "More magic! More magic!"

I can't use my healing energy, since I have no idea how much I'll have to expend on the Favored if they're wounded. But I can do a little water-wielding, since my energy well for that ability is separate. My magical senses tell me there are water pipes and spigots throughout the Réimse Ríoga, probably for the privies, or perhaps in case of fire. I can also feel barrels of water positioned here and there throughout the stands, with levered taps so thirsty audience members can get a drink. I center my focus on the barrel nearest me, drawing the water out through a small hole in its top.

As the stream of water glides upward in a graceful arc, the audience begins to hum with excitement. They've seen water-wielding before, I have no doubt, but probably not on this scale, since water wielders as powerful as me are usually Muted.

Since I'm a healer sworn to help and not harm, the Ricters who passed through my village simply gathered testimony of my character and let me remain unMuted. But as the King threatened, that could change at any time. Since my powers are separate, he could have one Muted and not the other.

I should enjoy the full extent of my abilities while I can. Why stand bored and idle when I could be having fun and entertaining everyone?

The sensation of the water, its undulating movements, its potential and power—it's so dearly familiar that tears of homesickness sting my eyes. I siphon water from a second barrel and pool it all into a shining liquid globe, floating high above the sandy floor. Then I unravel the globe, creating loops and spirals of glittering water, weaving them into increasingly complex patterns.

Next I flatten the liquid into a sheet and raise transparent mountains from the surface, an imitation of the horizon back home. The water swirls and reforms into dozens of galloping horses, then a school of shimmering fish, then a herd of Ashland fire stags. I send each group of creatures around the entirety of the stadium, over the heads of the enraptured audience, before calling the water back to me.

Last of all, I create something else—some*one* else. A tall figure in rippling robes, with features unmistakable despite their watery surface. A stories-high liquid sculpture of the Ash King.

The crowd roars with delight, rising in their seats while I make the figure of the Ash King spread his arms and wave.

A burst of pulse-pounding music resounds through the arena. The Favored are about to appear.

Quickly I whisk the water back into its barrels and resume my calm, subservient stance. I wish I knew what the Ash King thought of my display. Perhaps he'll rebuke me for it later. A delicate shiver passes over my body as I picture him bursting into my room, enraged and steaming, positively volcanic.

Am I actually looking forward to a conflict with him? Heartsfire, what is wrong with me?

"For this first challenge," booms a herald's voice, "the Favored have been asked to wear their finest and most luxurious attire. They will traverse the arena from end to end, and they will stand before the Ash King. Whoever receives his hand to kiss will remain in the competition. Those who do not receive his approval will be sent home."

That's *it*? They're just going to walk the length of the arena in their fanciest dresses? Not much of a challenge.

The seventeen Favored come out, one by one, a long procession of extravagant ballgowns and priceless jewels. I'm dressed in stark, pure white today—a one-piece garment that consists of flowing pants and two broad bands of material that travel diagonally from my hips to shoulders. The crisscrossed bands cover my breasts while exposing my cleavage and most of my lean stomach. My arms are lined with plain gold bracelets.

It's simple yet scandalous attire, and I voiced concerns about it when my maid handed the outfit to me. But she only said, "These are the clothes you were given for today." And I'm used to wearing even less in the fields, so I didn't complain any more.

In contrast with the Favored, I probably look rather plain and provincial, despite the glow of my burnished skin against the white cloth.

The instant the last Favored has taken her place in line, the doors slam shut, and most of the lights in the arena go out. A few people scream.

The Ash King rises, palms up, and sends a ball of red fire to the ceiling where it hangs ominously, bathing the space in crimson light. The entire Réimse Ríoga shakes, thundering and quaking as if a volcanic eruption is imminent. My fists tighten as I fight the urge to scream, to run, to be anywhere but here.

And then, up through the shifting sand, giant structures of iron explode all around me, all across the arena, rising taller and taller before locking into place.

It's an obstacle course more dreadful than anything I could have imagined. Whirring gears, rotating discs with razor edges, swaying rope bridges, churning spikes.

At the far end of the arena, in front of the Ash King's balcony, seventeen pillars shoot up from hidden trapdoors. A person stands atop each post. The volunteers I was told about.

The Ash King speaks, and a wind-wielder at his side magnifies his voice, sending it out across the crowd. "Any queen of mine must be willing to take risks, give up treasures, and sacrifice herself for the sake of her people. You must each navigate this gauntlet and rescue one citizen. Move quickly, because the victims are truly in peril, and time is short."

As he speaks, a viscous black liquid oozes from hidden tanks, pooling around the obstacles, around the pillars where the volunteers stand, and around the base of my platform. I don't know what the liquid is, but I'm sure the Favored don't want to find out—especially when something *alive* churns through the sludge, the ridges on its back appearing briefly before it submerges again. The crowd bellows, and a number of people shriek with delighted terror.

"Begin!" shouts the Ash King.

With a heart-stopping clunk, each volunteer's post begins to sink slowly into the ooze.

The Favored girls are squealing, gasping with shock as the audience roars at them to move, to act.

Morani is stripping off her gown. She's down to scanty undergarments, leaping onto the first obstacle, gripping bar after bar with her hands as she swings along above the ooze.

Round, creamy-skinned Leslynne with her beautiful golden hair is taking a different route. She has picked up her voluminous skirts and she's running, with surprisingly good balance, across a narrow beam. Khloe divests herself of her glittering skirts and follows Leslynne across the beam. Her eyes are even wider than usual—soft dark pools of terror.

Sabre uses her upper-body strength to follow Morani across the row of bars. Not to be outdone, Adalasia swings her lithe frame through a gap between spinning gears. One of them catches her skirts and rips half of them away, treating us all to a view of her long dark legs. Heartsfire, but I'd love to have legs like hers.

The other contestants are jumping into the fray now. Some take the time to strip, while others plunge boldly ahead, allowing their beautiful gowns to be ripped and wrecked by the sharp edges and grinding gears of the gauntlet.

Someone screams, and blood spatters across a metal post. One of the girls has cut her arm down to the bone. The churning machinery is moving faster now, propelled by magic or fuel—I'm not sure which.

The wounded girl is Diaza. She's still moving through the course, but I keep glancing at her, monitoring her progress. If she shows signs of flagging or serious distress, I'll need to send lines of magic through the gauntlet to heal her. Since they placed me in the center of everything, I should be able to do it from this distance.

Morani, Sabre, Khloe, and Leslynne are about halfway through the gauntlet now, nearly level with my position. Only one girl is left on the entry platform—a contestant whose name I don't remember. She's wailing, fussing about her dress, too proud to strip down and too fond of her gown to charge through the mayhem.

If she doesn't at least try, she'll be eliminated. And what will happen to the volunteer she was supposed to rescue?

A yelp of pain catches my ear, and I spin around to see Vanas standing on a beam, holding her head and leaning against a post. Something must have struck her skull; she looks dazed. She tries to move forward and falters, swaying toward the black ooze.

She's going to fall in.

I can't help her. Healing magic won't stop her fall, and I'm not allowed to interfere with water magic.

The crowd gasps collectively, then cries out as Vanas tumbles into the thick sludge.

The fall seems to reawaken her senses. She yells, black muck coating her neck and arms. With slippery fingers she struggles to grip the narrow beam and pull herself up.

A ridge of spikes whips past the edge of my platform, streaking toward Vanas. It rushes by her, brushing against her back, and she screams.

More shrieks from behind me. A couple more of the girls are bleeding now—nothing severe though. When I look back at Vanas, she has finally hauled herself onto the beam. Every part of her body except her face is slicked with oily black. Blood mingles with the ooze, streaming

132

from her shoulder blade, but she keeps moving ahead through the gauntlet.

This is chaos. This is horrible. My whole body is shaking. I'm whirling around and around, trying to watch everything at once, terrified that I'm going to miss something and then someone will die. I want to cry. I want to scream at the Ash King for allowing this, for putting me in the middle of it, for not telling me what to expect. My whole body vibrates with panicked energy, gold light winding around my fingers, ready to be sent where it's needed. I know my eyes must be glowing too, and I hope the odd effect doesn't distract any of the girls.

The volunteers atop the pillars are shouting now, their voices growing shrill as they sink lower and lower. That's when I realize there isn't just one spiked creature in the ooze; there are many snake-like monsters slithering through it, causing thick, ominous ripples on its viscous surface.

Adalasia has reached her volunteer. The moment she steps onto the pillar, its downward progression stops, and a rope slides down from the stadium ceiling. Adalasia grips it, and her volunteer hangs onto her as they both swing to safety, landing on a walkway right in front of the King's balcony.

Springing along on small light feet, Khloe takes a final leap and reaches her volunteer. She can't lift him, but they both grip the rope and manage to fly across the muck to the finalist's platform. Sabre grabs her volunteer around the waist and swings one-handed to the landing point.

Screams erupt from the crowd, and I glance to my right.

Teagan has just fallen, and an iron spike has impaled her neck. Blood pumps from the wound. Her eyes are wide, glassy, her mouth opening and closing like a fish.

I'm already unfurling my magic, gold light streaking toward the injury. But I can't heal her unless I can get her off that spike first.

Without thinking twice, I leap off my platform and into the gauntlet.

Idyllic though my home may look, it has its dangers. Volcanoes, of course, and the ash-burrowers—giant spiked snakes that like to nest near the mountains' roots. Between the smooth green fields there are ravines and rockfalls, poisonous plants and toxic insects.

I've done my share of running from danger.

But nothing I've experienced compares to the wild, heart-throbbing rush of racing through peril toward someone who is dying.

I don't even know how I make it through. Years of dashing across fields and working long hours have strengthened my legs—years of wielding water and harvesting plants have toned my arms—it all coalesces somehow, and I fly through the obstacles, ducking and darting, sprinting along a beam until I reach Teagan.

She's dying. I have mere seconds in which to save her.

I lift her off the spike, gritting my teeth against the horrific squelch of her flesh. Immediately I send my magic into the wound, sealing up the damage. The more energy I push into a healing, the faster it is, and I pour everything I have into Teagan. The platform under my knees is slick with blood, saturating my white pants. I don't care.

She's sealed up now, and the torn parts inside are fixed. I take a moment to replenish a bit of her blood, but the rest will have to wait.

Teagan sits up, blood-soaked hair sticking to her shoulders. "Thank you," she whispers.

"Go," I say.

She struggles to her feet, her dress hanging ragged from her body, and she leaps back into the fray.

I hesitate on the platform, gazing around. Nearly all the contestants have reached their marks now. One pair falls from their rope into the sludge and gets lacerated by the monsters—but they manage to haul themselves onto the finisher's walkway. They're screaming, bleeding, but not dying.

The girl who refused to participate is still back at the starting platform. All the volunteers except hers have been rescued, yet she stays put, sobbing. I feel sorry for her, but I'm angry, too. Her volunteer's pillar is almost submerged in the ooze—only a little of it is sticking out. The man atop the pillar has peed himself; urine soaks the front of his pants in a dark splotch, and suddenly I realize why he's so frightened.

Every toothy, razor-backed creature in the ooze has congregated around his post. When it sinks, he will be attacked by all of them. They will tear him apart, suck him under, drown him and devour him. I won't be able to fix him after that.

He is going to die.

I'm close enough to the end of the course that I can see the Ash King's cold, haughty features more clearly. "Do something!" I scream at him. "Stop this!"

I know he hears me, but he only stares, implacable.

With a frustrated shriek, I leap forward, grabbing onto a net of thorny chains and clambering across it while the tiny spikes stab my palms. Just like the diawen vines in the palm groves back home. I can do this.

Another jump, and I wobble, landing unsteadily on one of several stepping stones. The crowd's collective inhale gives me courage; they want me to do this. They want me to save that final man.

Six more steps, and a quick dance across a floor of whirling gears—my flimsy shoes are shredded and the gears slash my feet, but I push magic through the wounds as I run, healing my flesh and skin. The hems of my pants are tattered and bloodstained, and the material across my chest has shifted—I'm probably showing too much of my breasts. None of it matters.

All that matters is the life of the man whose feet are nearly in the sludge now. The monsters surge forward, snapping and slashing, as I gather my strength and fling myself across the final gap, landing on the pillar with the volunteer.

He's babbling, crying in pain as teeth and spines lacerate his ankles. But the pillar has stopped moving, and the rope has lowered.

"You have to hold onto the rope," I shout at the man. "I can't hold both of us, I'm not strong enough!"

Still gibbering, he grips the rope. My legs explode with pain as the monsters attack—I'm positive my left tendon has been cut, and the agony is so intense I can hardly think past it. I press magic to that spot while I snatch the rope and shove both of us off the pillar.

We're swinging too low. We're not going to make it.

Mentally I jerk water from the nearest drinking barrel and I shove it against our bodies, a powerful wave propelling us faster, higher, until we crash onto the finalists' platform in a mess of oily ooze and torn flesh and leaking blood.

"Rule violation!" screeches the King's herald. "Illegal use of magic in the arena."

I'm trembling on hands and knees, wrecked and wretched, even as I weave magic over the volunteer's shredded feet and send more tendrils of healing power out to the contestants on either side of me.

There's movement above, on the balcony. A scarlet-robed figure.

I look up into the Ash King's crimson eyes.

I must be a pitiable sight—eyes washed golden, dripping in gore, my clothes torn and wrenched askew, a web of magic spreading from my hands.

The herald is right—I used magic in the arena. Even if it was to save a life, I have no reason to believe the Ash King won't punish me.

"The Healer is not a contestant, and is therefore exempt from that rule," the Ash King says, in a loud, firm voice. "She has saved the remaining volunteer from certain death, and for that, she is to be commended."

And he stretches his hand toward me.

I take his hand in my blood-slicked one, and I kiss his fingertips.

He moves on immediately, giving his hand to the Favored—all except one. Then he announces the elimination of the girl who wouldn't participate, as well as the girl who fell into the muck with her volunteer. That leaves fifteen Favored women.

The First Challenge is over, and the crowds surge out of the stadium, chattering excitedly. I have no doubt today's events will be re-enacted over and over in common rooms and on street corners tonight.

While the arena is being drained and the monsters wrangled, contest aides pour from side doors and hustle the volunteers and the Favored backstage. They are all laid out on cots where their servants tend them until it's their turn to be healed.

I'm ordered to begin with the Favored who finished first, and to proceed by their ranking. But I ignore that directive and start with the worst injuries, whether Favored or volunteer, moving indiscriminately through the lineup. By the time all the cuts and contusions are mended, I'm scarcely able to stand upright.

"You'll have less strenuous day tomorrow," one of the contest managers announces to the Favored. It's the same woman who spoke to me about my responsibilities during the challenge. She barely looks at me; she must be displeased with my actions for some reason. "The next Challenge won't be as physical," she continues. "The King requested that we alternate between dangerous challenges and more cerebral ones."

"Small mercies," I whisper. At least my magic will have time to recharge.

With their healing complete, the Favored are wrapped in robes and ushered to fine carriages that will transport them back to the palace. I'm given a robe and told to wait, because apparently no one knows where the driver of my phaeton went. I'm tempted to drive the thing myself, but I've bent the rules far enough today. So I sit against the wall in the gloomy back room until someone finally takes me to the palace.

By then I'm covered in crunchy crusted blood under the robe. A servant escorts me to my room, where my maid has already prepared a bath.

"We heard what you did today," she says, taking the robe from my shoulders with almost reverent gentleness. "You're so brave, my lady, saving that man!"

"Anyone would have done it," I murmur.

"But anyone didn't," she says. "You did."

She helps me take off the ruined clothes, and then I dismiss her with my thanks. Once she's gone, I relieve myself quickly, thanking the Heartsfire I didn't piss in my pants during that ordeal.

As I sink into the tub, my eyes drift shut. The hot water is pure ecstasy.

I have a little healing energy left, and I use it to finish healing my feet and calves. Then I set the water in motion until it bubbles vigorously around me, and I relax into its pounding heat.

Moments later, a voice sounds outside the half-open door. "Healer?"

My weary heart can barely summon the energy for a flutter. "Yes, my Lord?"

He says something unintelligible, and I sigh, sinking further into the churning bubbles. With the water moving like this, he won't be able to see my body clearly, so I only hesitate for a moment before I call, "I can't hear you, Your Majesty. I'll be out soon—or if it's urgent, you can come in."

12

The Ash King doesn't enter my bathing room
immediately. Perhaps he's shocked that I would be so
forward as to invite him in. Perhaps I *am* forward. But I'm
too exhausted to care. I'm even too exhausted to cry,
although I want to, desperately. There's a raw ache in my
heart that can't be soothed by hot water or the softest bed.
I want my home, my room, my parents, my family. I want
a real hug from someone I know, someone who won't
judge me like Brayda or get distracted by my body, like
Rince.

The Ash King appears in the doorway, looking
haughty and uncomfortable. Only my shoulders show
above the bubbling water, but his cheeks are faintly
flushed, a fascinating contrast with the cool flow of his
white hair.

"You weren't supposed to get hurt," he says stiffly.

I vent a hard laugh. "What did you expect?"

"I expected you to stay where you were put and do
the healing magic from there."

"With challenges this dangerous, no one can predict
what's going to happen. I couldn't save Teagan without
first lifting her off that spike. Which is why I had to go
into the gauntlet."

"And the volunteer?"

"Saving him was human decency and common sense. Something that seems to be sadly lacking around here." I glare boldly at him.

"I didn't come in here to be insulted."

"Then why did you come?"

"I came—" he clears his throat— "to see if you were all right."

"You know I'm all right. I can heal myself." I rise a little higher in the bath, until the tops of my breasts are exposed. "Why are you really here, Your Majesty?"

His throat bobs as he swallows. "I'm here to request—no—*demand*—that you join everyone in the great hall for the banquet tonight."

"And who is 'everyone?'"

"The Favored, the visiting nobility, the contest officials, my advisors—"

My eyes widen. "You have friends?"

"I didn't say *friends*. I said *advisors*."

"Oh… well, do you have any close friends?" Another bit of information I can pass to the Undoing, perhaps.

But when I see the look in the King's eyes, I forget all about the anarchists.

"I *had* friends," he says quietly. "They all died. Enjoy your bath. I'll see you at dinner."

"Wait."

He halts, turning back.

"If you ever need to talk about them, I'll listen." Heartsfire, why did I say that? After all the misery and pain he orchestrated today—

But no one actually died. Everyone is all right. They're healed, they're whole, they're being well cared for. And to paraphrase the King himself, who wants a Queen who isn't willing to sacrifice life and limb for one of her subjects? Yes, there was pain involved in the challenge, but it will soon be forgotten.

The pain I see in the Ash King's eyes is the kind that can never heal.

Sympathy unfurls in my heart as I gaze at him. I'm glad I don't have much to report to the Undoing, because even after the day's trauma, I'm not sure I want this man dead.

Brayda would punch me on the spot if she could hear my thoughts right now.

"I don't talk about my past," says the Ash King.

"Maybe you should." I reach for the soap and pass it across my shoulders, along my arms. "Maybe if you did, you would be less... um, less..."

"Careful," he warns, crossing his arms. "You're talking to the King. Though you seem to have forgotten that, since you're bathing in front of me. Have you no concept of proper decorum?"

"You're the one who came into my room and spoke to me while I was bathing."

"I'm the King. I do whatever I fucking please. You're just a village girl."

"Well, this village girl just saved two lives *and* healed all your potential brides," I retort.

His eyes glow a fiercer crimson. "Believe me, I know," he says softly.

"Your eyes." I tilt my head, peering at him. "What does the glow mean?"

"Heightened emotions."

"What kind of emotions?"

"Emotions that do not concern you. You ask far too many questions."

"Me? No." I shake my head soberly, blinking innocently at him. "Just a few questions, like how does your magic work? Where does the fire come from? Why haven't you Muted yourself so you don't have to buy new bedroom furniture every month or so?"

He slams a palm against the doorpost. "You think I haven't tried to Mute myself? Do you honestly believe that wasn't the first thing I did after it happened?"

He doesn't have to explain what "it" is. He's talking about the massacre in the Ashlands.

"But everyone thinks you didn't try a Muting, that you don't care about what happened." I frown.

"I *let* them think that. A king who is powerful and fearsome is much more secure on his throne than one who is helpless, captive to his own uncontrollable magic. I want everyone to believe that I *choose* to keep my enormous power. The truth is, I would have stifled it long ago if I could. My skin simply won't accept the Muting tattoo. I'm impervious to my own fire, as you know, and while I'm not invincible, my flesh is difficult to damage. A tattoo won't hold. It vanishes within hours."

Mouth open, I stare at him.

"Don't tell anyone," he warns. "If people knew that I tried to Mute myself and couldn't, it would cause unrest. Better that they think me callous, cold, and fully in control. The only ones who know this secret are the two tattoo mages who tried to Mute me, and now you." He grips the edge of the doorpost. "Fuck. Why did I tell you about this?"

"I won't speak of it," I say, and my heart sinks at the lie, because I might tell Rince and Brayda. But how can I, when he looks so furiously wretched and so utterly alone?

He's breathing hard, a panicked light in his eyes. He prowls forward, menace in each step, and without warning he goes to one knee by the tub and wraps a hand around my neck—not tightly, but his fingers sting with heat. "If you speak a word of this, I will end you, do you understand? I'll do it personally, and I'll enjoy it."

Staring into those burning eyes, after everything today—I can't hold back anymore. My lip trembles and my eyes fill with tears.

The Ash King lets go of me immediately, alarmed. He backs away. "I'm sorry," he whispers.

Broken sobs escape me as he rushes out. I hug my knees and weep for everything he has taken from me.

I don't cry long. I finish bathing and grooming, and I summon my maid.

"I'm going to a banquet," I tell her. "And I need to look like a woman no one should dare to cross. How does this clothing allowance work? You've been bringing me a lot of clothes—have I reached my spending limit yet?"

"Oh, don't worry about that," she says. "The Ash King has told us we should provide you with any clothing you request, and as much of it as you want."

"When did he tell you this?"

"When you first arrived, my lady."

My chest tightens. Why show me such generosity? First the room beside his, then the royal ring, and now I find out he's given the servants orders to provide me with endless luxury, at least where clothes are concerned?

He likes me. It's the only explanation.

He invited me to his bed that first night in Aighda, and since then he has shown a marked interest in me. At least, I think he has. Perhaps he treats all the Favored with the same informal intimacy that usually characterizes our conversations.

Of course, he did threaten to kill me... and he burned a handprint on my chest. His herald promised my village would be razed to the ground if I didn't comply. *And* the Ash King says he might keep me here against my will even after the Calling of the Favored.

I don't know what to think. But I do know how I want to appear tonight—fully armored, with the soft places in my heart covered and protected against his crushing force. I won't let an unguarded moment or two derail me from my goal—to have him removed from power.

I hoped that maybe he could be Muted and deposed quietly, without an actual assassination. But with this new information about his physical qualities, that's looking less likely.

I'm escorted to the banquet by Owin. It's the first time I've seen him out of his usual armor; he's wearing a magnificent uniform of ash-gray. A stag with fiery scarlet antlers is embroidered across the breast. He guides me through the palace hallways into a banquet hall five times larger than the Lord Mayor's dining space back in Aighda.

Long tables glitter with amber glass and golden plates, a dozen chandeliers shimmer overhead, and the floor is a sprawl of glossy tiles. The tiles are oddly shaped, varying in color from red-brown to deep umber to pearlescent ivory and creamy yellow. As I examine them more closely, I realize they're not tiles at all; they are fragments of petrified wood, fitted together in a glorious polished mosaic.

Weary as I am, I can't help marveling at this room. But I lift my chin, conscious of my appearance and the strength I want to portray. My maid dressed me in a gown of bronze that nearly matches my skin. Far from the flowing, gauzy things I've worn so far, it has geometric panels that dramatize my shape. Fierce ridges of stiff metallic fabric jut from my hips and shoulders. My hair is upswept, fixed with sharp, glittering pins, and my eyelids and lashes glimmer with bronze paint and gold dust.

As Owin escorts me farther into the dining hall, I spot a cluster of the Favored, clad in magnificent gowns and elaborate jeweled headpieces. I turn toward them with an eager smile.

"I'm going to talk to them," I tell Owin. "I'll be fine. Thank you for escorting me."

He eyes the women uncertainly. "Are you sure?"

"Yes, thank you."

He shrugs and moves away, taking up a post by the wall.

I continue toward the Favored. After I healed everyone today, surely they'll be grateful, and maybe even want to be friends.

As I near them, though, I realize their smiles are anything but kind.

One of them sneers as she examines my outfit. "Don't you think that's a bit overdone, dear?"

"You do know you're not the queen, right?" another girl titters. "And you're not one of the Favored, either."

"Sweetie, I love the spotlight as much as any other woman, but really," adds a third girl. "Enough is enough. Stop trying so hard."

Khloe steps out from behind one of the girls. "Take it easy on Cailin. She saved lives today."

"We're just trying to help her realize how she's coming across," replies the first woman. "If you were making a fool of yourself in front of the entire kingdom, wouldn't you want someone to tell you the truth?"

Khloe's dark eyes take on a malignant sparkle. "You're just jealous because she looks more glamorous and queenly than all of you." She steers me away from the Favored, toward one of the long tables.

"They're right, aren't they?" I whisper. "I overdid it tonight, with this look."

"Not at all," Khloe says stoutly. "Most of them are wearing far more expensive gowns and flashier jewels than yours."

"I don't want all the attention. It's just been happening to me." I stare at her helplessly, willing her to understand.

Khloe shifts her stance and winces. "I can see that you mean well, Cailin, and you have the sweetest heart. But the displays of your magic, and your interactions with the Ash King, kissing his hand like you're one of the contestants—"

"He *offered* me his hand," I protest. "What should I have done, reject it? And I only did water magic before the challenge because I was so bored, and I felt awkward just standing there. Besides, everyone in the crowd seemed to enjoy it."

"The people like you," Khloe says. "No doubt about it. I think that's what concerns the Favored, that you're pulling focus from them, winning the hearts of the citizens without even meaning to. That, and the fact that *he* treats you differently." She nods toward the dining hall entrance, where the Ash King has just appeared, flanked by servants and guards.

He's wearing robes of metallic bronze over an ivory doublet decorated with gold. His pants are the same creamy fabric, and they match his boots, which are also threaded with gold.

"Did you intend for your outfit to coordinate with his?" Khloe whispers. "Because it does."

"I didn't plan for it." The words drift vaguely from my mouth, because I can't take my eyes off him. This whole time I knew he was handsome, of course, but now—he looks so strong, so tall, so utterly exquisite and regal—I want to crumple at his feet. But I strengthen myself with the memory of his hostile eyes, and his scorching hand at my neck, and his savage words.

He is not my friend, nor am I his. We are enemies, thrown together by his whim and a set of odd circumstances. My allegiance lies with my friends, my family, and the people of my village.

The King greets the Favored, actually smiling, gracing them with kisses on their cheeks or fingers. My stomach thrills and sickens at the same time, because I didn't realize he could be so charming. When he slides his arm around the waist of the girl who called me a fool, bile rises in my throat.

"How do we know where we're supposed to sit for dinner?" I ask Khloe.

"You'll probably be with the contest officials," she says. "If you'll excuse me—I'd like to greet him." She gives me an apologetic smile and moves away, toward the Ash King.

When he sees her, his face warms and softens. Of course it does. She's a precious darling. She's also seven years younger than him—eighteen to his twenty-five—and she's pregnant. But none of that is my business.

I won't stand alone in the center of the room, so I walk toward the edge of the space and pretend to be perusing the gilded engravings along the wall. I stand there a long time, until I've practically memorized every cottage, tree, monster, and milkmaid in the elaborate design.

Suddenly a warm palm grazes the bare skin of my back, the open space between the panels of my dress. It's the lightest touch, gone in a blink, but I can still feel the vibrating heat of it.

I turn, and there he is—the Ash King. But he's walking past me, arm in arm with one of the Favored, telling her the stories behind the engravings. It's Morani on his arm—the spiky-haired girl with the olive complexion, the one I healed of venereal disease. She laughs and squeezes his bicep as they walk, an intimate gesture that makes my stomach twist.

Something in my soul has shifted. I don't know when it happened—maybe when the Ash King held out his hand to me on the finalists' platform. I can't even define my feelings—there are too many of them spiraling and clashing in my heart, too many protests and counter-arguments clamoring in my mind.

I can't try to sort it out now. I simply have to be kind and poised while I get through this dinner. My focus must be on staying quiet and unnoticed. I can't do anything stupid, or anything that will draw attention.

All of which would be easier if the center of my back didn't still prickle with the memory of the Ash King's palm.

13

The banquet seems to last forever. I'm seated at the far end of the hall with the Calling officials and some of the contest staff. All of them seem either nervous or resentful around me at first—but throughout the many courses of the meal, I wear them down with smiles, jokes, and gentle questions about their personal lives.

By the time we're dismissed from the table, I feel good about the connections I've made, and two men have asked me to dance. One of them is a physik I noticed working behind the scenes after the challenge, keeping the contestants and volunteers comfortable until I could tend their wounds. He's a big fellow, perhaps ten years older than me, quiet and slow-spoken, with kind eyes. The other is a sharp, earnest little man about my age, with a blond mustache. He says he's part of the financial team for the competition—a bookkeeper.

The hall has become a little warm and stuffy during the meal, so a wind-wielder enters and cools the space with a fresh breeze. During our city tour, Owin told me that wind-wielders are in high demand in the city, especially during the heat of summer. Apparently the Ash King doesn't protest too loudly over their use in the mansions of the nobility or in the palace. I'm surprised he doesn't insist on a non-magical way to combat the summer heat, but maybe the breeze helps him keep his fire under control.

While the wind-wielder plies his talent, servants open three sets of tall doors into a ballroom with the same petrified wood flooring as the banquet hall. The wind-wielder's breeze flows through the doors, cooling that space as well.

The guests drift into the golden glow of the ballroom, where chandeliers cluster at the peak of the domed ceiling. One entire wall is a series of pointed windows with beautifully carved frames and stained-glass panes. Guards line the walls, and there are two people in Ricter uniforms, probably there to detect the presence of unexpected wielders who might wish harm to the King. At the far end of the room is a cluster of musicians playing a lovely dance tune.

Inwardly I bless the Ceannaire for giving me a few lessons in Capital-style dancing. Thanks to her, I can maneuver through the steps without making a fool of myself.

After my first two dances, another gentleman requests my hand for a dance, and then another. They all want to talk of my powers, where I came from, and how I came to be chosen for this role. Dance after dance, on and on it goes, until their faces, voices, and questions blur together in my mind. My heart is pounding and my brain is spinning.

"I need a moment," I murmur to my current partner, and I wander blindly through the crowd until I reach the wall of windows. Of course they are all locked tight, for the King's safety.

Desperate, I retreat to a dimly lit corner and lean against the back side of a pillar.

I press a hand to my chest, pushing against the ache of homesickness. So many people, so many eyes and hands and voices, yet I've never felt more alone.

When my heartbeat slows a little, I become aware that not far away, in an alcove half-draped by curtains, two people are sitting on a cushioned bench. My gaze traverses the length of a male leg—boots and pants of creamy leather embroidered with gold.

The King's back is angled toward me. He's holding the hand of the girl in the alcove with him. As I watch, he leans in and kisses her.

I suck in a tiny sharp breath.

His broad back stiffens under the fall of his white hair, and he breaks the kiss—starts to turn around.

I slide swiftly to the opposite side of the pillar and stand perfectly still, hoping it's wide enough to conceal me and my skirts.

I wait, breathless, watching the mesmerizing swirl of the dancers.

"Spying, are we?" That voice—fire beneath layers of ice.

The Ash King stands beside me, bracing a forearm against the pillar. The edge of his cloak brushes my bare shoulder.

"I'm not sure what you mean, Your Majesty. I was simply resting."

"No wonder you need a rest," he mutters. "You've been dancing with every low-born man at this infernal gathering."

He's been watching me. And this time, I can't pretend the shiver passing through my heart is fear. Nor can I let him guess what I'm feeling.

"Have you enjoyed your dances with the Favored?" I ask primly. "I assume your Queen will need to possess ballroom poise as well as bedroom talent. Do you plan to test both sets of skills before you choose a wife?"

"Are you asking if I plan to sleep with the Favored?"

"It's tradition, isn't it?" I keep staring at the swirl of colorful couples. "When there are five girls left, you get to bed all of them—one at a time, of course. I'm sure you're looking forward to that."

"Very much so. Too bad it's so far away." His fingertips trail up my arm, from wrist to elbow—a swift touch, gone in a moment. "I shall need release sooner than that."

"I'm sure your own hand will serve you quite well." Pushing myself off the pillar, I start to move away, but he blocks my path. His presence is heat and magnetism, compelling me to look at him—at his broad chest, swathed in shining bronze fabric—up a little further, to the cords of his throat, then to his savage jawline, his compressed mouth—all the way up to his eyes, black-fringed, shimmering with amber light.

"I frightened you earlier," he says, low. "I'm sorry for it."

My breath hitches. "My Lord, you need not apologize to one so far beneath you." With a half-curtsy, I'm moving away again when he seizes my wrist. His fingertips press the thin skin over my fluttering pulse, and I know he feels it—the betrayal of my own body, the frantic beat of my foolish heart.

"Dance with me." The words tear from him, as if he's been struggling to hold them back.

"I cannot. The Favored already hate me. They think I'm your mistress, that I'm trying to steal attention for myself." I back away. "If I want to survive this, I can't play your game anymore, Majesty."

"And what game is that? You're my subject—I'm requiring certain services of you, like healing my women and reporting your thoughts about them to me. That is all." His features are icing over; his chin lifts, and he gives me a supremely haughty look.

"Of course that's all." I pull free and move into the circling dancers. Not a moment too soon, because two of the Favored are making their way toward the King, hastening to beat each other to his side and secure the next dance.

Meanwhile, I thread through the crowd, gently declining more offers of a dance, and I wander alone through the palace until I find my own room. The defiant energy that carried me through the first part of the evening is gone now… it has ebbed away, and I feel the aching need to sleep like a ponderous weight dragging at my eyelids, like a heaviness deep in the pit of my stomach. My healing magic needs to recharge.

I disrobe and lie on the bed in my underthings, sketching the corridors and rooms I saw tonight, placing tiny X marks where the guards stood. In a handful of days, I'll need to decide what to do with this information, and with the King's secret—that he tried to Mute himself, and it did not work.

He is truly the most powerful wielder in the kingdom.

I must have fallen asleep, because when I surface to consciousness, my candles are puddles of wax in their silver tray, barely clinging to life. I can feel the edge of the notebook pressing into my face.

Groaning, I close it and push it under my pillow, muzzily trying to figure out what woke me. It's very late, probably after midnight. The ball must be over now.

A sound from the next room. A muffled clunk, like a drawer closing.

And then… a click, and the scrape of the curtained door—the door between my room and the Ash King's.

I don't even lift my head when he enters. I'm wearing a satin chemise and some very skimpy lace-trimmed panties that leave half my ass cheeks bare—I found them in my bureau. Lying on my stomach like this, in the dim candlelight, in these scanty clothes—I know the sight of me will tempt him, and I want it to. Maybe my mind is too blurry to think clearly, or maybe in this soft, drowsy space between sleep and waking, I can finally acknowledge what I really want.

He comes to my bedside, dressed in the same silky robe he wore the night we arrived at the palace. His hair is pulled back in a knot, leaving the planes of his handsome face bare. With my cheek pressed to the sheets, I look up at him, fill my eyes with the beauty of him—a beauty not mine. A beauty someone else will own and enjoy.

Perhaps I could enjoy it once first.

"Did you have fun," I murmur, "dancing with all the girls, pretending they weren't nearly torn apart by gears and eaten by monsters today?"

He flashes a quick smile. Someday I will make that smile stay.

The Ash King sinks onto the edge of my bed. "My advisors spoke to me tonight. Some of them want you to remain in your role. Others want me to send you home. They say you're causing too much of a stir."

"And what do you want?"

He reaches out, tentative, and brushes curls away from my temple. "What I want is rarely of consequence."

"I don't think that's true. You do what you want all the time."

"In small ways, yes. In larger matters, I must consider everyone but myself."

"You're sending me away, then."

His fingertips are tracing my nape now, trailing along the bare skin between my shoulder blades until they reach the satin of the chemise. "Do you want to leave?"

Yes. The answer rises automatically to my tongue, but I don't speak it, because it's no longer quite true. I've made a promise to Brayda and Rince—though I'm increasingly unsure about keeping it—and they expect me to stay in this role. Beyond that, in spite of how the Favored treated me tonight, I feel responsible for them. Judging by what I saw today, the women might not make it through the competition without me.

Perhaps they need someone more skilled than I am. Someone quicker, wiser. Maybe two healers, not just one.

"I'm easily replaced," I murmur, smoothing the sheet with my fingers.

"Not so. I've been looking for someone like you for weeks."

"You saw how close the girls came to death today. You need more than one healer for this contest."

He sighs. "There are few in the land, fewer than you'd think. Those that equal your power are already spoken for by the noble houses—they have allegiances, contracts, prejudices. They can't be trusted to be impartial. And others are too old, too young, or too volatile for the work. You are the perfect candidate, not only for the Calling, but also for the position of royal healer."

I sit up, the strap of the chemise sliding off my shoulder. His eyes drop to the exposed skin immediately, and his tongue passes briefly over his lip.

"Can we speak of this another time?" I ask in a shaky voice. "I'm honored, my Lord, but I'm tired. After today's events, and the stress of the evening—I feel weak. I'm afraid I will say something I shouldn't. Forgive me, Your Majesty."

He collects the fallen strap and moves it back onto my shoulder. His fingers drift from my skin slowly, as if they'd like to stay.

"The girls told me I'm trying too hard—that I'm purposely drawing attention to myself," I whisper. "Please believe me when I say that isn't true. I promise I will make better choices—I won't show off my magic—"

"But I love your magic, and so do the people," he says. "Let me calm the fears of the Favored, Healer. Continue to be exactly yourself, and you will have my protection."

Sighing, I lie down again, relaxing into my former position, on my stomach with my cheek against the sheets.

I hold his gaze and blink my lashes slowly.

That simple act is possibly the boldest, most wanton thing I've ever done—more daring than any sexual foray with Rince—because this is the *Ash King*, maker of the Ashlands, the volcanic lord of the land. And with that slow blink, I asked him to touch me.

The Ash King's breath is shallow, and his eyes glow molten.

He smooths his hand along my bare leg, starting just behind the knee and moving up, along my thigh, to the curve of my rear. The caress of his palm there sends a tingling warmth flooding over my skin, into the crevice between my legs.

Ever so slightly, I arch up into the touch.

14

At my reaction, the Ash King lets out a slow,
shuddering breath. His hand sweeps over the swell of my
ass—first one cheek, then the other, like he's savoring the
feel of my flesh.

I remain on my belly, hips tilted upward just a bit. I
can barely breathe.

Slowly he pushes the lace hem of the panties higher,
exposing more of one ass cheek. The movement tugs at
the fabric between my legs, drawing it tighter, and a ripple
of arousal rolls through me. The heat between my thighs
swells, every bit of my flesh sensitized, craving more,
more.

He rubs his palm over my rear again. Then, with his
fingertips, he traces slow circles, and each one sends a
vibrating swirl of pleasure through my lower belly.

I close my eyes, relishing the sensations. But a
moment later, he gives my bottom a light pat and rises
from the bed. "You are tired. Sleep." He reaches down for
a blanket and drapes it over my body. Quietly, he glides
back to his room.

Disappointment suffuses me, but it's softened by
weariness. I really do need to rest.

In the morning, I bathe and dress quickly, blushing
far too often at the memory of what happened between
me and the Ash King. We crossed a line, he and I—and

now that I'm not sleep-drunk, I vow internally that it won't happen again. In fact, I plan to pretend that it didn't happen at all. I did *not* let the Ash King fondle my nearly-naked rump. I didn't encourage such attentions, nor did I react to them.

Last night's conversation also made me realize I could be sent away at any time. It's unlikely, since I'm needed for the Calling, but it could happen if I make any more unintentional missteps. And while I would be happy to go home, there's something I want to do first.

My maid told me that the Favored are being tested on their knowledge of Bolcan's history today. It will be a fast-paced contest where they have to shout out the answers faster than their rivals, and the three women with the top scores will get personal time with His Volcanic Majesty. So I'm not needed, and no one will look for me today. It's the perfect day for my plan.

Technically I've been forbidden to go into the city without a guard, but when I order the phaeton and leave the palace, no one stops me. I simply behave as if I know exactly what I'm doing, and I feign the haughty, disdainful bearing of one of the Favored until I'm through the outer gates.

I'm free. Free. I could go anywhere, do anything.

Of course, if I run home, the Ash King will punish me and my village. He might not want to, and he might find a way to soften the punishment, but he'd have to retaliate somehow. If there's anything I've learned so far, it's that maintaining control is extremely important to him. I suppose it's like that for most people in roles of power and authority.

So instead of running back home, I order the phaeton driver to take me to the poorest section of town.

The driver twists in her seat and looks back at me, uncertain, but I give her a firm frown. "King's orders," I say.

She shrugs and guides the phaeton through the streets, past the Market of Uniquities, into a maze of dark, slipshod buildings. The smell of horse manure, rancid meat, *tobak* smoke, and sour wine fills my nostrils. Grime clings to the bricks and plaster, and when I step out of the phaeton, my boot lands in a puddle that looks like oil and piss.

"What's that building?" I ask the driver, pointing to a newish-looking structure of yellow brick, with white-framed windows.

"Palace-funded housing," she answers. "The King ordered the construction of new tenement buildings throughout this area, with low rates for those who can't afford anything better. There are palace-funded food stalls, too, and physik clinics."

"What about healers?"

"No healers. Just non-magical remedies and treatment. What's your business here, my lady, if I may ask? You said the King ordered this outing?"

"Um, yes."

The driver tilts her head, as if she hears deceit in my tone. She has angular features and shiny black hair beneath a broad-brimmed hat. "You're getting me into trouble, aren't you, Healer?"

I give her an apologetic smile. "Maybe. I want to provide healing to those who can't afford it. And I knew the King wouldn't agree, so—"

"So you lied to me. Do you know what he does to people who displease him?" She pulls aside her collar to reveal a small round scar on her shoulder. "That's from his finger. It was on fire at the time."

"What did you do to anger him?" I ask.

Her face hardens. "That's none of your business."

"You're right. It's not." I back away, upset with myself. Since when did I begin looking for reasons to excuse the Ash King's cruelty? "Please return for me in three hours' time."

The driver barely acknowledges me. She chirps to the horse, and the phaeton rattles away.

I wander along the street, gazing up in awe at the huge yellow tenement building. The Ash King has his faults, but at least he's trying to help the less fortunate. Whether his efforts are successful or not is beyond my knowledge; I'm not skilled at economics or the finer points of city management. All I know is, there are people in this sector who need my help, and I'm going to give it.

A little farther along the street is a public house, a place to buy drinks and food. As I approach, a skinny boy brings out an A-frame sign, sets it up by the door, and begins to write the day's menu on the slate sides in chalk.

The door to the public house is propped open, so I step inside. The space is so gloomy it takes my eyes a minute to adjust.

A hefty barmaid is moving chairs and tables around, setting up for the day.

"Good morning," I begin—but when she turns to me, her face lights up, and she exclaims, "Healer of the Favored! I was in the stands yesterday during the First Challenge! Won the ticket in a game of chud-lobber. Best day of my life." She throws both beefy arms around my neck. "Honored that you're here, my lady. Honored."

"Oh, no, please—it's not 'my lady.' Just Cailin. I'm from a farming village."

She clasps my shoulder with a broad hand. "I knew I liked you. What can I do for you, Cailin?"

"I'm looking for people to heal," I say simply.

"People to heal?" She puckers her lips. "Not sure many in these streets can afford your services, but—"

"No, no—not for money," I interject. "For free."

The barmaid stares. "You want to heal people for free. People around here?"

"Yes. Do you know of anyone who needs healing?"

She keeps staring at me. Despite the gloom, I can see tears shimmering in her eyes.

"I'm sorry," I gasp. "If that's offensive or something, I can go."

"Offensive?" she chokes out. "Please—please sit here." She drags a chair over to me. "I know at least a dozen people who could use your help." She looks toward the open door. "Boy! Run to Aunt Mag's house, and Master Daly's, and Rohu's place. Tell them the Healer of the Favored is here, and she's willing to heal for free!"

Five hours later, the crowd in the public house doesn't seem to have diminished at all. In fact, it has swelled beyond anything I could have predicted.

I've been healing everything from infected sores to swollen ankles to stomach ailments. I've repaired broken limbs, knitted torn flesh together, eased bruises, soothed headaches, and calmed colicky babies. And I pushed extra energy into each healing to speed the process along so I could have time for more people.

My energy reserves are dangerously low, far lower than they were yesterday after I healed the Favored. Once I drain my healing energy to a certain point, it starts to affect me physically. I've never learned exactly why, but my best guess is that my healing magic begins to draw on my actual life force to supplement itself.

My vision is beginning to grow hazy around the edges, and when I try to blink the haze away, it grows thicker. My fingers tremble as I splay them over the chest of a man with a heart problem. I can sense the blockage inside his artery—I just need a little more time to clear it.

He'll be my last one for the day.

But when I glance up, the room is still packed with people—sick people, injured people. People with pained eyes, hungry for my magic, desperate for relief.

"There are so many of them," I whisper to the barmaid, Herifwen.

She nods. "It is a big city. Lots of pain."

"Too much pain," I murmur, blinking. Shadows creep from the edges of my sight, crawling inward, but I grip the threads of my magic and focus as hard as I can.

The man with the heart ailment is healed now. He would have died in mere months without my help—now he'll live for years, if he takes care of himself.

I'm shaking so hard I can barely speak. I don't think I can move from the chair I'm sitting on. The only time I've been this low was during a plague, when I had to heal many people as fast as possible. After that incident, it took me a few days to refill my healing energy.

Tomorrow is another physical challenge for the Favored. My energy is too low—I'm not going to be ready.

How did I let it go this far? I kept telling myself, "Just one more"—I kept seeing pitiful bodies and sad faces, and I couldn't stop.

I can't stop.

Dazed, I stare at the woman who approaches me next. There's a baby in her arms—its eye is inflamed, leaking pus. She holds the child out to me, her eyes pleading.

"Just one more," I whisper.

But before I can draw on my magic again, a hasty royal fanfare sounds outside, ending in a screech of strangled notes, as if someone stopped the music by force.

Cold sweat breaks out across my forehead.

The next instant, the Ash King's tall frame fills the doorway.

He's dressed in black leather and metal, wearing one of his black-iron crowns, and his eyes are living flame.

Everyone in the public house gasps and cringes, moving out of his way as he strides toward me.

"Healer." His voice is cold as bones, hot as lava oozing through dark caverns. It cannot be both at once, yet somehow it is.

I blink at him, swaying in my seat.

His rage practically vibrates through the air. "You disobeyed my orders, Healer. You will be punished."

"Your Majesty." Herifwen sinks to her knees, lifting folded hands. "Please, she was only helping the injured. Healing the sick."

"She serves the Favored," he snaps. "Come, Healer."

With every bit of my remaining strength I manage to stand. But I collapse at once, my eyes rolling back in my head. My body trembles violently. Weakness, so much horrible weakness, flooding my limbs, turning them to quivering jelly.

Strong arms encircle me, lifting me. I'm clasped to a broad, hard chest—unforgiving plates of metal, stiff leather. I can't protest—I can't make a sound. I have to actually think about breathing, force my lungs to push the air in and out. In and out.

I'm being carried somewhere. Can't see. Sounds are muffled, except for the burning ice of one low voice. "What have you done to yourself?"

I can't answer him. But I want to.

I think I went too far this time.

I can't serve the Favored tomorrow—I'm sorry. I failed you.

I couldn't stop. These people need me.

Darkness swirls around me. Weakness weighs my limbs. And then the shaking starts again—spastic movements I can't control. The strong arms embrace me, hold me until the fit subsides.

We're in a jolting carriage for a long time… maybe forever…

Now there's something soft under me, over me.

And then, through the blur, a bloom of golden light, and an old man's cracked voice murmuring, "There, there, sweet child, you'll be all right. Took yourself down too low, that's all."

"You have to fix her." The second voice is familiar, but I've never heard it so full of fear. The Ash King's voice. I want to help him, to soothe his anxiety. I try to lift my hand, to reach out, but I can't move.

The aged voice again. "I will give her a little of my own energy. I can't spare much, but it should be enough to get her through this. Has she been trained?"

"From what I was told, she had no mentor in the healing craft," says the Ash King. "She is self-taught."

"She is extremely powerful," continues the aged voice. "As you know, my Lord, I have some skills as a Ricter as well as a healer. This girl's healing ability has a facet I've seen only twice before, one that is—"

The old man hesitates, and even in my weakened state I can sense that he's on the verge of telling my most dreadful secret. With every particle of strength I possess, I fight through the weakness, and I whisper, "No. No."

A wrinkled hand smooths my forehead. "All right, girl, all right. Hush now, don't distress yourself. You did a good thing today, but you need training and self-control. You have to know when to stop. I can teach you that."

The Ash King cracks a laugh. "Can you teach *me* that skill while you're at it, Jonald?"

"Your magic and motives are entirely different, my boy," says the ancient voice. "She did this because her heart is much bigger than her powers. Sweet child."

The old man presses his hand more firmly to my forehead. Something trickles into my body—warm liquid energy drizzling into my bones, slithering into my mind, strengthening my consciousness.

I'm still too weary to move, or to open my eyes, but my thoughts have clarified again, and my body isn't quaking.

"That's all I can spare," says the old man. "She needs rest."

"She won't be able to serve the Favored tomorrow, will she?"

"Certainly not," replies the old man. "You'll have to postpone the challenge."

The Ash King sighs. "Many of the girls already hate her. This won't help matters."

"I think she gained more friends than she lost today," replies the old man. "Loyal, grateful friends who are, perhaps, more worth having than a flock of twittering throne-seekers."

"You always put things into perspective, Jonald," says the Ash King.

"And Your Majesty permits an old man's bluntness, for which I'm grateful." The wrinkled palm leaves my forehead. "Perhaps this can be a secret challenge— observing which women of the Favored react charitably to your young Healer, and which ones treat her poorly."

There's a swishing of robes, a series of quiet footfalls, and the sound of a door closing.

Then the Ash King says, "Leave us," to someone.

"But my Lord," says a voice—a servant or a guard? "The Favored ladies who won special time with you are awaiting your presence."

"I'll be there shortly. Go."

More retreating footsteps, and the door closes again.

Cold rings and warm fingers brush against my forehead, stroking my hair.

And then, as I'm drifting into sleep—a soft press of lips just below my hairline.

15

The next morning I'm able to move and speak normally again, though my body is still weakened. I sit up in bed and eat the breakfast I'm brought. But I feel slightly sick every time I think about what I did.

I nearly died. I almost killed myself for those people.

It was stupid of me. I should have left when my energy got low; I could have come back another day to help the rest of them. Dead healers can't help anyone.

Shortly after noon, the Ash King flings open the door to my room and strides in. I'm wearing a scanty slip of a nightdress, so I tug the sheet up to my chin.

He quirks an eyebrow. "So modest today."

"I've had time to think about my recent choices, and to regret them."

He chews his lip, scanning the room. "You are better?"

"Yes. Your Majesty, I want to apologize for leaving the castle without your permission, and for spending too much of my powers. There were just so many people who needed—"

"Stop." He catches the bedpost in his hand, gripping it with such strength that it creaks and his knuckles turn white. "You almost killed yourself. I cannot forgive that. I'm in the middle of choosing my bride, Healer, and I am under constant threat from those pestilent anarchists with the Undoing. I don't need the extra stress of worrying about *you*."

"I'm sorry. Truly." I give him the most repentant, sorrowful look I can muster. "How did the Favored take the news that the Third Challenge is delayed?"

"Surprisingly well. I suppose they could tell you'd angered me. They're glad of the rift between us, and glad for another day's respite before the next perilous event."

The rift between us.

Why do those words bother me?

"Whom did you send home after the Second Challenge?" I ask.

He names a couple of the women I'm less familiar with, which means we're now at thirteen Favored in total. "Teagan, Vanas, and Axley were the winners," he says. "I spent time with each of them last night. I'm taking Diaza and Leslynne to the Market of Uniquities this afternoon, and having a private dinner with three other girls this evening."

"And who's your favorite so far?" I smile brightly, eagerly, but I'm sore inside—sore, and so very tired.

He walks to the bureau, where the jewels I wore the other night are still lying in their bed of white velvet. Usually my maid takes away the jewelry I've borrowed, probably to return it to a royal vault—but for some reason, she left the yellow diamonds in my room.

"You were right," says the Ash King, touching the gems with his fingertip. "I prefer Teagan. She is everything I want in a queen—intelligent, brave, determined, and beautiful. She has elegance and charm. She is diplomatic and kind."

It's all true. Truth is a pain-sharp blade, piercing the muscle of my heart, slicing deeper with every descriptive he uses for her.

"Anyone else?" I manage. "What about Khloe, or Sabre?"

"I truly believe Sabre could lift me bodily," he says, with a half-smile. "I respect that, and her courage. She's a well-read, well-traveled woman with a strong sense of loyalty to the crown. And her smile is stunning. Another excellent candidate. Now Khloe—" his face softens, and he smiles wider— "Khloe is a sweet treasure in a small package. When I'm with her, I find myself compelled to kiss her, and I want to make those big eyes of hers widen with delight, over and over."

This hurts. It hurts so much. Why did I ask him about the girls? I am moments away from breaking my promise and telling him Khloe is pregnant, just so he'll kick her out of the competition. But I clutch the sheet tighter, and I paint an encouraging smile on my face.

"All of these women have titles and connections to offer, as well as their other charms," the King continues, still examining the jewelry. "Teagan could strengthen my link to the border lands, and Khloe's family is powerful here in the Capital. Sabre has relatives in the South— choosing her would help my image among those who live near the Ashlands. Axley is perhaps the most well-connected of all—she comes from two ancient noble lines, both of which remain powerful influences in my Court."

"And that's important, of course," I murmur. "The power and influence. The connections and the noble blood. You have to take that into consideration."

"Yes," he muses. "I am forced to choose from a limited pool of women. At least I get to torture them a little first."

Something about that last comment annoys me—or perhaps my anger has been stirring this whole time, fueled by an entirely different emotion.

"You're cruel," I say abruptly.

The Ash King's head whips toward me. "You're just now realizing this?"

"No. I knew it before. But I've recently had more proof of it." I lift my chin, careless of the consequences for my defiance. "The phaeton driver showed me where you burned her."

He snorts. "She used to drive the royal carriage, until she showed up drunk to her post. I didn't realize she was inebriated until she nearly ran over two children in the street. She deserved a lasting memory of the incident. A permanent warning."

"Oh." Shock vibrates through me, but I steel myself against it and say, "Well—you burned me, here." I touch my chest.

"Burning you was cruel," he admits. "But I'd been told you could heal yourself."

"So why do it then?"

"I was angry. The way you spoke to me of what I did in the Ashlands, as if I were a murderous monster—it stung. I wanted to hurt you back—and I wanted to see your powers in action."

"By wounding me that night, you only confirmed my terrible impression of you."

"As if I care what you think of me." He speaks tight-lipped, his shoulders rigid. Fire flickers deep in his eyes. "Understand, Healer, that you are not forgiven, and that you will be punished for what you did in the city. And, recovered or not, you will serve the Favored in the Third Challenge tomorrow."

"Yes, Your Majesty." I give the words such a scornful twist that he strides to the bed, teeth bared.

He catches my face in his hand and pulls me toward him, bending until his nose brushes mine. "Watch yourself," he hisses.

He's gripping my cheeks, huffing angry breaths over my lips. I can taste his frustration; it tingles on my tongue.

Too close. He's too close. And whenever he is this close to me, neither of us seems capable of moving away immediately. We hover, caught in a panicked flutter of lashes and breaths and quivering lips—transfixed and trembling.

I nearly died, and life seems suddenly fragile as frost, prone to melting in a moment. Best to seize what pleasure we can when it appears.

I place my fingers over the back of the Ash King's hand. The tendons there are rigid as he grips my face, but at my touch they relax.

My mouth eases upward, the thin skin of my lips grazing his, just barely. The lightest of soft kisses, not even a kiss, really.

He exhales, sharp and hungry.

But I don't press in for a real kiss. I keep the touch light, my lips skimming his mouth. Waiting.

16

The Ash King doesn't kiss me. With his mouth
against mine he whispers, "I save my kisses for the women
I might marry. But if you want other parts of me, I'm
happy to oblige."

"I don't kiss kings who threaten me," I whisper back.
"And I don't fuck them either."

"That's too bad." He pulls back slowly. "I could make
you forget your own name."

"And I could make you forget the past," I reply.

The mutual challenge tightens the air between us. It's
like a child's game—a rope pulled taut, and we each hold
an end, straining, tugging—one gaining ground, then the
other. I'm not sure which of us will pull the other over the
edge. But I want to find out.

When the Ash King whirls and stalks from the room,
I collapse into my pillows. To escape thoughts of the King
on his outing with the girls, I spend the afternoon reading
more romance stories, an activity which makes me smile
but also leaves me hot, lustful, and frustrated.

While I'm picking at my dinner, a welcome distraction
arrives—a letter from my parents. I'm not sure how my
own message reached them so quickly, or how theirs got
back to me so fast. Either the King's messengers ride hard
or they use hawks for letter delivery. Or maybe there is

magic involved. No matter the reason, I'm thrilled to receive word from home.

Everyone is well in the village. My parents are relieved to hear that I'm all right, but they're worried, of course. In my letter, I included very strong words forbidding them from coming to the Capital to fetch me. Thankfully, it seems they took my warning to heart.

I write another message to them, telling as much as I can without revealing anything that could get them—or me—into trouble. At the end of the letter, I include a vague mention of meeting some old friends in the city. But I don't use Brayda's name, or Rince's.

With the letter sealed and handed off to a servant, I plop onto the bed again. Burying my mind deep in a fictional world is a blessed reprieve from the torment of my heart and soul. In fact, it's such a successful pastime that I barely notice the hours passing.

I've nearly finished a romance about a pirate and his captive when there's a tap on my door. Or rather, on *our* door—the door I share with the Ash King. Odd that he would knock—he usually enters without warning.

Quickly I arrange myself against the pillows and tug the neckline of my nightdress a little lower, so my full breasts are nicely on display. I push off the sheet and pose my bare legs artfully.

I want him to see what he's missing. And I've learned that no matter how much I tempt him, he won't force me. Not that he'd have to at this point—I feel rather like a puff-flower, whose seeds usually burst into a cloud of floating white motes at the slightest breath. A few touches between my legs, or a thick cock sliding inside me, and I'd shatter into bliss at once.

"Come in, Your Majesty," I say.

He saunters in, his magnificent body entirely bare except for a pair of gray undershorts. Three tiny orbs of fire rotate lazily above his head, bathing the planes of his chest and abs with a soft orange glow. His white hair is in a long braid down his back, with strands brushing his bold cheekbones.

He is altogether luscious. And he's tempting me on purpose, as I'm doing to him.

"I can't sleep," he says. "And I figured out how it could work."

He tosses a piece of paper onto the rose-colored blankets. I pick it up and examine the extremely graphic sketch of several naked people. It takes me a minute to realize he has drawn the group sex scene from the highwayman novel. The girl is lying belly-down with one man face-up beneath her and the other face-down on top of her—and then there's a third man standing behind and a fourth up front.

"Decent drawing skills, Your Majesty," I muse, willing myself not to blush. "But you've given far too much thought to this."

Despite my best efforts, my face is warming, and I'm seized by the compulsion to press my legs together. The panties under my nightdress are soaked.

The Ash King shrugs, sending his little fire orbs up to the ceiling of my room, where they spin lazily in a circle.

"Did you have a nice dinner with the girls?" I ask.

"Yes, but we ended the evening early because of tomorrow's challenge," he says. "And I can't sleep. Can your magic induce sleep?"

"I can normalize heart rates, soothe nerves, and calm inflammation, but I can't directly stimulate the production of chemicals in the body, nor can I alter brain function," I tell him.

"Fine," he growls. "I suppose I'll drink myself to sleep. I've already indulged in a couple glasses—care to join me in draining a whole bottle, or two?" He throws himself onto my bed and reaches for the pull-cord to summon the maid.

"Don't!" I lean over and grab his wrist. "Do you want her to see us like this? Think of the scandal."

He looks at me, a humorous smile hovering over his lips, his eyes flickering a warm amber. I can smell his wine-laced breath, which explains why he's in a more cordial and forgiving mood than he was earlier today.

Reclined beside him, I'm much too close to the expanse of his naked chest and his long bare legs. My gaze wanders up the beautiful sinewy lines of his outstretched arm, to the wrist I'm holding, then to the strong fingers poised around the bell-cord.

Slowly he pulls his arm back, bringing it close to his breast so that my knuckles brush his skin. "How else can I get to sleep?" His tone is huskier than usual. "I need my sleep, Healer, or I become somewhat volatile."

"I could—I could give you a massage. I'm rather good at them."

I wait with bated breath for him to make a comment about wanting a more intimate kind of massage, but he only regards me for a moment before rolling over onto his stomach. "Have at it, then."

"You know I'll be able to scan you while I'm doing this."

"I'm aware. You already know part of the secret I was trying to conceal—the intractable, unMutable nature of my flesh. The rest—well, Jonald tells me it's hard to describe. See for yourself, but don't ask me to explain it."

Curious, I hop off the bed and dip my fingers in the soothing herbed ointment my maid keeps on my dressing tray with the perfumes. Slicking the ointment over my fingers, I resume my seat and scoot nearer to him. His back is broad, so I have to reach awkwardly and angle my body as I press my fingers to his shoulders. It would be much easier to work on his muscles if I were astride him, but I'm not sure I have the boldness to try that.

At least, not yet.

I know every muscle group in the human body, though I have never learned all their correct names. I know them like a child knows the faces of dear relatives before she can pronounce their names or understand their place on the family tree.

The muscles at the curves of the Ash King's shoulders are hard as rocks, and not just from strength. This is a knotted anxiety, hard-baked into his flesh. There is extraordinary tension below the base of his neck and along the upper part of his spine. I rub those taut muscles with my thumbs, roll against the knots with the heels of my hands.

When I get to the slabs of muscle across his shoulder blades and back, I pummel them with my fists, knead them with my knuckles. My palms push through the tension, rubbing it away. As usual, my eyes drift shut as I work, and my other sense takes over—the instinct that tells me where the pain and damage are. He's harder to read than other patients—I have to concentrate more, as if there's an extra layer between the aura of his body and my senses.

I'm nearly replenished, but I don't dare use too much healing energy on him. I only allow a little to seep through his skin, seeking out inflammation to soothe. Or at least, I try to let it seep through—but I'm halted, as if by some barrier. Frowning, I push harder, breaking through the resistance.

The Ash King groans, and I gasp, because in the dark behind my eyelids I can see the interior of him, like a human-shaped furnace in my mind. I'm not a Ricter—I can't sense resonance. Whatever I'm seeing is beyond resonance, beyond anything a normal human or wielder possesses. Every one of his bones burns golden; his veins are threads of glowing scarlet, and his muscles are heated amber. Yet on the surface he looks and feels human. How is this possible?

I want to ask him what he is, but he told me not to. I have a feeling he doesn't really know. Or if he does, he isn't ready to tell me.

This is information the Undoing will want. And I should give it to them, because this man under my palms has killed thousands of people—*his* people. He burned them alive in their homes, in their fields and shops. And for what? No one knows. Some people give one reason, some another. But no one who was there that day survived, except for him.

As I continue palpating each muscle, I make an inner vow, sacred as my Healer's promise.

I will tell the Undoing *nothing* about the King until I've heard his version of the Ashlands massacre. Because despite his moments of cruelty, I can't imagine him murdering so many human beings purposefully, in cold blood. I can't believe it, or I don't want to.

Because I like him. I like the way he keeps coming to me, as if he can't help himself. I like his fascination with me, his obvious lust for my body. I like the way he keeps making exceptions for me and bending the rules.

I'm not blind. I see the way he overcompensates for his insecurities with terrifying lies and vindictive punishments. I see how he keeps everyone at a distance and wears a harsh, cold façade to frighten away those who creep too close. He is controlling, power-hungry, jealous, proud, changeful, and selfish. But he is also tentatively edging nearer to me, opening himself up little by little. Maybe because he wants to fuck me. Or maybe there is more to this pull between us.

Or perhaps I'm only wishing.

My hands move to his neck and shoulders again, easing the remaining tension before moving down, pressing along both sides of his spine. He sighs heavily and relaxes completely. I hadn't realized he was still holding so much tension until he lets it all go.

My fingers press around the base of his spine, then move to his rear, working over the material of his undershorts. I use the heel of my hand on those large muscles, pressing my other palm on top for deeper impact.

A moan breaks from the Ash King's mouth, and his whole body tenses again, as if he's embarrassed for letting that sound out.

"Sshh," I soothe him. "I'm the only one here. Let it all go."

He obeys, relaxing again, and I move to his thighs, then his calves.

I usually finish a massage by returning to the shoulders again. And now that we're both more comfortable with this, I want to try what I was too nervous to attempt earlier.

I position myself astride the narrowest part of the Ash King's waist, braced on my knees, and I rub his back and neck and arms thoroughly, evenly. My rear rests against his, and the brushing contact makes me wet again. To be honest, my arousal never really abated.

When I swing off him, there's a damp place on his skin where my underwear touched his back. I rub over it with my ointment-covered hands, hoping he won't notice. He's completely limp, his flushed face half sunk in the pillow and his eyes closed. Stripped of his usual haughty calm, he looks far younger than usual.

"Turn over," I tell him softly.

A frown line dents his brow. "I can't."

"Come on." I push at his shoulder.

"Very well." He sighs. "You asked for it."

The Ash King rolls over onto his back, arms relaxed at his sides. His arousal is pushing his undershorts into a pronounced peak, and there's a tiny damp spot on the fabric.

"We're going to work on those pectorals," I murmur as evenly as I can. My heart is beating so fast it's echoing in my ears, and my cheeks are fiery and tingling.

"Mm," says the Ash King, eyes still closed.

With him face-up, it's harder to focus on providing a simple massage. The muscles I'm pressing are so firm, yet the skin over them is so deliciously silky and hot. He's not flexing, but I can still see the subtle shapes of his abdominals, exquisitely sculpted. He's brimming with ferocious power, but at my touch, the molten lines of him have eased and cooled.

I skip the genital area and move to the muscles of his legs, working over them before dragging my thumbs along the inner thighs.

At the slow rub of my thumbs, his rigid length jerks beneath the undershorts, and his jaw tightens. But he says nothing, and he doesn't open his eyes.

He isn't asking me to pleasure him. And perhaps that is what tips me over the precipice into the valley of wicked, wanton impulses that have been racing through my mind ever since he yielded under my hands.

He wants release, but he won't ask. He's either too considerate or too proud for that—probably the latter.

I'm not ready to fully give in to him, either. I have too many questions.

But perhaps in the interest of healing… for the purpose of sleep and relaxation… there is something I can do.

17

"Say no anytime," I whisper. My hands press firmly against the ridges of the Ash King's hips. Some call them love handles. To me they are guiding lines, intersecting at the yearning center of him.

The heady, hazy, herbal scent of the ointment hovers thickly over his glossy skin, rising to tantalize my nostrils. We are linked by touch in a world of slow movements, where breath feathers into warm air suffused with candle-glow, and soft pillows cradle our beating hearts.

Gently I pull down his shorts, lifting the band away from his skin so his erection can bob free. The Ash King's penis is solid, not overly thick, but a healthy girth and a perfect length, with a slight upward curve and a neatly shaped head. I'm seized with the primal urge to lick it, but I have a little restraint left, so I don't touch it at all. I touch him everywhere but there. My thumbs rub over his abdominals, my fingertips press into the hollows of his hips, the heels of my hands roll along his thighs.

The King talked of pleasurable torture once. I'm showing him that I know exactly how to do such things. I once teased Rince almost to the peak, over and over again, for two hours as we lay hidden in a grassy hollow by a stream. I would bring him to the edge and then stop, while he writhed and begged so beautifully. I did that over and over. By the end, his skin was coated with sweat and he was whimpering, entirely helpless to my lightest touch. When release finally came, it was exquisite to watch.

I smooth my palms over the Ash King's pectorals again—only this time I circle his nipples and roll them gently between my fingers. His head tilts back, muscles along his jaw flexing, and his cock dips again.

I work my way lower. His stomach is rock-hard and ridged now, taut with impending release. I mold my palms to each muscle, enjoying them on the way down. This time, when I reach his cock, I curl my hand around it and stroke upward once, firmly, and then let go.

The Ash King lets out a broken gasp, twitching helplessly.

I love that sound. I want to hear it over and over—I don't think I will ever be tired of it.

But I dare not take too long with him, or I will lose my nerve. I will begin to think of my village, and how this act of mine, secret though it is, might be a kind of betrayal. Rince would look at me with such deep disgust and disappointment; Brayda might actually cut my fingers off—oh gods.

I did it—I made the mistake of *thinking*, and now—

My gaze travels the Ash King's powerful body, motionless except for his quick breaths. He's lovely like this, bathed in soft warm light. His eyes are still closed—he is blind to everything but the sensations I'm giving him.

This man is my king. Ruler of the entire kingdom. Murderer and punisher. Wielder of a power that could raze the lands I love. Why do I struggle to grasp that reality in this moment? Why can't I see anything but a weary, lonely man who comes to me with hunger and hope in his eyes?

His hands are splayed rigid against the sheets. I want to pick one of them up, caress the tendons, circle those prominent male knuckles—but that would be too tender, too intimate. I am massaging him, helping him sleep. That is all.

My fingers are still slippery from the ointment. I slide both hands over his hard length, one stroking the shaft, the other polishing the tip. After a few moments, I switch to one hand and pump firmly, with an expert press of my thumb in a sensitive place just beneath the head. My other hand cups his balls, massaging them gently.

He comes with a low cry, his release sprinkling his own stomach and chest. A violent clenching of every muscle in his incredible body, and then he goes boneless in my bed, his handsome face perfectly smooth.

"See," he whispers. "I don't ejaculate lava."

He overheard Teagan and I talking during the journey to the Capital, before I realized how keen his ears were.

I smile at the memory, soothing him with a few more comforting strokes along the softening shaft.

"Your massage is complete, Your Majesty," I say. "Do you think you can sleep now?"

"If I can manage to move from here to my own bed. Which I must, since my guards check on me now and then through the night."

"That must be annoying." I slide off the bed and take a cloth from the dressing table.

"It is, sometimes." He catches the cloth I toss to him and wipes his body with it. "Tonight I told them not to disturb me for a couple of hours. I had plans to seduce you, you see."

"Really?" I give him my most innocent, wide-eyed look of surprise. "Gracious gods."

"After so many denials, I did not expect to succeed." He regards me keenly.

I bristle a little. "You didn't succeed."

"I suppose not. A challenge for another day, then."

"You told me you were only interested in my magic."

"Kings are experts in matters of delicate deceit."

"And that is one reason I decline, my Lord. Tonight was a mercy of mine, to help you sleep. Nothing more."

"Mercy?" His cheeks crease as he grins, the widest smile I've seen from him. "It felt precious near to cruelty. You've practiced that torturous art before, yes?"

"I have a past, as you do."

At the pointed reminder, his smile vanishes, and I almost regret the comment. But I need to put distance between us again, or he might never leave my bed.

"I will see you at the Third Challenge tomorrow, Healer," says the Ash King, rising and moving to the door between our rooms. "Rest well. You will need all your strength."

The tiny orbs of fire linger near my ceiling for a little while once he's gone. But eventually they wink out, one at a time, and the room feels colder without them.

18

"This is madness," I say under my breath.

I'm fairly sure every would-be royal bride is thinking the same thing. Today's challenge takes place in an enormous open field, ringed by a tall fence of thick metal bars. The bars are set wide enough for a person to slip out through them, but not wide enough for *anything else* to escape.

Anything else like the thirteen monsters locked in thirteen cages at the far end of the field.

I've seen beasts like these in a book before. They're rare, denizens of an older world, creatures who now haunt the caves of the south-eastern mountains. They are called ollpheists.

Their blunted skulls sweep back low, with barely any space for their miniscule brains. They look eyeless from this distance. Their faces are blank and featureless except for their wide, fanged mouths which stretch upward at the corners in a perpetual, horrifying smile. Spikes of bone protrude from their elbows, knees, hips and spines. One of them even has a ring of spikes on its stomach. Some of them stand two-legged, claws outstretched, while others remain on all fours, pawing the turf. A serrated tail whips from the hindquarters of each shaggy beast.

I'm glad to be far away from the ollpheists, standing just behind the row of women. The Favored are not in gowns today; they're dressed for activity, or perhaps for battle. Morani wears a jaunty suit of black leather, the perfect complement to her spiked black hair. Leslynne's creamy skin and soft curves are protected by armor whose metal plates gleam in the afternoon light. Diaza's freckled face is half covered by goggles to protect her eyes, and she wears glossy brown leather.

I scan the rest of them: Teagan with her red braid and light chainmail, Khloe in white leather, Sabre in a bulky armored vest with her huge biceps bare. Adalasia, her lean dark arms banded with scarlet wrapping, her hands covered with metal-knuckled gloves. Samay, in black from head to toe. Vanas, thickly clad in padded armor. Axley, in silver armor as uncompromising as her sharp face, flanked by the three other women who tend to shadow her.

None of the Favored were allowed to bring weapons onto the field, and the crowd sitting in the stands seems keenly, rapaciously aware of this fact. They lean forward on their wooden benches and shout for their favorites, which might be encouraging if any contestant could actually discern her name amid the tumultuous roar.

The audience is hoping for bloodshed, craving the violence of the spectacle. And blood they will have. But it's my job to see that the wounds are not fatal.

The Ash King walks out onto the field, surrounded by guards, and halts before the line of the Favored. I'm strangely panicked about him being there, exposed to possible attacks from the Undoing. There are three rings of security fences around this area, and everyone coming and going is checked for weapons—but still. Someone might have slipped a weapon through. And I can't forget what Rince said—that the Undoing has someone on the inside, possibly even a contestant.

I can't imagine any of the women I know being one of the rebels. They are all members of the privileged class. What motive would they have to end the King and destroy the monarchy?

"For this challenge," says the King's herald, "The Favored will learn to handle and subdue an ollpheist."

The crowd gasps and murmurs, and several of the women grow visibly more tense.

Subdue? Not kill?

The Ash King steps forward. "Any Queen of mine must have the ability to defuse dangerous situations and handle volatile people without resorting to violence. That is why you have no weapons with which to face these beasts. But you will have help." He lifts his hand, and thirteen people walk out onto the field, each clad in padded armor similar to Vanas's gear.

"These are the ollpheists' trainers," the King continues. "They teach the beasts to respond to simple commands. They will explain how to handle the creatures, and you will be given several minutes to practice."

He sweeps the line of women with unmerciful eyes. "One at a time, you will stand in the field while the ollpheist you practiced with is released. An ollpheist's first instinct will be to kill you and eat you, but if you've paid attention during practice, you'll know what to do. You must maintain control of your ollpheist until that hourglass is empty." He points to a platform where a servant stands beside an enormous hourglass filled with crimson sand. "If you cannot handle your beast and your life is threatened, you may defend yourself. But extra points will be given to those who maintain control. Anyone who steps through the fence and leaves the ring before time is up will be sent home."

This is even more dangerous and ridiculous than I thought. Those horrible monsters have *trainers*? I shudder.

"Excuse me, Healer?"

I turn to the servant who spoke. "Yes?"

"The King said you're to ride this horse during the challenge. He's a strong, fast fellow, and doesn't spook around monsters." The boy offers me the reins of a tall, burly stallion.

"Thank you." I take the reins and mount. It's a relief to know that I won't be on the ground during this exercise. I'll be able to move around the ring where I'm needed, and I'll be up high, which is better for visibility and safety. But I'm still not happy about being in this field with thirteen savage monsters and thirteen vulnerable human bodies, even if the girls are being tested one at a time.

I was wrong about the noble women being soft. Most of them are physically stronger than I expected. But despite the strength and training they may have, they're weaponless, and no match for these toothy creatures. Why would the Ash King do this?

He's walking along the line, greeting each of the Favored with the cool elegance that's so typical of him in a public setting. He is warmest to Khloe and Teagan, and I'm sure the other girls notice.

To his credit, he seems to have calmed the fears of the contestants during his personal time with them. They aren't terrified of his very presence like they were on the first day.

When he reaches the end of the line, he walks up to me. I'm in the unusual position of being taller than him, thanks to my horse's height, and I can't help enjoying the fact.

"You're smiling?" His mouth twitches at the corner. "Not terrified?"

"Oh, I'm terrified. For myself, and for them. But I like being up here on high, while you are—" I catch myself, remembering the guards nearby. "You look magnificent today, your Majesty."

"I do, rather." He stretches out his arms, the breeze ruffling his flame-colored cloak and the wide sleeves of his shirt.

His vanity piques me a little, even though I encouraged it. "This is a deadly challenge, my Lord." I let a tinge of rebuke enter my tone, and the guard nearest me bristles, clenching his fist.

The Ash King quiets him with a sharp gesture, still holding my gaze. "As I said, any Queen of mine must be able to calm volatile people. They must know how to deal with monsters."

There's an intensity to his eyes, a pointed significance to his words. And suddenly I understand.

He's the monster. He wants to be sure that these women would have the courage and presence of mind to handle him should he get out of control. His future wife will have to deal with his occasional flame-outs, whether in public or in private.

The King and his retinue are moving away, out of the field and into the private box that has been constructed for him, from which he will view the event.

As I watch him go, I think of flames swelling in his throat, licking between his teeth—and I think of my water magic pouring through him, quenching the fire.

I have already learned how to deal with the monster.

Once the field is clear, the Favored pair off with
trainers. Most of the trainers speak low, and even though I
ride closer, I can't quite catch what they're saying. But
Leslynne's trainer is a pleasant-looking woman with
naturally loud tones, and I sidle my horse toward the pair
of them, trying to hear everything I can. If I'm going to be
out in the field when these beasts are set free, I need to
know what to expect.

"Ollpheists don't like bright light," says the trainer.
"See how they keep ducking their heads, bobbing them up
and down? They're not happy about the sun. If old
Hesham—that's my ollpheist—if he charges you, you get
the sun at your back and he'll think twice about running
into that blaze of light. Stay out of shadows. The beasties
are cowards, so they'll go for the smallest target in the area,
the easiest prey. Given a choice between you and that
healer on horseback, they'll go for you every time."

Leslynne nods, her blue eyes wide.

"Now let's practice our approach," says the trainer.
"Make yourself as big as you can by holding your arms out
from your body, like this." She spreads her arms wide. "If
you get into real trouble, use this sound." She gives a
throaty, croaking call. "That means 'sundown,' and signals
that it's time to rest. Try it."

Leslynne tries the call, with limited success. The
trainer winces. "Let's forget about that, then. The
'sundown' cry is very close to their calls for danger or

food. Takes a long time working with these beasts to differentiate the cries. Now we're going to approach Hesham, and I'll tell you what commands he knows. Arms out wide—yes, like that—and stomp on the ground so he'll feel you coming and know that you're a formidable presence. They're big into vibrations and sound waves, these beasties. Right then—in we go!"

The trainer and Leslynne stomp toward an ollpheist cage, arms spread wide. Laughter trickles through the crowd at the odd spectacle, but they stop laughing when Morani and her trainer begin a similar approach. I don't want to ride too close and jeopardize the girls' concentration, so I hang back, just close enough to rush in if I'm needed.

Morani's ollpheist stands perfectly still until she and the trainer have nearly reached the cage, and then it lunges, crashing against the bars. Morani screams, and the monster squalls with rage when it can't get to her. The trainer shouts, stomping the ground and making rhythmic jerking motions with his arms until the creature settles down.

That first charge and scream takes everyone's mood from apprehension to terror. I can sense the desperation from the women. Khloe is openly sobbing, her narrow shoulders shaking while her trainer tries awkwardly to comfort her.

As I ride closer, I can hear her crying, "I don't want to do this. I can't do this."

"Khloe." I swing down from the horse and take her shoulders. "Khloe, do you want to be here? Do you want him?" I point to the Ash King.

"I—I—I—think so," she gasps through sobs.

"Then you can do this. Your trainer is here to help you. You don't have to make the beast do any tricks, okay?

Just stay on the field and survive until the hourglass runs out. I won't let you die. Trust me."

I can't slow her pulse or calm her nerves with my magic—that wouldn't be fair to the other girls—but I give her my most confident smile before mounting my horse again. She wipes her eyes and nods as the trainer continues to explain his preferred strategy for handling an ollpheist.

By the end of the practice session, a few of the contestants have managed to make an ollpheist lie down or turn around, while others can't get too close to the cage without their beast trying to break out and eat them. Apparently every ollpheist has a different temperament, just like people do. And the Favored have no choice about which one they must wrangle. They've each been assigned a number and a corresponding cage.

At last the girls and trainers are pulled out of the field, and the herald repeats the rules—stay on the field with the unchained beast until the time is up. Stepping outside the fence means automatic disqualification from the contest. Survival is the minimum expectation, with bonus points for being able to calm or control the ollpheist. The girl with the top score gets personal time with the King.

The herald holds a bowl up to the Ash King, and he selects a scrap of paper. "Teagan," he says.

White-faced, Teagan nods and steps back through the fence. A trainer runs out and unlatches the corresponding ollpheist's cage, then races back to safety. I clutch the reins of my horse, conscious of the sweat coating my palms and the center of my back. Like some of the Favored, I'm wearing heavy leather today, from neck to wrists to toes, and I hate it.

What I wouldn't give to be back in the potsava fields, dancing through crumbly dark soil while guiding sprays of

199

glittering water over the plants. I wish I could deliver Elisse's baby—I've been monitoring her progress and the child's for months, and I feel deeply connected to both of them. But it will be the midwife from Ranis who handles the birth, because I'm here, watching the noble daughters of the land face off against monsters.

A servant on the upper platform pushes the huge hourglass until it turns upside-down, and red sand begins to flow.

Teagan lingers near the fence, and for a second I wonder if she's going to play it safe and stay near the edge until time runs out.

But then, her ollpheist nudges the cage door and discovers it's free.

It charges immediately, straight for Teagan.

My first impulse is to spur my horse forward and intercept the beast, to get between it and Teagan. It's all I can do to hold myself back.

Teagan stomps her feet, arms spread wide. She yells at the creature, but her cry is shrill with fear.

It's not stopping. It's going to crash straight into her.

At the last second she dives aside and rolls, and the ollpheist smashes headfirst into the bars. It staggers, stunned.

Teagan repeats the maneuver twice more before the creature learns its lesson. It approaches her more cautiously the fourth time, and when she shouts at it, it sinks into a submissive crouch. A bell rings, signaling the end of Teagan's test. The palace wind-wielder and two trainers wrangle the monster back into its cage, and the next Favored steps into the field.

Each girl has a different way of dealing with the ollpheists. When it's Diaza's turn and her monster's cage is unlocked, she runs straight for the cage and climbs lightly up its side. She spends her time perched atop the cage, out of the monster's reach, while it rages below.

Sabre fails to subdue her monster despite lots of stamping and shouting, so she takes it on head-to-head, delivering punches that could fell a man. She keeps the beast's jaws at bay, barely, until time is up.

Axley faces her beast with a savage courage that I have to admire, even though I don't like her. The ollpheist must recognize the spirit of a dominant predator in her, because it submits immediately. It even turns in a full circle at her command, though in the process its tail grazes her stomach.

One of Axley's trio of friends doesn't fare so well— she's immediately chased out of the ring. Two guards escort her away. Morani, Leslynne, and Adalasia all show some level of control over their beasts.

Several of the girls endure injuries of one kind or another—mostly scrapes and bruises, from what I can tell. Samay suffers a broken arm and deep lacerations when her ollpheist attacks her—but just as I'm about to charge in and help, she manages to roll from beneath the creature's paws and keep running until her time is up. When the bell rings, she stumbles off the field, her clawed face dripping blood. I check on her quickly, but since the wounds aren't life-threatening, I can't heal her until after all the Favored have competed.

Khloe is the last contestant to endure the challenge. She has to wait while Samay's raging monster is pushed back into its cage by the wind-wielder and a few trainers with spiked poles. That beast seems to be the strongest and most bloodthirsty by far. Thankfully Khloe's creature is smaller and more docile.

As her monster's cage is unlatched, Khloe hesitates in the center of the field. Maybe she's trying to decide on a strategy.

When her monster begins to pace toward her, Khloe trembles, but she holds her ground. The beast shakes its head, strings of saliva swaying from its fangs. Its furry shoulders are matted with something dark—I hope it's just mud. It snarls, and Khloe spreads her arms and stamps her small foot petulantly on the ground.

"Enough!" she shouts. "I'm just as scared as you are. Sit down so we can get through this!" She mimics the jerky hand signs her trainer taught her.

To my shock, the ollpheist obeys her. Its hindquarters plunk down and it sits there, its horrible head swinging from side to side.

Khloe maintains her stance, speaking firmly to the creature whenever it starts to get up. "No, you don't. You stay put."

Her tone is sharp, but I can hear a companionable note in it. She connected with the beast somehow, despite her fear.

I risk a look toward the Ash King. He's standing up, smiling eagerly and proudly at Khloe.

Pain lances straight through my beating heart, so sharp I can't breathe for a second.

He loves her. At the end, he's going to choose her.

They will do so well together. She's perfect for him.

I should tell him she's carrying another man's child. She'd be eliminated immediately. Of course, I might get in trouble too, for concealing the truth this long. But at least she'd be out of the running, away from him.

What is wrong with me? I'm not this girl. I don't scheme the downfall of anybody, much less someone I actually like.

This is what being near the Ash King has done to me. It has turned me into someone jealous and sneaky.

I'm better than this.

A creaking sound shatters my reverie. There's a disturbance in one of the cages—Samay's vicious monster, unhappy at being confined again, is smashing itself against the cage door.

Which pops open.

Heartsfire. Oh gods.

The door must not have been latched correctly.

With a guttural bellow, Samay's ollpheist launches itself toward Khloe.

19

I urge my horse forward, desperate to get between
Khloe and the oncoming beast. The horse has been brave
so far—beyond some snorting and pawing, he hasn't
fussed about the monsters that have been prowling the
ring for the past few hours. But what I'm asking of him
now is too much. He squeals and snorts, shuffling
backward, refusing to approach the big ollpheist.

Khloe has her hands full with one ollpheist. There's
no way she can wrangle two. Her beast is already getting
more riled up at the presence of the second monster.

I swing off my horse and run toward Khloe. Out of
the corner of my eye I see the wind-wielder and the
trainers moving through the fence, ready to intervene, but
the Ash King bellows, "Wait!"

My body feels like it's on fire, frenzied chemicals
fueling my survival instinct. These beasts go for the
smallest prey, which means I have to *make* this monster
focus on me instead of Khloe. If I make it mad enough, it
will chase me instead of her.

I step right into its path and spread my arms, and I
stamp my feet as hard as I can, until pain shoots through
my shins.

"Stop, you big coward!" I shout. "Fucking stop!"

The ollpheist is close enough for me to glimpse its
beady eyes, half-buried in clumps of fur. Its attention is on

me now, and it slows to a halt. But then it begins tearing up clods of dirt, preparing for another attack.

I'm too far from the outer fence to try Teagan's strategy. But I sidle to the right, slowly, and the creature turns to keep me in its sightline—until the late afternoon sun flashes over my shoulder, into its eyes. It screeches, pawing at its head.

Samay tried a few commands on this one during her session. They didn't work, probably because her voice was so thin with fear and her body language was anything but dominant. My voice probably won't be any better, but I have to try something.

I could flash gold healing light in the monster's eyes. I could siphon water from the drinking barrels and whip it into submission. But something inside me wants to know I'm capable of this, that I can conquer the beast without my magic.

The sun's fiery glare heats my back and shoulders. My neck is slick with sweat, and my nostrils fill with the hazy scent of hot leather, the acrid smell of my own body, the aroma of freshly clawed earth and grass.

I stretch both arms up and out, as if I'm embracing the sky, and I walk toward the beast.

Diaza removed herself from her beast's rage. Teagan let hers smash its own skull until it was too dizzy to defy her. But Khloe—Khloe made a sort of connection with hers. It's still obeying her firm commands, despite the ongoing standoff between me and the second monster.

My ollpheist lowers its head, those upturned jaws sagging wide. A snarl rips from its throat as it lopes forward.

"Can you even understand me?" I shout. "You want to kill, to eat. Well, guess what—the quickest way to dinner is you getting back inside that cage. Then this ridiculous challenge can be over, and we can *all* go home to eat. I'm sure your trainer will feed you something nice."

The beast tenses for a spring, and I hold out both hands and bark, "Stop!"

The ollpheist skids to a halt in front of me and roars, spraying spittle from its fangs. It swipes at me with a paw, but I don't move, not even when the tips of the claws rake across my chest. Pain sears through my flesh, but I force myself to step forward, slamming my boot to the ground, a tangible threat that reverberates through the turf.

The monster withdraws a step, like it's confused about why I don't scream and run like Samay did.

"I'm not afraid of you." My voice is low and firm, but I know a certain gifted pair of ears in the audience can hear every word. "You think you're so big and scary, that no one can handle being around you, but that's not true. You can't hurt me, because I'll heal and I'll come back, every time. Everything you want—you can have it if you just give in. If you submit to me."

The ollpheist slashes me again, my arm this time. I keep walking through the haze of pain, through the sensation of my own blood soaking my clothes, dripping on the turf.

When the creature squalls, I bare my teeth in a smile, because I can hear the difference in its voice now. This isn't a raging scream; it's more of a "who-is-this-scary-girl-and-why-doesn't-she-run-when-I-hurt-her" scream. The monster scuffles backward as I keep prowling forward, caging it against the bars of the outer fence. Beyond those bars is the royal box.

"See there," I murmur. "You're not so terrifying after all." And I lift my eyes, just for a moment, and meet the scarlet gaze of the Ash King.

The ollpheist cringes down against the bars, quieting. A bell cracks the porcelain silence.

After healing myself, I mend the wounds of the Favored one at a time. Samay is first, since her injuries are the worst. I begin with her face and discover that her eyeball has been sheared in half, her jaw is broken, and a claw ripped right through her lip. I soothe the pain receptors and slowly rebuild all the layers of tissue until she looks as beautiful as ever. Then I work on knitting her arm bone back together.

"Thank you, Healer," she says. "I want you to know that I'm sorry for what I've said about you."

"I didn't hear any of it, so there's nothing to forgive." With the arm fixed, I move to her chest, scanning for more injuries. She's got two broken ribs.

"But I feel bad for laughing with the others," Samay says. "Axley and her girls joke about you all the time. She really hates you."

I pinch my lips together, trying not to respond. At least Axley has lost two of her poisonous little friends in this challenge. One of them stepped out of the ring, and the Ash King eliminated another at the end. Which leaves just eleven women in the contest.

With my fingers splayed over Samay's body, I scan her again, top to toe. "You're fine now," I tell her. "Perfectly whole."

"That's a relief. If I can ever do anything to thank you," she says, sliding off the table.

"What's your ability?" I point to the temporary Muting tattoo on her ankle.

She smiles a little. "I can change the temperature around me while I remain unaffected. It's a limited power—I can't freeze people solid or burn them up—but I can make them feel very uncomfortable. If my resonance had been any stronger, I would have been permanently Muted."

"None of the other girls have wielding powers?"

"Not that I've noticed."

I nod. "The Ricters would have caught it if someone was trying to hide their magic."

She winces. "Not necessarily. There are ways to fool the Ricters, or bribe them."

She leaves with a brief smile, as if she's glad to escape the conversation.

So not only is there a spy for the Undoing in the palace—possibly among the Favored—but she could also be hiding unknown powers. Wonderful.

As I heal the girls, I slip in a few questions that I hope sound harmless and conversational. Have they ever traveled beyond the borders of our kingdom? If not, would they like to? Casually I complain a little about the lack of internationally imported goods in the city markets, but I stop short of asking what the girls think of our country's isolationist policies.

They're all fairly guarded in their answers, but nothing really rings false. Morani offers to get me in touch with a black-market dealer of international goods. It's a good-natured gesture, and also the only comment that's potentially treasonous. I decline as gracefully as I can. She's lucky I don't plan on telling the King about her black-market connection. Though I wonder if many of the nobility secretly purchase international goods despite the trade ban. Those with money and privilege seem to find ways around every law, while the poor have no choice but to submit.

At last Axley arrives for her healing. She strips and lies down on the table, her mouth a grim red line and her sharp eyes fixed on the ceiling. "A few scratches," she says. "I'd rather heal naturally, on my own, but the King insisted I come to you."

"Are you sure it's only scratches?" I let my hand float above her bruised stomach. "You were struck by your ollpheist's tail, harder than I thought, it seems."

"Just scratches," she grits out.

But it's not. I can sense that something inside her is bleeding copiously. If it's not fixed, she'll be dead in a few hours.

"You have internal bleeding," I tell her. "It'll take me a little while to mend it."

"I really don't have time for this. I placed first in the challenge and I'm supposed to get one-on-one time with the Ash King immediately after this. Every minute counts." She pushes herself up.

"Lie down, please," I say in my calmest healer voice. "It's my job to ensure you're completely healthy."

"Like you care," she snaps. "Rose Room whore."

My whole body tenses.

I could let her walk out of here and die. It would serve her bitchy ass right.

But I took a vow.

"If you don't agree to the healing, I'll have to speak to the King," I say evenly. "Whatever problems you have with me, please believe that I take my duties very seriously. I would never harm you. And if you don't let me do this, you won't last the day."

Axley stares at me, then nods once. "Hurry up with it, then. I have to meet someone before I join His Majesty, and I'm already late."

"Meet someone?"

"None of your business."

"Of course." I let the gold lines unwind from my hands and sink into her flesh, seeking out the contusions and lacerations, sealing and healing them. I replenish some of the lost blood as well, but not all of it. Let her feel a little weak during her time with the Ash King.

My last patient is Khloe. She flies into the room and hugs me tightly around the neck. "Cailin! You saved me. My pretty knight on the chestnut horse. Maybe I should be falling for you instead of the Ash King."

I squeeze her tightly, laughing. "I'm flattered. And if I liked girls, I'd be all over you."

"Ever tried?" she asks, with a sly smile.

"No—you?"

"Yes. It's so different from being with a man. Softer and wetter, mostly." She giggles. "And they know exactly what to do. But I like men, too—especially men like Perish. He's got those muscles and that elegant face— gods." She fakes a swoon.

It takes me a moment to realize she's talking about the Ash King. My shock must show on my face, because she blushes and says, "Oh, yes—he told me I could call him by his first name."

"So you two are getting close?" I avoid her eyes as I scan her body for injuries.

Her face darkens a little. "I know what you're thinking. The pregnancy thing. I'd made up my mind to end it, actually—and then today, when I was out there, facing those monsters, I realized I wasn't so much scared for myself as for this one." She places a protective hand over her belly. "I want this child, Cailin. Whoever they are—they're mine, and I won't give them up."

My heart warms, but I can't help speaking the truth she needs to hear. "You'll have to tell the King, then."

"I know." She presses her fingertips to her brow, kneading it. "It's just so hard. He'll probably kick me out of the contest. And I can't be kicked out, Cailin. I have to stay. I *need* to be here. Can you give me just a little longer? Please?"

My brows pinch together. "I can see him falling for you, Khloe. Is it fair to make him love you without giving him all the information?"

"Love is love," she protests. "It can overcome anything."

With those earnest, innocent dark eyes shining into mine, I can't bear to deny or contradict her.

"A little more time," I promise, and a smile like pure sunshine breaks over her face.

But a creeping sensation of dread stays with me long after the healing sessions are done.

20

During the banquet that night, Axley sits at a private table in the corner with the King. When we're all dismissed, we go up to a long lounge on the third floor of the central wing. The room opens onto a well-guarded balcony on which couples can promenade—a balcony shielded by trees so there are no clear lines of sight from other windows or rooftops to this spot. As always, security is paramount.

There are quiet nooks and soft sofas throughout the lounge, too. It's a space made for drinks, quiet conversations, and secret kisses. With a sweep and shiver of bows over strings, a small group of musicians serenades the gathered guests.

I encounter several of my acquaintances from the other evening—my dance partners and the contest officials I befriended—and it's nice to hear their pleasant greetings. Most of the nobility and advisors are still pointedly ignoring me, probably because they've heard about my quarters in the Rose Room. For a city so dedicated to free love, they're being unfairly judgmental about my supposed connection to the Ash King.

I'm wearing a simple blue backless gown tonight, with a couple pieces of jewelry. My hair is pinned up neatly. Nothing about the ensemble invites censure, yet people I pass still break into significant whispers of which I can't catch more than a few worrying words like "mistress... scheming... bewitched... not fair... scandalous."

Finally I escape to the long balcony. I walk to its far end, where a veil of ivy throws a corner bench into deep shadow. I'm lucky no lovers have found this spot yet.

Tucking myself into the dark corner, I close my eyes and inhale the scent of fresh green leaves and summery night air. I toe off my shoes and sweep my bare soles over the smooth stone floor of the balcony, wishing it was the worn cobbles of the village square.

Homesickness knots my belly so tightly I feel physically ill. I want my home so badly. I've lost myself here—I've wandered from who I knew myself to be. I have to get back to my truth. I have to remember that I'm not Cailin of the Undoing, or Cailin the Keeper of Secrets, or Cailin the Healer who spies on her patients for the King. And I'm certainly not Cailin who might be falling for the wicked murderous Ash King.

I'm just Cailin, water-wielder for her people, healer to the surrounding villages, daughter to loving parents, big sister to the neighbor children, mentee of the Ceannaire.

And I want to go home.

Two figures glide through the gold-lit doors of the lounge, stepping out onto the balcony.

"See that no one disturbs us," mutters a low voice to one of the guards.

It's the Ash King. And the girl with him is Axley.

He pushes her against the wall, in the shadowed space between two of the lounge windows. I curl myself tighter into my dark corner, pain pulsing through every beat of my heart.

I should make myself known. I shouldn't watch this.

But I stay quiet, and I stare.

213

The Ash King kisses Axley, his mouth wide open to hers, his cheeks sucking in slightly as he plunges his tongue into her mouth. Her thin, elegant fingers arch against his shoulder, nearly piercing the fine material of his shirt. His hips grind against hers, urgent, desperate. She rakes the hem of his shirt up, her nails grazing his back beneath his white hair.

There are guards posted all along this balcony. They can see everything. How far is the King going to take this tryst?

Pretty damn far, apparently. She's reaching for his pants, undoing buttons between harsh kisses. His hand sweeps over her breast.

He's supposed to wait until there are five girls left before he sleeps with any of them. My fingernails dent my palms deeply, an echo to the agony in my heart.

This is what happens when I say no. He finds someone else.

But I don't want him to want anyone else.

The King and Axley keep kissing. His pants are entirely open now, but when she reaches inside them, he pushes himself back from her.

"No," he says. "Gods—no." He runs a hand through his white hair, tossing it slightly, a frustrated gesture. He strides to the balcony's edge and sets both palms on the stone balustrade, hunched over and breathing hard.

Behind his back, Axley rolls her eyes. She tugs her neckline down a bit further and pushes up her breasts. Then she approaches him, rubbing his back with one hand. "What is it, my king?" she croons. "Do I not please you?"

He doesn't answer, and she slides her hand down to his rear, squeezing lightly. "You know a union with me would be politically beneficial, as well as physically pleasurable. Why can we not send the rest of these girls home?"

"Because I have committed to this process, and I will see it through," he says.

She's silent for a moment, and when she speaks again, her voice has changed. "Is it that countrified Mayor's daughter Teagan? Or the teenage girl with the big brown eyes?" She snorts a laugh. "I didn't know you were attracted to mere children, my Lord."

Fire erupts at the King's fingertips.

Alarmed, Axley backs away. "I didn't mean—I was only pointing out the age difference between you and Khloe. I didn't intend—"

"You intended what you always intend—harm, and your own self-interest," growls the Ash King, prowling toward her as she retreats.

"I've offended you," she gasps. "Forgive me, Your Majesty—I went too far. I forgot my place. Please—" She crumples at his feet, the bustles of her fine dress crinkling. Her back is to me now, but from the way her shoulders shake, I suspect she's crying. And with good reason—the Ash King's eyes are pure living flame, sockets completely engulfed in fire. There's a telltale glow along his throat, too. He's losing control again.

"Go!" he chokes out. "Go!"

Axley scrambles to her feet and flees into the palace.

The Ash King grips the balustrade and vomits fire upward, streaming it into the sky until it vanishes, leaving only a crackling heat and the bitter, stinging smell of spent magic.

None of the guards have moved. And I have not made a sound.

The King hangs over the balcony's edge, panting.

And then one of the guards coughs slightly.

In one furious stride, the Ash King has him by the throat, armor and all, and he throws the guard bodily over the railing. I hear the armored man crash to the stone pavers below.

The other guards don't react at all.

A moment later, there's a groan from below, and anxious voices float up, muttering about taking the guard to a healer. I'm guessing they mean Jonald, the old palace healer, not me.

The King whirls with a curse and strides back inside.

A few moments later, when I dare to move again, I sneak back into the lounge as well. Thankfully the King doesn't see me enter. He doesn't know that I witnessed his lust and his cruelty.

He's not someone I should like, or understand, or want.

Axley is smiling and circulating through the crowd, chatting gaily as if nothing happened. Somehow, her makeup isn't smudged at all, not by the kissing or by the tears. Perhaps one of her maids fixed it for her.

"We need lively entertainment! Someone should sing for us," pipes up a well-dressed man, raising his glass.

"Are you volunteering, Lord Bayner?" asks someone else, and a laugh ripples through the room.

"Not me, not me," Lord Bayner chuckles. "But perhaps His Majesty would grace us with a song? Oh, he has a marvelous voice, just marvelous. You must sing for us, Your Majesty. For the girls. A treat for the Favored."

"Oh yes," simper a few of the women. "Sing for us, Your Majesty, please."

It's all I can do not to roll my eyes at them, though I'm deeply curious to hear him sing.

"If the Favored request it," the Ash King says, with his usual cold grace.

He speaks to the musicians. They nod and start to play, a delicate ripple of notes.

The Ash King begins to sing.

At first I can't believe what I'm hearing. There must be something wrong with my ears. Or maybe I'm not familiar with the song? No, it's one I've heard before.

There's no other explanation—the Ash King is a terrible singer.

He's horribly off key, and every phrase or two he hits a note that's so wrong my skin crawls. I love music, and to hear a song butchered this way—it's almost physically painful.

I glance around, wondering if everyone else hears what I'm hearing. They all have rapt smiles on their faces, but when I look closely I can tell that some of those smiles are looking a bit forced, a bit pained. It's not just me, then. Everyone knows he can't sing. Yet they're faking admiration. Some of them are even nodding along or swaying to the music. The courtiers and nobles don't flinch, not even when the King's voice wavers or skews into the wrong register.

Slowly I creep backward, toward the doors that lead to the hallway. I can sneak out of here while everyone else is pretending to be awed by his terrible voice.

I slip out of the bright lounge and into the gloom of the corridor just as the song ends on a quavering note that's just so incredibly *painful.* Applause rattles the room behind me, and I hear the Favored shrilling over each other, trying to deliver saccharine compliments to the King.

Grimacing, I slink away, while someone calls out for Teagan to sing next. The first notes of a new song echo along the hall, and I slow my steps, convinced that I've escaped.

Until a male hand brushes upward, along my spine.

"Why do you wear these dresses?" The Ash King's voice is low, barely above a whisper. "Are you trying to drive me insane?"

I freeze, my breath hitching. Why did he leave the lounge? Teagan's song won't distract the guests for long; they'll be looking for him any minute.

He runs his knuckles down my spine and then up again, a slow graze that ignites every vertebrae I have. "Did you like my song?"

"I—um, objectively, there is—well, subjectively, I would say—" *Stop stumbling around, Cailin! You need to be diplomatic. He just threw someone off a balcony for coughing.*

"There is something so charming about a performer earnestly doing their best," I tell him. "Sincerity is the loveliest music of all, don't you think?"

It's something the Ceannaire said once; not original with me, but the King doesn't need to know that.

His hand leaves my back, and he moves around to examine my face. I give him my brightest smile.

"Well done. You've given me the diplomatic answer," he says. "Now for the real one."

I suck in a breath and glance around for anyone who might object to pure honesty before the King. There are armored guards standing motionless along the hallway, but none of them are very near to us.

So I look the Ash King right in the eyes, and I say, "You are a dreadful singer. You can't carry a tune. You can't hold the notes properly. There are children in my village who have better breath control. It's too bad, because your speaking voice is so nice. But you can't sing."

For a long moment he stares at me, his features rigid. My heart thunders, and I begin to sweat a little.

Then his mouth relaxes into a wry smile. "I know I can't sing."

"Oh thank the gods," I gasp, pressing a hand to my chest. "I thought maybe you didn't realize it."

"No, I'm well aware, which is why I never sing before others. But I'll let you in on a little secret—tonight is the Fourth Challenge. Lord Bayner was in on it—I asked him to urge me to sing, and to tell everyone how wonderful my voice is. And then I watched the Favored, to see their reactions. I'll be talking to each of them about it, to see how they respond. I won't tell them it was a test until the end of the evening."

"Oh," I murmur, my mind racing. "That's—that's actually very clever, Your Majesty."

"Thank you," he says dryly. "Occasionally I do something mildly intelligent. And now to see what the other ladies thought of my song."

He grins and takes a few steps toward the lounge before I say, "You came to me first."

The King stops without turning around. "What?"

"You came to me first, to see how I would respond. Why? I'm not one of the Favored."

"No," he says quietly. "You are not."

"But if I was," I say, trying not to sound breathless, "did I pass the test?"

"Diplomacy when it was needed, honesty when it was required. Yes, you passed."

Back in my room, I keep picturing the magnificent flex of the King's body as he threw an entire adult man in armor off the third-floor balcony. It was horrible. *Horrible.* Not strangely, darkly attractive. I am not tantalized by the thought that he could pick me up bodily in one hand. Nor am I reveling in the fact that he said no to sex with Axley.

I suspect the King will come to me again tonight, once he has finished with the other women. I'm not sure what I want or what I hope for—just his confusing, tantalizing presence, I suppose. Nothing more. Maybe I'll confront him about what I saw—rage at him a little.

I indulge in a bath, expecting to wait a couple of hours for him, but a few seconds after I step out of the tub, I hear the door between our rooms opening. Frantic, I snatch a towel and wrap it around myself just before he appears in the open doorway of the bathing room.

He props a forearm against the frame and takes in the sight of me. "Healer."

"Your Majesty," I breathe.

The front of his pants is stretched tight, a pronounced shape obvious beneath the fabric, and he keeps shifting, moving constantly, as if he can't bear to stand still. I'm barefoot instead of in heels, so he looks taller than ever—truly majestic. There's a restless, heated lust rolling off him, a raw male dominance so intense I can almost taste it. He wants sex. He said no to Axley, and now he has come to me.

My thighs and belly tighten at the thought, and my heartbeat kicks up.

"Take it off." He gestures sharply at the towel.

"No, thank you." I retreat out of reach.

He cocks an eyebrow. "So shy, after what you did to me the other night?"

"I told you that was a one-time mercy because you couldn't sleep. There's nothing more between us, and can never be anything more."

A long sigh emanates from him. "This again, Healer? I am not looking for *more between us,* merely for a mutual release of the urge we both feel. There is no shame in taking pleasure together. I know you despise me, and you know I can't love you or marry you. Yet our bodies react to each other, as is natural for two beautiful, powerful people. Why should we not indulge that craving?"

"Because then they'll be right," I murmur. "I will be the cheap mistress in the Rose Room, the one the girls fear will take your heart, even if they win the throne."

"I promise you won't win my heart or my throne. I will abide by the tradition of royalty marrying nobility. And I would not give my heart to someone who disapproves of me as thoroughly as you do. So there's no issue."

"But what we know to be true and what everyone else thinks are two different things," I protest. "Even if you repeated that declaration to the Favored, they might not believe you. There's plenty of suspicion around me due to my placement in these quarters, and I have my honor to think of."

"Your reputation is already soiled in that respect, Healer. I ensured that when I placed you in this room." He gives me a sly smile. "No one will believe I haven't tasted the pretty little treasure next-door, no matter how much you might protest. Since they already think us guilty, why shouldn't we allow ourselves this diversion?"

My face heats, and I grip my towel tighter. "You did this on purpose. You put me in the Rose Room so you could weaken my resolve."

"Guilty." He saunters toward me, his sheet of white hair swaying, sinuous as a serpent. His eyes are hooded, glowing richly red with lecherous thirst. His voice softens, circling me like a snake's coils. "Do you feel your resolve weakening, Healer? Just once, let me come inside you. I promise you'll have a good time."

He's so close now that I have to press my back against the wall to put some distance between us.

"Why are you so fixated on me when you could have anyone else?" I ask.

"I'm not sure." He braces a palm near my head, leaning in. "Perhaps I crave one last conquest before I'm chained to one of these noblewomen for the rest of my life."

"Chained?" I lift an eyebrow. "Your father didn't think much of marital chains."

"I suppose not. He indulged himself with a mistress—sometimes more than one." Heat from his body suffuses the air between us, warm on my damp skin. "What do you think, Healer? Shall I keep you in this room once I'm married?" He picks up a lock of my wet hair, winding it around his fingers. "Shall I pay you visits and receive delightful massages?"

222

"Is that what you would do?" I counter. "Do you want to treat your wife as your father treated his?"

A spasm of quick pain ripples through his gaze. "No," he says quietly. "Once I marry, I will be true to my wife, even if it kills me."

"Then you will be miserable and resentful," I murmur. "Faithfulness to one partner is an old-fashioned notion these days, especially in this city."

"Yet I still believe in it." There's a raw note in his tone that makes me wonder about his past, whether a lover was ever disloyal to him.

I do not judge a couple who share partners openly or find pleasure wherever they like—as long as it is done with full knowledge and consent of both parties, not with secrecy and deceit. But it's not a choice I would make for myself.

"What about the Favored?" I ask. "Have you talked to them about your thoughts on marriage and fidelity?"

The Ash King shoves himself away from me. "I intended this to be a seduction, and here we are, having a serious conversation." He scoffs a little. "No, I haven't talked to them."

"You should, before you eliminate anyone else. You need to know who shares your views on the subject."

"And what are *your* thoughts on the matter? Not that I care," he adds hastily. "I'm simply curious."

Emotions surge inside me, so strong I can't look at him. I look down at the tile floor, biting my lip. "I would never share the man I love. He would be mine only, mine always. And I would be entirely his."

I already knew that truth about myself, and I've felt it more strongly than ever during this competition.

The Ash King stands silent, while I continue staring at the blue and white tiles.

After a moment he says quietly, "I eliminated Vanas tonight. She was brutally honest about the song, which I liked, but she lacked the diplomacy I need from a wife. My bride will have to deal delicately with pompous, arrogant fools at court, and I don't believe Vanas can handle that. She is lovely, though. It was a difficult decision."

I nod without speaking.

"Tomorrow will be an activity day for me and the girls," he continues in the same soft, quiet voice, as if there's something fragile in the room and he's trying not to shatter it. "First there will be training and exercise, and then we'll be enjoying some art. You should join us, in case anyone sprains an ankle or has a fainting spell."

There's the faintest hint of humor in his tone, a tentative lure as he tries to draw me out.

"I will be present and observe in my role as Healer, Your Majesty," I reply.

"Very good. I will see you tomorrow, then."

Only after the Ash King returns to his room do I realize that I didn't confront him at all—not about the interlude with Axley, or his temper tantrum when he tossed the man from the balcony, or his decision to hold back the trainers and let me handle an ollpheist on my own.

He kept Axley in the competition, even after she insulted him on the balcony. Yet he eliminated Vanas, a good-hearted person who was only guilty of honesty.

And then he dared to tell me, *You won't win my heart or my throne.*

As if I want his stupid heart or his godsdamned throne. He should be so lucky.

He tore me from my home and threatened to keep me here indefinitely, even after the competition. And what's in this for me, other than clothes and lodging? I've not seen a coin of the promised compensation.

And he stole my neighbor's horse. Stole it. When he has everything and everyone at his disposal.

I keep stewing over everything while I put on a nightdress and braid my hair. The longer I think about it, the angrier I get, until I'm positive I won't be able to sleep until I confront him. I have to let him know what I feel, how much I resent every decision he's made tonight.

I march over to the door between our rooms and try the handle.

I expected it to be locked. I didn't expect the handle to bend so easily or the door to swing open so quickly.

And now I can't retreat.

Oh gods—I'm probably going to be incinerated.

But I've come this far, so I steel myself with my righteous rage, and I step boldly into his room.

21

The Ash King's chamber is far more sparsely furnished than I expected, probably because he tends to set his possessions on fire from time to time. He lies in the center of the huge bed, bare-chested, propped on pillows, with a book in his hands and his pale hair in a messy knot.

He's staring at me, completely shocked by my entrance.

"You almost let me die today," I accuse him.

He closes the book. "And?"

"And? And—I didn't like it. That wasn't right. What happened to me not getting hurt during the challenges?"

"I wanted to see if you could handle the ollpheist." His gaze is a blade edged with fire. "I knew you would heal yourself if you were injured. And I had a backup healer in the stands, as you suggested, just in case something went badly wrong."

"Badly wrong—like if I almost died." I scoff. "You want me to believe you regret the past, but you still don't care about others. You beat your guards with fire whips and throw people off balconies."

His face tenses. "How do you—"

"How do I know about that? Because I was sitting in the corner of the balcony during your passionate interlude with the fair Axley." I'm trembling all over now, and my voice shakes with the intensity of my rage.

"You're jealous." There's a triumphant, predatorial gleam in his scarlet eyes.

"No." I shake my head. "I'm angry. I'm angry because I'm homesick and I have no idea when I'll get to go back to my village. And I'm worried if I do go back to my village, these women won't be properly cared for. I'm also worried about the poor of this city, those who can't afford a healer. And speaking of affording things, you haven't paid me like you promised. I would like my payment, and I would like different lodgings. I don't care how small and simple the lodgings are—I can't stay in the Rose Room. I want to maintain my dignity where you are concerned."

"Which is why you came in here dressed in *that*." He cocks an eyebrow at my skimpy nightdress. "I thought you swore you'd never seduce me." He rises from the bed, and a bolt of thrilling shock courses through me as I realize he's entirely naked.

"I'm not seducing you," I gasp. "I'm yelling at you."

"By all means, continue. It's working for me." He halts by the bedpost, his lithe, powerful body angled against it.

The door of the bedroom opens, and a guard pokes his head in. "Your Majesty? Is everything all right? We heard shouting."

"Get out," the King snaps, "and stay out." He shoots a fireball from his palm, and the guard beats a hasty retreat, slamming the door just in time.

"You see? *That* is what I'm talking about." I point at the sizzling scorch mark on the door. "That was unnecessary. You frightened him, when the only thing he's guilty of is checking on you, protecting you. You're so rude."

"Yes," he says, nodding, smirking. "I'm very rude."

"And selfish." I step toward him for emphasis. "And cruel."

"Selfish and cruel. Both true."

Whatever self-destructive spirit has gripped me and throttled my better judgment, she seems determined to go for the King's jugular. "And you're a mass murderer."

His mouth twitches in a snarl. "And you *want* me. You want the murderer of thousands—the wicked, cruel, selfish monster. That's why you're really angry, Healer—admit it, or I'll make you scream the words." He stalks forward, his hands gloved in flame.

I jerk water from a large urn nearby and whip his fingers with it, snuffing out the flames. "I don't want you. I hate you."

He lights his fingers again, a gauntlet of flame gloving his right hand to the wrist. He reaches for me, but I intercept with a ball of water. His fiery hand passes through it, extinguishing with a hiss. I condense the steam, forming a glimmering liquid shield in front of myself.

"Admit it." He runs his fingertips through my shield, creating ripples.

"No." I swallow hard, pushing with the water, shoving him back.

"I could end you, you know."

"Try it then."

Flames shoot from his palms, hissing against my water-shield until it starts to boil and bubble. I reinforce it with more water from the urn, but I'm not fast enough and the shield explodes, spattering both of us with boiling drops.

I cry out in pain, and he hisses through his teeth, shoving me against the wall. His skin is dotted with red blisters. Somehow, the magic of my water melded with the magic of his fire, and it managed to wound him despite his impervious skin.

"I thought you took a vow of healing," he growls. "You hurt me."

"You hurt *yourself*," I retort. Palms to his bare chest, I shove him with all my might. "Asshole."

His brows rise. I'm fairly sure no one has dared to call him names to his face for a long time.

"You should remember your place, Healer." His hands close on my upper arms, each finger glowing, searing my skin in hot bands. I shriek a little, panting with the pain. He crushes me to the wall again, grinding his hips against mine. He's rock-hard, his erection pressing through my nightdress.

"Fight back," he whispers. "Fight me, Cailin. Defend yourself."

I jerk against his grip, but I'm not strong enough, so I draw more water, lashing his back with stinging whips of it until he lets go. The watery whips hover at my back, curling around me like protective tentacles.

"There she is," says the King, pulling back, while his eyes burst into hot blue flame. "There's the water goddess I've been waiting for."

He attacks me with lashes of fire, slicing through my liquid tentacles—but each one reforms as quickly as his fire passes through it. I wrap both his ankles with water and jerk him flat on his back. Breath leaves him in a sharp grunt, and he looks so astonished that I laugh. When he meets my eyes, I swear there's the ghost of a grin on his lips.

He rises, the fiery whips gone, and for a moment I think he's done fighting me. But then his entire naked body begins to glow molten, like an ember stoked to fresh fierce heat. Even his hair is aflame, though it doesn't burn.

Incandescent, white-hot with flickering amber edges, the Ash King stalks toward me.

I empty the urn and pull more water from his washstand. As he charges, I encase myself completely, head to toe, in a shimmering suit of water.

We crash together, fire and water sizzling into steam, both of us crying out with the pain of it. Somehow, when his heat and my water combine, I can *hurt* him. And that makes me strangely elated.

He collapses to the floor, gasping, weakened by an agony he's not used to. I'm tangled with him, limbs lashing and struggling. We're wet and scorched at the same time, hair dripping, breaths cracking sharp from singed lips. His cheeks are scarlet, his eyes bloodshot.

But his fire is out.

I look into his face, and I realize with sudden heat that I'm astride him. His erection is pinned between us, and since I'm not wearing anything beneath the nightdress, his cock is pressed directly against my bare center. That firm column of flesh rolling between my legs is so wildly stimulating that I inhale, sharp and tight.

The King goes very still under me. He's been dismantled by our joint magic, his skin raw from the searing steam.

Very slowly, I angle my hips and rock forward along his length. My eyes close at the thrilling contact.

The Ash King lunges upright and flips me over onto my back with passionate force. The breath slams out of my lungs, and a line of sharp pleasure traces through my belly.

The heat of us hangs thick and humid in the air—lust and seared skin and the faint scent of soap from my bath.

He's breathing hard. Loops of his white hair have loosened from their knot, and they brush his cheekbones as he kneels astride me, his gaze devouring me with vicious intensity.

With exquisite control, he flakes my nightdress to ash. And now I'm naked, scorched in places from the steam, my skin beaded with water and covered with soot.

He doesn't seem to care. He brushes aside the ashes and cups my breast, while a hiss of satisfaction leaks through his gritted teeth.

I knock his hand away and he recoils, startled regret flaring through his eyes as he allows me to sit up. His lips part—he's on the brink of an apology.

Impulsively, trembling with a blazing lust I can't quench, I seize both his wrists and pull his hands to my chest, pressing them hard over my breasts.

"I hate you," I whisper, my eyes stinging with tears.

"I hate you more." He almost kisses me, but he turns aside at the last second. His teeth scrape along my cheekbone, while one of his hands moves from my breast to dive between us, rough and eager, discovering the liquid need between my legs.

"Admit it," he seethes, toying with my clit. "You want me."

When I don't answer, he pinches, just hard enough to sting.

I gasp and grip his shoulders, sinking my nails into his skin. I've been soft-hearted Cailin the healer for so long, healing my pain and that of others, soothing everything and everyone—and I love being that person, because she is *me*—but this wild thing of pain and passion is also me, and somehow it feels wretchedly good to *hurt* with him.

231

The Ash King flings me backward onto the floor again. His body hovers over me while his fingers slither, quick and merciless and tantalizing, along my folds. His scarlet eyes blaze into mine. "Submit," he orders. "Your body has already told the truth. Admit that you want me."

I buck against his hand and lift myself on my elbows, pressing my breasts to his chest, my mouth grazing his lips. "Make me."

"Gods-fuck." His face wrenches with an expression of near agony before relaxing again. "I almost came just then, you rebellious village brat."

"My apologies, Your Majesty," I whisper savagely.

"Stop talking," he chokes out. "Either I come all over your body or inside it. Your choice."

I sink back against the tiled floor, spreading my thighs wide, pressing my ankles against the small of his back to pull him closer, lining up his tip with my center.

"If you're wondering," he breathes, "I take a tonic. I cannot risk having illegitimate heirs with random women."

My heart flinches, because by doing this I am making myself one of the random women. But I don't want to stop. Maybe, like he said, we can just have pleasure together, without any other expectation or attachment. Maybe—*ah*—and then I stop thinking of anything besides his long cock pushing inside me.

I arch with the force of the pleasure, a breathless shriek breaking from me. The Ash King groans and slams in hard. He slides back until he almost slips out, then slams in again—and I squeal, my fingers raking against the floor, because my brain is about to explode with pleasure, I'm quivering, shaking, spasming right on the edge—

The Ash King pulls out and gives me the most wicked smile I've ever seen—teeth like knives and starlight.

"How does that feel, Healer? Do you like being teased?" He lifts my leg, pressing his mouth to my inner thigh. "I could feel your body fluttering around my cock. You're almost there. I think a single touch would finish it."

"I detest you," I whimper, squirming. "You're a horrible person."

He laughs and grips my shoulders, pulling my limp, shuddering body upright with him. The hot, wet tip of him pokes against my stomach.

Incensed, out of my mind with thwarted desire, I slap his cheek. "Cruel bastard."

It's a weak slap, because I can't shake the grip of my vow. He chuckles hoarsely and leans in, nuzzling my face with his. The craving to kiss him is almost too much to resist. But a kiss would mean something else entirely, to both of us. It's something we can't give to each other.

"Tell me you want me." His forehead presses to mine. "Tell me you want me in spite of it all."

I can't look at him while I say it, so I put my arms around his neck, my chest soft against his hard muscles. With my mouth to his ear I whisper, "I want you in spite of it all."

With a guttural sound of triumph, he throws me face-down on his bed. He jerks my hips up and pulls me back onto his cock, ramming into me so hard and fast that he's grunting harshly with the effort, with the sheer violence of it.

I can't take it anymore—I scream, arching as my body explodes in the most potent orgasm of my life. It tears through me, rips me open with sheer white-hot bliss. The

King tucks three fingers into my open mouth to quiet me. He keeps thrusting until he shatters, and deep groans vibrate through his whole body as he comes inside me.

"Oh gods," he's panting, moaning. "Oh gods. Cailin—Cailin, gods, I can't—"

"I know," I whimper against the sheets. "I know."

With one final shudder, he pulls out of me and crashes onto the bed at my side.

Slowly, slowly, Cailin the healer resurfaces, and the feral stranger who attacked the Ash King sinks back into the deep places of my soul.

I let magic sift through my skin, healing my burn marks and bruises. And then I heal the Ash King, where he lies belly-down and utterly spent on the bed beside me.

As I heal him, I realize he's asleep, and I sigh with relief. Now I can slip away, back to my own room. I can clean up and forget that I did this.

Or maybe I'd rather not forget. Because I don't regret it, and I'm not ashamed of it. Violent and hateful and strange as it was, we both needed it.

I said what I wanted to say. And maybe we didn't resolve things, exactly—but at least he didn't kill me. And I feel—purged, and sated, deeply, refreshingly, all the way down to my bones. Like a fierce, festering, painful thing inside me has been softened and eased.

I think I've been wanting to fuck him since he branded my chest with his burning hand.

And that makes me a terrible, terrible person. I should feel worse about this. I should not feel thoroughly soothed and relaxed.

I leave him there and tiptoe back to my room, where I wash myself off and put on a longer, more proper nightdress before climbing into bed.

Strangely, I'm able to sleep.

I take breakfast in my room the next morning, but I can't eat much because my stomach keeps jumping with "what ifs." What if he comes into my room to talk? What will he say? What will I say? How does last night change things between us?

How did it change *me*?

When I think of him pouring fire into the forest, burning his attackers, burning Brayda's face—and when I remember him pounding into me, releasing inside me—I feel sick.

I've never done anything this morally questionable in my life. I'm *good*. It's who I am, who I'm proud to be. I help people, I don't screw cruel, wicked kings on the floor amid the aftermath of our clashing magic.

It can't happen again.

With that resolve in mind, I dress myself in simple clothing—plain trousers, a blue shirt, a high-collared vest with toggles up the front. Not a hint of cleavage. My maid braids my hair and pins it tightly to my head.

"Are you all right, my lady?" she asks.

"Just Cailin," I say for the hundredth time. "I'm fine. The Ash King and the Favored are training and exercising this morning, and I'm supposed to observe, in case anyone gets hurt."

"Very good, my lady," she answers. "I can take you to the activity grounds that the Favored have been using."

She leads me through the wing where the Favored reside, past the examination room I used a few days ago, then through the garden. At the far end of the garden is a walled square, paved with stones and lined with several motionless guards. There's an expanse of sandy dirt in the center of the area—a combat ring. A long, low building forms one side of the square.

"There are weapons and weights in there," says my maid, pointing to the building. "This area is for sparring and dueling. And that is for agility training." She gestures to an array of posts, beams, bars, ropes, and wheels along the right side of the square.

It's an obstacle course like the one in the First Challenge, only not in perpetual motion, and not as lethal. Four people are swinging across the bars, leaping the gaps, ducking under the beams. Axley, with a body like a tight-coiled spring, whips through the obstacles. Teagan dashes across the tops of several posts and then climbs a rope net, every movement lithe and graceful. Khloe dances along a beam barefoot. And the Ash King, shirtless, climbs a post and then leaps to catch a bar, swinging hand over hand across a gap and landing sure-footed on the narrow step beyond. His skin shines in the morning light, sinew and sculpted muscle. A long white braid trails down his spine.

At the sight of him, a ripple of panicked delight rolls through my stomach and chest.

My maid squeezes my arm lightly, and I glance at her, surprised. Her eyes are bright with awareness. "I must tend to my duties. Enjoy yourself."

"Not much chance of that." I release a breathless laugh.

She hesitates, then whispers, so quietly I can barely hear her, "Don't chase him. Make him come to you."

She's gone before I can respond. Hers was the tiniest of whispers, so I don't think the Ash King could hear her. I suppose the servants know of his hearing ability, and they've learned to account for it.

I'm still watching my maid's retreating form and mulling over her words when two feet thump into the dirt nearby—someone leaping from the obstacle course and landing not far from me.

When I turn, the King is looming over me, mouth curved in a smirk. "Healer."

As I curtsy, I keep my face immobile and my voice cool. "Your Majesty."

He's practically glowing today, vibrant, brimming with an unusual energy. And at first I think it's for me.

But then Khloe runs up to us, shouting, "I did the entire course without falling!" and he catches her, picks her up, and captures her excited squeal with his mouth.

She has opened a part of him that none of the other girls have been able to touch. That *I* haven't been able to touch. He's rutting *playful* with her.

The King sets Khloe down immediately when Axley leaves the obstacle course and approaches us. Several of the other Favored arrive through the garden gate, while Sabre and Morani come from the weapons building. They're already sweating and panting as if they've had a rigorous practice session. At last all ten of the remaining women are gathered.

"Some of you have made use of these facilities before today," the Ash King says. "But this morning, all of you should spend a few hours honing your skills. Trust me when I say, you'll need all the strength and skill you have for tomorrow's challenge."

"Team combat," says Leslynne under her breath. "It's got to be."

She's standing right at my elbow, but she doesn't look at me or greet me. In fact, most of the women seem determined to pretend I don't exist. Only Khloe smiles at me, while Teagan and Samay offer brief nods.

For the next hour, I sit on a shady bench between two of the guards and watch the girls train. They rotate through the obstacle course, the combat ring, and the exercise building. The Ash King participates a little, but mostly he prowls in a slow circle, watching them spar or climb.

Adalasia and Diaza make a particularly glorious and graceful pair as they practice swordfighting. The sun flashes off their blades, gleams on the different shades of their brown skin, glitters in their black hair. They battle with an unrelenting ferocity that soon draws the other girls to watch. Neither one wants to give in, and the blows begin to rain faster, the clang and scrape of the blades exploding in the quiet morning. Breath hisses through their clenched teeth, and now and then one of them cries out with the effort of blocking an attack or delivering a blow.

I lean forward on my bench, gripping the stone edge. They're going at it so fiercely now that one of them is bound to get hurt.

Sure enough, Diaza sidesteps and drives her sword beneath Adalasia's guard, right into her side.

She stops herself—the blade doesn't go in far, but Adalasia screams. As Diaza jerks the blade back, blood pulses from the wound, spattering onto the dirt.

I leap up and dart forward, magic already slithering from my fingertips. The gold tendrils dive into Adalasia's wound, staunching the blood.

"Come here," I tell her. "I can heal you."

But Adalasia vents another scream and charges at Diaza, who's turning away. Diaza barely has a second to lift her sword and block the blow.

"Enough!" shouts the Ash King, and the two women freeze, glaring and seething at each other.

"I think it's time for a new kind of training," says the King. "Healer, when you're done repairing Adalasia's wound, we'll need you for practice."

Some of the women murmur at that, and Axley scoffs openly. "Why would we need her?"

I move over to Adalasia and focus on mending her wound, while studiously avoiding the King's eyes. But I'm all ears, desperately curious how he'll answer.

"As some of you know, our Healer disobeyed me recently," says the Ash King. "She took a phaeton without permission and went into the city. She spent all her healing magic on unworthy citizens and left nothing for her duties to the Favored. And she nearly died. All of which displeased me greatly." His tone darkens with vindictive heat. I can practically feel the apprehension of the girls at that change in tone. Casual though he might sometimes be with them, they haven't forgotten his terrifying side. I suspect he likes to remind them of it now and then, as he did with Axley yesterday.

"I told the Healer she would be punished for her carelessness and disobedience," says the Ash King. "Perhaps she thought I'd forgotten, or that I'd grown suddenly soft and merciful. Not so."

He's right. I thought he'd decided to spare me. I swallow hard, pushing more magic into Adalasia's wound so I can seal it up quickly. Not that I want to hasten my punishment, but I can't bear not knowing what it is.

I risk a glance at the Favored. They're all watching either me or the King, a dreadful interest and eagerness painted across their features.

"What say you, my ladies?" says the King, stretching out both arms. "Would you like to help me punish the Healer?"

22

If the people of my village could see me now...

I would be mortified, and they would vengefully attack the Ash King and get themselves burned to bones.

I'm tied to an enormous wooden target at the end of the archery range behind the weapons building. My wrists and ankles are bound tight, stretching my legs and arms wide. And I've been stripped down to my corset and pantalettes. So much for dressing modestly today.

At the end of the shooting lane, the ten Favored women are preparing their bows and arrows. Their voices are somewhat softened by distance, and I'm glad. I'd rather not hear the comments they're making about me, about this situation.

"Each of you will take three shots," says the Ash King, loudly enough for me to hear. "No arrows should land above her shoulders. The one to come closest to her skin without breaking it wins a private lunch with me. But if your aim is off—well, she can heal herself." He gives the girls a wolfish smile, and they smirk and giggle in response—all except for Khloe, who looks paler than usual, and Teagan, who frowns at the King but doesn't speak.

The King is humiliating me on purpose. Is he doing this because he regrets what happened between us? Or because I was cold to him this morning? Maybe he's simply proving he doesn't care about me at all, that I was just another one-night conquest to him.

Seems like he could have found a way to do all those things without tying me to a board and letting his would-be wives shoot arrows at me.

"If your Majesty pleases," says Axley, her voice raised for my benefit. "I'd like the first three shots."

"By all means." The King makes a sweeping, inviting gesture toward me.

I hate this. I hate the rough grind of the wood grain against the skin of my back. I hate the chafing of the ropes against my wrists. But the burn of the sun against my bronzed skin is familiar—and to be honest, I'm more comfortable in my underthings that I have been in any of the fancy gowns I've worn lately. I close my eyes, letting my head tip back against the board, savoring the heat of the morning as it soaks into my body.

With my eyes closed to the King and his women, I can shift their murmuring voices to the back of my mind and focus on the sweet twitter of a bird somewhere nearby. I can feel the dirt of the archery lane under my bound, bare feet. A strong herbal scent, almost minty, wafts from a nearby flowerbed. Cedars form a hedge-wall behind the target, and I inhale their sharp, spicy fragrance.

A sharp whine, and something thunks into the board, right at the curve of my waist. It passed so close I felt the whisper of its edge against my skin.

My eyes pop open.

Axley's first arrow. Its green-tipped feather shivers slightly from the force of the shot. It landed precisely at my waistline, nearly touching me but not quite.

Axley meets my eyes, and her mouth bends in a rigid smile.

She's an expert shot. And she might have just won the King's challenge. She gets two more arrows, but I'm not sure how she can do any better.

She nocks another green-tipped arrow. Pulls back the bow again.

And fires a second arrow directly into my thigh.

The pain is horrific, but I don't scream—I only gasp, tears starting in my eyes. I try to push the arrow out with magic, but I can't. This is no splinter. I'll have to wait until they're all done shooting, then pull the arrow out and heal myself.

"Oh my," says Axley loudly, touching her fingertips to her mouth. "I'm so sorry. My aim wasn't very good that time."

"Try to do better," says the Ash King grimly.

She pulls the bow again.

Watching the arrow speed toward me is the most terrifying thing I've experienced. My heart is racing, and a nervous sweat breaks out over my body.

The third arrow slices my cheek, nicking my ear and ramming into the wood beside my head. I suck in a sharp breath, sending magic to heal the wounds. But the blood still coats my cheek and wets the side of my neck, under my ear.

"Nothing above the shoulders," snarls the King. "Axley, you're disqualified from winning the prize."

"My humble apologies, your Majesty." She sinks into a docile curtsy. "I don't know what happened."

Despite her apology, it's clear she is a skilled markswoman. She proved it with her first shot, so I would know that the next two were purposeful.

It doesn't make sense for her to antagonize me like this. I'm the Healer, for the gods' sake. What if she's injured in the next challenge and I decide to leave part of the job undone, to let her suffer or die?

Or maybe she knows I wouldn't do that. Maybe she and the others are counting on my healer's vow to protect them. I suppose they're right. I'm not sure I could find it in my heart to leave any of them in pain or danger when it was in my power to help.

But everyone is a mountain, as the Ceannaire said— even me. Anyone can be pushed too far. Perhaps I need to remind them of that.

Samay steps up, preparing for her first shot. Mentally I search for water, but there's been no rain for a couple of days, and the most I can sense is a little dew, nearly dried. I can't use sweat, tears, or blood—it's too blended, not pure enough for wielding.

There is one other defense I could use. The reverse side of my healing power. I can make these women hurt whenever they hurt me. I can corrode them, make blisters erupt on their bodies, reverse the healing magic I've done for them.

But I won't. I can't let these people change me.

Samay's first arrow thunks near my elbow. Her second skims my thigh, drawing blood, and she swears. She's actually trying for the private lunch with the King. Her third arrow goes wide, missing my hip by a handsbreadth.

I notice Axley whispering to a few of the other girls, and as the next one steps up to take a turn, Axley smiles, serpentlike.

I stand helpless against the target as arrows whistle toward me, slicing my leg, my hip, and my elbow. One scrapes along my ribs. Another slits the flesh of my upper arm. The worst ones actually sink into my flesh—my calf, my hand, my stomach, my shoulder.

I can heal the lacerations and scrapes, but the ones where an arrow is actually lodged in my flesh—those I can't fix until the arrows are out. I grit my teeth, soothing my own pain each time it flares up, trying to hold the blood at bay.

Teagan and Khloe shoot carefully, attempting to win the time with the King, but the others are more intent on making me hurt—even Sabre and Leslynne. There's a desperate hunger in their eyes, the look of cornered prey. It's as if they don't see me anymore—they see everything standing between them and the crown. With these arrows, they're pinning their fears, their anxieties, all the pressure and pain, onto me, onto the target.

Meanwhile the Ash King stands with his arms folded across his bare chest, his handsome face hard as stone and his hair a white halo in the sunlight. No hint of what he's thinking or feeling.

So far, since Axley was disqualified, Teagan's arrow is the one most likely to win. It's lodged against my right breast, and it didn't break the skin. I hope she wins.

The only person left to shoot is the last woman of Axley's toxic trio—the only one who hasn't been eliminated yet. She's called Beaori.

She nocks an arrow and exchanges a look with Axley.

Her first arrow sings through the air and slashes my leg. I seethe through the pain for a second before sending more magic to calm and heal it. I'm holding nearly a dozen threads of magic in place at once now, easing the pain and staunching the blood around the embedded arrows. I need time and space to get these arrows out and make myself whole again.

Beaori aims, anchoring the bowstring near her mouth, and lets the second arrow fly.

It sails toward me and strikes right between my spread legs, narrowly missing some very tender parts. The other girls gasp and I look up at Beaori, incensed.

She grimaces like she's mad that she missed, and she readies another arrow.

Beaori plans to shoot me in the crotch—that much is clear. And even though I could heal myself afterward, I'm not about to allow that.

I gather what little dew I can access, creating a fine mist. My hands are bound, but with a twitch of my finger I whisk the moisture across the archery lane just as Beaori's third arrow flies. I'm no wind-wielder, but the mist is just enough to push the arrow off course. It thumps into the wood by my hip.

"The punishment is over," says the King.

"It isn't fair," Beaori says. "She can ease her own pain, so it wasn't really a punishment at all."

I clench my teeth. *The next time you need my help, just wait…*

The Ash King grabs Beaori by the chin, tilting her face up to his. "Anything else you'd like to complain about?" Heat shimmers along the lines of his body, and a sudden tension simmers in the air. Khloe grips Teagan's arm.

Beaori murmurs something I can't hear, but it must be sufficiently apologetic, because the King lets her go and commands, "Train for another hour, and then Teagan will lunch with me. Everyone else, meet us in the upper gallery of the West Wing after the meal. Oh, and someone free the Healer so she can mend herself."

He stalks away, toward the palace, not toward the training square.

Sabre unties the ropes holding me, while Khloe and Teagan tug the arrows from my flesh. As each arrow leaves my body, I let healing magic flow through the wound. It will take a little time to mend everything.

I stumble along the archery lane and pick up my clothes. As I'm walking away, through the garden, I hear Teagan say, "This is a good reminder for all of us about who we're dealing with."

"Careful how you speak of His Majesty," Axley interjects. "You're perilously close to treason."

"It's not treason, it's reality," Khloe snaps. "He let all of us do *that* to her. And he didn't flinch once."

"True," says Axley. "Maybe she overstepped, and he finally realized she needed to be put in her place. She walks around like she's high-born, when she's nothing but a grimy village whore."

I round the corner of the hedge and limp along the path, not caring to listen anymore. What they think of me doesn't matter. Shouldn't matter.

I pass the flowerbed where I once stood with my feet in the earth, where the Ash King called me "vagabond." The medical examination room is close by, so I slip inside, toss my clothes on the floor, and hoist myself onto the edge of a cot. I don't want to lie down—that feels too vulnerable a position for this East Wing full of poisonous noblewomen and their servants. But I can't stand either, so I sit, and let the pain surface in my thigh wound. There's something clarifying about the agony—it helps me perceive the wound more fully and seal the area faster. I don't worry about conserving energy—I use as much as I want, intent on speeding up the healing.

The windows in the room are closed, shuttered, and draped, so my healing glow is the only light in the darkness. Lines of gold sew the lacerated tissues of my hand, my calf, my stomach, my shoulder, my thigh.

The door swings open slightly, admitting pale light and a dark figure.

"Cailin." The Ash King steps into the room and closes the door behind him. He's wearing a tunic now.

I turn my face away, inhaling a broken breath that sounds far too much like a sob.

"I didn't think they would take it that far," he says.

"You gave them a chance to hurt the woman they've mocked and despised for days." My voice breaks. "Of course they took it too far."

"I had a reason for doing this. A few reasons, in fact. You can hate me for it, but you need to hear why I did it."

I take another hitching breath. I don't dare speak again or I will sob outright. Pinching my lips together, I coalesce my energy, finishing the healing process for my leg wounds.

"The servants have told me the antagonism between the contestants is growing stronger," says the Ash King. "The stakes of this contest are high, and the families of these women are willing to do anything it takes to place their daughters on the throne. There have been murders and suicides during the Calling of the Favored in the past, and we nearly had a murder in the combat ring today. I needed the girls to shift their animosity from each other to a new target, a common enemy."

"Me." I shake my head, running my fingers over the newly flawless skin of my thigh. "Heartsfire, this job just keeps getting worse."

"Does it really?" He moves closer, stepping between my knees, pushing them farther apart. "I thought perhaps you enjoyed one of the recent perks of the role."

"Not at all," I shake my head vigorously.

"No?" He leans in, fingertips trailing along my jawline. "So that scream last night—that was—"

"Horror," I say. "Pure horror and self-loathing."

"Ah." His voice deepens, quiet and molten as the silent flow of lava down a mountainside. "And the quiver of your body, the way you tightened around me when I was inside you—that wasn't the best pleasure of your life?"

He's all around me, over me, cradling me with his presence, filling my lungs with his scent—spicy smoke and charcoal, heat and sweat and darkness. His body calls to mine, pulls me inexorably closer.

But his servants tied me to a target. His women shot me full of holes. And now he's fishing for compliments about the pleasure he gave me?

"You think very highly of yourself, Majesty," I manage.

"I truly don't," he says, and I look up in time to see the agony of truth in his eyes. A mere flicker, and then gone.

Something warms and widens inside me, flooding forward, reaching out to him. So much pain, and he keeps it all carefully hidden away. There is no magic with which he can soothe it.

I'm nearly healed now, pain-free again. I can afford to relent a little. "So you put me through that to keep the girls in line. To keep them from killing each other."

"For that, and for one other reason. You see, if we want to repair your precious reputation, we have to throw them off the scent. They have to think we hate each other."

"We *do* hate each other."

"Of course we do." His hand glides up my back. "Would you like to *hate me* again tonight?"

My mouth is dry, but other parts of me are definitely not. "Only if you hate me harder."

The Ash King's broad hands close over my hips, fingers grazing my bare skin. "But then again, why wait until tonight?" He presses inward between my legs, opening my core to him. The loose pants he wore while training jut out in the front, the covered tip of his cock pressing against my tingling center through the delicate fabric of my underwear.

I want nothing more than to make my clothes and his vanish entirely so he can sink inside me. I'm still angry with him for the "punishment," but I'm also violently, vibrantly awake, pulsing with a lust stronger than any I've ever felt. Perhaps, where he's concerned, anger and sex are linked.

"Not here," I manage. "Guards outside—people could walk in—"

His hands slide up to my waist and tighten. He sets his forehead against mine. "I want you. And you want me—I can feel you shaking. I know you're wet for me."

I grip his shoulders, closing my eyes. "Tonight."

"Very well. I'll see you this afternoon for the art session with the girls, yes?"

"As Your Majesty wishes."

He tilts his head, bringing his mouth perilously close to mine. For a moment we stay, breathing in each other's exhaled lust.

Then he leaves. And I'm left trembling and wanting in the dark. Which feels terribly prophetic for the end of all this, when he chooses someone else.

It's just sex between us, and yet it isn't. Not for me. For me it's a constant force tugging me to him against my will, against my better judgment, against what I know of his character.

Except that with him, I always have the sense that there is *more* to know. Deep places to explore, secrets to unfold. Like when Brayda and Rince and I used to climb higher than we were supposed to, along the ridges and slopes of Analoir Doiteain, our home mountain. We found the strangest things, like huge black waterfalls of frozen stone, formed when lava poured over a rock edge and cooled while in motion. We collected speckled granite, pock-marked pumice, glossy obsidian, peppered andesite. So many different types of rock, each with its own coloring and facets. And every rock I found only made me love our mountain more. Perhaps, when it comes to me and the Ash King, secrets could be like those rocks.

If I'm going to sleep with him again tonight—and possibly more times after that—I need to find a way to assuage my guilt, to justify what I feel for him. I must discover more about his past, and I need to do that without pushing too hard and making him recoil from me. He's skittish and reactive, and more sensitive than he wants people to think.

Once I'm fully healed and dressed, I lunch alone, nibbling salted tomatoes and buttered bread in a quiet nook of the garden, with my feet in the soil. Afterward I wash up and reluctantly make my way to the gallery the King mentioned, where he and the Favored will "enjoy some art."

The gallery is an airy space, its floors adorned with rectangles of yellow sunshine from a dozen tall windows. On the opposite wall hang paintings, portraits, and sketches of varying sizes—all of them fascinating and enticing to me. Other than the creation of objects from petrified wood, there's little art in my village.

I've never been particularly artistic, and my parents didn't force it. Nor did they make me learn the art of shaping and polishing the petrified wood, after they realized my affinity lay with outdoor work, with water and leaves and soil.

I can make beautiful things with water, but I admire those who can create lasting pieces with ink or paint. I walk the gallery slowly, toward the seating area where the Favored cluster on couches. Their pastel gowns, jeweled headpieces, and chinking teacups are a far cry from this morning's sweat and toil.

Halfway along the room, someone has set up three long tables with trays, pots of glue, and bins of small colored pebbles and chips of glass. There's a chair set close to the central table, and another chair opposite, facing it. More chairs line the outer two tables.

"Cailin." One of the armored guards stationed along the wall steps forward, blue eyes glinting through his helmet.

"Owin." I squeeze his outstretched hand, smiling. "It's good to see you."

He pulls off his helmet and ruffles his sweaty hair. "Curse this confounded thing. I hate wearing it."

"I wonder sometimes if you're really cut out to be a guard." I reach up and smooth aside a stray lock.

"I wonder that too." The corners of his eyes crinkle as he smiles. "But I do like this posting. It means I'm close to the King."

I lift an eyebrow. "But he whipped you."

"He went easy on me. And since then he's been indifferent, which coming from him means we're best friends." Another grin. "He even asked me if I knew any portrait artists in the city who could use a wealthy patron. So I did you a favor."

"What favor?"

"You told me how you got interrupted when you and your friend in the alley were—" He waggles his eyebrows significantly. "Well, I figured you deserve another chance at—ahem, *connecting*—with your old lover."

"Old lover?" I echo, confused—and then his meaning clarifies in my mind.

The mosaic supplies—art—portraits—my friend from the alley—

Oh gods.

Rince. My former lover, my friend, zealous servant of the Undoing, advocate for the death of the King…

Rince is here, in the palace.

23

I hear voices behind me, entering the gallery, and I turn, my heart dropping like a stone into my stomach. One of the King's stewards is escorting Rince into the room.

"We have everything set up, just as you requested," says the steward. "You'll sit here, and the ladies will sit there, one at a time, to have their portraits made. Meanwhile the other ladies will be working on mosaics of their own."

"That's fantastic. Everything is exactly right." Rince's dark eyes have already locked with mine. "Will His Majesty be joining us?"

"A bit later, yes. He's still with one of the Favored."

The Ash King is still with Teagan? That's a long lunch. What are they talking about? Or maybe they aren't talking at all. Is he kissing her? Touching her?

I haul my thoughts away from that subject and focus on Rince. He's my immediate problem.

Rince wants to kill the Ash King, and today is the perfect opportunity.

He can't kill the King. I'm not done with the King yet.

Rince is still watching me, walking toward me. Owin backs away, nodding encouragingly before jamming the helmet back on his head and retreating to his post by the wall.

"Cailin the Healer." Rince bows to me. "I am a great admirer of yours. I wonder if I might have a few moments of your time?"

"The Healer of the Favored is very busy," begins the steward, but I interrupt him. "I can spare a few moments. The ladies are finishing their tea anyway." I smile ingratiatingly at the steward.

"You're from the borderlands, yes?" says Rince to me. "I have some very fine obsidian glass here from your region. Would you like to see?" He lifts the satchel he's carrying.

A leather satchel. Anything could be sewn into it— explosives, knives, poisoned darts. I hope the King's guards checked it thoroughly before they let Rince bring it in here.

"Of course I'd like to see. Let's go nearer to the windows. Better light." Keeping my face neutrally pleasant, I take Rince's elbow and guide him toward a window far from the steward and the Favored and Owin.

We stand facing the light with our backs to the room, and he pulls out a palmful of gleaming obsidian. Under his breath he says, "It's wonderful that you're here. I wasn't sure I'd see you. But this is perfect. Now we don't have to meet at the tea shop. I heard you got in trouble for going into the city alone." He presses a hand over mine briefly. "Did they really use you for target practice? Heartsfire, Cailin. But it all ends today. You'll get to witness his final moments."

My heart jerks. "How did you know about the target practice? That happened this morning."

Rince only smiles.

There can be no doubt now. One of the Favored is with the Undoing, and she has spoken to Rince today.

But he just arrived, and all the Favored appear to have been in this room together for a while. The only one absent is Teagan. Is she really with the Ash King, or did she and Rince manage a brief meeting right before he entered the gallery?

No, it can't be Teagan. Maybe one of the ladies told a maid about the archery incident, and the news traveled through the palace to Rince's contact. Or maybe—

"Cailin." Rince is frowning at me now. "Did you hear me? It ends today."

A sick chill floods my body. "Keep your voice down. The Ash King has magically gifted hearing."

Rince's eyes widen. "Really?"

"Yes."

"That would explain how two of our infiltrators were caught in the past few months. Gods. Thank you, Cailin. That's valuable information. Not that it matters now." He lowers his voice, excitement coursing through his whisper. "The Ash King will be dead within the hour."

Nausea swells in my throat. "How?"

"These stones. They're explosives. Enough to take out this whole gallery."

I suck in a startled breath. "But—that will kill everyone in the room, not just the King."

Rince nods soberly. "I'm willing to yield my life to the cause. But if you'd rather step out before I do it—"

"No!" I take his fingers, folding them gently over the rocks. "Rince, you can't die for this."

"I knew I might have to sacrifice everything for the cause, Cailin. Why do you think I greeted you like I did in that alley? I've been living on the edge of death for a while now, and it makes the momentary pleasures all the sweeter. This is my day, my time. I can end him here, now."

"No," I whisper brokenly. "Rince—I care about you. If you die—gods, your parents, Rince. Think of them."

"They'll be proud of me. So will Brayda and my friends. So should you." He frowns again. "What's this really about, Cailin? I thought you believed in this too."

"You expect me to be *happy* that my best friend wants to kill himself?" I voice a breathless laugh, glancing quickly over my shoulder. Still no one nearby, but the steward is looking restless. We need to finish this conversation quickly.

I can't let Rince die—and I can't let him kill the Ash King, or the Favored women.

"Think of those girls." I jerk my head toward the Favored. "You'll be killing them too. They're innocent."

His frown deepens. "They're complicit in all this. Part of the toxic system, the monarchy and the nobility. Their goal is to become partners with a murderer and an oppressor, which makes them just as guilty as he is."

I whimper a little, desperate, my hands balled into fists. What can I say to persuade him? I could raise the alarm and tell everyone what he plans, but then he might set off the explosives immediately, killing me, himself, most of the Favored, Owin, the steward, and the other guards. Even if the guards manage to grab him before he can trigger the explosion, Rince will be dragged away, tortured, and executed.

My only way out of this is to convince him not to act yet. And I have a handful of seconds to do it.

24

Every nerve in my body is taut with terror. Rince holds in his palm the element of the King's death, and his own. The toll in collateral damage will be terrible.

"Rince," I breathe. "You can't kill the King with those."

He narrows his dark eyes at me. "Why not?"

"You know he can light himself on fire and not burn, right? He's impervious. Practically indestructible. There's something different about him, about his anatomy—something I haven't figured out yet."

I can't tell Rince that I was able to hurt the Ash King. I haven't even figured out how, or why, because when I quenched the fire from his throat it didn't harm him—it cooled and soothed him. But perhaps, wielded by my hand, my water has intent. Perhaps I wanted to hurt him yesterday, and the water I wielded was infused with that desire. Does that mean I've broken my healer's vow?

Rince chews his lip. "Are you sure about this?"

"I scanned him, Rince. He's going to be very tough to kill. I don't think an explosion is the right way to go here. What if you died, and your undercover contact died, while the King lived? What a waste that would be! We can't risk it."

Rince's features sag with disappointment, and my heart leaps, because he's starting to believe me. "The blast might not kill him, but it could weaken him. Injure him."

"They'd only force me or the palace healer to fix him. Listen, Rince—I'm deep on the inside. Let me work on this problem a little longer, figure out what's going on with his anatomy and his magical qualities."

"I might be able to give you a little time," he says grudgingly. "A few more days."

"Another week," I counter.

"Fine. One more week. But I need more than a body scan, Cailin. I need a possible solution."

I scramble for something to say, and I blurt out, "Poison. The internal kind, not the type absorbed through the skin. He'd have to ingest it. It could work."

"And you could get him to drink it?"

I grit my teeth. "I told you—my vow—I can't do that."

"Hm." He shakes his head. "You mean well, Cailin, but your values are grossly misplaced."

"One week," I whisper. "I'll have more information by then—I can focus on how food and drink is tested and delivered to him. And already I have notes and sketches for you, marked with times and guard postings." Part of me doesn't want to hand over those notes—but I have to give Rince something tangible. I'm trying to save many lives here, including the lives of my first lover and my new one.

Rince's expression shifts at the mention of the notes. "That's something, I suppose."

"Give me time," I say. "Meet me after the portraits, and I'll hand over what I've collected so far. Just don't be an impatient idiot and destroy our only chance of really making this happen."

He grins at me, brief and bright. "Impatient idiot, eh? Now you sound like the Cailin of my childhood."

I grin back.

As we're smiling at each other, the King enters the gallery, and the Favored greet him with a cooing chorus of saccharine voices.

Teagan isn't with him. Did he send her home?

That's the least of my worries. My biggest fear right now is that Rince will change his mind sometime during this art session and blow us all to pieces. I'm not sure if the King would survive an explosion, but hopefully I was convincing enough to hold Rince at bay. He has known me a long time, and he would have caught me in a straight-up lie; but I mixed my words with truth, so I think he believed me.

Rince turns from me and moves to greet the King, with a graceful, humble demeanor that almost makes me laugh even as my stomach churns. I settle my nausea with a little magic, and I suppress my heart rate slightly. I need the nerves and adrenaline to keep me sharp and attuned to the situation, but I have to be calm enough to appear normal, as if nothing's wrong.

Teagan enters shortly afterward, and the portrait sessions begin. Thanks to a pair of court musicians in the corner, the gallery soon fills with delicate song, and my tension eases a little.

Rince is charm incarnate with his wide smiles, quick fingers, and velvety voice. He teaches the girls the basics of creating a mosaic, and for those who've done something similar he provides extra tips to make the art more realistic and complex. He's good at this—suave and skilled. I can tell he's met many people in various scenarios since he left our little village, and I can't help watching him.

There's pride in my heart, but it's mixed with horror and shock, that he would end his life to take out the King. I always knew he was devoted to the cause, but this is beyond anything I thought he'd do. Attempt an assassination, yes—but actively commit suicide to achieve it? It makes me so sad that I ache inside, every breath dragging painfully through my chest.

I'm conscious of the Ash King circling the girls, eyeing their work with a kind of tolerant approval, but I barely glance at him. I'm too occupied with reading Rince's face, trying to discern any miniscule change that might spell our imminent doom.

When I finally do glance at the King, he's watching me watch Rince. And he doesn't look pleased.

At last, after three tense hours, Rince has completed the mosaic portrait of every Favored woman. The girls make their obeisance to the King and leave to dress for dinner, while I remain in my chair in the seating area, waiting for Rince to pack up his things.

The King lingers as well, running one bejeweled finger along the edge of a portrait tray. His hair is unbound today, a snowy river over the dark gray suit he wears. A silver band is his only crown. It looks much more comfortable than the black ones he sometimes wears. Thin-beaten as the iron is, those other crowns must get terribly heavy.

"Where are you from?" the King asks Rince. "I've not seen your work before."

My gut twists, and I clutch the arms of my chair. *No, stop talking to him. Just walk away, please. He could kill you right now.*

I'm not sure which of the men I'm more terrified for. Rince half-smiles as he turns to face the King. "I'm from the same town as Cailin."

Shock runs cold through my veins. I did not expect him to give a truthful answer. Shouldn't Rince have a secret identity, a fake hometown?

"Is that so?" The Ash King glances at me, his features cool and remote. "Old friends, the two of you?"

"Childhood friends, Your Majesty, and more." Rince gives me a warm smile. "If you would kindly permit, I'd like to stay a little longer to speak with your Healer. She and I have not seen each other for a long time. Though we did have a brief encounter in the city the other day."

"Did you now?" The King speaks through tight lips, and his eyes flicker scarlet. "That must have been when she was out with Owin, the guardsman who recommended you."

Why is Rince telling the King all of this? I suppose there's no obvious connection between him and the Undoing. Still, revealing his real identity feels dangerous, for him and for me.

Maybe that is part of Rince's plan—establishing the connection between us, so if he's outed as part of the Undoing, I'll be implicated as well.

Perhaps he didn't entirely trust my words today, after all.

"By all means, speak to the Healer," the Ash King says brusquely. "Enjoy some time together. And you must come back again sometime to visit with her. Gods know she has few friends in this place."

He stalks out, leaving Rince and me alone. Well... alone with the ever-present guards.

I rise, meeting Rince halfway as he walks toward me. "Let's go to my room," I say, low.

I lead Rince through the palace, along the corridor of the central wing. Owin and another guard trail us watchfully.

When we reach my bedroom door, the second guard clears his throat. "Healer, it is a grave breach of security for anyone else to be allowed in the room adjoining the King's. Only you and your maids are permitted in the Rose Room."

"But you heard the King," I say. "He gave us permission to enjoy some time together." I lend a sultry significance to the words. "Would you prefer we do that here, in the hall?"

"No, my lady," says the guard.

"You could post someone at the door between the rooms," I suggest. "Just for a little while. This won't take long. Never does, with this one." I nudge Rince with my elbow.

He splays his fingers over his chest, assuming a look of mock offense. "My poor pride is wounded. Though I will say, speed does not matter as long as the object of the game is achieved for both players."

"And you always win the game." I give Rince my best adoring expression.

"Oh, let them go in," Owin says to his fellow guard. "There are guards along the hall, and one of us can watch the inner door, as she said. I volunteer."

"Naughty," I gasp. "You want to listen."

"Not so, my lady." Owin gives me a wink. "I promise to cover my ears."

The second guard yields, and I hurry Rince into my room before he can change his mind.

The moment the door closes behind us, I tug him to the bathing room and close that door, too. I turn on the spigot for the tub, push Rince against the wall, and rise on tiptoe, placing my mouth against his ear.

"What were you thinking, telling the King who you really are?" My words are barely audible, barely above a breath. I have no idea if the King is in his room or not, but I'm taking no chances.

Rince wraps my body in his arms, pulling me tight against him. His breath is soft and warm against my ear. "I had to be honest about my identity, Cailin. Do you think the King would trust the recommendation of a single guard and allow a complete stranger into the palace? No. When I was approached about showing my talents to the Favored, I knew I would be questioned and my records would be checked before they would allow me through the gates. So I told them my true name and origins, but not my current associations, of course. They examined my records thoroughly and searched me for weapons, but they underestimated the cleverness of the Undoing and its servants." He pats the satchel at his side.

And then he has the nerve to kiss me. His soft lips seal over mine, and his tongue probes for entrance. I wait, moving my lips slightly, expecting to feel the same humming warmth and tingling excitement I always felt with him.

But I don't. I feel—mildly pleasant at best.

I pull away, wiping my mouth. "I should give you the sketches and notes."

"Yes, we should do that first."

First? Does he really expect something intimate to happen between us before he leaves?

Am I going to allow it?

266

I turn off the water, and he follows me to the bedroom. I dig the notebook from its hiding place behind my headboard and pull out the pages I've finished. "It's not much, but maybe it will help."

"Thank you, Cailin." He folds the pages small and tucks them into an inner pocket of his vest.

Then, slowly, he moves into my space.

I let Rince enfold me in his arms, and for a moment I relax against that familiar chest, breathing him in. But he smells different now. He's not the boy who shifted from friend to something else on the day I turned sixteen, when he persuaded me to show him my breasts. He's not the boy who put his fingers in me at seventeen, or who took my virginity on my eighteenth birthday. He's not the boy whose body I learned and enjoyed for the next few years, until he left me.

He doesn't smell like resin and rain-washed earth anymore. He smells like *tobak* smoke, paste from his artwork, and an unfamiliar perfume.

"It's good to see you," I murmur. "But…" I look up at him, shaking my head.

"Are you sure?" He looks disappointed.

"I'm sure."

He sighs. "If we go out there now, the guards will think I'm far too quick to my pleasure, as you said."

"But I know the truth. You can last a long time, with the right touch."

"Mmm." His eyes close briefly, and I know he's remembering those hours we spent in the grass by the stream. "Best day of my life, I do believe."

"Really?" My heart, sore and strained, heals a little at those words.

"Really." He kisses my cheek.

"I'll tell the guards you gave me a good one. Better yet—" I tilt back my head and release loud orgasmic cries. "Oh gods. Oh I'm coming—I'm—oh, Rince—you're the best lay in the kingdom, the very best!"

Rince claps a hand over his mouth to stifle a laugh. Silently laughing myself, I reach up to his ear and whisper, "I'm glad you didn't die today."

He sobers, pulling back and cupping my shoulders. He whispers, "Do as you've promised, Cailin. Remember, our mission is saving lives. Saving the kingdom. To do that, there must be sacrifice. There's more here at stake than you know, and I have powerful people on my side too, people to whom I must answer. They won't be pleased with either of us if you prove untrustworthy."

My mouth opens, surprise stealing my words. Before I can cobble together a response, Rince opens the door and hurries out, pretending to adjust his pants.

I shut the door behind him and lean against it, shaken to my core.

What Rince said to me wasn't exactly a threat—more of a warning. Still, I'm worried that I've inadvertently gotten deeper into the political scene than I ever wanted to be. Why couldn't the King have just left me alone? What made him choose me? He's never mentioned who told him about me, or what they said. I should ask him.

There's no banquet tonight—just a dinner for the King and the Favored. Tomorrow will be another challenge—a violent one, judging from the King's comments today.

I order food to my room and eat quickly before wandering out into the palace. I want to explore a bit more. It's such a beautiful, enormous place, yet I've only visited a few areas of it.

I don't ask for guidance. If I get lost, I'll just ask one of the omnipresent servants or guards to help me find my way again. It feels delightfully adventurous to wander the halls alone. I've explored the outdoors many times back home, but I've never had the opportunity to meander through a building as large and complex as this one.

Barefoot, dressed in a simple gown, I follow the main halls—the wide spacious corridors where most of the traffic of palace life happens, the ones that smell faintly of that cloying royal incense.

I pursue a broad hallway to its very end and take a quaint side stairway, which twists up and up, then spits me out into a narrow passage that smells old and stale. The faded red carpet here is threadbare, thin. I pad along it, taking a strange comfort in the fact that it isn't as plush and rich like everything else I've seen here. There's a lamp burning near the stairs, but the rest of the hallway is dark, so I light the small lamp I brought with me and hold it high.

The white plaster walls give way to painted brick, interspersed by doors of golden wood bracketed with black iron. Most are locked, but one of them yields, revealing a musty, dusty room, garnished with cobwebs.

At the end of that hallway, a metal stairway takes me down, down, down, and I weave through several short corridors, ducking around tight corners and jumping when my lamp makes the shadows dance in deep-set doorways. There's not a servant or a guard to be seen in this area of the palace. Strange. I suppose the King never comes here, so there's no need for it.

Ahead, there's a new section—walls paneled with glossy dark wood, cheerful lamps in sconces, the murmur of voices. I pass what looks to be a common room for the servants. Down another hallway there are storage areas with hundreds of wooden shelves, all completely stocked with goods for the care of the household. There's a door marked "Fur Closet" and another marked "Linens." Stone steps descend to a lower hall, possibly holding the cold-cellars, but I skip that one and move on.

The few servants I pass give me curious looks, and some smile. One of them, a kind-looking woman who reminds me of my mother, stops me with a gentle, "Can I help you, Healer?"

"I'm exploring," I tell her. "Is that all right?"

"It is in my opinion, but Mistress Effelin might have a different view if she sees you wandering down here. Is there anything special you wanted to see?"

"Well, I—" I hesitate, glancing around. "I was curious about artifacts, books—maybe information on magic?"

The woman's expression turns cautious. "Well, His Majesty doesn't cater to the study of magic, as you know. He's had bad experiences with it, you see. Fears it, you might say."

"I've always been taught that understanding a thing can help you fear it less."

"That's a good thought, my lady. But it's not my place to speak on the King's opinion. I will say that if you're interested in magic of the kind you wield, you might speak with Jonald, the palace healer. He's getting on in years now, and a bit soft in the mind at times, but he's a kindly soul. Tends to talk a bit more than he should about the old days. Could be interesting." She gives me a mischievous smile.

"I'd love to. Is it too late to see him now, do you think?"

"He does go to his rest early, but he's usually reading around this time. He'll be glad of the company. Come on, I'll take you to him."

"Thank you. What's your name? And please call me Cailin."

"Well, Cailin, I'm Dottred, or Dot for short. I manage some of the servants, the cleaning staff mostly."

"Important work," I say. "That must be quite the job in a big place like this."

"Oh, it never ends." She shakes her head, laughing lightly. "This way."

Dot leads me down a hall. "You know, the King himself used to hang around in the servants' quarters when he was a child. I was a young maid then, and sometimes I'd be called to tote him back to the nursery. He was just Prince Perish then."

It's strange to hear the Ash King's real name, and stranger still to think of him being a child. "Did he always have the white hair?"

"From birth. Had that temper of his from birth, too. Made for quite the interesting time." She points to a black smudge low on the wall, and another further on. "He made those when he was about seven years old, when his gift for fire manifested. One time a servant started to paint over the marks, and Mistress Effelin shouted at him to leave it. So there they stay. Fond of him, she was."

I never thought how it must have been for those who knew the Ash King as a child, when they found out about the Ashlands massacre. It must have hurt them so badly, knowing that the little prince they loved did such a dreadful thing.

Cautiously I venture, "Where were you, when—when you found out about the Ashlands?"

Ahead of me, Dot's back stiffens.

"I'm sorry," I say quickly. "I shouldn't have asked. It's just—I remember where I was. In the fields. Someone came to get me and the other workers, and we all went to the village square. Our Ceannaire told us what she'd heard, and some people who had relatives in the South cried. There weren't many details about what happened."

"Many would like to know more about it," says Dot. "But the King's word on it is the King's word."

"What did he say, when he came back from the South?"

"He said the rebellion had been quelled, and our enemies were gone. And that was all he said." Dot mounts half a dozen steps, while I hurry up after her. "We have to trust that he knew something we didn't. And whether he did or not, the throne was his by blood-right."

She doesn't speak aloud what everyone was thinking in those days—that the man who burned so much of the South could have easily destroyed the rest of the kingdom had anyone tried to challenge him. Perhaps if they'd coordinated their efforts, the nobility could have deposed him. What did he promise them to ensure their loyalty?

Dot seems to be done with the subject, eager to hand me off to the old healer. "We put Jonald on this floor because it's on a level with most of the living areas where he might be needed." She pauses outside a door, patting a wheeled chair parked nearby. "One of us pushes him around, and sometimes when there are stairs, the guards carry him. This place wasn't built with the old folk in mind. Too many ups and downs and crooked corners."

She raps on the door. "Jonald? May we come in?"

A pause, and then a cracked voice says, "Who's we?"

I recognize that voice. This man pulled me back from the edge of death. It's about time I thanked him for it. I feel suddenly regretful that I didn't seek him out before.

"It's Dot, Jonald," Dot calls through the door. "And I've got the Healer of the Favored here. She'd like to speak with you."

Something scrapes in the room, and then there's the rhythmic tapping of a cane or walking stick, approaching the door. It opens, and a thin white-haired man peers at me. He's toothless, smacking his lips over pink gums. "Healer of the Favored, eh? Good to see you, child. I'll just put my teeth back in, and we'll have a nice chat."

25

The Healer's quarters are cushioned and comfortable, with flames crackling merrily in a small fireplace. Once his teeth are in again, he settles himself in a plump armchair and gestures for me to take the opposite chair near the hearth.

"I can call for more tea," he offers.

"No, thank you, I'm fine. I wanted to tell you how grateful I am for what you did for me, saving my life."

"Of course, of course. It's what we do, isn't it? Well… most of us." He watches me with a gaze that's surprisingly sharp for his age. There's a film that often covers aged eyes, but he's had those scaly cells removed for better clarity.

"Can you heal yourself?" I ask.

"No, my dear. That's a special gift only certain healers possess—you among them."

I nod, swallowing hard as I prepare to broach the sensitive topic I want to discuss. "When you were healing me, you mentioned that you have some skills as a Ricter."

"Not exactly," he says. "The average Ricter can discern someone's level of magical power, but not the specific gift or its facets. For that, they have to rely on testimony from others who know the gifted person. In my case, my Ricter talent and my healer gift blend, allowing me to read the facets of other healers' powers."

"So," I draw a deep breath. "You know. About me."

He nods. "As well as healing others and yourself, you can do the opposite. You can corrode and destroy. You can return healed wounds to their damaged state. It's an ability I've only seen twice before. One of those men was permanently Muted by the Ash King's grandfather."

"They did Mutings that long ago? I thought it was a recent thing."

"The Ash King's Ricters are much harsher with Mutings," says Jonald. "In the old times, there was more magical freedom. But after everything His Majesty endured, you can understand why he would want to curtail magic."

"That's what Dot said." I lean forward in my chair. "She told me he's suffered from the effects of strong, uncontrolled magic. His own, obviously, but she seemed to hint there was more to it."

The old man sighs, picking up his teacup with a tremulous hand. I wait while he sips from it and sets it back down with a rattling chink. "You grew up in the borderlands, yes? Far west of here?"

"Yes."

"Then you were spared the horror of the Cheimhold Invasion."

"I knew of it," I say. "I was eighteen. We were scared, in my village—scared that the trouble would come our way."

"The trouble came here." Jonald jabs his chair with a bent-knuckled finger for emphasis. "It came from the North mountains. It came from our closest ally and strongest trading partner. There was no warning, no hint of animosity or greed on their part. No sign that they wanted to overtake our country and absorb us into theirs. We were unprepared."

"It must have been horrible," I murmur.

His wrinkled lips shake for a moment, and tears shimmer in his eyes. "You cannot understand," he says, "what it means for a young prince to have his home city torn open. The Triune Arch was broken by magic. Parts of the city were destroyed. Whole villages between here and the northern border were slaughtered. People forget…"

His voice trembles, and he takes a moment to steady himself, lips working. "They remember the fire of the young prince. But they forget what destroyed him, inside. They forget the true enemy."

I wait, tense and listening with all my might. I feel as if I'm on a cliff's edge, poised on the brink of some awful truth.

"I'll tell you something." Jonald lifts a shaking hand. "I'm not supposed to tell, but you'll keep this secret, because I know yours. Among the invaders was the second man I've met with your kind of power. A Rotter, a man who could corrode bodies. He wielded lines of black magic, not gold, and he killed many of our soldiers. He worked his way through the fray to King Prillian, Perish's father. And he rotted him. Rotted him, child, do you understand? You cannot conceive the horror I felt seeing my king, my oldest friend, with parts of him corroded and seeping, as if he was a living corpse. His bones, so brittle they would snap at the slightest impact."

"Gods," I choke.

"I kept him alive as long as I could. For nearly a year I tried to mend him, and other healers tried as well. But that kind of magic can only be reversed by the healer who wrought it."

"I didn't know," I breathe.

"No one was told the King's true condition, or what had produced it. That was the young prince's decision. He did not want the healers of our kingdom to be suspected of concealing such dark power. He was afraid people might panic and hunt down healers out of fear. But because of that incident, and the breaking of the arch by the Cheimhold wind-wielders, Prince Perish changed the levels of permissible magic, forbid its study or expansion, and extended the powers of the Ricters."

Jonald sips from his cup again. "As King Prillian lay ill, the prince took the reins of the kingdom. He was not alone—he had his two cousins and seven of his closest friends to support him. A band of ten they were, inseparable. Strong. They rode together to quell the unrest growing in the South. Our kingdom was fragile, still recovering from the invasion. We could not afford attackers from without *and* within."

"What happened?" I breathe. "Do you know why he did it? Why he burned everything?"

"When he came back, he would only say that our enemies were defeated. It was obvious he'd lost control, but he would never admit to that. He wants to seem strong, you see. Like his father." Jonald's watery eyes lift to mine. "We never told his father what he'd done. The king was suffering enough—he'd been lingering on the brink of death for almost a year by then. He died shortly after the Ashlands Massacre. After Perish took the crown, he closed the borders. Ended most of the trade, focused on becoming an insular, self-sustaining nation, with very little help from magic or other countries."

I've never heard the tale told like this. I've never been able to connect the invasion, the former King's illness, and the tragedy in the South the way Jonald does.

"It's fascinating," I say slowly, "how a person's perspective on something changes the memory of it. Does that make sense? I'm not sure I'm saying it right."

The old healer nods. "Memories are fragile things, most fickle when they stem from a collective consciousness. Yet they are also the foundation on which we construct our truth. When a warped memory is crystallized into stone, and people build upon it, the future is skewed as well."

After several moments of quiet thought, during which we both stare into the flickering fire, Jonald and I talk of healing magic. I've barely spoken to anyone else who possesses my ability, and I realize I have a voracious appetite for learning more about my powers. But there's too much to discuss in one night, and I can tell that the elderly man is tiring. He's beginning to struggle to find his words, and that seems to frustrate him.

"I should go," I tell him, rising. "But thank you so much for speaking with me. I wonder if I could return sometime? I have so much more to learn, and you are a treasury of wisdom."

"Silver-tongued girl." He smiles. "Of course you may come back. I'd be delighted."

"Thank you!" Impulsively, I hug him. "Anything I can do for you before I go? I'd be happy to soothe any aches you may feel."

His wrinkled face brightens. "That would be a delight. The King will hire me a healer whenever I need it, of course, but I don't like to bother him. And there's only so much that magic can do for this old body anyway. But I won't say no to a little treatment."

"It would be a pleasure," I tell him. "I owe you, remember?"

I angle myself more fully toward him in the chair and extend my hands, letting my eyes drift shut while my magical senses expand, seeking out any pain or malfunction in his body. I can feel the slowing of organs and cells, the unstoppable march of time carrying him toward the end. There's nothing I can do to halt that systemic, natural progression, but I can ease his way, extend his time a little.

With my magic, I calm the inflamed joints, ease the function of bowels and kidneys, strengthen the heart muscle. In the process I discover several spots of mutated cells in his body—small tumors that are bound to grow rapidly. I've encountered this kind of disease in people before. It's not something my healing magic can fix, but suddenly I wonder if the other side of my ability might be useful here. With it, I could potentially erode those tumors, erase the mutating cells.

As I'm considering the possibility, I can feel something shifting, changing inside me. When I open my eyes, I'm horrified to see the lines of my golden magic darkening to black. Quickly I withdraw all my power, sucking it back into myself.

Jonald's eyes were closed—he didn't see the dark magic uncurling from my hands.

I leap up, forcing a bright smile. "I have to go, but I hope that helps! Thank you again, so much!" I pick up the lamp I brought with me, and I bolt from the room.

I stand in the hallway, trembling so hard I can barely hold the lamp. It's been so long since I used that side of myself—I forgot how it felt. My corrosion magic is a rush of sweet darkness through my veins, and addictive, vindictive potency. What did Jonald call wielders of my kind? Rotters. I am a Rotter.

I don't like it. It's a disgusting name for a disgusting power. Why did I think, even for a moment, of using it on Jonald? What if I'd destroyed more than just the tumors? What if it had gone too far? I could have accidentally killed him, in the horrible way King Prillian was killed.

How awful it must have been for Perish, watching his father's decayed body struggle to cling to life, watching the healers try in vain to save him for all those months. And then the mysterious incident in the Ashlands—Perish was the only one to come back, which means he lost his cousins and his friends in that inferno, along with many of his citizens. And when he returned, his father died as well.

The sheer loss he suffered—loss of his magical control, loss of his loved ones—no wonder he's so guarded. No wonder he has erected so many shields between him and everyone else. The shields are there to protect others from his magic, yes—but they're also in place to guard a wounded heart.

Still pondering what I've learned, I wander the corridors until I find a major artery of the castle again. I follow it slowly, lost in thought, passing the occasional guard along the way. It must be so boring to be a guard in a place like this. Hours of standing still with nothing to do. Sometimes I wonder if all the suits of armor really have guards in them, or if some of them are just for show. I suppose I should figure that out, for the benefit of the Undoing.

I'm becoming increasingly certain that I don't want to help the rebels at all. But Rince hinted there might be some sort of retaliation if I back out now. And I can't keep making excuses and stringing Rince along, because eventually his contact inside the palace will make a move. Before she does, I must figure out who she is so I can protect Perish—the Ash King—from her.

Or I could tell Perish everything. But if I do that, he might want me to turn informant against Rince and Brayda. He'll want to use me to trap them. I won't allow that—I won't permit my friends to be caught and tortured for information.

Which means I'm stuck between the throne and the anarchists, and I have no idea what to do.

Unexpectedly, my stomach rumbles. I ate early, and it's quite late now—besides which, I tend to get hungry when I'm worried.

A couple days ago my maid told me there's a secret pantry in the central wing. It's in the upstairs hallway at the very end, past my room, past the King's suite, and beyond several other chambers that used to house royal family members. The servants store dry goods there—crackers, cookies, candied fruit—so they don't have to go all the way to the kitchens when a royal wants a snack.

It takes me a while to find my way back to the right corridor, but when I do, I walk past the shadowy figures of the guards and head straight for the secret pantry. It's exactly where my maid said it would be—right behind a portrait of the Ash King's great-grandfather and his husband.

The door is narrow, but the room beyond is larger than I expected, big enough for several people to stand comfortably. I set my lamp on a half-empty shelf and inspect the contents of the place—wrapped cheeses, crisp crackers, bottles of wine, tins of cookies, boxes of tea. A wholesome scent of cinnamon and herbs pervades the room, and my stomach growls again. I pry open a tin and sneak a cookie. It's delicious—crumbly and buttery.

The door of the pantry creaks, and I whip around, startled and guilty, brushing cookie crumbs from my lips.

A hooded figure stands in the doorway.

26

"I'm so sorry," I say to the shadowy stranger. "My maid told me about this pantry—I thought it would be all right if I—if I…" My voice trails off as the figure advances. The glow of the lamp glimmers on a dark, velvety robe. The person's face is in shadow, but the fingers are male, strong and lined with rings. A wisp of silver-white hair slips from beneath the hood.

"Your Majesty," I say, relieved. But my relief dissipates when he grips the neckline of my dress and yanks me closer to him. His eyes burn orange in the recesses of the hood.

"We had an arrangement," he hisses. "You said you'd meet me tonight. You weren't in your room."

"I was exploring the castle."

His hood falls back, his beautiful, harsh face bared to me. His voice is hoarse with rage. "What else were you exploring?"

Why is he so angry? Desperately I search for water—there's some in jugs on one of the shelves. If I can get over there and unstopper one of them, I'll have something to protect myself.

"I'm not sure what you're talking about," I say. "I walked through some older parts of the castle, found the servants' quarters, talked to Jonald—"

"Jonald? Why?"

"He's a healer, I'm a healer—we have things to talk about—gods!" I whimper as he hauls me closer still. His fingers are smoking, burning through the fabric of my dress.

"You'll ruin it!" I gasp.

A growl is my only answer. He rips the weakened fabric, tearing my gown wide open down the center. It's a thicker material, so I didn't wear a corset under it, and now my breasts are bared to him, peaked with sudden, illicit need. I suck in a sharp breath, my core tingling and heating in spite of my fear.

"What are you doing?" I whisper.

"Shut up." He shoves me back, and my shoulders crash into a cupboard door. The King lunges forward, crushing me to the wood, raking up my skirts. Frantic and rough, his fingers catch my underwear and drag it down. He parts his robe, his erection jutting through the opening.

He pauses for two seconds—just enough time for me to protest what he's about to do. When I don't object, he seizes one of my legs and pins it up, arched, against the cupboard, exposing my opening to him.

"Not that I'm complaining," I whisper, wrapping my arms around his neck, "but what is this about?"

He grabs one of my wrists and slams it against the wall above my head. "Don't fucking touch me," he snaps, eyes flaming brighter.

Shocked, I pull back my other hand. I'm pinned against the cupboards by my wrist and thigh, splayed open for him, and despite my fear of his new mood, I'm violently aroused.

He drives into me without warning, and I voice a tiny shriek. He grinds his brow against mine, skull on skull, so hard it hurts. "Shut. Up." He's shaking. Whatever emotions are rolling through his body, they're overpowering him completely.

His hips jerk forward, ramming his length deeper inside me. "I'm going to drive the memory of his cock out of you," he hisses. His body slams against mine, over and over, dark velvet and hard muscles burning like heated iron. "You won't remember it. I'm the damn king. I don't fucking share, Cailin."

"Heartsfire... is this about Rince? The artist?"

He vents a guttural sound of rage, brimming with ruinous promise, and he batters into me, a frenzy of hard thrusts. I can barely think through the vicious onslaught, through the lewd wet sounds his body is making with mine. I'm flushing, liquefying. Exquisite lines of tingling pleasure snake through my belly, twining, twisting, tightening—

The Ash King releases my wrist and grips my face, glaring into my eyes, his face contorted with passion. Nothing elegant or controlled about him now. "Don't think about him," he growls.

"*You* need to stop thinking about him." In spite of his order, I reach for him, cupping his head in my hands. "Listen—I didn't sleep with that artist today."

The Ash King shoves himself up me, so deep and brutal that I gasp, because he hit some tremulous glowing spot inside me and I'm poised, quivering, pinned in place by a scorching, suspended ecstasy I can't quite reach. I desperately want him to thrust again, but he stills for a moment.

"The guards heard you," he says darkly. "They told me."

"It was fake. I used to sleep with him, back home, and I was going to today, but then—I couldn't go through with it. I faked those sounds so he wouldn't be embarrassed." I never intended to sleep with Rince this afternoon, but it's the only plausible excuse for him coming to my room.

The Ash King holds me to the wall with his cock and hips, still clutching my jaw. "You're lying."

"I'm not." I twist my head, jerking free of the face grip. "I promise I'm not."

Slowly he pulls back a little and thrusts into me again so hard I squeal, shivering on the verge of a climax. "Swear it."

"I swear on the Heartsfire of my home mountain."

"A stupid vow."

Savagely I dig my fingers into the muscles of his shoulders. "That's our most sacred vow, bastard."

He catches my thighs and hooks my legs over his hips. I'm losing my mind to the heat of his hard flesh surging deep inside me, and I whimper, helpless, needy, hitching myself farther onto his length.

"Still hate me?" he whispers, with one more slow slick thrust, deep, so deep.

"So much—I hate you so—gods, I'm coming... I'm coming..." The tingling blaze of the orgasm floods through me, and I convulse around him, gasping. He cries out, too, his heart thundering against my breast. I can feel the rhythmic spasms of his release and mine, synchronized.

I can't kiss him. I won't. I want to.

He has to kiss me first.

I press my cheek to his, relishing the smooth warmth of his skin. I breathe him in, the sweating, panicked, passionate heat of him, the dark essence of his jealousy. Nothing has ever tasted sweeter to me.

But he's unfair too. Expecting me to be only his, while he belongs to the other girls, to the Favored.

"You're so selfish," I whisper.

"I know." His palm strokes my thigh.

"I hate that about you."

A long, shuddering inhale, then he says, "I hate how you despise me, when you don't know me at all."

"So tell me," I breathe against his ear. "Help me know you."

"No. This is just sex."

"Of course. It's sex and secrets."

He chuckles, runs a hand over my hair. Then he eases out of me and we separate.

"We dripped on the floor," I whisper, scandalized.

"Get your snack," he says. "I'll clean it up and come to you. Don't wander off before I get there."

Holding my ruined dress together, I carry some cheese, crackers and wine back to my room. My insides have that warm, tender glow I always get after thorough lovemaking. Quickly I put on a nightdress and shove the ruined gown under my bed. Maybe I can have my maid smuggle it to the refuse bin tomorrow.

The Ash King comes to my room in his velvety robe, with his snowy hair pouring over one shoulder. He sits on my bed, and I pass him a bit of cheese on a cracker.

"What secrets do you crave, Healer?" he says, inspecting the food rather than looking at me.

"Whatever you need to tell."

But what I really want is for him to tell me the one secret he has told no one else.

He pops the cracker into his mouth and chews thoughtfully while I take two mugs from the washstand and pour wine into them.

"They say you never get drunk." I hand him a mug.

"I do. But not outside the walls of the palace. I don't want liquor to make me slow and stupid around any of these cutthroat nobles." He swirls the wine, wincing. "Wine from a mug, Healer? Seems wrong. I have glasses in my room."

I quirk an eyebrow at him and drink from my own mug, a clear challenge. He smiles a little and sips. "I lost my mother a few years before the Cheimhold Invasion."

It's such an abrupt beginning that I nearly choke on my swallow of wine. But I manage to get it down, and to nod compassionately. "How did it happen?"

"Riding accident. The horse threw her, and she broke her neck. No healer around at the time. Once the consciousness slips from the body, it's too late, as I'm sure you know."

I nod, picturing glassy eyes and sagging mouths, skin pocked with plague boils. People I didn't reach in time.

I take another swallow of wine.

"After her death, my aunt was like a mother to me," the King says. "She and her two sons, my cousins—they lived here in the palace with my father and I. I don't remember my uncle—he died long ago."

So much death. He's felt so much grief, and it hurts me.

"I cannot describe the invasion, Cailin," he says, and my heart jumps at my name, my actual *name*, falling so easily from his mouth. It's one of a few precious times he has said it, rather than calling me "Healer."

"It was the worst time of my life," he muses, still avoiding my eyes. "To see people with whom I'd trained, caroused, and laughed—to see them falling, one after another, and I couldn't save them—to watch the Triune Arch be broken. To witness my father being corroded, rotted by the foulest of dark magic—" He sets his mug down on the tray and rises from the bed, stalking the room. His fingertips flicker with fire.

The idea of that wielder, that Rotter, makes him so angry. What would he think of me, if he knew what I can do?

I draw water from the washstand, inwardly blessing my maid for always keeping the pitchers full—and I create a glimmering liquid hand, which I guide toward him. The watery fingers lace with his, quenching the flame without causing the burning, hissing steam that scorched us both before.

So my intent does matter, then. If I'm defending myself, repulsing an attack, that strength of purpose infuses the water, changes its quality somehow. And when my intent is to calm, to soothe, the water does exactly that, and no more.

"I've heard tales of the invasion," I say, careful not to betray what Jonald shared with me. "A terrible time. I'm sorry you had to be in the center of it."

"I'd never had to fight before that day. I fought during training, of course—but not with deadly intent. I had never killed anyone. We were at peace, you see. But during the invasion I killed, and I killed, and still they kept coming."

"You fought them off, though," I murmur. "You and the army. You stopped it."

"Yes, they retreated, but we didn't stop anything." He whirls to face me, fire glowing through the tendons of his throat.

I rise from the bed and take another mug from the washstand, guiding water into it. "Drink," I tell him. "No more wine, or things could get rather explosive."

As he gulps the water down, the dangerous glow fades.

"How does your water hurt me *and* ease me?" he asks, low.

"I've been trying to figure that out. I'd have to ask another water-wielder, but I can only guess that my intent affects the characteristics of the water itself." I risk a bold look into his eyes. "If only someone would allow more magical learning and research…"

He turns away, scoffing impatiently. "Ah, yes. The part where you believe that because I came inside you, you get to instruct me, *change* me."

"Don't be so crude. You know I'm right."

"You aren't, though. The more freedom wielders have to explore their magic, the deeper they delve into sick, wrong, twisted applications that should never be thought of, or allowed to exist."

"Greater knowledge and understanding is never wrong," I counter. "Evil doesn't come from magic, but from people's hearts."

"You think I don't know that?" He vents a harsh laugh. "I know it better than anyone else in this whole kingdom."

"Is that so? Enlighten me, oh Great All-knowing One."

"You want to know? Fine. Sit." He points to the bed, eyes blazing.

I'm not afraid to challenge him, but this is not the right moment. He's wavering on the brink of divulging something momentous to me—I can feel it. If I play my cards right, he will tell me everything.

27

I sit, folding my hands in my lap, while the Ash King resumes his pacing back and forth across my bedroom.

"It was months after the invasion. My father was rotting away, cursed by a disgusting wretch of a two-faced Cheimhold wielder, so I had to take on the responsibilities of the kingdom. I received word of an uprising in the south—anarchists who wanted to overthrow the crown while my father was weak. This kingdom was already shaken to its foundations by the recent invasion—we could not afford to be divided from within. So I took a company of soldiers and nine of my closest friends with me to the South. Those nine had battled beside me during the invasion, and I trusted each of them with my whole heart. My two cousins were among them."

He pulls his long hair over his shoulder and begins braiding it, messily, nervously, as he's walking back and forth.

"When we reached the southern city of Irafhen, we disguised ourselves, spied among the people, and discovered a terrible truth—that Cheimhold had been funding the anarchists. When the invasion failed, they decided to destabilize our kingdom from within. Money, weapons, supplies—vast quantities of support for the rebels was coming through our northern borders and being channeled to the Undoing in the South."

My stomach does a sick roll of dread. The Undoing was supported and funded by our enemies? Do Rince and Brayda know this?

"Is Cheimhold still funding the anarchists?" I ask.

"If they are, they're doing it with much greater difficulty. Why do you think I closed the borders and cut off trade? We cannot trust anyone, not even those who appear to be our allies. Better to be insular and self-sufficient, dependent on no one."

His fists are clenched so tightly I can see white bone through the skin of his knuckles.

"My friends and I discovered that the Undoing was woven into all levels of society in Irafhen, and indeed throughout the whole southern part of the kingdom," he continues. "They were lying to my people. The citizens, gullible and terrified, were swallowing every untruth. I was at a loss, unsure how to purge the instigators and arrange peace. And then my cousin Nikkan suggested a banquet to which we could invite the leaders of the southern towns and talk things over. He said we might be able to devise a way to pacify the Undoing."

The hollowness of his tone tells me we're nearing the tragic end of the tale. With trembling fingers I lift my mug of wine and take a few slow sips.

The King looks at me, embers of old pain glowing deep in his dark eyes. "The Undoing is skilled at persuading the young and the reckless. So very clever with words and promises. They create the most fervent of zealots."

Rince's eager face leaps into my mind, and I swallow hard, averting my gaze.

"I didn't know they had touched someone I loved," the Ash King continues quietly. "Not until my cousin

Nikkan, my brother, my fellow warrior—he rose from the banquet table and shouted, 'To the glory of anarchy!' and smashed a strange-looking bottle. A powdery green smoke curled from the shards, spreading through the room and seeping out the doors and windows into the air. All around the table, my friends fell, choking, frothing, dying. As his own lungs spasmed from the poison, Nikkan slit the throat of the healer who had accompanied us. Not that the healer could have saved us anyway—most healers cannot counter the effect of toxins."

"Heartsfire," I breathe.

"The leaders of every southern city died at once, alongside my friends. And that was not the end of it. The toxin was a magical one, devised in Cheimhold. It crawled from person to person like a plague, and each body it touched served as fuel, enabling it to spread farther. Within hours, the entire city was infected—people dropping and dying in the street, in their houses. Only those with allegiance to the rebels had been given an antidote."

"How did you survive?"

His fingers close around the bedpost. "I was able to burn the poison out of my lungs. I had to keep doing it over and over, as more toxin seeped into my body—and I was weakening from lack of clean air, but I managed to find one of the surviving rebels. I forced him to show me where he'd hidden a spare dose of the antidote. I wanted more of the antidote to save my people—but he said there was no more, and no time."

The Ash King picks up his mug of wine again and drinks it all down, despite my earlier warning. "And he was right. I dragged him with me through the city. They were all dead—everyone except the traitors who knew of the attack. The toxin was like nothing I've seen before or since. One breath, a handful of seconds, and the victims died in contorted agony."

I nod, my throat tight with emotion.

"I went back and fetched my horse from the stables of the Lord Mayor," the Ash King continues. "The magical toxin did not harm the animals—a small mercy. With my rebel prisoner, I rode out of the city. We were nearly shot down by rebels as we rode. Once we cleared the city walls, I saw green fumes sweeping across the land, leaping from farmhouse to roadside inn and to villages beyond. This was a plague designed to destroy all life in our kingdom, leaving it thinly populated by those with allegiance to the Undoing. I could not allow it time to spread any farther. So I rode to the edge of the toxic fog, and then I released my magic."

"You burned everything," I whisper.

"A cleansing fire, destroying the bodies, the plague itself, and every traitor, along with their families. All the animals, the buildings, the possessions, the crops—I wiped it all away. Once I began I could not stop. My anger and pain were too great."

The ceramic mug is heating in his hand, its glaze melting. "I cannot describe the overwhelming power I felt during those hours. I was unleashed, yes—but more than that, I was connected to the land, to the fires of every southern mountain. I could perceive the edges of the magical plague, as you might perceive the edges of a wound. I made sure that I burned it all, and more."

"Your cousin, Nikkan—he didn't take the antidote?"

"No. Perhaps he did not wish to live past that single act of manic devotion to his wretched cause." The Ash King's jaw tightens, and his eyes glimmer with unshed tears. After a moment he says, "The rebel I took prisoner—he said the poison had taken years to develop and was difficult to make. He said it required the soul essence of many wielders, and he promised that Cheimhold had no more of it. They planned to let it fester within our kingdom, confined by our mountainous borders, until it wore off in a few days—and then they would enter without resistance and take possession of Bolcan."

"You killed the prisoner, of course."

"Burned him like a candle, and took immense pleasure in it." The Ash King's smile is dark, dreadful. "I'd promised to let him live if he told me everything he knew. I lied."

"I don't understand why you didn't tell everyone else in the kingdom what really happened," I venture. "Why let them think you slaughtered so many people without reason?"

"Telling the truth would only have caused a panic," he says. "Think about it. A magical poison that kills within seconds, with no remaining doses of antidote, and no other cure? Imagine the paranoia that would have ensued—a pointless panic, because I eradicated both the toxin and the rebels. The threat was gone."

"But there's more to it than that, isn't there?" I ask softly. "Your cousin."

"Yes, I wanted to protect his name. To keep anyone from knowing what he did, who he had become. My aunt believes that I killed her sons, and she hates me. Moved out of the palace the day after I returned, and hasn't spoken to me since. Better she despise me than know the truth—that her son was a traitor. I may have destroyed the cities and killed the rebels, but he was responsible for everyone else. Thousands of our people. Five years later, and I still do not understand why he did it."

The Ash King sits heavily on the bed. "I didn't want to leave my friends there, Cailin. You don't know what it's like to be dining with your truest comrades, the companions you love most in all the world, and to watch their smiles vanish and their eyes change from humor to terror. I dream about it often. Sometimes I resist sleep for fear of the dreams."

I shove the tray of food aside and scoot nearer to him, placing my hand on his shoulder. But it's not enough, so I wrap my arms around him.

"You can't tell anyone," he says.

"I won't."

"They're all so frightened of me," he whispers. "Even the people I've known since I was a child. They don't see me anymore. They only see what I've done. I lost everything to that massacre, everything. My people are waiting for me to explode again. And I won't lie—it's a possibility. Something was unlocked inside me that day—I drew upon power I should have never accessed, and it changed me, down to my very bones. You saw the proof of that, inside my body."

I grip him tighter. "You saved the rest of the kingdom. You should tell everyone how it really happened."

"You think they would believe me after all this time?" He looks down into my face, his eyes sorrowful. "I've waited too long now. If I was going to tell the truth, I should have done so after the Ashlands massacre. But I did not. I kept it all to myself. I shut down every avenue of access into this kingdom, and my strategy worked. I am feared, not only by my people, but by our enemies. Word of what I did spread into Cheimhold itself. They do not dare attack us again, by any means, lest the Ash King of Bolcan burn them to dust."

"I'm not afraid of you," I tell him.

"You are." He sighs, setting his chin on my hair. "I've seen it in your eyes."

"Maybe sometimes," I concede. "Especially at first. Less often now."

I try to keep the next words back, but they slip out anyway. "Have you told any of the Favored about this?"

He shakes off my embrace and glares at me. "The telling of a tale doesn't make you special."

I should be hurt by that caustic comment, but instead a smile spreads over my face. I can't stop grinning. "I'm the only one you've told."

"Don't look so damn pleased with yourself." He's trying to be stern, but I can tell he's fighting a smile, so I let my whole heart shine through my eyes. For a moment, I'm as vulnerable with him as he has been with me. His gaze brightens, a tender glow suffusing his eyes.

This conversation is far more intimate than anything physical we've done, and we both know it.

"I want you beside me," he says, and my heart leaps. "In my bed," he hastens to say. "I want you to sleep beside me tonight. I think you could keep away the dreams."

I take a moment to breathe through my disappointment, to separate my affection for him from my personal pride.

Delicately I shift away from him, so our bodies are no longer touching. "I had a stuffed fire-weasel when I was a child. I used to cuddle it whenever I was frightened in the dark. An inanimate thing, without heart or feelings. Strange how it gave me so much comfort."

The King stares at me as if he thinks I've gone mad.

"If you need comfort," I say crisply, "may I suggest your Majesty finds a pillow to hug? Or perhaps the palace seamstress can sew you a stuffed fire-weasel. I only sleep beside men who are committed to me—heart, soul, and body."

He rises abruptly and walks to the door between our rooms. "But our other arrangement remains?" he asks, without turning around.

"Sex and secrets," I murmur with a smile. "Yes. It remains. But I'm not sure I despise you quite as passionately as before."

"A pity," he replies. "I shall have to reawaken your hatred somehow. It's so refreshing."

"I'm sure you'll find some way to anger me," I say dryly.

"Rest well, Healer. My potential brides are battling each other tomorrow, and it will be bloody. You'll need your full strength."

And with the swiftest of fleeting smiles over his shoulder, he leaves my room.

Once he's gone, I eat far too many crackers with cheese and drink another two mugs of wine. Without the wine's soothing influence, I'm sure I would not be able to sleep. My mind has broadened, my perspective has changed, and I'm left with a multitude of important questions.

Should I keep the King's confidence, or should I find a way to contact Rince and tell him what I've learned? If he knew the truth, surely he would realize, as I have, that the King is far less menacing than we thought. His strict laws have reasons behind them, and most of the people he burned in the southern lands were already dead, killed by the Undoing, with the shadow of Cheimhold behind it all.

But why should Rince believe me? What proof do I have beyond the word of the very King who has the power to destroy an entire region? Brayda would deny it all, and claim that it was a trick. She'd say the King told me that story just to soften me up, to secure my loyalty.

But it was no trick. He was holding back powerful emotions the whole time he spoke to me—genuine emotions of sorrow, betrayal, anger, and pain.

Does he make all the right choices? No. Were each of his decisions without fault? Also no. Is he sometimes arrogant, cruel, reactive, and harsh? Certainly. But he does not deserve the death that the rebels want to give him. He's doing his best to protect the kingdom.

I can't break my ties to the Undoing. Rince warned of possible consequences if I tried—and I need to keep my ear to the door, to find out if they are still being supported by our enemies in Cheimhold. If I can prove that, I'll have something with which to convince my friends. Maybe I can get Brayda and Rince away from the rebels before they are manipulated into killing themselves for a false cause.

And before any of that, I need to find out which of the ten remaining contestants is an anarchist sympathizer. Because I'll throw myself in the fires of Analoir Doiteain before I let her assassinate the man I'm beginning to love.

28

I thought I'd learned not to underestimate the Favored—their skill, their savagery.

But watching them battle each other in the Réimse Ríoga is a revelation.

They fight one on one, and they are allowed to request any weapon they please. The first two matches are already over—Sabre bested Morani after a long fight, and Adalasia beat Samay easily. Sabre, Morani, and Samay came out of the matches with terrible wounds—I'm still working on reconstructing the slab of flesh that was sheared off Sabre's shoulder by Morani's scythe. Sabre and I stand together at the edge of the arena so I can keep an eye on the fight between Teagan and Beaori.

Beaori plays dirty, and I suspect she's going to try something nasty before the match is done. Technically there are no rules—anything goes, short of actually killing your opponent. But I've noticed the other girls behaving with honor—giving the other fighter a moment to pick up her weapon if she drops it, not biting or pulling hair, that sort of thing.

I don't expect Beaori to show such mercy.

My fingers hover near Sabre's wounded shoulder, the golden light doing its work while I try to divide my focus between healing and watchfulness.

Teagan is fighting with a long, thin sword and a short knife. I remember the skill with which she fought during the rebel attack on our way to the Capital. On her own two feet, with enough freedom to move, she's even more talented—graceful, ruthless, with technique that looks perfect to my untrained eyes.

But Beaori is equally dangerous. She wields a long chain with a curved knife at each end. The two women are shining with sweat, clad in little more than leather vests and pants cut to mid-thigh. My maid, Enna, brought me similar attire this morning—a blue bandeau and blue shorts, with a leather vest that's a size too small for me and deepens my cleavage dramatically.

When I raised my eyebrows, Enna offered me an alternative outfit with more coverage; but I decided to wear the scanty outfit after all. The clothes the King selected for me are reminiscent of the ones I wore when I first met him. Perhaps I should despise him for dressing me to his pleasure; but I find it charming.

I risk taking my eyes off the fighting pair and glance in the direction of his balcony. He's standing at its edge, leaning eagerly forward. What man wouldn't enjoy watching two strong, beautiful women fight for him?

He made it clear at the beginning of this challenge that at least two of the Favored—possibly more—would be leaving the competition afterward. That declaration has made the matches even more frenzied. Which was no doubt his intent.

A cry startles me. When I look back at the fighters, my lungs constrict and my blood runs cold.

One of Beaori's knives has hooked into Teagan's back. It's lodged in her spine. She's choking, white-faced. Her hand loosens, and her sword falls to the sand.

Beaori doesn't hesitate. She jerks on the handle of her other knife, yanking the chain short, wrapping it around and around her own arm as she pulls Teagan closer. Teagan falls—she's being dragged through the dirt by the blade in her spine.

Beaori hauls her nearer, right to her feet. She reaches down and grips Teagan's red braid, jerking her head up.

But Teagan still grips her knife, and she slashes across the back of Beaori's ankle. Beaori screams with rage and pain. She nearly falls, but she manages to stand on one leg, and her second blade whips toward Teagan's neck.

I yell, leaping forward—but Teagan rolls out of the way just in time.

Sabre catches me with her good arm. "You can't interfere, Healer."

"She's going to kill Teagan!"

"Maybe not. And if she does, she'll be eliminated."

I jerk against her grip. "Is that all you care about? One less rival?"

Sabre lets me go, fixing me with a stern look. "I didn't come to the Calling to make friends. I came to win the throne."

"Why?" I resume healing her, pushing frantic energy into her muscles so I can finish the task and focus on the fighters, who are both tangled in the dirt, stabbing at each other. Sooner or later one of them will secure a killing hold, at which point they are supposed to stop and wait for the match to be called.

"Why?" Sabre scoffs. "Why would anyone want a throne? Renown and riches for me, power and prestige for my family, a handsome husband in my bed, a legacy of children who will continue to reign. And there are things I want to change."

My ears perk up at that. I finish the healing of Sabre's shoulder and watch Teagan slash Beaori's cheek before trying to crawl away. It's a miracle Teagan is still fighting. More than a miracle, really. With a blade lodged in that part of her spine, she shouldn't be able to move at all.

My stomach drops.

Not a miracle. Magic.

Heartsfire.

Is Teagan hiding a special power?

She did survive a massive wound to the neck during the gauntlet challenge. I considered it luck that I reached her in time before she bled out, but maybe it was more than that. Maybe any other girl would have died within seconds, not minutes.

Teagan's parents are wealthy—they could have paid a Ricter to look the other way and not report any latent abilities. They also could have paid off the Ricters who have circulated through the palace parties during the Calling, though that seems less likely.

I can't say anything, not without proof. I will investigate later.

Right now, I have more questions for Sabre. "What things do you want to change if you become queen?"

"Everything is too restricted," she mutters. "Magic, commerce, taxes. I want to loosen all the laws and border restrictions."

Does Sabre realize how treasonous her words are? How close they sound to the philosophy of the Undoing?

When I questioned the girls before, Sabre was diplomatic in her answers. And when the Ash King spoke of her, he mentioned her firm loyalty to the crown. But she comes from the South, near the Ashlands. Perhaps she expressed exaggerated loyalty so he wouldn't suspect her of any anarchist leanings.

Whatever the reason, she's being a little too open about her political views now, probably because of the blood loss and the blow to the head she suffered during her match. Those injuries will have to wait until all the fights are over. I can't spend all my healer power on one person, when I have no way of knowing the extent of the other injuries I'll have to treat.

"Go lie down in the back room, please," I tell her crisply. "I'll take care of your blood loss and head wound later."

"But I want to see the other matches."

"Go. Healer's orders."

Grumbling, she shuffles unsteadily toward the arena exit.

I turn back to the fight just in time to see a bloodied Teagan plunging her knife into Beaori's breast.

29

Teagan halts mid-stab, bloody spit flying through her clenched teeth with every hissed breath. She's astride Beaori, and Beaori doesn't try to throw her off. That was the killing blow.

The King's herald calls the match in Teagan's favor, and contest aides hurry forward to help the battered contestants to the sidelines. I scan Beaori's wound quickly—Teagan's knife sliced through the flesh of the breast, but didn't get near the heart. I seal off the blood flow from that injury and the ankle wound, but I don't heal them completely yet. That will come later.

"Can you do anything about the pain, Healer?" Beaori's voice is thick with agony.

I meet her gaze, remembering the look on her face as she aimed her arrows at me. "I've done all I can for now," I tell her sweetly. "I need to conserve my energy."

Fury sparks in her eyes.

Before she can say anything else, I turn away and approach Teagan. She lies in the shadow of the arena wall, on her side. Her face and hair are coated with blood and grime.

A contest aide kneels beside her, his fingers fluttering anxiously over the hilt of Beaori's hooked knife, which protrudes between Teagan's shoulder blades. "Should I pull it out?" he asks.

"In a moment." I kneel beside her as well, sending tendrils of my magic into the wound, probing down to the spinal cord and vertebrae. As I thought. She should have been paralyzed by this. The match should have gone to Beaori.

Teagan blinks at me through blood-matted eyelashes, and in her green eyes I read awareness and fear. She knows that I know.

Maybe she is counting on our previous history to keep me silent. After all, I know her family. I've healed them. It's not a strong connection—I don't owe any allegiance there, like the other healers who serve nobility—but suddenly I understand why the King was so anxious to find someone unconnected, someone without bias.

Perhaps I'm not as unbiased as either of us thought. Because I want Teagan to win. Or I did, until this moment. Lies, bribes, and unfair advantages—is that the kind of queen the Ash King needs?

"Pull it out," I tell the aide. He grips the weapon and tugs it out of her spine with difficulty—it's stuck in the bone. Once it's out, I tell him to take it away and clean it. He obeys, and Teagan and I are left alone for a few moments.

Alone is relative in this situation—we're still in the arena, within full view of the crowd of onlookers. But they're distracted for the moment, watching the cleanup of the combat site as workers collect Teagan's sword, rake away the bloodstained sand, and scatter fresh sand in its place. A trio of jugglers walk from one end of the arena to the other, leaping and cartwheeling as they go.

As I seal Teagan's wound, I bend close to her ear. "What is it? Your ability?"

"Survival," she whispers. "When you healed me from plague last year, I'd already been sick with it for much longer than the others. I simply—didn't die. I can't heal myself or anyone else. But while mortal wounds and illnesses do affect me, they don't kill me. My spirit hangs on. My brain keeps functioning even when it shouldn't."

"It's an unfair advantage," I whisper. "A Ricter should have caught it."

"It's a barely detectable talent. Only a very powerful Ricter can identify it." Her cracked lips tighten.

"Your father paid off a Ricter," I say. "Maybe more than one."

"Don't tell the King, Cailin. Please." She fumbles for my hand, squeezing it. "I would make a good queen. You know I would."

"It was you, wasn't it?" I say quietly. "You told the Ash King about me somehow. Not personally, because then he would have suspected a connection—no, you hired someone else to tell him about me. You wanted me in this position, so I'd feel obliged to keep your secret if I discovered it."

She closes her eyes. "I *hoped* you would keep it, yes. I consider us friends."

I barely know her, and she's putting me in this position? I'm already keeping a secret for Khloe—can I conceal this for Teagan?

"If friendship isn't enough," she whispers, so low I can barely hear her. "I'm willing to add a monetary incentive."

I'm spared from answering, because two aides are approaching. "If Lady Teagan is stable, we'll move her to the recovery room," one of them offers.

312

"She's stable," I answer. But I don't deaden her pain, either. Maybe it's cruel of me to punish her and Beaori like this, but I've fulfilled my responsibilities—they won't die, and they'll be fully healed soon. They both deserve a little pain while they wait.

If Teagan hadn't offered me a bribe, I might have considered keeping her secret. But the bribery suggestion offended me deeply. The Ash King is depending on me to be fair and objective. He wants me to tell him everything I learn about the girls, and so far I haven't been forthright enough with him.

After this challenge, I'm going to tell him everything.

In the remaining matches, Diaza triumphs narrowly over Axley, and Khloe surprises everyone by knocking Leslynne out cold within a few minutes. Axley and Diaza are both badly wounded, so I heal them enough to get them on their feet.

Then all ten of the Favored line up before the King's balcony.

"You fought well today," he says. "And I know some of you are still suffering. I will not make you wait for my decision. You may all remain here until you are completely healed, but afterward, Beaori, Morani, and Samay must leave the Calling and return to their homes. They are no longer counted among the Favored."

Murmurs of shock, disappointment, or joy ripple through the audience. Each onlooker has a favorite contestant, and for some of them, their favorite lost her chance at the throne today. People in the crowd shout the names of the remaining women, an endless echo of "Khloe" and "Teagan" and "Axley" and "Cailin" —

Wait. Cailin?

I listen harder, certain I must be mistaken.

There is no mistake. Voices in the crowd are shouting my name, most of them coming from the upper tiers of the arena, where the cheapest seats are. The common folk are calling for me. I'm not sure why—perhaps because I didn't perform any magic before this round? Maybe they're disappointed about that.

Ever since the first few shouts of my name, more people seem to have been emboldened to speak it. In fact, so many are shouting "Cailin" now that the heads of the Favored women begin to turn toward me. And their expressions are not favorable.

Gracious gods. I want to crawl under something. I want to huddle in the shadow of the arena wall, slip through the exit into the back room and hide.

But a secret part of me is darkly delighted, too. My pulse quickens, racing through my veins like an ash-burrower through its tunnel. Instead of cowering I straighten my shoulders, smile, and lift my head.

And I risk one glance at the Ash King.

He's looking at me, eyes scarlet and narrowed. Then he surveys the crowd before lifting his hands, signaling for quiet.

The audience falls silent.

"What would you have of the Healer?" he asks. "A display of water magic? Or perhaps—a show of her combat skills?"

I stifle a sharp gasp. I have no combat skills.

But the King isn't done. "Perhaps both?" He gives his people a rare smile, and their roar of approval pummels my ears. "Ah, but our Healer is sworn to help and not harm, except in defense of herself or others. She cannot engage in offensive combat."

A hum of disappointment from the crowd.

"Shall we provide her with the proper motivation then?" The Ash King's smile is wider, crueler, and I remember his words to me: *I shall have to reawaken your hatred somehow. It's so refreshing.*

What the Heartsfire is he about to suggest?

"My guards will tie the eliminated Favored to three posts in the center of the arena," says the King. "The Healer will defend them from my attacks. If she can do so successfully for a half-turn of the hourglass, she wins a most enviable prize…"

The crowd quiets, anticipation hovering thick in the air.

"If a single flame of mine touches any of the three women, the Healer loses the challenge," says the Ash King. "But if she protects them effectively, she may replace one of them as a Favored contestant in the Calling."

Silence coils through the arena, thick and deadly as smoke.

I can't breathe.

A frantic sweat breaks out over my entire body. My stomach is dipping, rolling.

Mutters slither through the audience, surging to a roar of astonishment, anger, and approval, all mingled. Two men and a woman in the King's box rise abruptly and step forward, murmuring to him. Advisors, most likely, suggesting that he rethink this.

Not that any of them imagine for one second that I could win. The idea is laughable. This is the Ash King, maker of the scorched Ashlands, wielder of fires beyond scale or comprehension.

He knows I'm going to lose. He risks nothing by this, because I have no chance at defeating him.

Everyone else must know I'm doomed to fail, too. But the Favored are furious, nonetheless, and though most of the crowd is wild with excitement, and some of the finely-clad folk in the front rows look highly displeased.

I stare up at the King, there on his balcony above me, toying with our lives like he toys with his fire orbs—idly, thoughtlessly. Whatever happened to him proving that he hates me? He has just given me a strange mark of his favor, opening a chance for me to compete—I can hardly think the words—to be his *bride*.

But is it really a mark of his favor, or something far worse?

What if he hurts me? Scorches me? Humiliates me by winning the match in the first few seconds?

Unpredictable as this move may seem to everyone else, I know him better now. He always has a plan, a strategy, some plot to manipulate everyone. Naïve he may have been five years ago, but he's had half a decade to become the clever serpent of a man that he is now.

I won't know what his play is until we face each other in the center of the Réimse Ríoga.

30

My fingernails dig into my palms as contest aides
carry barrels of water into the arena. I stand in front of the
three tall wooden posts, set in a triangular formation.
Beaori, Morani, and Samay are bound to those posts, and
judging by their faces, they're furious about it. None of
them are entirely healed yet, and in addition to the
humiliation of being eliminated, they're being forced to
endure this spectacle, this added danger.

The Ash King is cruel. His reputation for swift
retribution and fiery punishment is well known. They were
fools if they expected anything else from him.

Maybe I'm a fool too. A worse fool, because I
thought he and I were building something, and this plan of
his doesn't make any sense. The whole thing is pointless if
he intends to beat me quickly anyway.

What if he lets me win? My foolish heart does a tiny
twirl at the thought, at the idea that he might actually
entertain the idea of placing me in the contest. It would be
proof that he thinks me worthy of his heart and throne.

But he can't let me win the match, not with everyone
watching. The nobles wouldn't allow me to join the
Calling, and despite his power, he has to consider what the
high-born citizens and his advisors say.

And do I really want to be one of those women,
struggling and sweating, seducing and simpering, trying to

claw past each other and grasp the crown? I prefer what he and I have right now. It's private, special, tender—at least I thought it was.

Maybe he regrets telling me his secrets.

The servants leave the arena, and the Ash King strides in through a side entrance. He has stripped to the waist, every muscle glowing in the light from his own swarm of fire-orbs drifting far overhead, near the arena ceiling.

The King is greeted with a royal fanfare and with worshipful cries from thousands of throats. He inspires reverence the way only a young, merciless ruler can. His blend of beauty, magic, and cruelty is what makes him so powerful, so unassailable.

In his hand he wields his sword, Witherbrand. It's already alight with orange flame, and that makes me nervous. Surely he wouldn't strike me with it. He can't damage me too much, or I won't have enough energy to fix myself *and* finish healing the girls.

I draw water from the nearby barrels, slightly reassured by how much there is. At least I'll have plenty to work with.

The King is putting himself at risk here too, because as we both learned, if I intend to hurt him, and I mingle my water with his fire, I can cause damage. That's a vulnerability he probably doesn't want disclosed to the kingdom. He's trusting me to defend only, not attack—to keep my intent pure and harmless.

Last time we fought, we were in close quarters. This time, he stops a good thirty paces away from me and nods to the timekeeper and the herald.

"Ready," the herald calls. "And—begin."

A streak of fire races from the tip of Witherbrand, streaming toward me like water shot through a reed. I intercept it with a wall of liquid, recapturing and condensing the droplets after they hiss into steam. I need to conserve every bit of water if I'm going to have a chance.

Next the Ash King opens his palm, releasing dozens more of those little fiery orbs he favors. They come whizzing through the air, missiles aimed straight for the three captive women, but I form a sphere of glimmering water around them, and the tiny orbs hammer harmlessly against it.

Blades of spinning fire, writhing snakes of flame, more fiery pellets, great churning orbs of blue heat—he sends them all at me, one after another. The air is acrid with the sting of magic. Sweat films my bare limbs. Tendrils of my hair have come loose, sticking to my neck and shoulders.

I can tell the Ash King holding back, giving me time to defend against each attack. Tempting me to believe that maybe, somehow, I can win.

I wasn't asked whether I wanted to participate or not. I was simply escorted onto the field by one of the contest managers, the sour-faced woman who already disapproves of me.

What if I yielded? I could give up the match and bow before the Ash King, murmuring some nonsense about how I'm not worthy to face him like an equal.

But I discard the thought instantly. Village girl though I am, I'm his equal—maybe not in magic, but in every other way.

I won't relent. He will have to take this victory from me.

My arms are toned from long days of wielding water in the fields, so exhaustion isn't a problem for me. But the King doesn't use his magic often; he is constantly restraining it. Maybe his stamina isn't as great as mine. Maybe I can outlast him.

Or maybe I should put him on the defensive.

He sends another volley of fireballs my way, and this time, in addition to shielding the girls, I send whips of water snaking across the arena toward him—not to harm him, but to restrain him. The liquid ropes coil around him faster and faster, whirling into a funnel that blurs his form. The crowd shouts with surprise, and I smile.

But the next second he walks out of the hurricane, surrounded and shielded by a firestorm of his own. He tosses Witherbrand down and lifts both palms.

The arena fills with fire—flames racing along its edge, spreading, rushing inward toward the three bound women and me. I soak the sand around us and raise a thick shield of protective water, but the fire is too hot, too fierce. Blue flames soar high over our heads, pressing against the ever-shrinking sphere of my liquid magic.

I've helped the King control his fire before. Perhaps that gave me a false sense of my own power compared with his. During those moments, he was fighting to control himself, and my magic was just the extra bit of help he needed for the task. I was able to curb the fire only because he wanted me to, because he was already exercising a monumental amount of self-control against it. When he willingly unfetters his power, nothing can stop him. Not me, not anyone.

There is no defense against a man like this, against power like this. But I fight him anyway, until all my water is scorching steam. My eyes sting with the heat, and I feel as if I'm boiling in my own skin.

The oncoming fire halts, and a quivering tongue of flame stretches out and lashes Beaori across the arm. She squeals sharply at the pain.

The Ash King has won.

Immediately all the flames withdraw, lowering like servants succumbing to their master. This time, at least, they are completely in his control, and they dissipate into smoke.

The crowd expresses thunderous approval for the King's triumph. His pants are smoke-stained, spattered with tiny holes from his own sparks, but somehow he still manages to look regal. He picks up Witherbrand and lifts a hand for silence—and when the audience doesn't immediately obey, he sends up a shower of explosive orbs that shatter with hissing violence over the heads of the people.

A repentant hush falls immediately.

"Lest you all believe that I did this lightly or thoughtlessly," he says, "Let me be clear—the outcome of this match was never in question. I do not place bets with the throne."

He strides rapidly along the center of the arena, Witherbrand flaming in his hand. "The Calling is not a game to be won. It is a grueling test of worthiness. The women here are suffering on your behalf, striving to prove themselves worthy of *you*, the people of Bolcan. Do not diminish their birthright, their strength, and their competence by praising their names alongside the names of others who are not part of the Calling."

Others like me.

Those words—it feels as if he has wrapped my heart in fiery fingers and squeezed.

He keeps walking, right up to me, smelling of smoke and fire. "There is a time, however, for praising the dutiful servants of the crown. And this moment is such a time." He grips my wrist, raising it high. "The Healer of the Favored," he shouts. "She did not win, but she did well."

At his nod of permission, the crowd applauds.

It's torture standing beside him, inhaling the raw masculine scent of his bare skin, feeling the strength of his grip, the heat of his body. *Not mine, not mine.*

I want to cry. So I let a few tears escape, and I smile through them.

The crowd will think they are joyful tears because my King has acknowledged my efforts. Not heartbroken tears because the man I love will not love me back.

Yes, I love him.

I love him, I love him…

I love you… My heart cries after him as he releases me and strides away.

My heart keeps bleeding those words while the three eliminated women are unbound, while we all return to the recovery room. I mend the wounds of the Favored, replenish their blood, and make them flawless. Like the volcano concealing a pool of lava at its core while green fields grow on its shoulders, I keep my face placid, pleasant, calm—and still my heart cries.

I love you.

Not mine, not mine.

31

I'm exhausted yet again. Drained nearly empty, though not as dangerously low as I was after my healing session with the people of the city. I don't spend long in the bath because I'm afraid I might fall asleep in the warm water.

After staggering from the bathing chamber into my room, I tug the covers down and collapse on my bed, still wrapped in the towel. My maid brought food, but I don't touch the tray at my bedside. I'm too heartsore to eat.

And now there is no activity to distract me, nothing to keep the events of the day from spinning through my head, over and over, the way I've watched my parents polishing stones or pieces of petrified wood over and over until their gloss is perfect.

Today the Ash King introduced the idea of me and him, together, into the people's minds—which incites a tiny flare of hope in my heart. Yet he humiliated me, too, rebuking the audience for calling my name. He knew— everyone knew—I had no chance of beating him. There was never a real possibility of my becoming one of the Favored.

I don't know whether to be flattered, furious, hurt, embarrassed, or some of each.

I'm on my back, eyes half-closed, so when three fiery orbs drift across the dark wood of my bedroom ceiling, I notice at once. The Ash King must have opened the door very quietly. I didn't hear him come in.

"Go away," I murmur.

"You fought well," he says. "Almost as if you wanted to win." There's a tentative, questioning note in his voice.

"I wasn't given the option of declining, so I put on a good show for the people. As you did." I turn my head on the pillow, and the sight of him is a fresh wave of pain and pleasure. He's wearing a loosely wrapped tunic and pants, both dark, and there's a cloak draped over his shoulders. It's early evening, after all—he probably has plans for private time with one of the remaining Favored.

Perhaps I should tell him the secrets I know about the women. But I'm not feeling very generous at the moment.

"I had to do it," he says, advancing. His eyes linger on the towel, where my breasts swell against the soft folded edge.

"I understand. You can't have your people calling the name of a village vagabond in the same breath as the names of the high-born." Bitterness tinges my tone. "I'm good enough to serve the Favored, good enough for you to bed, and worthless beyond that."

"You're angling for compliments and reassurance." His brow arches.

"I can't exist on duty alone," I murmur. "Back home I was loved as well as needed. People cared about me, and they showed it. I miss that. I miss nurturing the crops and watching them respond to my magic. I miss wandering the slopes and ravines, picking up strange rocks, finding fire salamanders in the little smoky crevices near the peak of Analoir Doiteain. I miss watching my parents come home arm in arm, dirt-stained and laughing together, delighted over some piece of petrified wood or magnificent geode they found, talking of what they planned to do with it. I miss going with them to towns on market days and providing my healing magic to anyone who needed my help."

I focus on the fiery orbs circling near the ceiling, but I'm conscious of the King standing at the edge of my bed, arms folded, listening.

"I miss the Ceannaire. She's the leader of our village, and she tutored me—taught me most of what I know. My mother used to laugh when the Ceannaire taught me courtly manners and dance steps and modes of address. My mother knew I was happy in our village, that I would never want to leave. But the Ceannaire always said that one day I would need those lessons in etiquette and proper speech. I may not be nearly as refined as the Favored, but I'm no dirt-grubbing halfwit."

Still he doesn't answer, and I sit up, clutching the towel, growing angrier by the minute. I like to think of myself as a kind, caring, even-tempered person, but *gods*, he makes me more furious than anyone I've met in my entire life.

"I won't do it," I say. "I won't stay here and be your royal healer. The people of my region need me, and I need them. I won't be a ghost of myself, starved for love, trapped in this palace, bound to this broken city." I get to my feet, my cheeks burning, my fists curled tightly around the edge of the towel. "After the Calling I'm going home, and if you want to keep me here, you're going to have to chain me up or kill me."

His eyes flame, and he slides his hand along my neck, past the corner of my jaw, sinking his fingers into my damp hair. "You forget who you're speaking to," he says, low and dangerous, cupping my nape. He's drawing me closer, and I let my head fall back, tipping my face up to his.

"I know exactly who I'm speaking to," I whisper. "A cruel, selfish, arrogant man who uses, punishes, and manipulates people. I don't like you. I pity your future bride."

"Is that so?" he snarls softly, his mouth nearly grazing mine.

"Yes. I hate what you did to me today. I'm sure those women you eliminated hate you too, for putting them in that position, treating them like common captives. Their families won't like it."

"They know the rules. When they came to the Calling, they knew that suffering would be part of it."

"But you enjoy it," I hiss in his face. "You like making people suffer. What would your parents say—"

His face changes, and I realize with sickening dread that I took it a step too far. His eyes aren't even eyes anymore—they're pools of whirling fire. One of his hands is still cupping the back of my skull, and with the other he squeezes my face. His breath gusts painfully hot against my lips.

"How dare you?" His voice is lethal power, savage fury. "I told you what I've been through, how much I've lost. You think I *want* to make my people suffer? That I enjoy it? I do it to make them stronger. I do it to test their mettle. Everything I do has a reason, Cailin. Everything has a purpose, for the good of this kingdom and its citizens. There is only one thing I do for myself, purely for the joy it brings me."

His fingers compress my cheeks harder, and my lips are pushed into a pout by the force of his grip. When we were children, Rince and Brayda and I used to squish our own cheeks and make faces at each other, just like this—and when I imagine how my face must look right now, a bubble of laughter rises inside me. I can't help it.

He must see the merriment in my eyes, because his own widen abruptly, and the flames fade somewhat.

"What is the joyful thing you do for yourself?" I say through my bulging lips.

His mouth twitches, and sparks of humor dance in his gaze. "Gods, Cailin." With a hoarse chuckle, he relaxes his fingers, cupping my face instead of squeezing it, and I smile at him.

How can I be so furious with him one moment, and feel nothing but ridiculous joy the next?

Joy—he said the one thing brings him *joy*, not just pleasure. There's a difference.

I hope the *one thing* is me.

He's still looking at my mouth with a dazed craving that's unmistakable. He wants to kiss me.

I can't allow him to do that. If he kisses me and then marries someone else, I won't be able to bear it.

"Shouldn't you be spending time with the Favored?" I whisper.

"They are resting after their grueling day," he says. "I thought it best to give them time to discuss what happened during the challenge without me around. I'll see them tomorrow."

I nod, expecting him to ask for sex. Perhaps afterward, if he does his part well, I'll tell him the secrets I'm holding for the Favored.

The Ash King shifts his thumb, stroking it across my lips. Then he inhales sharply and shakes himself, as if he has come to an abrupt decision.

"Get dressed," he says. "There is something I want to show you."

I choose the simplest of the dresses I've been given since my arrival—a dark blue one with a scooped neckline, a form-fitting bodice, and swishy skirts. Naughtily I omit any underthings, because I have a suspicion that my King will want access to me sometime tonight. And despite everything that happened today, I crave him. I have the strangest feeling that sinking onto him, being entwined with him, would make everything right and solid and whole again.

I love him even when I hate him. I need him in every way. And if he does not try to seduce me, I will do everything in my power to tempt him.

I've barely finished dressing when the Ash King opens the door between our rooms and leans in. "Count to one hundred and then meet me in the pantry."

I assume he means the one down the hall, behind the painting, where he treated me with such delicious roughness after he thought I'd slept with Rince. Strange how my exhaustion has sloughed away. My heart beats fast, and every nerve is alight with eagerness. What does he want to show me?

After counting to a hundred, I wander out of my room, nodding at the guards in what I hope is a casual, nonchalant manner. When I reach the painting that conceals the pantry, there's a guard outside it.

"The King is currently occupying this room," he says, and I smile at the sound of Owin's voice.

"I know," I murmur. "I'm supposed to meet him here."

In the opening of his helmet, Owin's eyes widen. "So you really are sleeping with him. I didn't think the rumors were true."

"They weren't, until—" I wince. "Never mind. Just let me pass, please."

"My shift is up soon," he says. "I can leave this post unguarded, if you prefer not to have someone listening in on your—festivities."

I can't see how any harm will come to the King in the pantry, so I shrug. "As you wish."

Owin's eyes crinkle at the corners as he smiles. "Enjoy yourself, Healer."

"Thank you." I sweep primly past him and duck into the pantry, closing the secret door behind me.

The shelves are uplit by three tiny fire orbs circling over the King's palm. The light flashes on his rings.

"What are we doing?" I whisper. "I enjoyed our interlude here last time, but don't you think a bed would be more comfortable?"

"You think I brought you here to fuck you?" His low chuckle vibrates along my skin, tingling between my legs. "No, Healer. Put this on." He hands me a cloak identical to his. "Are you too tired to walk a while?"

"I'm fine." Truthfully I'm not sure how long I can last, but the illicit delight of being with him like this is too much to resist.

While I put on the cloak, he walks to the back corner of the pantry and adjusts a few things on a shelf before reaching into some dark recess. There's a flare of his fire magic and a series of clicking sounds—and then an entire section of shelving swings outward, like a door opening. Stale, dank air wafts up from the dark tunnel beyond.

A secret passage. Depending on where it leads, this is the kind of information the Undoing would kill to possess.

"We must be quiet," the Ash King says. "This tunnel passes between rooms, and in some places the walls are thin."

I follow him inside, and he leans past me to pull the secret door shut. For a moment our bodies are aligned, and my skin hums with the intensity of his nearness.

But he continues along the passage, guiding fire orbs ahead of us to light the way.

We walk and walk, descend some steps and walk more, until it feels as if we've gone far enough to be outside the palace.

Suddenly the Ash King holds up his hand, and I halt. He's frozen, listening.

I creep toward him. "What do you hear?"

"On the other side of this wall is a parlor where the Favored sometimes gather," he whispers back. "I can hear some of them speaking now."

"If you can spy on them like this, why ask me to observe them for you?"

He presses two fingertips to my mouth, tilting his head toward the wall. I can hear nothing, and it frustrates me.

"Who is it? What are they saying?"

"Axley, Leslynne, and Diaza. They are speaking of the time when there will be five of them left, and I will bed each one to see who is most agreeable to me."

My lungs contract. Slowly I shift away from him. "What fun that will be for you."

He cuts a glance at me. "Jealous?"

"Not at all." I swallow, trying to moisten my dry mouth.

He keeps walking, and after a while I risk a question. "Which one do you most look forward to bedding?"

"Why are you asking me that?"

"Curiosity." Because I'm trying to prove I'm not jealous, and because I have a sick desire to know. "My bet would be Axley. You were all over her the other night on the balcony. Or maybe Khloe, since you've apparently kissed her a lot."

"Only a few times."

"Have you kissed them all?"

"I did not kiss all the Favored candidates, but I've kissed the seven remaining women, at least once each."

Something twitches inside me—a knot of corruption uncoiling, sending out viperous threads. When I look down at my hands, my fingertips are darkening, and thin black lines are slithering out of them.

Panicked, I tighten my grip on my magic, hauling it back in, crushing it down. This is the second time recently that the darker side of my healing powers has surfaced. Not a good sign.

"You seem very interested in my physical relationships with the Favored, Healer," says the King. "Perhaps you'd care to observe a coupling or two. Would that bother you, watching me take pleasure from someone else?"

There's a challenge in his tone. He's testing me, making sure I don't have unrealistic expectations about our relationship. Which I do, of course, though I barely let myself think them, and I certainly can't let him know.

"Of course it wouldn't bother me," I say lightly. "Heartsfire, I'll even hold the woman's legs open for you."

"Filthy words, kitten."

A thrill runs through my heart at the endearment. But his cloaked back continues moving along the tunnel, and he says nothing else for a while.

When he speaks again, it's to ask about my village, specifically its crops and production rates. At first I disclose the information grudgingly, but soon he transitions from economic inquiries to quiet questions about my parents and my fellow villagers. I find myself relaxing, telling him all sorts of details about my home life. It feels good to speak of familiar things, and it feels even better to know he is listening.

His attention softens the pain of knowing that his body is soon going to be sampled by others. I know he's been with women before me, but somehow it's worse anticipating what he'll do with the Favored. So I try not to think of it, and instead I tell him the most humorous stories from my childhood, smiling secretly at his back whenever something I say makes him laugh.

Once though, when I'm telling him about my parents' frequent forays in search of new materials and their long hours working together in their shop, he turns around, a frown etched between his brows. "Did they neglect you? Your parents?"

"No, of course not…" But I hesitate, pondering. "They're very much in love, after all these years. In love with each other and with their work. But even when they were away, I never doubted that they loved me too. And when you live in a village as close-knit as ours, everyone is family. Everyone cares for each other—young, old, or in-between. I wasn't neglected."

But his words give me a new perspective on myself, and shed fresh light on my hunger for open affection and appreciation from people, lots of people. Maybe my parents were a little too absorbed with their work and each other. Maybe they handed me off to others a little too readily, allowed me a bit too much dangerous freedom running the slopes of our mountain.

Maybe there are caverns within myself that I have not yet explored. And maybe it alarms me a little that the Ash King saw straight into those deeper places, without my making the slightest effort to reveal them.

We walk for perhaps another hour, then duck through another door with a very low lintel. There's a final squeeze along a tight passage, and then the Ash King applies heat to a strange-looking lock, and we exit through one final door.

The room we're in is dark, too dark for the light of his fire orbs to reach far, but by the feel of the air I can tell we're in a large space.

"What is this place?" I whisper.

"A private vault of the Justice Building."

"We're in the Justice Building? Gods, how far did we walk?"

"Far." He leads me to another door that unlocks in answer to his fire magic. "This building is magically sealed at night, and its exterior is well-guarded. We do not have to be quiet now."

"Magically sealed? I thought you disliked using magic for things. You prefer that everyone operate without it, yes? But apparently you make exceptions for air circulation in the palace, and for this."

He looks down at me, his eyes glinting. "I have people working on non-magical air circulation systems for the palace, and others designing mechanics that would operate on some type of fuel—the details are beyond my understanding, but they assure me that progress is being made. We will not always be dependent on wind-wielders to cool the palace."

"I'm not complaining," I tell him as we walk down a wide, empty hallway. "I appreciate the cool air flowing through the vents in my room. I imagine the wielder can set it in motion and then it circulates on its own for a few days, yes? That's how my water magic worked back home—the irrigation patterns I set in the fields would flow for a couple of days before I had to redo them. Of course the fields are so large and numerous that by the time I finished with all of them, the first ones usually needed tending again."

"Did you not tire of it? The constant labor?"

"I love being outside. I love the earth, the plants, the views—and other villagers were always at work nearby too, hoeing or weeding. We sang and told stories. And we'd finish our labor by mid-afternoon, so we had time for other pursuits. It was perfect."

The Ash King's pace slows. The hand that swings at his side curls into a fist. "You could not be happy anywhere else, then. In any other role."

If he's asking me if I will stay on as the royal healer, my answer is still no. Not for the reasons he believes, but because of one simple truth—I cannot bear to watch him marry someone else and live with her.

"When this is over," I say quietly. "I will collect my payment and return home."

"Your payment, yes. Did you like it?"

"What do you mean?"

"The yellow diamonds I had sent to your room. They were my mother's, and they are yours to keep."

I stop walking.

Those jewels are worth more than my entire home village and all its crops.

"But—that's too much," I breathe.

The Ash King halts several paces away. Amid the shadows of the great stone pillars that flank this gallery, he is uplit by the three tiny orbs circling around him—a cloaked figure swathed in hazy amber light.

"You deserve it," he says, his voice floating through the cool emptiness of the hall.

I hover in the darkness just beyond the orbs' glow, conscious that if I step closer, he will be able to see my emotions much too clearly.

"I don't understand you," I murmur. "I don't know what you want from me."

"Come with me," he says, "and perhaps you will. Just a little farther. We are almost there."

32

The Ash King guides me through more gloomy,
echoing corridors of stone, with ceilings that soar high into
blackness. Finally we emerge into a large room with
colonnades down either side and lots of benches flanking a
central aisle. At the head of the chamber is a raised
platform with half a dozen broad steps leading up to it.
And on that platform is a magnificent throne crafted from
a gigantic piece of petrified wood.

I gasp and rush forward. "This fragment came from
the ravines near my village. It was cut and polished by
Ceardai, the finest lapidary in this kingdom! I wish I'd been
able to meet him before he passed to the afterlife—but to
see this—Heartsfire, just to see his work in person—"

I hurry up the steps and circle the throne, marveling
at the natural curve of the back, the neat crafting of the
armrests. The design embraces the natural shape of the
wood, with as few cuts as possible interfering with its
beauty.

"Is it comfortable?" I ask the King, without taking
my eyes off the throne. "Imagine the size of the ancient
tree that yielded this! Gods, I love it. It's just as beautiful as
I imagined."

"There is one thing that could make it more
beautiful." The Ash King's voice is as cool as ever, but

there's a heat simmering within it that makes me turn and look at him.

He mounts the steps, sending his fire orbs up to float high above our heads. Then his warm hands close around my waist, and he's lifting me bodily, placing me on the cushioned seat of the throne.

I'm speechless, my throat dry and my heart hammering violently.

The Ash King steps back to survey me, cocking his head. "Just one improvement. Remove the dress."

My pulse stutters, but I rise and obey, removing my cloak first. I have to reach back awkwardly to undo the buttons of the dress.

The King doesn't offer to help. His jaw is locked, and his eyes burn orange.

As I step out of the dress, I realize that I haven't been fully bared to him like this before—at least not without a lot of smudged ash and seared places all over my body. Now there is nothing covering me. I stand defenseless, naked in the Ash King's throne room.

A few weeks ago, I could never have imagined such a thing.

I am deeply grateful that neither my village family nor my friends in the Undoing can see me now.

"I've always wanted to fuck a woman on this throne," the Ash King says. "Ever since I was about fifteen, when the idea first entered my head."

I swallow hard. Of course that's all he wants—to use me to fulfill an illicit youthful fantasy of his.

"Sit," he says. "And spread your legs."

When I hesitate, he lifts an eyebrow. "Denying me again?"

Narrowing my eyes rebelliously, I sit, with all the grace I can muster. Secretly I'm thrilled to be sitting on this masterpiece, in my dress or out of it. But I keep my legs pressed together.

He throws off his cloak and stalks nearer, his eyes hungry. "Stubborn village girl." He places both hands on my knees and leans in. Silky white hair trails over my thigh. "Let me in, Healer."

His nose drifts lightly against mine, his dark lashes sweeping up, then down as he looks first into my eyes, then at my lips. I'm breathing his air. Each tense breath of his is mine.

He could make me do it. He could be rough, like he was last time. But he simply hovers, his handsome profile, his scent, his skin, his body completing the command for him, tempting me to obey.

Heart pounding, I move my legs slowly apart.

He huffs a triumphant breath and moves back, taking in the sight of me splayed open on his throne. Frantic tingles of wicked euphoria trace along my clit, rippling through my belly, peaking my breasts. I shift my thighs farther apart and push two fingers between the lips of my sex, spreading them wide.

"Do I please Your Majesty?" I murmur.

He lifts his gaze from my sex to my face and says, "Always," in a tone so tender I can hardly bear it.

He doesn't remove his clothes.

He's moving in, kneeling between my legs—

This cannot be happening.

The Ash King himself, His Royal Majesty, Perish the son of Prillian, Ard Rí of Bolcan and High Vanquisher of her enemies, is pressing his mouth into the heated center of me.

He touches his tongue to my clit, flicking the tip, and I whimper, arching against the polished back of the throne. He chuckles, a warm breath of delight, and begins to enjoy me in earnest.

Tenderly he explores with his tongue, dipping into every delicate seam, tracing each sensitive fold. He puckers his lips, sucking gently at my clit, then kissing me, over and over, every bit of my sex. There's something desperate in the way he does it, a fevered ache that echoes in my own soul.

"I am sorry about today, Cailin." He nuzzles into my sex, breathing me in, nibbling along my folds. Rince was never this eager—he preferred using his fingers, not his face—but the King seems to delight in pleasuring me this way.

I'm writhing, wide awake and flooded with sensation, every nerve alight, desire pooling at my core. He licks through the wetness and presses more suckling kisses to that perfect spot. I close my eyes, my entire consciousness focused on nurturing the bead of pleasure that's condensing, brightening, right at the tip of my clit—he starts to flicker his tongue, a rapid patter against the sensitive nub. My thighs and belly are tightening—I'm coming—I'm coming on the Ash King's throne, while he kneels at my feet.

"Yes, kitten," he croons, rocking back on his heels to watch me pant and spasm. "Oh yes. Look at you, beautiful. You're perfect."

"I can't bear it, I can't," I whisper, bucking as the ecstasy spirals through me. I need to be held, I need—I need him. "Please—please, Perish—"

I reach for him, and he surges forward with fire in his eyes and kisses me.

His mouth envelops my faint cries, his hands rush over my body. I release a sob, winding my arms around his neck. He's joining me on the throne now, pulling me into his lap, cradling me against him, and the whole time our mouths never part. I am illuminated inside, widening and sparkling, thrilling with the pleasure and with the joy of kissing him. I release a bit of my healing light and wind it around him as I lock my body more tightly to his.

He tastes like smoke and secrets, like wine and wickedness. I want to devour him. His tongue is a silky flame in my mouth, his teeth are the edge of a cliff I'd gladly leap from if it means I can do this forever.

But we have to breathe, and so we part, gasping.

Perish sweeps both hands down over my hair, cupping my face, looking into my eyes. I can see the reflection of my golden irises in his scarlet ones.

"You," he says, hoarse and ragged. "You."

33

When the Ash King says "You" in that tone—there's something thrillingly significant in the word. But I don't dare hope for what it could mean.

So I wait silently, sliding my fingers through his beautiful silver-white hair, sitting naked on his lap as he devours my face with his eyes.

"You belong to yourself," he says. "I will not hold you here after the Calling. And you do not know what it costs me to say that."

I touch his mouth with a fingertip, tracing the shape of his lips. "I wish I could bring you home with me. I would dress you in simple clothes, a field worker's garb, and we would run barefoot through the potsava fields. I would show you a volcano with a fire that rivals your own. We live on the edge of danger, you see. My village is under constant threat from that mountain, but even if it destroyed us, we would not blame or hate it, because it has given us such a good life."

I'm not sure why there are tears in my eyes, but his are wet, too.

"That sounds perfect," he whispers. "And you love this mountain, the one that could kill you without meaning to?"

I press my palm over his heart. "I do."

"The mountain would give you everything in its power." He leans in, lips brushing mine. "But the one thing a mountain cannot do is move. It cannot give up its place, or abandon those who depend on it."

I kiss him, slow and soft, my heart full to the brim and sweetly aching. "A person might be persuaded to move from one mountain to another, if she could be sure that the new mountain would belong to her alone."

He leans back, staring at me with shocked gladness. "Do you mean that? You said you didn't want any of this. You only want to return home."

"And I do want to go home. But perhaps not forever. I have a suspicion everything would feel smaller and lonelier than it used to."

"Smaller and lonelier." His hand glides along the curve of my waist. "Yes."

We are on the verge of something tremulous and exquisite and tender. He kissed me, and I opened the door a bit farther. It's up to him to push it wider still.

But I'm desperate. So I nudge him a little. "What is this?" I whisper. "Still sex and secrets?"

He vents a shaky laugh. "I think you know the answer."

"In spite of today, in the arena?"

"In spite of that, and because of it. Fighting you today, I was also fighting myself, and I realized that I wanted you to win. I couldn't allow it, but with all my heart I wished for it."

I can't look at him. My every nerve is taut, and my whole being craves his next words.

"I do not want any woman's mouth or body if it isn't yours," he says quietly. "I trust you as I've trusted no one in years, Cailin. Everything about you sings to me. You're intelligent, diplomatic yet sharp-tongued, kind-hearted to a fault. And you find the humor in everything. Leaving aside your lack of noble blood, you would make the perfect queen."

"You trust me?" I bite my lip, guilt warring with the joy in my heart.

"Yes."

I slide off his lap, and reluctantly he lets me go.

He trusts me. This man who has been betrayed by allies, by his family—he trusts me, the girl with ties to the Undoing, the girl who promised to help the murderous rebels destroy him.

His trust, his affection, the vague possibility of a future with him—it's all I've wanted, for longer than I would admit. And now that I have it, I don't feel worthy.

Clenching my teeth to force back the tears, I walk to my discarded dress and step into the skirts. I know the Ash King's body craves release—I felt him, rock-hard under his trousers, while I sat on his lap. But he doesn't protest as I clothe myself.

"It's strange," he says. "I always feel more settled when I sit here, on this throne. I am more balanced, more in control of my magic. I feel the same way during banquets at the palace, and when I'm on my balcony at the Réimse Ríoga."

"Maybe sitting down helps you stay calm?" I arch a brow at him.

"I'm not sure. I feel more controlled during dances at the palace, too. It's very odd. If I knew what common element those places have, perhaps I could begin to understand my magic better." He approaches me from behind and wordlessly begins to fasten the buttons for me.

"Your parents didn't have magic?"

"No. But my grandfather did. He had fire magic like mine, but he never used it. Few people knew of his gift."

"He was the foundling, yes? The one adopted by the two kings?"

"Yes."

"And where did they find him?"

"They were on holiday in the Southern Mountains, and they returned from a ride one day with a baby. Said they found him crying in an empty cave. They asked about him in the villages nearby, but no one claimed him. They brought him back, christened him as their high-born son, and that was that."

"No one complained?"

"If they did, their complaints were useless, because the kings' minds were set." He clears my hair away from my nape and kisses my neck, inhaling deeply as he does so.

"So truthfully, you're no more noble than I am."

"Ah, but my grandfather and my father married high-born women." He kisses just beneath the corner of my jaw.

"Still, you're one quarter commoner. Or one-quarter vagabond, if you prefer."

He chuckles against my neck.

"I need to tell you something," I murmur, my eyes drifting shut as I relish the sensation of his mouth on my skin, his hands cupping my hips.

"Hm," he replies, still kissing me.

"Teagan has an ability. It's a low-level one, a strange sort of magical exception, I suppose, only detectable by a powerful Ricter. She's been hiding it through bribery, and maybe by staying away from the Ricters at the palace parties—I'm not sure how she managed to conceal it this long. She tried to bribe me to keep her secret, but I can't withhold the knowledge from you."

"How long have you known of this?" His tone is dark.

"I realized it today, when the blade lodged in her spine. She should have been dead or paralyzed, but her body kept functioning, helping her survive against Beaori. She told me it was the same when she had the plague—she was sick, but she didn't die. Her body manifests some symptoms of sickness or injury, but not others. It keeps functioning normally despite wounds or illness that should have a major impact or lethal consequences. A survival power, she calls it."

"So Beaori should have won the match."

"Yes."

Silently the Ash King picks up our cloaks from the floor and hands mine to me.

I drape it around my shoulders. "How did you first hear about me?"

"What does that have to do with Teagan's ability?"

"Just tell me. Please."

"I was meeting with a few Ricters in a city not far from Aighda," he says. "That meeting had been set for months, and since I would be near Aighda anyway, I'd decided to escort Teagan to the Calling personally. One of the Ricters at the meeting mentioned you. She spoke very highly of your generosity, the sweetness of your nature, and your loving disposition. A natural talent, she said, powerful and self-trained, unconnected to any noble family. I had begun to despair of finding the right Healer for the Calling, and you sounded like the perfect candidate. I decided to go and fetch you immediately."

"That must have been the same Ricter that Teagan's father bribed to conceal her ability," I muse. "Teagan probably asked her—or paid her—to tell you about me. Teagan hoped that if I did discover her secret during the Calling, I'd keep it quiet because of our previous friendly connection."

He sighs deeply, running his fingers through his pale hair. "I'll have to disqualify her. Is there anything else I should know?"

"Sabre appears to have a private political agenda." I repeat the words she spoke to me in the arena. "I'm not sure she's connected to the anarchists, but she shares some of their ideology."

"You should have told me about that immediately." Five tiny flames spurt to life at the ends of his fingers, and I tense, waiting for punishment. But he only says, "In the time we've known each other, I've withheld things from you as well, so I will not rebuke you for this. But if you know anything else, Cailin, tell me now."

My mind fills with things I should confess: Rince's near-suicide and assassination attempt, the Undoing and their plans, Khloe's pregnancy.

But Khloe's secret isn't mine to speak. And revealing Rince's connection to the Undoing could make the Ash King suspect me as well—and I can't let that happen, not when he has finally admitted the connection between us, not when I finally have hope that maybe, maybe—

"There is nothing else," I tell him.

"Good." He reaches inside his cloak. "Then take this. Before we return to the palace, you and I are going to have a little more fun."

I look down at the object in his hand. It's a full-face mask, darkly metallic, with cutouts for the mouth and eyes.

"There's a festival in the city tonight," he says. "The Ruse Wake. Most people will be masked, so you and I can walk among them."

"Is that safe? And this building is magically sealed. How will we get out?"

"I have my own private exit, which responds only to my magic," he replies. "And once we're in the streets, our masks will protect us. Besides, you and I are the most powerful wielders in this city—perhaps in the entire kingdom. Even if someone should guess who we are and attempt an attack, we can defend ourselves."

He binds his white hair into a knot and then puts the mask on, tying it at the back of his head and pulling up the hood of his cloak. "What do you say, Healer? Are you ready to see a different side of the Capital?"

The Ash King ties my mask for me, and he wraps his strong, warm fingers around mine as we approach a side exit of the Justice Building. A few expertly wielded fireballs, and we're leaving the building, whisking across a shadowed alley before the oncoming patrol spots us. The Ash King pulls me against him, and we stand together in the darkness while the guards tromp past, completing their rounds.

Then he guides me along the alley and out into the streets of Cawn.

We have not resolved the matter of his impending choice. I'm not sure if he plans to continue the competition and sleep with the Favored even though he claims he doesn't want to.

Maybe he'll find a way to include me in the contest. After all, I've completed most of the challenges so far. Or maybe he'll declare an end to the Calling and announce that I'm his choice.

Or perhaps he will sleep on it, and bow to what he believes to be his duty, and continue with the Calling as planned, rejecting me and choosing one of the Favored.

He didn't actually say he loves me. But he came precariously close to it. Though his face is masked, I sense a difference in him—an excitement, a lightness that's contagious. I squeeze his hand, and when he looks down at me, I smile, knowing he'll read the sparkle in my eyes and know I'm happy to be here with him.

The deeper we wander into the City, the brighter and more colorful everything is. Masked revelers jostle and dance between booths strung with fluttering pennants. Perish produces coin from an inner pocket and buys a bag of sugared nuts.

I snatch it from him. "I'll test them first, to be sure they aren't poisoned."

"Sneakthief," he says, grinning. "You just want the first bite."

"Guilty." I pop a nut between my lips. My eyes close as warm sugar crunches and melts, as the rich nutty flavor fills my mouth. "Heartsfire, I think I like this better than your tongue."

"I'm deeply offended." He snatches the bag from me and eats one himself. "Gods, you're right. They taste so much better than your sweet, wet—"

"Hush!" I shove a few more nuts into his mouth, and he laughs, louder than I've ever heard him laugh before. We step aside, out of the flow of people, and drift into a square where three wielders are doing a small display of elemental magic: water, air, and fire working together. They're nowhere near as powerful as the King and I are, but their clever use of the elements in combination is fascinating.

People gasp and cheer and laugh, music jingles from another show farther along the road, and sparks from the fire magic float high into the black sky before winking out among the white stars.

Standing at the back of the crowd, with my shoulder pressed to the Ash King's arm, sharing a snack with him and watching the magical display, I'm the happiest I've ever been. Weariness tugs at me, but I'm too full of joy to yield to it.

I'm happier now than I was with Rince by the stream. Happier than when the Ceannaire was teaching me dance steps. Happier than I ever was on a market day back home. Happier than those rare occasions when my parents laid aside their work to read to me or sing with me.

I'm happiest now. Because of him. The Ash King.

"It feels odd, eating something my servants haven't tested and brought to me," he says.

"I've never noticed anyone tasting the food for you."

"It's tested in the kitchen, and then a trusted servant brings my portion straight to me. I have five servants assigned specifically to that task, and they rotate the responsibility."

"And they can't be bribed?"

"Do you wish to poison me, kitten?"

"Of course not!" My cheeks are reddening. "I'm asking out of concern for you." Which is the truth. I would never pass this information to the Undoing, not now. Not even if they tried to torture it out of me.

"My tasters have all been with the palace for years, and they are loyal," he says. "There are also observers in the kitchen, and guards nearby to keep an eye on who comes and goes. I suppose there is a flaw in every system, but it has worked smoothly so far. I'm not dead yet." He digs in the nearly empty bag for another nut. After popping it into his mouth, he inspects his sugar-coated fingers.

"Here, let me." I take his wrist gently and guide his fingers between my lips, sucking each one slowly.

His pupils dilate, and a telltale glow lights his eyes.

"Shit," I whisper. "Stop that."

"Stop what?"

"Your eyes are glowing. They'll give you away."

He shuts his eyes quickly. "I can't help it. I'm aroused. You had to lick my fingers in that sensuous way, you abominable village brat…"

I turn him toward me and pull his hood further around his face. "Your eyes glow when you're aroused?"

"As I told you, they glow when I feel strong emotions. Arousal, frustration, jealousy, anger—love." His lashes blink apart, and his gaze meets mine. Through the holes of the mask, his irises shine a deep, rich orange.

My stomach does a dizzy twirl. "We need to get you somewhere else until this wears off," I murmur. "Where can we go?"

"A tryst booth?" He slow-blinks at me. "I've never used one, but I've had them installed throughout the city.

Before I did that, people would simply couple on street corners or in alleys. It was a problem."

"Gods." I swallow hard at the thought. "Do you know where the nearest one is?"

"Of course I do." He bends, his mouth brushing my temple. "I'm the King, sweetheart."

"Hush, you fool," I breathe, lifting my mouth to his ear. "Do you want to be assassinated?"

"I'd rather not. Especially when I've just begun to taste you, little vagabond."

The space between my legs is growing warmer and wetter by the second. "Lead on, then," I murmur. "Let's have a tryst."

34

A few streets over, there's an entire row of tryst booths along a street intermittently lit by glazed pink lanterns The booths are constructed of wood, with curtains of heavy dark-purple fabric draped over the doors. When the Ash King and I peer inside one, we discover a small room with a padded bench.

"My bare ass is not touching that," I whisper, grimacing. "Imagine all the fluids."

"This from the woman who came to me dirt-stained and glistening with sweat."

"It wasn't all sweat," I say primly. "Some of it was water."

"Whatever it was, you were filthy and wet. I wanted to throw you down in that dusty square and tear those little blue shorts off you."

Shocked, I stare at him. "You did?"

"Of course I did." He pulls the curtain shut behind us and slides both hands under my cloak, running them up my waist, along my sides, over my breasts. My skin tightens with need, and I sigh, yearning toward him.

He moves closer, lowering his voice. "And then when you kept smiling at the oddest moments—well. I had to have you."

I tip my face up, my mouth hovering near his. My fingers pass lightly between his legs, grazing the rigid length under his trousers. "It must have frustrated you when you could not have me. Did it make you hard, Your Majesty? Did you touch yourself and think of me?"

He exhales a long, shuddering breath and grips my upper arms. "Gods, Cailin."

I tease open the fastenings of his pants, wiggle my fingers inside, and circle the hot, satiny length of his cock. I tug it out and touch the tip, pressing gently. One long stroke along the side, from base to head. The King's hands tighten on my arms.

"Lately I've forgotten to make the proper obeisance," I whisper. "Allow me to correct that omission now, Your Majesty."

"I love those words on your tongue," he whispers, as I remove my mask and sink to my knees.

I lick him first, relishing the smooth, salty heat of his skin. And then I run his length all the way into my mouth, taking him as deep as I can. He voices a shattered groan and reaches up to grip the wooden beam overhead with both hands.

I work him quickly, my head bobbing as my lips pump along his shaft. I tuck my fingers into his pants, cupping his balls. His whole body strains and heaves, and he makes the sweetest sounds—quick helpless moans of pleasure. The overhead beam of the booth groans with the pressure his powerful arms are exerting on it.

Just to torture him, I remove my mouth and fingers, and he cries out, his cock twitching helplessly, naked and yearning. When I slide him into the warm comfort of my mouth again, he nearly sobs as he comes apart for me. He quakes with the force of his climax, jetting heat across my tongue, down my throat.

I want to do this with him over and over for years. Forever.

He puts himself away and refastens his pants. But the glow in his eyes has only dimmed a little. Planting himself on the padded bench, he pats the triangle of space between his spread legs. "Come here, Healer."

I sit down, nestling my ass against him. He hums with pleasure and tilts my head aside so he can kiss my neck again. Then he leans me back, supporting me with his left arm while his right hand rakes up my skirts, delving beneath them.

"Wicked woman," he murmurs at my ear, as his fingers lightly caress my bare sex. "You knew I would want to pet this pretty little kitten tonight, didn't you?"

My only answer is a soft moan, because his fingernail is teasing a certain delicate spot, circling slowly. His hand glides through my folds, and then he dips the two central fingers inside me, his palm pressed flat against my mound. I am helpless to that hold, and when he curls his fingers slightly and begins a rhythmic pumping motion, I voice several short, breathless screams because it feels so good—how does this feel so good?

I'm soaked and swollen, and the sound of his hand slapping against me is so loud I should be embarrassed, especially since only thin partitions separate us from the street. But I can't bring myself to care. He is breaking me down, working me to the limit.

"Are you coming, kitten?" he breathes roughly in my ear. "I can feel you squeezing my fingers. Come undone for me, sweetheart. Come for your King."

He nuzzles my cheek, whispering more filthy encouragement, and when he grinds the heel of his hand hard against my clit, I break. Spirals of glorious bliss twirl outward from his hand through my sex, my belly, along my spine. I arch, squealing softly, and he croons, "Yes, kitten, yes. Gods, I adore you, you beautiful thing."

A deeper thrill races through me at those words. Mutely I seek his mouth, and he kisses me, accepting the last few whimpers and moans as I recover from the ecstasy.

Afterward, I replace my mask and let my skirts fall back into place, even though my inner parts are still wet and warm and tremulous. The King shows me a compartment under the padded bench where a special type of soap is stored. "It is mixed with alcohol, and cleans without water," he tells me. We rub our hands with it before leaving the booth.

The street outside is bathed in clean night air, but as we walk past the pinkish glazed lamps, I notice that each one is redolent with royal incense.

"The smell of royal incense doesn't bother me as much now," I remark. "When I first came to the city, I hated it."

"I dislike it too," he admits. "Too rich, too cloying."

"Then why not change it?"

"My mother chose the blend, not long after she married my father."

"Oh." I take his hand, squeezing it lightly. "Then I will learn to appreciate it."

We're out in the festival again, passing booths where craftspeople wave their goods aloft, shouting to passersby. There are plenty of items related to the Calling of the Favored, and I'm shocked to see a few different artists hawking "portraits of the Healer" and other items inked with my likeness—cloth bags, handkerchiefs, tunics, and tapestries. Many vendors offer golden "Healer ribbons" alongside their regular wares.

Now that I've seen the ribbons, I begin to notice how many festival guests are wearing the bits of gold fabric in their hair or around their wrists. It's enough to make me blush deeply beneath my mask.

Perish darts aside and swaps a coin for a gold ribbon. "Tie it around my wrist for me," he says with a wink. "I want the Healer to know I fancy her."

"I think she knows," I murmur, winding it around his forearm and tying a neat knot.

But my heart is wary of happiness. The Ruse Wake festival feels like an alternate world, like something from a beautiful dream. He adores me now, but how will he treat me tomorrow, when reality resumes?

Perish points out a memorial wall bedecked with colorful silken ribbons and bunches of flowers. "The people we lost during the invasion," he says simply.

"Is the Ruse Wake for them?"

"Not officially. It is a long-standing festival in Cawn, dating back over a century. The idea is to release so much joy that we frighten away the spirits of death and decay, with the goal of prolonging the summer warmth and the growing season. A silly superstition."

"But a charming one. Oh, look! Petrified wood!" I tug Perish toward a booth featuring glossy carvings, unhewn chunks of marbleized wood, and gleaming slabs engraved with images.

The booth owner is a wizened old woman with a cheery smile. "I'm about to pack up for the night, dears. These old bones be aching. But take a quick look, if you like."

The impulse to soothe her pain rises in me, natural and inevitable. "Can you keep a secret?" I ask.

Her eyes narrow, but then she smiles again. "You don't get to be as old as I am without picking up a few secrets along the way, sweetkin."

Cautiously I send a couple threads of golden healing magic toward her. They soak into her body, seeking out inflammation, calming the nerves that spark with pain.

The old woman's eyes widen and soften. "A healer?" she whispers.

"Hush." I press a finger to my lips. "Your wares are beautifully crafted and polished. And I've never seen these hues before—streaks of green and blue in the wood. Where do the materials come from?"

"From the Ashlands," she says. "There are hidden crevices where special varieties of this wood may be found. I know all the places, since my family has lived in the Southern mountains for years. They're all dead now, of course, thanks to the Ash King."

The King's fingers twitch in my hand.

"Surely you don't gather the wood yourself," I say.

"Ah no, my dear. My apprentices make the journey to obtain these materials. They do most of the polishing, too. But I still do the carving."

"It's lovely work." I run a fingertip over the smooth surface of one piece, tracing the dark etchings, reveling in the rough, familiar texture of the fossilized bark at the edges.

"Since you gave me a secret, I'll give you a story." The old woman points to a piece of polished wood, daintily etched with six tall, spindly figures with their hands upraised. Over their heads are symbols—a flame, a drop of water, a curl of air, a forklike design, a sun, and a pattern of dots and leaves.

"They say the gods once roamed the mountain ranges of the world—the high places," the old woman continues. "Hlín, Hœnir, Eostra, Macha, Diancecht, and Nehalennia. They loved humans and gave some of them special powers which live on in the wielders of this land. On rare occasions they bred with mortals and produced new wielders with fresh divine blood, more powerful than others—the Numenai."

Her wrinkled finger moves to another slab of petrified wood. This one features a figure bowed over, holding its head in its hands.

"The Numenai appeared as normal wielders until some significant event in their lives," she says. "A great loss or a great love could awaken the divine strength of a Numen, causing them to become supremely powerful and volatile. When that happened, tragedy often followed. As in the case of the Numen Kyr-sharis. When her children were slaughtered, she felt her powers growing beyond her control, so she wandered beyond the Altagoni Mountains and released her magic. That place is still cursed and broken to this day, down to its very bones. It is called the Bloodsalt."

My heart is beating so loudly I'm sure the Ash King must be able to hear it. "How long ago did that happen?"

"Oh, centuries ago, my dear. That sort of thing doesn't happen anymore—in fact, some claim it never did. The gods are long gone, if they ever existed. And I haven't heard anyone speak of the Numenai in years. Only my grandmother, and she is long dead, gods bless her."

"I have certainly never heard such a tale," says the Ash King. His voice is low and hollow. It doesn't sound like him.

"Was there anything that could help a Numen control their powers?" I ask. "Did your grandmother speak of talismans, tattoos, perhaps some meditative practice?"

The old woman's bleary eyes narrow. "It's a story, dear. Even if it was once true, there are no such beings now."

"Really?" I raise my eyebrows, shocked that she doesn't see it. "You can't think of one? Not one person with enough power to ruin an entire section of land?"

"Time to go," says the Ash King. "Thank you, madam." He places two coins on the woman's table.

"My grandmother used to say that a crystallized memory could stabilize magical resonance," says the craftswoman, picking up the payment. "I have no idea what she meant. Where does one find a crystallized memory?" She laughs, testing the edge of a gold coin with her teeth. "Here, have one each." She hands me two rings of polished petrified wood, one small and one large.

"Thank you," I call back to her as the Ash King pulls me away.

He's walking fast, towing me through the crowd of gaudily masked faces.

"You didn't have to be rude," I protest. "She clearly didn't make the connection."

He yanks me aside, into the mouth of an alley. "Why has no one told me of this before?" He's breathing hard, teeth clenched.

"Maybe because it sounds like a children's bedtime story. Or maybe because approaching you and asking if you are part god sounds rather silly."

"Silly. Of course." He strikes a palm against the wall. "Ridiculous. Untrue."

"Not necessarily. It would explain a lot. Your grandfather's mysterious origins, for one thing. His true power didn't surface because he didn't experience the trauma that you did."

"What of my father?" he snaps. "He had no powers, or he would have used them in defense of this kingdom."

"You know as well as I do that magic can lie dormant for a generation or two."

"Yes, but—no. This isn't possible."

"It would explain what I see when I scan you," I murmur. "And why your powers suddenly took a great leap forward in potency, after the invasion and the—the betrayal you suffered."

"What did she mean by crystallized memory?" He turns burning, anguished eyes to mine.

"I'm not sure." Impulsively I take his left hand and slide the ring of petrified wood onto the only unadorned finger—his heartline finger. "A perfect fit, see?"

He stares at his hand. "It doesn't go with the others."

It's true. All his other rings are of precious metals. "I still like it. And look—we match." I place the smaller ring on my own heartline finger.

He's breathing easier now, and the hectic fire in his eyes fades a little. He picks up my hand. My fingers look so small and brown compared to his, and I love the contrast.

Slowly he lifts my knuckles to his mouth and kisses them, a long press of his lips. "We should return. I've kept you out too late, and you were already exhausted. I apologize for my selfishness."

"Don't apologize," I whisper. "This has been the best night of my life."

35

It's nearly noon when I wake. When I ring for my maid, Enna, she hurries in eagerly, brimming with the latest Favored gossip. Apparently the Ash King wasted no time in confronting both Teagan and Sabre and sending them home this morning. I'm not sure what I expected from him, but I didn't think he'd act so abruptly. I wish I'd had a chance to speak with Teagan first, though I'm not sure what I would have said to her.

"Just five Favored left now," Enna says. "Adalasia, Khloe, Axley, Leslynne, and Diaza. You know what that means." She meets my eyes in the mirror, and her gaze is curious, questioning.

"The King gets to bed them all." I make a wry face as she fastens my dress.

"How do you feel about that?" she asks, low.

"Am I that obvious?" I sigh, picking up a comb from the dresser and plucking its tines idly.

"There is something between you two," she answers with a smile. "The whole kingdom knows it."

"But what the King did yesterday—what he said—"

"You mean when he offered you a chance to be one of the Favored, and then took it away? His orders that people should not chant your name along with those of the high-born?" She laughs. "That incident only made everyone love you more. Perhaps the nobles took him seriously and approved of his words, but no one else did."

My pulse quickens. "I don't think he can defy the nobility, even if he wants to."

"He's the King," she replies. "Perhaps he can find a way."

Once I've dressed and eaten, I make my way to the wing where the Favored reside. I've decided to ask Khloe to tell the Ash King about her pregnancy; otherwise I'll have to do it. If Perish and I are to have a future—which seems increasingly, thrillingly possible—we should have as few secrets as possible between us.

After inquiring for Khloe among the servants, I'm shown to her private suite. She's lounging on a flowery sofa, nibbling at pink-frosted cakes and sipping tea. A book lies open on her lap, its pages fluttering lightly in the breeze from the window.

When she sees me, her face lights up. "Cailin! How lovely to have a visit from you. Please sit down."

"How are you feeling?" I ask, settling into a nearby chair. "When I scanned and healed you yesterday, the baby seemed well."

"Oh yes. I feel perfectly fine." Her smile fades a little as she inspects my face. "You're going to tell the King, aren't you?"

"Not yet. But you should. Khloe, we are down to five girls. You must give him all the information he needs to make his choice. If you don't inform him of your pregnancy, I'll have to."

For a moment, her eyes take on a steely, calculating look. Or perhaps I imagined it, because the next moment the expression is gone, replaced by her usual soft sweetness. "It was you, wasn't it? You said something that made him send Teagan and Sabre away."

"Teagan and Sabre were sent away because of secrets they kept from the King," I say. "I don't want the same thing to happen to you. If you're honest with him, he might keep you here. But if he finds out some other way, he'll be furious."

She skims the floral pattern of the upholstery with a fingernail. "I should think you'd want me gone. Everyone knows you want him for yourself. I didn't believe it of you at first—I thought the other girls were simply being cruel. But now I think they were right to be jealous."

I purse my lips, unsure what to say.

"I'm not jealous, though," she adds. "I've thought it through, and I believe I have the perfect solution. The King needs a high-born bride to pacify the nobility. But who's to say he couldn't take a second bride, one favored by the people?"

A dreadful thrill runs through my heart. "The monarchs of Bolcan have only ever had one spouse."

"But triads and groups are normal throughout the kingdom," she says. "This could be a first among the royals. It would make everyone happy. You and I like each other, and we both like him. We could take turns with him—or perhaps enjoy pleasure all together." Leaning forward, she touches the back of my hand. "I know you find me pretty and pleasant, and I think you're beautiful. We could have such fun. Promise me you'll consider it, and that you'll suggest it to him. Trust me, it is the best possible resolution to all this."

I swallow hard. "I will tell the King about your idea, if you promise to tell him about the baby."

"I will," she says. "We have a week without challenges, to allow him time to bed the five Favored. And during the day he'll be spending extra private time with each of us. I'm sure I'll have a chance to tell him."

My gut curdles, soured by what I've agreed to suggest to the King. I know he desires to be faithful to his spouse—no mistresses or trysts. But would he consider a triad marriage? Would *I* consider it, if it's the only way I can have him? I could be both healer and queen. And I would have the freedom to travel home sometimes, to see my parents and spend time in my village.

I rise from the chair, forcing a smile. "I should go."

"Oh, before you do—" Khloe sets aside the book and leaps up. "I was saving this for my night with His Majesty, but I want you to have it, as a promise from me that I'm invested in this—in us." She cups my cheek briefly before hurrying to her dressing table. After a moment she returns with a tiny enameled pot. "This is a pleasure-enhancing lip stain," she says. "It tastes delicious, and it has these lovely tingly properties. Spread it on your mouth and his, and whatever body part you kiss will be titillated even more. I hope to enjoy it with you two someday."

She bounces onto her tiptoes and gives me a delicate kiss on the lips. It's sweet, and she's charming, but I don't feel excited or hopeful. The thought of sharing the Ash King's love with anyone else opens a hollow wound inside me. Maybe I could learn to like it. But as I leave Khloe's rooms with the pot of lip stain, my heart feels sore and heavy.

In the evening, I'm invited to dine with the King and the Favored. It's a smaller group than the previous banquets. The Ash King—or whoever plans the seating for these affairs—placed me near the foot of the great table, and I soon discover that I'm surrounded, not by nobles, but by skilled artisans and well-known merchants. My interest perks as they discuss their art and their businesses, and I nearly forget about Khloe's proposal.

This time, I notice the servant who brings the Ash King's portion to the table. The system of food delivery seems safe enough, though I wonder about the food in the upstairs pantry, near the royal chambers. That food is only protected by the hidden door behind the painting, and the presence of the guards in the hallway. Who brings the stores up to the pantry from the kitchen? I hope they test all the edibles and drinks before stocking them on the shelves.

Soon the Undoing will approach me again, either through Rince or someone else. The Calling is drawing to a close, and a Queen must be selected. If the rebels want to make a move against the King, they'll need the information I've gathered, especially if their ally among the Favored has already been sent home.

I don't plan to give them any information that would help them kill Perish. And if they attack him, I'll protect him with every bit of power I have in me. But I can't help remembering Rince's words: *There's more here at stake than you know, and I have powerful people on my side too, people to whom I must answer. They won't be pleased with either of us if you prove untrustworthy.*

As much as I want to protect the Ash King, and as much as I'd like to purge every last secret between us, I don't want Rince and Brayda to be arrested, tortured, or imprisoned. I know how deeply the King hates the Undoing. When it comes to rebels, invaders, and potential risk to his kingdom, he can be terribly cruel.

How will he react if he finds out I was in league with them, even if it was a temporary, half-hearted alliance?

What will the anarchist leaders do to me when they realize I'm not going to help them?

After the banquet, the King dances with the Favored in the adjoining ballroom. It's a merry dance, one that allows for the frequent switching of partners, so none of the five women feel neglected. I can't help but smile watching them, though a dark, possessive part of me wishes I could send them all away and make him mine alone.

The Ash King seems more buoyant than usual, and he glances at me frequently, with a sparkle in his eyes as if he's sharing unspoken secrets. It's enough to salve my jealousy until later that evening, when the dinner party has ended and everyone retires to their quarters.

I've barely had time to freshen up in the privy when Perish breezes into my room, shirtless, with his hair unbound. He smells like royal incense and wood smoke, and when he kisses me, he tastes both savory and sweet, like the gravy we had at dinner and the sugared cakes we enjoyed afterward.

"Tonight I am going to fuck you properly," he says, his voice husky with desire. "In a bed, with both of us naked."

"First I have two things to tell you." He's already trying to peel off my clothes, so I wriggle away, holding out both hands to fend him off. "One of the Favored will come to you tomorrow, or the next day, with a secret to share. I know of it already, but it isn't mine to speak, and I would ask that you show her mercy."

His face sobers, but his eyes are still alight. "If it's about Khloe's baby, I already know."

"What?" My jaw drops. "You know? How?"

"I've known for a while. I was hugging her once, and beyond her own heartbeat I could hear another fainter one."

"And you didn't send her away?"

"Why should I?"

"Because she is carrying someone else's child."

"And that only matters if she loves the father of the child. Which I was going to ascertain eventually, but I was derailed from my intent by a certain vagabond Healer who proved irresistible—come *here*, kitten."

He darts toward me, a wicked gleam in his eyes, but I retreat quickly. "Not until I tell you what Khloe suggested to me today. She has noticed the connection between you and me, and she said she would be willing to marry both of us. A triad. She would be the queen the nobles want, and I would be the one the people like. You would be able to bed either of us, or both of us."

He halts, gripping the bedpost. "Is that what you want?"

"It's the perfect solution, Perish." I force the words out—the vulnerable, fragile words I can't take back. "Unless you're willing to defy the nobility and marry a commoner, this is the only way. You can have one of the Favored, and you can have—me."

His face softens, his mouth curving up at one side. "A perfect solution. So why do you look as if you're about to vomit?"

"I don't," I gasp. "I'm only—adjusting to the idea. Others can make it work seamlessly—we should be able to do that as well."

"Marriage to multiple partners isn't for everyone, kitten."

I'm breathing too quick, too shallow, and I can't seem to stop. I sink onto the edge of the bed, trying to calm myself. "But if not a triad, then—then you will marry one of them, and I—what will I do?"

Perish approaches and sinks to one knee, gathering my hands in his. I fill my eyes with him, with that finely turned profile, those handsome features I've admired since the day he came to my village to fetch me.

"I will have you and you alone," he says quietly. "I told you I want you. I want you grimy and soil-stained, shining with sweat under the sun, on your knees and palms in an open field while I take you from behind. I want you secretly in some broom-stuffed closet while servants look for us outside. I want you splayed on my bed—I want to feel your tremors when you come on my tongue. I want you against the garden wall and on the desk in my library. I want your mouth on my cock while I sit on my throne. I want you now, in your youth and beauty, and I want you years from now, when we're both slow and sagging."

He's kissing every one of my fingers, punctuating his beautiful filthy words. "I want your intelligence and your diplomacy. I want that immense, generous, sweet, good heart of yours. I want your smiles and your laughter, your courage and your compassion. I want the ruthless side of you, too—your jealousy and your vindictive impulses, your anger and your ferocity—the shade of darkness that makes your light brighter."

Perish reaches up, running a fingertip along my forehead. "I will say it plainly, to erase that worry from your brow. If you would do me the honor of accepting me, you will be my queen. You have only to say the word, and I will make it happen. I will try to do it diplomatically, without angering the nobles, but if I must anger them, so be it. And as I said before—I do not share, Cailin, nor would I ask you to do so. It will be you and me. Always. No one between us."

My whole body is shaking, and tears are gathering in my eyes. I can't respond, so I only nod. The Ash King smiles and touches my trembling lips.

"I need words, kitten," he says softly. "Because if you do not want a throne, I might leave mine for you."

The enormity of that statement shocks me, loosens my tongue.

"No," I manage. "I would never ask that of you. I know how seriously you take your role, how much you want to protect this kingdom. Without you, we would probably be conquered by now. And while I think you could loosen the restrictions a little, I understand why you set them in place. If I can have the freedom to spend time at home when I need it, without a swarm of bodyguards trampling the fields when I need to be alone, then I can agree to this, I think."

"I will order the guards to walk barefoot, softly." His face is sober, but his eyes twinkle.

"Perish. I am serious. I don't want to be a queen who is followed around by bodyguards and curbed from doing anything reckless. Nor do I want to be confined to parlors and dining halls."

"You can be exactly the kind of queen you want to be."

"I can go into the city and heal people whenever I want?"

He grimaces. "As long as you've learned your lesson, and you don't drain your energy as low as you did last time."

"Trust me, I have learned."

"Then yes. Yes to everything. Yes, over and over, as long as I live, if I can have this one 'yes' from you, right now. Will you be my Favored one, Cailin, my everything, my queen, my wife?"

I take a moment. Just a moment, to let the reality of it soak into my being, that this is happening, that the Ash King himself is asking me to marry him.

That I, Cailin Roghnaithe, of the village Leanbh near Analoir Doiteain, have the chance to be queen.

I would be lying if I said I didn't care about that part. To be able to influence policy and decisions, to have a hand in making life better for those who suffer—that is a supreme incentive to say yes.

But greater still is the other treasure I'll receive—this beautiful, broken man at my feet, this lonely warrior, this strong King who has been carrying all the weight by himself for too long. This man with the powerful body and destructive magic, with the clever tongue and sinful mouth.

I want him. I love him.

Extricating my hands from his, I place my palms on his cheeks, and I kiss his forehead.

Then, looking into his glowing eyes, I say, "Yes."

And I mean it with all my heart.

Perish lunges for my mouth, bears me backward onto the bed under an avalanche of his kisses. And for a while there is nothing but his lips, his breath, the tantalizing brush of his skin against mine. The space between us is a haze of golden happiness, blurred by desire.

He's fumbling with my clothes again, but his fingers are trembling. "Fuck. What have you done to me?" A shaky laugh. "I am never overwhelmed like this, except by my own magic."

Grinning, I wriggle out from under him. "I'll do it." I remove all my clothes, slowly, while he watches from the bed. His cheeks are flushed, and there's a warning glow in his throat.

"Do you need water from me?" I ask.

He closes his eyes and takes a moment to focus, and the fire dims again. "I think I'm all right."

"Just to be sure…" I guide water into a mug for him, and he rises to take it. "Oh, and I nearly forgot. This lip stain is supposed to enhance pleasure. You spread it on your mouth and then kiss anywhere, and it tingles. I'm told it's a delightful sensation."

"Is that so?" He finishes the water and shucks off his pants. "Let's give it a try, then."

I don't tell him where the cosmetic came from, because I feel slightly guilty about using it, especially since Khloe will not be joining us in a triad marriage. But it *was* a gift, and truthfully I'm eager to experience the heightened sensations Khloe promised.

After removing the lid, I spread a bit of the creamy, rosy stain across my lips and then drop to my knees. I kiss the head of Perish's cock before taking it in my mouth.

"Oh gods." He shudders, sinking his fingers into my hair. "It's tingling, like you said. It feels wonderful. Give me some. You need to feel this."

I pull my mouth off him, rise, and hold out the little pot. He dips a finger in and daubs his lips liberally. Then, with a lecherous glance at me, he swipes a generous dollop onto his tongue. I turn hot all over, anticipating where his tongue might be headed.

He ducks to kiss my nipples, and immediately I feel the cream activating, tingling through my skin.

"Oh," I breathe. "That is amazing."

The Ash King suckles my right breast gently, then trails kisses down my belly. His pale hair is a silken curtain against my skin. He's leaning against me—sliding downward—but he's not kissing or licking me anymore.

He's collapsing.

Something is wrong.

36

Perish slumps to the floor, on his side, with his white hair spilled around him. Breath wheezes faintly through his lungs.

My own throat is swelling, tightening—it feels as if someone's huge hand has grasped my neck and they're compressing, intent on choking me to death. My lips are burning, burning as the cosmetic soaks through the thin skin.

Poison.

My heart pounds slow, huge, and heavy—so sickeningly, frighteningly heavy. Slower. Slower.

My muscles are giving out, legs wobbling, weakening. I'm sinking onto the rug at Perish's side. Foggily I search for my healing magic, but it can't help—not against poison.

"Burn—it—out," I wheeze, but Perish is unconscious. He can't hear me—he ingested more of the lip stain than I did—actually put it in his mouth—oh gods…

The poison is working deeper—I can feel it seeping into my bloodstream, corrupting the particles of my blood one at a time.

My healing magic cannot help us. But maybe my Rotter magic can.

I drag another breath through my failing lungs, and I focus every bit of my consciousness on the poisoned particles in my blood, the ones that are signaling my body to shut down. I send the black corrosive tendrils of my alternate magic to attack those cells—there are many of them, and they're multiplying fast.

Destroy destroy destroy—I corrode each poisoned cell, exploding them into nothing, into harmless motes floating through my veins—but that leaves me without the blood volume my body needs. My heart flutters and falters, a terrifying sensation, and strange sparks dance before my eyes.

I have only moments before I pass out, and we both die.

With my healing magic, I replicate the healthy blood in my arteries, pushing all my energy to do it faster, faster, until I have just enough to survive.

Dragging myself closer to Perish, I spread my naked body over his. I need to be able to sense every bit of him.

My eyes close as I focus on his skin, pressing through that nearly impervious barrier to the glowing muscle and bone beneath. His inner light is dimming, and his heart is failing, slowing. Nearly all his blood is poisoned—I can feel the toxin eating the healthy cells, spreading through his limbs at a frightening rate, signaling his organs to stop functioning. A normal man would have already succumbed, but thanks to his magical nature and his possible godly heritage, he is still here. He is not dead yet.

Black corrosive magic floods from me into him, destroying his blood supply in one great blast of dark power.

His heart stops.

I swallow hard, terrified as I scan his form. The damage I caused was more extensive than I intended. I haven't used this power, I can't control it as precisely as I want to—oh gods, I may have killed him. I have to fix him. I have to heal him *fast*, before it's too late.

I pour healing magic into his body, a violent rush of golden energy, repairing the half-rotted veins and the withered blood vessels. Then I fill up his arteries with fresh blood, as many cells as I can generate—*hurry, hurry, hurry*. My limbs tremble against his bare skin—my consciousness dims as my well of healing energy wanes.

"No," I whimper aloud. "No."

I will not pass out. I will finish this.

His body is healed, but his heart hasn't started beating again. Frantic, I thump against his chest with my fist. "Please," I sob. "Please, gods. You're a mountain, Perish, and mountains don't die. They endure. You—have to—live." I punctuate each word with a blow. "Do—not—die." I press my mouth to his and blow air into his lungs, as deeply as I can.

The air leaks from his lips, unused, and tears blur my eyes. Weakness saturates my body, and I slump against him.

And then he inhales, sharply enough to startle me. I roll off his chest and press my ear to his heart.

The soft thump-thump is the most beautiful sound I've ever heard.

He's still unconscious, and his breathing is barely perceptible, but he's alive.

Now that I've purged the poison and he's stable, I need to summon the guards and get help—and tell them where the toxin came from—

"I thought you might wriggle out of this somehow," says a voice close behind me.

I start to turn, but an arm locks around my throat, and the tip of a knife lodges beneath my chin.

"Scream and you die," says Khloe brightly. .

"You," I breathe. "You did this. You almost killed both of us."

"I didn't *want* to kill you," she says. "Rince tells me you're on our side. But I didn't have a choice. I couldn't get the toxin into him any other way. He wouldn't kiss me—hasn't kissed any of us in a while—and I gambled that he must be saving himself for you. I was right."

With surprising strength for her small form, she pulls me to my feet, still holding the knife to my neck. "So you managed to save yourself, but he's dead, yes? The poison was designed to be absorbed through the body's membranes, the thinnest and most delicate skin—you kissed him, I'm guessing? Maybe sucked his dick a little?"

"That's none of your business. But yes, he's dead," I lie, keeping my voice as steady as I can. "How did you get into his room?"

"The guards let me in. I told them I'd been summoned for my night of passion with the Ash King." She snickers. "It's the final five, so they believed me, of course. Now the question is, Cailin—whose side are you really on? The monarchy, or the Undoing? Because I need to make sure he's really dead, and I need both hands free to do that. I can kill you right now, or I can let you go if you promise to stay quiet."

"I'm with the Undoing," I say quietly. "Sure, I'm a little upset that you nearly killed me as well as the wicked king—but I'm glad he's dead. You spared me the trouble of eliminating him myself."

"Ah yes, your healer's vow." Khloe's grip tightens, and the knife pricks my skin. "Rince believes that's the only reason you refused to assassinate His Horrific Majesty. But I have a suspicion you're actually in love with the man."

"The sex wasn't bad. But love?" I force a laugh. "I've been playing a part, just like you. How could I love someone like him?"

The knife falls away, and she steps back. "No one could. He's a tyrant and a monster. And I'm not trusting to the poison—I'm going to cut his head off, impervious or not. Want to help?"

"Do you have an extra knife?"

Khloe grins, throwing off her silky robe and reaching under the short skirt of her nightdress. From a sheath strapped to her thigh, she extracts another dagger. "It will take some sawing, especially when we get to the spine, but the certainty of his death is worth it. Rince has poisoned the guards by the sluice gate in the northeast corner of the back gardens. That's our way out. We'll meet him there once this is done."

"Perfect," I say, taking the knife. As she leans over the Ash King, I create a long whip of water from the washstand and slice it toward her. The lash strikes her hand, and she drops her dagger with a faint cry.

But I don't stop. I wield the water savagely, screaming as I whip her with it, over and over. She backs away, cowering, trying to shield her face.

It takes the guards a moment to enter the room. Perhaps they aren't sure if my screams are of the sexual kind. But within seconds they're rushing in. Two of them seize Khloe and me while others rush to the King's side.

Owin is among them. He takes off his helmet and approaches me, eyes narrowed. "What happened?"

"The Healer has poisoned the Ash King," Khloe says, her large brown eyes liquid with feigned sorrow. "She killed him. She is a spy for the rebels, and she—she killed the man I love." She breaks into sobs that sound so heartbreakingly real they almost fool me.

"It's not true," I say quietly. "He was poisoned, yes, but Khloe gave me the toxin. She claimed it was a harmless lip stain to enhance lovemaking. You'll find that he isn't dead, as she believes. I saved his life. You'll also find that she has sheaths strapped to her thighs, where she was concealing weapons she certainly wouldn't need for a night of passion with His Majesty."

"Is the King breathing?" barks the guard who's restraining me.

Another guard, kneeling at the King's side, looks up and nods.

"But that's not possible," Khloe gasps. "You couldn't have saved him. Healers can't eradicate poison, certainly not one as potent as this. We designed it to—"

She clamps her mouth shut, but she has said enough. The guard holding me lets go. "You heard her confession, men," he says. "Take the Favored woman to the dungeon. His Majesty will deal with her when he wakes." He turns to me. "Thank you, Healer. You saved the kingdom tonight."

Owin snatches a blanket from the bed and approaches me. "Put this around yourself," he whispers.

I forgot that I'm naked. "Thank you." I pull the blanket around my body.

As the guards drag Khloe from the room, she spits at me. "Traitor. Liar." Then she grins. "We were prepared for this, you know. Say hello to your parents for me. I expect you'll see them soon. Whether they're dead or alive is up to you."

Her laughter echoes along the corridor, fading into silence.

Khloe's words send a spike of nauseating dread into my gut. I run to the closet and pull on the first clothes I find. It's difficult to get away—the King's guards keep pelting me with questions—but at last I escape the room, on the pretext of going to consult with Jonald the healer about the potential aftereffects of the poison on the King's body.

Except instead of going to Jonald, I leave the palace through the wing where the Favored reside, and I make my way to one of the gates of the inner wall surrounding the palace. When I tell the guards I want to walk in the outer gardens, they exchange quizzical looks, but they don't protest. I am the Healer of the Favored after all, and I wear a palace ring, a sign of the King's goodwill.

Unfamiliar as I am with the layout of the grounds, it takes me nearly an hour to locate the sluice gate in the northeast corner of the back gardens. I follow a damp depression in the ground to a stone-lined drainage trench, and then I tromp through heavy foliage, breaking twigs off bushes in my haste. The drainage trench empties into a wider stream that exits the palace grounds via a dark tunnel.

I brush aside branches, spitting out a leaf that somehow got into my mouth. Bushes rake at my arms as I forge a path to the tunnel. Finally I give up trying to stay dry and I slosh through the shallow water, down the dark arched passage, until I reach the sluice gate. The tunnel continues beyond it, cutting through the thick outer walls of the fortress.

"Khloe?" A sharp whisper from the other side of the gate. The whisper chills me as thoroughly as the night breeze gusting through the tunnel.

It's too dark for me to see who the person is. I have a little healing magic left, so I release a thin ribbon of golden light. As it snakes through the bars, its glow illuminates Rince's face.

"Cailin." Surprise colors his tone. "Where is Khloe?"

Hurt and betrayal tighten my chest. "Did you know she planned to kill me as well as the King?"

"I knew there was a chance you wouldn't make it, Cailin, but I hoped you would. I wanted Khloe to tell you about the poison so you could protect yourself, but if you'd known what it was, you wouldn't have used it on him, because of your vow. Am I wrong?"

I clench my teeth.

"It had to be this way." Rince's velvety tones flow through the bars, thicker and richer than the gurgling water. "You understand, don't you? For the cause, Cailin, for the kingdom. You must tell me—did we succeed? Is the tyrant dead?"

"You killed people to get into this tunnel," I say. "The guards. You murdered them."

"Cailin. Is he dead?"

"No."

A frustrated sigh bursts from him. "Gods! And Khloe?"

"She's been taken to the dungeon."

"Then she is lost to us. But you—your cover is preserved? The Ash King doesn't suspect you?"

"I won't harm him."

Rince vents an angry growl. "Cailin, you're being foolish. I know the vow you made, and I understand the allure of good sex—but false pride and a little pleasure aren't worth risking the future of the entire kingdom. Can't you see how selfish you're being?"

"No!" I hiss, pressing my forehead to the cold, wet metal of the gate. "You're being fooled, Rince. You don't have all the information." I know I promised not to tell, but this is the only way I can think of, the only thing that might sway my friend. Quickly I tell Rince the Ash King's story, explaining about the Undoing's connection to Cheimhold. "You're working for the enemy, Rince."

"Lies," he scoffs. "The King's lies. I wouldn't have thought you'd be so gullible, *mo stór.*"

"Don't call me that. I'm not your treasure anymore."

He's silent for a moment. My healing light has faded, and we both stand in the dark, on opposite sides of the gate, with the cold wind rushing over bodies, carrying the scent of mildew from the damp walls.

"I cannot extract you," says Rince. "Khloe was supposed to bring melting acid to weaken the gate. It's her own special recipe. I have a few men with me, but not enough to knock these bars loose."

"Getting out of the palace isn't a problem for me. I'm not a prisoner. Nor am I a collaborator who requires extraction."

"Oh, but you are." There's a darkness in his tone that scares me, and reminds me why I came out here in the first place.

"Before they dragged Khloe away, she said something about my parents." My grip on the bars tightens, as if I can draw strength from the chilled metal. I'm still weak, suffering from blood loss, and I have little healing energy left. I need to rest.

"Our leader didn't think you'd come through for us," Rince says hollowly. "I made him promise to use Khloe against the King first, and if she couldn't kill him, we'd fall back to you. And we knew you wouldn't agree to kill him by your own hand unless you had a powerful incentive."

"Rince," I breathe. "What have you done?"

"I invited your parents to Cawn," he says. "They were intercepted and escorted to our headquarters."

"Heartsfire." I sag against the gate. "No. Oh no. Rince, how could you?"

He crouches on the opposite side of the bars, reaching through them to grip my shoulder. "Listen, they're fine, Cailin. They're safe. I won't let anything happen to them. You don't think I would, do you? I've known them since I was little. Think of it as a reward. When you do the right thing, you get to see them."

"The right thing—Rince—you—" But I can't formulate anything logical or reasonable. Tonight has been too much. The Ash King's offer of a life with him, his near-death, Khloe's betrayal, and now—now my parents are in the hands of the Undoing, the merciless rebels who sided with Cheimhold and created the toxin that killed thousands.

"You have to do it tonight," says Rince. "I'll wait here a little longer. Kill the King, get the melting acid from

Khloe's room, and return to me. I'll get you out safely, and we'll reunite you with your parents. You'll be a hero of the people, Cailin. Everyone already loves you. Destroy the King who forced you to serve him, end the man who used and humiliated you—and the people will love you even more. We'll burn the monarchy and create something new, something better."

"And if I don't?"

He reaches farther through the bars, taking my chin and turning my face toward his. "I warned you," he says sorrowfully. "I work for very powerful and dedicated people. If you fail, your parents will pay the price."

"How do I know you really have them?"

Rince reaches into his pocket and pulls out a thick ring, set with a tiny starstone. When he breathes on it, it glows fiercely bright for several seconds, like a miniature star. I've seen it a thousand times. My father uses it to check the quality of gems and crystals.

"Bastard," I hiss through my tears. "That belongs to my father. Give it to me."

Rince's fingers curl around the ring. "Give me the King's head, and I will. If not, I'll return to headquarters and inform our leader that you failed. And just in case you think of telling the King about this, I'll send one of my men back to the Undoing with a message—that if I don't return by dawn, they should kill your father immediately, and save your mother for future leverage."

"How do you expect me to assassinate the Ash King?" Rince doesn't know about my Rotter magic. This is my last chance for his mercy—if he thinks there's no way for me to kill the King, maybe he'll relent.

"You're resourceful. I trust you'll find a way to end him." He rises, backing away from the bars. "Do it now, Cailin, or your parents die."

37

I stagger back to the palace, wandering white-faced
through the inner gates, ignoring the guards who ask me if
I'm all right.

I have no idea if Perish is conscious again. If he is, I
could tell him what's happening. He might be able to send
guards to follow Rince back to the Undoing's headquarters
and rescue my family. But if the guards are spotted, and
Rince leads them astray, my parents will die at dawn. If
Rince is taken into palace custody, my parents will die at
dawn.

I can't see a way out of this. I'm too weary, too weak.

Despair is the only thing propping me up as I stumble
back into the royal corridor and make my way to Perish's
room. Bodyguards and servants are still bustling in and
out, and farther along the hallway a cluster of the King's
advisers are speaking in low tones.

"Is he awake?" I ask a passing servant, but she
doesn't appear to hear me.

A guard grips me by the elbow. Owin. "I thought you
were fetching Jonald," he says.

"I got lost," I murmur. "And then when I found
Jonald's room, he wouldn't answer the door. His hearing
isn't good, I think. Old age, you know?"

Owin accepts the lie, nodding. "You should check on
the King. He still seems weak."

"I will." A lump rises in my throat, and I swallow it down. "Can you clear his room? I'm drained pretty low, and I need space to concentrate and complete the healing."

"Of course." Owin nods again, eagerly. "Anything you need."

As he speaks to the other guards and servants, I enter Perish's room, drifting to his bedside like someone walking in a dream. He is splayed against silken sheets, their dark-gray sheen a startling contrast to his pale skin and moon-white hair.

The room has been cleared, and Owin shuts the door, leaving me alone with my decision.

I can't kill him, because I love him. I love him more than I love my parents. Which sounds strange and wrong, but it's inescapably true.

But I love my parents as well, so much. They are gentle people, fervent in their art, generous to others. They love me. They love our mountain and its gifts. They don't deserve to die simply because their daughter was stupid enough to get tangled in a web she didn't fully understand.

I can't allow them to die.

But Perish—the kingdom needs him. Without him, our enemies might rise against us once more, and this time they might win.

There has to be another way. But time is so short. Rince will have sent the messenger back to his overseers by now. They will be counting the minutes until they can shed my parents' blood. I have to kill the King quietly, leave the palace, and go back to the Undoing with Rince.

I won't do that. My heart would never survive it.

What is wrong with me? Am I really prioritizing the life of a man I recently met over the lives of the man and woman who birthed me and loved me for years? My parents would be so hurt, so disappointed to know that I would spare the Ash King and let them die.

What sort of despicable daughter am I?

I could kill the Ash King right now, and save my family.

As if my magic is responding to my thoughts, black tendrils unfurl from my fingertips, slithering across the prone form on the bed. I barely have to flex my will at all, and those dark ribbons begin to coil around the Ash King's hand, writhing along his wrist, corroding his skin. They lace around his neck, rotting through flesh until I can see the tendons, the red muscle blackening. Magic crawls across his mouth, eating away his lips down to his teeth.

I should not have used this magic at all. It's at the surface now, too eager, too powerful, like a gnawing, clawing creature wrenching at its chains, slavering for death and for blood.

What am I doing?

I'm hurting the man I love.

Frantically I drag the magic away from him, hauling it back inside me.

I'm still trying to retract it when the Ash King's eyes flare open.

He sees the blackness flowing from my hands. Lifts his own rotted fingers, jointed bones with rags of glistening flesh and withered skin. A faint gasp issues from his ruined jaws.

"No," I whimper. "No." And with a mighty effort I suck it all back in—all the corrosion. I've used nearly all my healing magic—using any more will hurt me, but I don't care. I thrust every last bit of my energy into his body, repairing his perfect lips, his strong throat, his precious fingers. Pain wracks my nerves, and my vision gutters, blackness crawling at its edges.

"I'm sorry," I gasp. "I'm sorry, Perish, I'm sorry."

The look in his eyes shatters my heart. Shock, horror, and the agony of betrayal—he has every right to feel them all.

I am the thing that he hates. A Rotter, like the one who killed his father.

And I tried to kill him just now. Or my magic did, which is the same thing.

I am, and have always been, his enemy.

"You're one of them," he wheezes. "Aren't you? You're—a Rotter. And a rebel. You want me dead. You've wanted me dead—all this time—spying for them—"

"No." A jumble of words pours out of me. "No, I'm not one of them. My friends are, and they asked me to spy on you, but only after I got here. I told them I wouldn't be their assassin. I thought they were right about you, about the kingdom—but then you told me your secrets, and I realized they were wrong about everything. As for my Rotter magic—it saved you from the poison. Khloe poisoned both of us with the lip stain, and then she tried to stab you—you can ask the guards. I don't use my Rotter magic, Perish, I *won't* use it—I *can't* hurt you. I love you."

He reaches for me.

I move closer with a sob of relief, placing my hands in his.

With a clawing wrench, he tears the rings from my fingers—the palace ring he gave me, and the wooden ring from the Ruse Wake.

Sparks flicker deep in his cavernous dark eyes. "This is over."

My face crumples. "No."

His breathing is labored, his voice faint. "It would have been bad enough rejecting all the noble daughters for a barefoot village girl—but how can I marry the anarchist sympathizer who tried to kill me?"

I cup both hands over my mouth, tears streaming down my cheeks. I'm breaking apart. Dying, corroding, rotting inside.

"Go," he says. "No one else has to know of this. I will not kill you or imprison you—I could not bear that—but you must go. Leave, and do not return. I never want to see you again."

"Perish," I whisper.

But he drags himself up on his elbows and speaks one more word on a hot gust of angry breath. "Go!"

I'm barely conscious of what I'm doing. But I manage to keep my face calm as I leave the king's quarters and make my way to the hall where the Favored reside. Khloe's room is empty—her maids are sleeping in their own chambers. I wonder if they knew of her true allegiance to the Undoing. I wonder if her family knows, or if, like Perish's cousin, she kept it secret from everyone. She would have had to conceal it, or she could not have made it this far in the competition. Once word of her treachery gets out, her family's reputation will be ruined.

In the back of a drawer full of underthings, I find the container with the melting acid. I leave the palace's inner walls by a different route this time, and I hurry to the sluice gate, stumbling with exhaustion. My eyes are dry. I have no more energy for tears. As I limp along the dark tunnel toward the gate, my vision keeps clouding over.

Rince is still there, a black silhouette in the gloom. "Is it done?"

"Yes." I push the bottle of acid through the bars. He catches it as I collapse, and my vision finally fades into darkness.

My mouth tastes terrible. Like the skin of a potsava root before it has been washed. Dry and mealy, with a hint of sourness. I'm not sure how long I was unconscious; I've regained some of my healing energy, but certainly not all of it.

Pain thrums at the side of my skull, near my temple. Maybe I hit my head when I passed out—when I collapsed in the tunnel near the sluice gate, with Rince—

My eyes fly open.

There's a face peering into mine—pale, lightly freckled, with piercing pale-blue eyes. An attractive man, not quite to his fortieth year. Red hair waves across his brow and reddish scruff colors his jawline. His lips are thin, and the edges of his coat's high collar are worn and frayed.

"Cailin," he says, smiling far too widely. "Healer to the Ash King. Welcome to the Capital headquarters of the Undoing."

I suck in a sharp breath and struggle to a sitting position.

"You're lovely, aren't you?" He laughs lightly, running a knuckle along a lock of my hair. "I've seen the sketches, but in person—my *gods*."

"Why am I here?"

He doesn't answer. Keeps smiling. "You can try to water-wield. It won't work. We're on the third floor of this building, and we cleared the place of water. That was a job, let me tell you. Very inconvenient. Troublesome. Like most of what you've done for our cause, eh? Which is very little." His grin widens.

I don't like him. He's talking in a friendly, conversational tone—bright eyes and a sunny expression. But there's a tightness around those eyes, fangs concealed behind that smile.

I scan the room—a large one, studded with wooden support posts and lamplit tables. The twenty or so people I can see are hurriedly packing a few crates and some bundles. There's litter scattered across the floor, as if more items and supplies were here, but they've already been packed up and carried away. At the far end of the room are four narrow windows. It's still black night outside.

The red-haired man—whom I assume is the leader of the anarchists in this city—is right. There is no water that I can sense, anywhere around. Everything is dry as dust. How I wish I could wield mixed or impure liquids—tears, sweat, wine, piss, or even blood. But my magic will only work with water. If there was some mud around, I could possibly lift some water particles from it as long as it was recently dampened—but there is nothing. Not a drop I can use.

I look to my right, and there, bound and kneeling, are my parents. They're horribly thin, and their wrists are raw from the ropes. They've been tied like this for a while, maybe for days. How long has the Undoing been holding them here?

Sickening realization strikes at my heart. I've been lounging in the palace, dancing, doing magic, sleeping with the King, while my parents were in the hands of the anarchists.

That knowledge is almost more than I can bear. Almost enough to make me wish I had killed Perish... no. No, no, never that. No matter how furious he is with me, he's *alive*, because of me, and that is a tiny flame of triumph in my heart.

Two burly women stand nearby, ready to intervene if the two prisoners try to escape. My father and mother don't speak to me, but their tearful eyes tell me all I need to know. They love me. They don't blame me for this.

I have to save them.

"Please let them go," I tell the red-haired man. "I did what you asked. The King is dead."

He taps a finger to his mouth. "Yes. You told Rince you killed the Ass King—forgive me, I believe you call him the 'Ash King.' We've a different name for here." He chuckles. "But it's been a few hours since you were brought to me, and we've received no such reports. No confirmation. Do you want to know what I think, gorgeous? I think you're lying."

"I'm not."

"So you believe in the cause then? You fully support the defeat of the monarchy and the uplifting of a new order in its place?"

"Of course I do."

"Interesting, interesting. Because Rince told me a story when he brought you here—something you told him, I believe. Some royal propaganda the Ass King stuffed into your head while he was stuffing your holes." He winks and chucks my chin. "Seems as if you believed that shitload of lies about what happened in the Ashlands, and you were trying to get Rince to believe it too. But he's smarter than that, you see. Rince is a faithful believer, a loyal defender of the true Bolcan. He can't be swayed by the lies of royals and nobles."

"That's because you've soaked his brain in your radicalism," I snap. "You've turned his passion for our kingdom into something foul and self-destructive."

The anarchist leader clicks his tongue, stroking my hair as one might pet a child. "From village wielder to whore of the King. Quite a climb, little one. But you're wading in waters too deep for you."

Quick as thought, he twists his hand, and his gentle petting turns into a searingly painful death-grip on my hair.

My mother whimpers quietly, then cringes as one of her guards takes a threatening step forward.

"Triniden." It's Rince's voice, velvety as ever, threaded with concern. He walks forward from a shadowed corner. Behind him stands Brayda, her scarred face tight and emotionless. If she cares about my fate, she doesn't show it.

"You promised you wouldn't hurt her." Rince's handsome features are taut, his eyes pleading.

"And I won't, if she can provide proof that the Ass King is dead," Triniden says softly. He tightens his grip until I whimper, leans down until his hot breath fills my ear. "Can you provide proof, little whore? How exactly did you kill the King?"

"I—I cut his throat."

"Did you now? And walked away without a speck of blood on you? Without raising any alarms? You simply cut his throat and walked out of the palace? You hear that, everyone?"

Disbelieving laughter ripples around the room.

Heartsfire. I shouldn't have chosen throat-cutting as the lie. There's no use trying to fool him now. "Fine. I didn't kill the King. Punish me, and let my parents go. Please."

"But Cailin, I can't let you go." Triniden gives me a little shake and lowers his voice, speaking with confidential cheerfulness. "I'm very angry with you. Because of you, the Ass King has my lover and my unborn child."

"Your child?" I gasp. "You mean—Khloe—and you?"

"Yes." His voice drops lower. "You see, the Ass King and I have one thing in common. We both know that the best way to ensure a woman's loyalty is to fuck her, and keep fucking her. And if you want to hold her loyalty for years, you go one step further and breed her. That's what I did with sweet little Khloe. I want her back, her and that baby. They're mine. I'll be damned if I let the fucking Ass King have them."

"You could trade me for them," I whisper. "The Ash King cares about me. He'll make a deal. And I'll cooperate, if you let my parents go."

"You think he cares about you? Oh. Oh, you're more stupid than I thought." He laughs, releasing my hair. "You'll cooperate either way. I don't need to trade you. We've got people who are skilled at prison breaks. Isn't that right, Wirtun?"

A figure nearby turns from the box he's packing, and my stomach drops. It's the man I healed in the torture room. The Cheimhold spy. His mouth presses tighter as he looks at me, but he only nods to Triniden.

"See? We got Wirtun out of the King's prison. Had to, because he'd collected too much helpful information to be left festering in there."

"Information you plan to pass along to Cheimhold?" I say loudly. "That's where he's from, isn't he?"

Several of the rebels turn, startled, and Triniden smiles widely at them, shaking his head. "No, he's not. She's lying. It's all her whore mouth is good for, besides the Ass King's cock."

"The Ash King himself said Wirtun was a Cheimhold spy," I continue, still loudly enough for the others to hear. "So either Wirtun confessed falsely under torture, or he told *the truth* under torture. If it's the truth, Wirtun fooled you into thinking he's from Bolcan." I stare hard at Triniden. "That, or you knew of his ties to Cheimhold all along, and you didn't tell your people."

An uneasy murmur rolls through the room.

"Once we're clear of all this, I will investigate the matter," Triniden announces. "Though I suspect the Healer is as skilled a deceiver as the Ass King himself. We should give no credence to anything she says. The point is, we got Wirtun out of prison, and we will break out our beloved Khloe too. She has risked too much for the cause to be left in that murderer's bloodstained hands!"

The anarchists respond with quiet cheers before returning to their work.

The rebel leader puts his mouth close to my ear again. "I would kill you right now," he says in a companionable tone. "But I can't waste a gifted Healer, so you'll be coming with us. You'll spend the rest of your life serving our cause, healing our people. But we can't risk you using your water-wielding to try to escape, so Pye over there is going to Mute the water side of your magic. He'll create the tattoo while you speak the vow, and you will never wield water again. Because only the tattoo mage who Mutes you has the power to reverse it. Though I'm sure you know that already."

Panic courses through my veins. "I won't say the vow."

"Oh, but you will," Triniden hisses. "Did you ever wonder how the Ass King's Ricters control people so easily, why the wielders they Mute don't make more of a fuss? The Ricters threaten their families, you see."

He rises, crosses the room to where my parents are kneeling, and grips my father's hair, jerking his head back.

"Serji, lend me your weapon," Triniden says, and one of the largest rebels hands over a gigantic sword, broader than Witherbrand. "If you resist the Muting, Healer, I will lop off your father's head. If you try to heal him, or if you keep resisting, I'll do the same to your mother. See how that works?"

An agonized sob wrenches from my mother, and tears burn in my own eyes.

I could use my Rotter magic now. I could hurt these people until they let us go. But if I let it flow again, I'm not sure I can control it. What if I hurt my parents, or Rince? And there are so many people in this room—what if I don't Rot them fast enough and they kill my parents before I can stop them? If I'm not quick enough, and the Undoing finds out about that darker power of mine, they'll either kill me on the spot or force me to use Rotter magic against the people of Bolcan—against my King.

No, I have to submit and accept the Muting tattoo for my water magic. I have no choice. Maybe later there will be a chance to use my Rotter magic to escape.

"Don't hurt them." My voice is thread-thin. "Please. I'll speak the vow."

The tattoo takes a while, and it hurts more than I anticipated, but though I cry silently, I don't scream. As directed, I speak a binding vow never to use my water magic again, in any way, for any purpose. If I try to wield water, the tattoo will cause me pain, and if I keep trying, it will kill me, unless it is removed first.

I've heard that most Muted wielders get to choose their tattoo. Pye doesn't ask what tattoo design I want—he just inks a simple spiral shape on my inner wrist. I assume it worked, but even if I wanted to test it, there is no water here.

Water-wielding has been such an intrinsic part of me, ever since I was very young, and now it's gone. I can't grasp the reality of what I've lost yet; I have more urgent things to think about.

"Finished." Pye puts away his ink, needles, and other implements and leaves my side.

Triniden returns and grabs my wrist, inspecting the tattoo. "Now that it's done, we can move out. Since Rince was foolish enough to bring the girl here, I have no doubt the Ass King's men will be close behind."

"We weren't followed," says Rince. "If they'd followed us, they would be here by now."

"Of course you were followed. You thought you could poison three sentinels and not be noticed? Here's what I would do, were I the captain of the palace guard—I'd send a couple spies after you, and then once I found your hiding place, I'd return to the palace to tell the King. He'd want to take us down personally, so he'd need time to prepare a company and ride all the way here—and we're quite a distance from the palace. Which leaves us with just enough time to get out before he arrives. I suggest you start carrying the rest of those crates downstairs," he shouts to his people. "We can't afford to lose all of this. Brayda, get the Healer up and keep a hold on her."

Brayda pulls me to my feet and moves behind me, gripping my upper arms.

"Don't do this," I whisper to her. "Remember what we are to each other."

She doesn't reply.

"Come quietly, and it will be all right." Rince steps in front of me, touching my cheek gently. Under his breath he says, "I'm sorry, Cailin—"

"Don't apologize to her," Brayda hisses.

"Now, before we run with our new Healer prize, we need to get rid of the dead weight." Triniden hefts the big sword, posing with it dramatically, almost jokingly. For a second I fear he's going to strike Rince with it. Apparently Rince fears so too, because he retreats, eyes wide. Brayda's grip tightens on my arms.

"Not you, boy," Triniden says, with a peal of merry laughter.

Then he whirls and strikes off my father's head.

And my mother's.

My brain stutters. Refuses to accept the sight of their bodies slumping aside, their heads rolling to a stop, the

403

blood—the blood—like lava, spewing across the floor—volcanic, horrific—

Everyone is a mountain.

Rince is voicing a shaky protest. "They were going to be our leverage, to get her to comply."

"You and Brayda are her childhood friends. You will serve as leverage if we need it," says Triniden. "Bring her."

The others in the room are sneaking glances our way, but they don't protest the slaughter of the hostages. They've seen their leader do this before. They've seen him kill people, innocent people—my people. The people of Bolcan.

My shuddering, bleeding soul stills. Solidifies into impenetrable rock, hard as a mountainside.

The Undoing will not win. They will not take my kingdom.

I will see them undone.

Everyone is a mountain.

I am a mountain, a volcano with secret depths.

And with a dark and terrible scream, I erupt.

My hidden Rotter magic is voracious. It leaps from my body like black vines, flinging outward and coiling around each person in the room.

My vision changes, like a tinted glass dropping over my eyes, sapping the color from the world. Screams tear from throats as the magic sloughs away skin, melts flesh, eats down to bone. There is a vast, cosmic well of energy within me, and I cannot restrain it.

Brayda is on the floor, gasping as sores bubble over her arms. Rince is caught in a blast of my magic, roaring in agony, his fingers decaying, his skin corrupted. There's someone behind him—someone using his body as a shield. But I cannot change the course of the magic. I can only let it feed.

When I destroyed the poison in the Ash King, I was in partial control. Less so when I was in his room and I rotted his hand and face.

Now I have no control. I am galvanized, hypnotized—a conduit for more raw, terrible power than I have ever managed in my life.

I am not ready for this. I cannot stop this.

My body jerks. My spine arches and my limbs go rigid as the corrosive magic spews out of me and brings the bodies down, one after another, each one a spider's prey cocooned in black webs and tethered to me by rippling, shadowy tendrils.

A crash somewhere below. Shouts, and the clang of swords.

The distraction snaps a connection inside me, and suddenly my thoughts clarify and my vision clears. The Rotter magic festers and fights as I pull it back, but it is returning, slowly, leaving the dead and dying in its wake.

The door to the room bursts open, and the Ash King strides in, clad in his splendid black armor.

His eyes meet mine, flaming with fury—but the fury changes to shock as he stares around at the receding strands of my corrosive magic.

"Cailin," he says hoarsely. "What have you done?"

My gaze drops to Brayda, glassy-eyed, a destroyed carcass. Near her, lying on top of someone else, is Rince's body, his flesh slowly oozing.

What have I done?

My vow. I've broken my healer's vow.

I have killed my friends.

Rince's eyelids blink. He's alive in that rotted husk. Barely.

The person underneath Rince's body shoves him aside violently and rises, dripping with gore. Triniden. The side of his face is ruined, putrefied, his jawbone exposed. He's holding the big sword, still scarlet with my parents' blood.

The blade whips toward me.

A flash of pain through my neck.

My body won't respond—

I'm falling, I am—severed.

The Ash King screams.

38

I have heard that a person's brain remains active even when the head is cut off. I've seen it happen with chickens.

With my head separated from my body, I can't speak, but I am still *here*.

Two people are screaming—one in mortal agony, the other with boundless rage. Against my brow and my hair, I feel the heat from a blast of streaming fire somewhere nearby.

My head has rolled aside, my eyes fixed with shock. I'm gazing at the face of Wirtun, the Cheimhold spy whose tortured body I once healed. He is partly Rotted, his face sagging and seeping, but he's moving, crawling toward me.

He reaches out—what is he doing? He is cupping my head with his corroded fingers. Setting my severed neck against my body—gods, my body, I can sense my body again. Now that I'm nearer to it, I can feel the wound, the gap between me and—the rest of me.

My healing power usually flows through my fingers, but it is centered in my mind, connected to my eyes. I focus my last spasming thoughts, calling upon the well of healing power that's still there inside my consciousness— not fully recharged, but *there*, thanks to the few hours I was unconscious. With every bit of force I can muster, I push healing magic into that narrow gap in my neck.

I fuse the spine first. Then I reattach the veins, the arteries. Each restored connection strengthens and speeds the healing. Rapidly I sew the nerves together, link the tendons and tissues, restore the windpipe. I'm repairing the skin now, replenishing the blood I lost, spurring my heart to pump and my lungs to haul in air.

I'm working faster than I've ever worked in my life. I'll be exhausted after this—nearly depleted again—but I'll be alive.

There's fire spewing through the room, streams of it arching across my body. One stream catches the Cheimhold spy's half-rotted corpse and he burns to ash. The flames from his carcass singe the skin of my arm.

He saved me, and I will never be able to thank him.

Only one voice is screaming now, cold fury and tormented rage. That single mighty voice is the source of all the fire. The Ash King is burning everything in the room, because he thinks I'm dead. He might end up burning me, too, unless I can get his attention.

I still can't speak. Can't scream. My body is in a shocked state, paralyzed, all energies focused on healing.

I repair my vocal cords last of all, and I manage to force one tiny word out.

"Perish."

He stops roaring, and the streaming fire gutters, falters.

Praise the gods for his enhanced hearing.

"Perish," I whisper again.

"Cailin?" He crashes to my side, sweeps an arm outward to extinguish the remaining flames. "Guards!" he roars.

Cautiously his guards enter the room and cluster around us. He must have told them to wait while he dealt with the rebels. It's a small comfort that none of them witnessed my terrible magic.

"Cailin. Cailin." The Ash King keeps repeating my name in a voice that is raw from screaming. His hands hover over my neck and face, as if he fears my head will fall off at a mere touch.

"Open the windows," says one of the guards—Owin's voice. "Let's get some fresh air in here, clear the smoke."

Some of the guards hurry away to help him.

Gingerly the Ash King lifts my head onto his lap, touching the healed skin of my neck. "How?" he says. "He killed you. You were—gods, Cailin, you were gone."

"Not quite," I whisper. "Perish—what I did to you—I—I'm sorry—"

"You helped me destroy a threat to the crown," he says tightly. "It was well done."

"I can't control my magic, Perish," I murmur, so low only he can hear me. "It's out now, and I can't—I can't—"

"Kitten." He takes my hand in his, lifts it to his mouth. "I know." His voice is deep, sincere, tinged with anguish. "I know. I understand, better than anyone."

"Do I still have to go away from you?" I whisper.

He lets out a broken laugh. "No, love."

"Thank the gods." I sigh, closing my eyes.

"I reacted in fear, Cailin. You can't imagine what I felt when I woke, when I saw what you are. But you saved me, and once I had time to think, I realized that the magic you carry doesn't matter. It is a risk and a danger, but so is mine. Your heart is the same, and I still want it, if you can forgive me for sending you away. Hate me if you must—I can bear that—but don't leave me."

"Never." I look up at him again, just to assure myself that he's really here, that I'm safe. "How did you find me?"

"The captain of the guard told me about three dead sentinels near the sluice gate in the outer wall. His best trackers followed them and then reported back to me at the palace. I was ready to ride the moment the trackers returned."

"That's almost exactly what Triniden said would happen."

"We have been hunting the leader of the Cawn rebels for years. He was a cunning adversary who would have escaped, if not for you." Perish's tone darkens a little. "I must ask why, when I sent you away, did you go straight to the Undoing? If, as you say, you were not truly in league with them, how did you know where to meet them?"

"Khloe told me the route she was supposed to take to escape after the poisoning attempt," I say. "She thought I was on her side at the time. But I wouldn't have gone to the Undoing at all, except they kidnapped my parents—oh gods—my *parents*—"

I lunge from his lap so quickly my head spins and I nearly vomit. I suck in several quick breaths, blinking until my vision clears, and I crawl to the spot where my parents lie.

I collapse beside them, sobbing.

Their bodies are a mess—decapitated, rotted, and burned. They are thrice dead, and with my energies so low from healing myself, there is no way I can fix them.

"I didn't know," Perish says. His tone is tinged with sickened horror. "Cailin, I—"

"You couldn't have known they were here. You didn't kill them—Triniden did. And then I rotted them

411

because I couldn't control my magic." I can barely whisper through my tight throat.

Perish draws me against him. "Don't speak of your magic again, not here," he whispers. "We will talk of it later. We're fortunate no one else saw you use it. All anyone needs to know is that you were knocked unconscious at the palace and taken as a hostage by the Undoing. I came to your rescue, and together we defeated the rebels."

It's truth, mixed with a lie, and with my new understanding of politics, I can see how it will sway the people in our favor. After this, they will be even more eager to accept me as Queen, to embrace the monarchy, and to repudiate the deeds of the Undoing. Even the nobles will think twice before rejecting me, after hearing such a tale of courage and love.

I should be glad for it—and in a way, I am. When I'm with Perish, there is part of me that is always deeply, quietly joyful. But there's a wound inside me, too—the space my parents occupied, torn open and bleeding.

"I can't be your queen right away," I murmur against his neck. "I need to mourn them."

"Yes, for as long as you need. They will be given a memorial ceremony fit for Bolcan's greatest heroes."

"Oh no." I grimace, shaking my head. "It's so sweet of you, but they wouldn't want that. I know exactly what they would want." I reach up to kiss his cheek. "Please bring them with us and light their funeral pyre yourself once we're back at the palace. Then we'll collect the ashes. When the dust settles on all of this, we're going to take them home."

39

When someone dies, everyone expects you to perform your grief for them. They watch your reactions carefully, to see how your emotions fit into their personal construct of how loss and sorrow should look.

I perform the grief I know the people want to see. The soft sadness. The tears.

But my true grief runs deeper. It is wilder, angrier.

The memory of my vengeance is the only thing that helps. When I hurt so badly I can't breathe, I remember how I killed the man who killed my parents, and my lungs loosen.

Heralds travel through the Capital and the entire kingdom, announcing the temporary suspension of the Calling of the Favored due to Khloe's assassination attempt on the King. She is tried in the Justice Building and sentenced to life imprisonment. Harsh, but it isn't death. Perhaps the twisted thinking of the anarchists can be unraveled from her mind, and she can be pardoned one day. Her baby will be born in the women's prison of Cawn, in the section reserved for inmates with tiny children. In five years, Khloe will have a choice—to keep the child with her, or yield it for adoption.

I healed Rince on that terrible night, just enough for him to survive. I finished the healing the next day, once my magic was mostly restored. He is in the King's prison too, but like Khloe, I hope to pardon him someday, when I believe he is truly sorry for the harm he caused.

No other anarchists survived that night. I know there are more rebels out there, recruiting more vulnerable, bright-eyed young people to join their cause. When I eventually obtain Perish's consent, I plan to share the truth of the Ashlands with the entire kingdom. Maybe then the people of Bolcan will realize what a hero their king truly is, and what he has done for them. But that will have to wait until Perish is ready. And the first person with whom he will need to share the truth is his estranged aunt.

Two weeks after the attempt on his life, the Ash King hosts a gathering in the Réimse Ríoga, where hired actors perform the story of our love for a crowd larger than any the arena has ever seen. I sit beside him, watching it unfold, crying into his shoulder a few times.

It's a sensationalized version, to be sure, with the elements and timing slightly altered. There is much no one will ever know—like the way his knuckles grazed my back in the banquet hall, or how he rutted me jealously against that cabinet in the pantry. But the King knows the power of a story, of a memory created and crystallized into the stone for a new foundation, a new future. I like to think of this foundation stone as petrified wood—alive and growing, then calcified into marbled beauty by the fire and darkness we endured.

And suddenly it clicks together—the story the old woman told us. Crystallized memory. Stabilizing resonance.

The throne in the Justice Building. The King's official seat on the royal balcony in the Réimse Ríoga. The flooring of the banquet hall and the ballroom. The ring that calmed his mood the moment I put it on him. The rings that helped me subdue and direct my Rotter magic until the King ripped them off me.

All made of petrified wood. Ancient memory, crystallized. Linked, perhaps, to a time when gods walked the mountains.

It's so ridiculously simple. I squeeze Perish's arm, and he looks over at me, eyes glowing with sympathetic emotion. Perhaps he thinks I'm wrapped up in the show, reacting to the moment of Khloe's treachery as it's being played out before us.

I can hardly wait to tell him my discovery. Perhaps, if the petrified wood works for him, it will work for me as well, and I won't have to spend every conscious moment reining in my corrosive darkness.

All my life I've lived around those beautiful pieces of ancient wood. Perhaps they influenced me more than I knew as I taught myself how to control and use my powers.

When the play is over, the Ash King rises, drawing me to my feet with him. It's the moment he and I have prepared for and talked about, but I'm still trembling with excitement, joy, and a deep, deep sorrow that my parents will never know of this.

"The Calling of the Favored ends today," the Ash King says. "I have found the woman who will be my bride. You've seen her bravery and compassion during the challenges. You've heard the tale today, how she won my heart entirely. To the noble women who invested their time and showed their mettle so beautifully during this competition—you have my utmost respect and my best wishes for your future happiness. I hope you will forgive this concession to true love, and welcome your new intended Queen, the Healer of the Favored, Cailin Roghnaithe of Leanbh, on the slopes of Analoir Doiteain."

His final words are drowned in a mighty ocean of applause.

The Ash King places a crown of golden interwoven branches on my head, and we kiss to even more thunderous cheers and applause. Then I turn to the people and lift my hands, carefully holding my darker powers in check while I let golden magic flood from my fingers. Ribbons of healing light ripple over the audience, and the King sends out thousands of tiny fiery orbs that dissolve into glimmering sparks. The shower of our joined magic bursts over the people.

It is an exquisite moment.

But my favorite moment comes two weeks later.

40

Perish and I walk to the peak of Analoir Doiteain in the company of my village, my family. Jonald is with us, newly freed from the tumors infesting his body. The bracelets of petrified wood that now adorn my arms enable me to guide my Rotter magic precisely, and I am beginning to use it for good—secretly for now, but one day I will share the truth with our people. I will show them that incredible power need not be feared.

Perish wears glossy cuffs of petrified wood, etched with fire-stags. He has not had an uncontrollable episode of fire magic since he began to wear them, and the difference in him is magnificent. His eyes still change and glow with his emotions, and he is still as powerful as ever—but his resonance is synchronized and stabilized by these fossilized elements, salvaged from the very heart of our land.

Are we descended from gods, he and I? Do the gods still exist, walking on the other side of sight, entering our world just long enough to share their power through a tryst or two? We will never know, nor does it matter, because we have each other.

I have lost my parents, but as I look around at the precious familiar faces from my village, I know that I still have my family. A much larger one now—an entire kingdom, since I will be Queen soon. Not everyone is glad of that, but Perish says I will win over the remaining objectors—and if not, he doesn't "give a fuck what they think because I'm the damn king, and I'll marry whoever I want and they'll like it, or they can move to Cheimhold."

I think of his words as I lift the urn containing my parents' ashes, and I look over at him with a small smile. He smiles back with an indulgent shake of his head, and I know he's thinking that I always smile at the most inappropriate times.

But I'm strangely happy. And this happiness, too, is part of my grief.

Each person from my village walks by and takes a bit of the ash. Perish and I gather the final handfuls, and together we release them into the wind. The hot breath of Analoir Doiteain carries my parents' ashes upward and away. They will fall upon our fields, and they will be part of this land, of us, forever.

We descend the mountain, soft songs wending along the procession as we walk. Back in the village, a feast is being prepared. But I am not expected to help with the cooking, nor do I want to. The sun is setting over my mountain, over this land of memories, and I would like to make one more memory before the day ends.

Owin is my willing conspirator, distracting the other bodyguards while I pull the Ash King into the space between two houses. It's the spot from which I peeked at him for the first time on that first day.

I pull off his stiff, heavy coat and unbutton his vest.

"Cailin," he says apprehensively. "Here? With your people in the village square just a few steps away? Have you lost your mind?"

"Take off your boots and your socks. I command it."

"You're not Queen yet," he grumbles, but he obeys.

I survey him critically. He's standing before me in black pants and a creamy, blousy silk shirt. "Not enough." I unbuckle his sword belt and lay Witherbrand on top of a barrel. "Roll up your pants and your shirtsleeves. Untuck the shirt a bit, and loosen the band in your hair. There— now you're perfect."

He gives me a haughty smirk. "You're trying to turn me into a commoner."

"You're handsome enough as a king," I tell him. "But as a feral farm boy—gods. You're rutting irresistible. If you'd come to me like this that first day, I'd have gotten wet just looking at you. You could have ploughed my field anytime."

His smile is incandescent, so beautiful I almost can't breathe.

I seize his hand and pull him with me, along the dirt track leading out of the village and up to the fields. As my bare feet sink into the first crumbly rows of soil, I release a long breath of delight.

"Come on!" I release his hand and run.

He keeps up with me easily as I lead him up the slopes, to a point where we can see the village below, smoke feathering from its chimneys, with the entire sky sprawling above, awash with sunset orange and pink and blue. To our left rises the mountain, dark and powerful, an ever-present reminder of our mortality—which makes life here all the sweeter.

"Would you have scorched my village?" I ask. "If I had refused to come with you?"

"A little of it, maybe."

"Cruel man."

"Kings sometimes have to be cruel." He sighs, taking in the view. "It's beautiful, Cailin. I can see why you love it. I'm sorry that you cannot wield the water here, as you used to. You don't speak of it, but I know you miss it. If only I had asked questions before I burned everyone—your parents, that Cheimhold spy, the tattoo mage who Muted you—"

His face is darkening, and I can't bear it.

"Perish." I press my hand to his cheek, turn his face toward me. "Time flows on. Set the memory aside. You and I—we've both made terrible mistakes, big and small. We can only move forward and do better."

He nods, his features relaxing.

"And you don't have to be sorry about burning up that tattoo mage. He was already rotted when you burned him. Besides, I found a way around the rule."

I shift one of my wooden bracelets aside, revealing bare unmarred skin where my Muting tattoo used to be.

Perish seizes my arm. "What? How is this possible?"

"I Rotted the skin where the tattoo was, and then I healed myself. It hurt, but it was worth it." I grin at him, and he meets my eyes, astonished glee sparking in his gaze.

There's a rivulet of water nearby, a thin stream left over from the work of Evan, the water-wielder from Kuisp, who's been helping my village in my absence. I pull on that stream, sensing its tether to the river far down the slopes. I've grown stronger since I've been gone, and it seems easier than ever to draw the water to me. I divide it into thin, glittering ribbons and raise it high, surrounding us with a dancing, swaying veil of liquid streams, crisscrossing each other and arching over us. The bright glow of the setting sun sparkles in the shifting water, turning it to jeweled amber.

"Cailin, you wonder." The Ash King pulls me in, melds his smooth warm lips to mine. His hot, wet tongue swirls through my mouth, and fierce need spikes at my core.

We've made love in a real bed many times now—he's been my comfort in every way these past few weeks. But I love seducing him in unexpected places. Or maybe he's seducing me.

I lace my arms around his neck, licking lightly along his cheekbone. He releases a shuddering sigh, urging his hips closer to mine, and I smile, because he's so hard for me, like always.

"Take me here," I whisper. "Right here in the field, where I was when you called for me."

He hesitates. "Are you sure?"

He's asking, delicately, if this is appropriate, given the goodbye we've just said to my parents.

"I can feel their spirits," I murmur. "I want them to know I'm happy. Please, Perish—love me here."

"Anywhere and always." He presses a tender kiss to my mouth and lays me down on the rich soil, amid the dancing veil of the water. I don't have to move my fingers to wield it—it maintains a shimmering shield around us while Perish folds up my skirts and draws my pantalettes down my legs. He unbuttons his pants and settles against me as I open for him.

I love the moment when he first pushes inside me—it feels new every time, a parting of my inner self to let him in. He eases in and out of me with a slow, steady, utterly tantalizing rhythm. With each surge of his hard length through my body, I'm swelling, warming, liquefying for him, aching for more.

He slips out and drags the head of his cock through my slickness before gliding into me again.

"Gods, Cailin," he says raggedly. "Every time. Every time you feel so good I can hardly believe it."

"Harder," I plead, and I touch my chest.

He understands immediately, planting his right hand in the place where he once burned me. He lets his palm heat my skin, not painfully, just enough to make me gasp with pleasure. Then he sweeps it lower, over my breasts. My legs curl tight on either side of his waist.

Perish straightens, cupping my bottom with both hands, lifting my hips and thrusting harder, while I throw my arms above my head and give myself up to the beauty of the sky, the scent of the fresh earth, and the sight of my King fucking me deep and sweet. He looks magnificent like this, with the fiery sky behind him and his fiery eyes fixed on me. Thrills pulse through my clit, over and over, intensifying with every thrust. I'm so close.

"Kiss me again," I say, and he comes down to me, aligning his body with mine, his hips rocking while he savors my mouth.

On impulse, I push against his shoulder, and he lets me roll us both over until I'm on top with my skirts scattered over us. His lips part and his eyes glaze over with pleasure, with admiration. I sink onto him so deep that a cry of infinite bliss escapes me. I ride him there in the fields, while a flock of birds soar from a faraway cluster of feathery palms and fly toward the mountain.

The Ash King is tensing under me, rhythmic male groans breaking from his mouth. I can feel his thick shaft twitching, throbbing. His abdomen contracts as he suddenly sits halfway up, reaches for me, jiggles my clit rapidly with two warm fingertips. The shock of that clever touch finishes me, and I come hard, shrieking breathlessly as the sun sinks behind the mountain, as he erupts into his own bliss with a deep cry.

Perish falls back, splayed on the earth, still pulsing inside me while I clench around him. I'm gasping, shining, my hands braced on his chest. When I release the veil of water, it falls in a shower of drops, soaking into the soil.

We're filthy in more ways than one, scarred and sorrowful in places that will never quite heal. But we have precious memories, crystallized both in the Capital and in this place, and we will make more together, a lifetime of them.

I trace the Ash King's nose, fondle the edge of his sharp jaw. "I love you," I tell him.

The glow in his eyes matches the sunset. "And I love you—Your Majesty."

MORE BOOKS

by

REBECCA F. KENNEY

The IMMORTAL WARRIORS adult fantasy romance series

Jack Frost
The Gargoyle Prince

Wendy, Darling (Neverland Fae Book 1)
Captain Pan (Neverland Fae Book 2)

Hades: God of the Dead
Apollo: God of the Sun

Related Content: *The Horseman of Sleepy Hollow*

The PANDEMIC MONSTERS trilogy

The Vampires Will Save You
The Chimera Will Claim You
The Monster Will Rescue You

The SAVAGE SEAS books

The Teeth in the Tide
The Demons in the Deep

These Wretched Wings (A Savage Seas Universe novel)

The DARK RULERS adult fantasy romance series
Bride to the Fiend Prince
Captive of the Pirate King
Prize of the Warlord
The Warlord's Treasure
Healer to the Ash King

The KORRIGAN trilogy
Korrigan (Book 1), *Druid* (Book 2), and *Samhain* (Book 3)

The INFERNAL CONTESTS adult fantasy romance series
Interior Design for Demons
Infernal Trials for Humans

MORE BOOKS
Lair of Thieves and Foxes (medieval French romantic fantasy/folklore retelling)

Her Dreadful Will (contemporary witchy villain romance)

The Monsters of Music (a YA gender-swapped Phantom of the Opera retelling)